Fortuné Du Boisgobey, Dorothy Craigie, Graham Greene

Thieving Fingers

Fortuné Du Boisgobey, Dorothy Craigie, Graham Greene

Thieving Fingers

ISBN/EAN: 9783337376758

Printed in Europe, USA, Canada, Australia, Japan

Cover: Foto ©Andreas Hilbeck / pixelio.de

More available books at **www.hansebooks.com**

DU BOISGOBEY'S SENSATIONAL NOVELS.

XX.

THIEVING FINGERS.

By FORTUNÉ DU BOISGOBEY.

———◆———

LONDON:

VIZETELLY & CO., 16 HENRIETTA STREET,
COVENT GARDEN.
1889.

THIEVING FINGERS.

I.

THE night is dark, and the rain, which is falling in torrents all over Paris, dashes fiercely against the windows of a small isolated house at the end of the Boulevard Voltaire, near the Place du Trône. A small house, not a villa, for it consists of but a ground floor, an upper storey, and an attic—no court-yard, no steps, no iron gate, nothing save a fence on the side next the street, and behind this primitive enclosure an unkempt patch of ground bounded by kitchen gardens. The architect has not even taken the trouble to provide a foundation. The structure rises from the ground, as if it had been brought there already built. It is occupied, however, for there is a light in one of the windows of the ground floor.

Who can live there? No capitalist, certainly, for his money would not be safe there. A tradesman? No customer would come so far to patronize him. This uninviting abode would best suit some old misanthrope, who might hide himself there like an owl in his tower, or possibly some impoverished family of the middle classes, reduced to a bare livelihood and cultivating vegetables to eke out their meagre daily pittance. Such at least was the opinion of the passers-by who saw this structure standing there like a huge boulder in the middle of a field, and so, too, thought the neighbours, who scarcely knew the inmates of the shabby dwelling by sight. They were all greatly mistaken, however, and they need only have crossed the threshold of the house to see that outward appearances were deceitful, and that the place was at least comfortably, if not luxuriously, furnished.

The lighted window was that of a little sitting-room, containing a number of handsome arm-chairs of different forms, to say nothing of a low Turkish divan, bright with gay coloured cushions. A good fire blazed in the grate, although it was April, and on the mantel-shelf, instead of the gilt clock, such a favourite with retired grocers, there was a bronze statuette bearing the signature of a famous artist.

The floor was covered with a Smyrna carpet, and there were door hangings of a fawn-tinted silken fabric, whilst in the middle of the room there stood a large square table that did not harmonize very well with the rest of the furniture—a real work-table strewn with large sheets of drawing-paper, rulers, pencils and compasses. And it was evidently there for use, not for ornament—it indeed served as a work-table for a man who sat perched on a stool, bending over a tracing of which he was carefully measuring the dimensions. Opposite him sat a young lady embroidering by the soft light of a shaded lamp. The man was at least fifty years of age, with thick, dark hair streaked with silver, a long grey beard, and large, brilliant eyes that lit up a rather careworn face. The young lady was beautiful, though her thoughtful and somewhat virile beauty was of a type that made her look older than she really was to a casual observer ; still her twenty summers were unmistakably imprinted on her face, which was as fresh as a spring flower, whilst her figure was characterized by the supple round-ness of early womanhood.   She was steadily embroidering without lifting her eyes from her work, and the silence was broken only by the growl of the storm which was bursting over Paris.

"What weather !" she murmured at last, dropping her work into her lap.   "I should feel afraid if I were alone.   Do you notice how the house shakes ?   I really fear that it will tumble down one of these days."

"It will last a month longer, I guess," replied the man, laughing, "and in less than a month, my dear Camille, you will be living in a handsome suite of rooms in a fashionable part of the city pending the purchase of a château ; for, now that I have secured the means of introducing my patent, our fortune is made."

"So you told me, father ; but I have not yet succeeded in accustoming myself to the idea that we shall be rich."

"We are rich already, for I received this morning a first instalment of twenty thousand francs ; and that is a mere trifle in comparison with the full amount that my invention will yield.   You know that the number of steam engines in the world is almost beyond calculation, and in a little while they will all be paying tribute to me, for not one of them will be able to do without the Monistrol condenser.   And only to think that I had been working for twenty years without any practical results whatever, when I met that worthy fellow Gémozac, who opened his purse to give me the means of making a practical application of my system.   I am no longer troubled by any fears of failure now.   But let me finish this drawing, which I must show to my partner to-morrow morning.   It is ten o'clock already, and when I have finished, I shall still have to find a hiding-place for the twenty crisp thousand-franc notes I received to-day.   I am so little in the habit of having money that I don't know where to put it.   We haven't a safe here."

"Have you the money about you ?" inquired Camille.

"Yes, here it is," said Monistrol, laying the banknotes on the table.

"You had better lock them up in my wardrobe for the night ; but de-posit them at some bank to-morrow.   I shall not be easy while the money is in our possession.   This house is at the mercy of the first thief that comes by ; and if an attempt were made to murder us, no one would hear our cries for help, for the Boulevard Voltaire is deserted at night-time."

"Not this evening at least, my dear, for the ginger-bread fair is in pro-gress on the Place du Trône, and it draws a crowd even in this bad weather.   Listen, you can hear the music now."

And in fact the wind did bring to their ears snatches of music from the brass bands that were playing noisily in front of the circus tents.

"Besides, before going up to my room, I shall carefully bolt the outside door," continued Monistrol.   "Now go on with your embroidery, my child, while I finish my work.   It won't take me long."

The father and daughter resumed their occupations ; the father eagerly, the daughter half reluctantly.   Camille's fingers plied her needle in and out, it is true, but her attention was no longer with her work.   She was thinking of the brilliant future that was opening before her, and of the peaceful, quiet life she was about to leave ; she already began to think with regret of the modest existence in which she had been so happy, for the cares and responsibilities that accompany wealth frightened her.

Camille had no ambition, and she was extremely nervous, so that she found herself in much the same state of mind as a man who is about to embark for an unknown country, and who would prefer to remain in his native village. Her over-excited imagination showed her only the dangers of the voyage, and she had a vague presentiment of approaching misfortune.

All at once a light sound, an almost imperceptible cracking, made her start. One would have thought that some one was moving cautiously in the adjoining dining-room, which was only separated from the little parlour by the door-hangings. She was afraid to disturb her father, who was absorbed in his work, and who had heard nothing; but, raising her head, she looked and listened attentively. At first, she perceived nothing unusual, and, as the sound ceased, she was about to resume her work, when she suddenly thought she saw a black hand glide between the two curtains that draped the doorway.

Was it really a hand, that dark mark that had so suddenly appeared upon the light curtain? Camille doubted it at first, though she was at a loss to explain this strange apparition. She even thought that she must be the victim of an optical illusion. The fire had begun to smoulder, and by the dim light of the shaded lamp it was difficult for her to clearly distinguish objects at the further end of the room.

She tried to close her eyes, but could not, so irresistible was the fascination that this mysterious dark mark exercised over her. It looked like a huge spider with long legs, and it did not stir. Was it the claw of some fantastic animal? Camille was no coward, and yet she felt her blood freezing in her veins.

Monistrol, who was sitting with his back to the door, worked away at his drawing with unflagging zeal. By dint of persistent scrutiny, Camille finally succeeded in distinguishing that it was a hand that had parted the curtains—a hand with fingers as knotty and as crooked as the claws of a crab, while the thumb, which was widely separated from the fingers, was of extraordinary length, and ended in a long, hooked nail, like the talon of a vulture. Just then, in the opening between the curtains, Camille saw something which she took for the blade of a dagger glittering in the darkness. "Look, father! Help!" she shrieked wildly, pointing to the door.

On hearing this unexpected call, Monistrol hastily turned, but he had not time to rise. With a single bound—the bound of a panther—the man who had been hiding in the dining-room sprung upon him. One hand—the same gigantic hand that Camille had espied—seized hold of the roll of bank-notes; whilst the other clutched the throat of the unfortunate inventor, who overturned the lamp in his struggle to rise.

Camille sprung forward to defend her father, but the thief repulsed her with a vigorous kick that sent her reeling to the floor. She did not lose courage, however, but again rose to her feet almost instantly. However, the room was now enshrouded in darkness, and if she could hear the sound of scuffling and of laboured breathing, she could see nothing,

She finally succeeded in groping her way back to the table, but found it would be necessary to reach the other side of it to seize the wretch who was holding Monistrol. She succeeded in doing so, and then tried to catch hold of the thief by his coat; but it was of some smooth, slippery fabric, upon which she was utterly unable to secure a hold, though, strange to say, her fingers occasionally came in contact with some small, sharp excrescences

which she broke away with her nails. Still the thief seemed to slip between her fingers like an eel, and she tore her hands terribly.

He made no attempt to hurt her, his object evidently being to overcome
Monistrol's resistance, and make his escape with the money. The struggle
did not last long. The inventor soon relaxed his hold with a groan, and then
flinging him heavily to the floor, the thief hastily fled.

His work was accomplished. He had secured the twenty thousand
francs, and he only thought of making his escape without paying any
further attention to the young girl whom he supposed incapable of pursuing
him. He was mistaken, however. Camille supposed that her father was
only stunned, for he had not given any cry on falling ; a strong man seldom
dies of a fall, and the thief had used no weapons save his hands.

"Follow me, father !" she cried. "He shall not escape us." And she
rushed after the scoundrel, who had already reached the hall.

He fled through the front doorway, which he had left open on entering,
ran rapidly across the garden between the house and the fence, cleared the
latter at a bound, and darted up the Boulevard Voltaire in the direction
of the Place du Trône. This was exactly what Camille wished, for she
said to herself that she should certainly find some policemen to arrest the
audacious rascal where the fair was being carried on.

The great thing now was not to allow him to distance her. Fortunately,
she had good legs and no foolish prejudices. She cared little about the fact
that she wore a dressing-gown and slippers, and did not fear remark. Her
father, instead of bringing her up like a fine lady, had early taught her to
help herself. She kept the house and did the cooking, bought the pro-
visions, and feared nothing, not even the street gallants, who at times
pestered her with foolish remarks.

The intense desire she had to overtake the thief was due not so much to
grief at the loss of the money, but to the fact that her father needed it to
perfect the invention upon which he based all his hopes. She felt sure of
being able to recover it, and it never once occurred to her that it would
have been better for her to pay him attention than to save his little fortune.
She even imagined that he was already upon his feet, and would join her
and help her to arrest the man whom she had not lost sight of, though he
could run much faster than she could.

The rain had ceased, and the merry-makers who had sought shelter during the downpour, were again crowding the Place du Trône. The parades
had begun again ; there was a harsh braying of trombones and a clashing
of cymbals, indeed the hubbub was so great that it would have drowned
Camille's voice completely, had she attempted to cry : "Stop, thief !"

The man ran swiftly on, but whenever he passed a street-lamp she could
see him distinctly. He was a tall, stalwart fellow, that is as nearly as she
could judge, for he was enveloped from head to foot in a long waterproof
coat. She now understood how he had managed to escape her hold whenever she had attempted to seize him.

This was no time for retrospection, however. The man had reached the
square, and instead of directing his course towards the centre, he turned
to the left, towards a large shanty. Camille was now close upon him, and
she followed him into this dark and deserted corner without stopping to
ask herself if the thief might not be lying in wait there to seize and strangle
her ; and this danger was the more to be dreaded from the fact that he had
paused beside the rough wooden structure as if waiting to assail her.
However, Camille had gone too far to draw back.

"Ah, wretch! I have you," she cried, darting forward, and she was about to seize him when he suddenly disappeared. She heard the sharp click of a hastily closed door, and then she realised that the scoundrel must belong to the company of acrobats that was performing in this shanty which he had just entered by a side door. Camille could not follow him by the same route, but there was nothing to prevent her from passing through the public entrance, and securing the thief's arrest during the performance.

"I did not see his face," she said to herself, "but I am sure I should recognise his hands."

She did not reflect that the fellow might re-open the side door and make off while she was going round the building, nor did she think it strange that her father had not yet overtaken her. She was so excited that she had lost all power of reflection. Without losing a second, she slipped between the building and a booth where some people were selling macaroons, and passing round the corner, found herself in the midst of a crowd that had gathered in front of a platform lighted by half a dozen oil lamps, and upon which six musicians, dressed as Polish Lancers, were playing, whilst a woman in short skirts was walking to and fro with a wand in her hand, like a fairy in a spectacular drama. The performance had begun, but the place was probably not full, for the ticket-seller was bawling at the top of his voice : "Walk in, gentlemen, walk in and see the last performance of the celebrated Zig-Zag of the Beni-Dig-Dig tribe. Take your tickets. General admission only twenty-five centimes. Reserved seats fifty centimes —and only one penny for soldiers !"

The woman took up the refrain in a shrill falsetto, boldly eyeing the crowd the while, and tapping a little urchin, dressed as a clown, who was making frightful grimaces. However, the pressing invitation did not appear to have much effect, for the loungers seemed in no haste to enter. Some of them were admiring the fairy, who was a black-eyed brunette, with well formed limbs, and really pretty in spite of her hard expression ; others were teasing a big bull dog who responded by barking furiously.

Camille, undaunted, forced her way through the crowd and reached the steps leading to the entrance at the same time as two young men, whose attire indicated that they were gentlemen of fashion who had come to the fair for a spree, after dining at some stylish restaurant a long way from the Place du Trône. They paused in astonishment on perceiving Camille, whose great beauty was apparent, despite the disorderly condition of her toilet, and they hastily stepped aside to let her pass. She did so, climbed the rickety steps, and on reaching the platform went straight to the doorway, which was guarded by an old, toothless hag, who exclaimed in a husky voice : "It's ten sous for a reserved seat, my little lady."

Camille put her hand in her pocket, found nothing, and made a despairing gesture on recollecting that she had neglected to provide herself with some silver before starting out to recover her father's twenty thousand francs.

The old woman understood her gesture and remarked, with a sneer : "One can't see the show for nothing, my dear. Ask those gentlemen to pay your way in." And as she spoke, she pointed to the two young men who were just behind Camille.

"Here is money for three," said the taller of the two gentlemen, throwing a five-franc piece into the old hag's tray, which was covered merely with coppers.

Camille did not stop to thank him, but hastened inside without looking back to see if the two fine gentlemen were following her. Vacant seats were plentiful, and she seated herself on the first row of benches, near a party of counterjumpers and shop girls who were eating oranges and talking very loud.

The assemblage was a most disorderly one. The occupants of the reserved seats were laughing noisily; while the other spectators, principally workmen, common soldiers and nurses, were hooting, cock crowing, and imitating animals. But clear and shrill above all this clamour there rose cries of: "Zig-Zag, Zig-Zag! It's Zig-Zag's turn now. Where is Zig-Zag? What has become of the rascal? Has he gone to see his sweetheart?" and so on. Zig-Zag was evidently a great favourite with the audience, and Zig-Zag was late; he had failed to discharge his obligations as an artist.

Camille, almost stunned by the uproar, now for the first time realised her folly in rushing rashly into this show. The thief had certainly entered the building, but how could she reasonably hope to find him in such a crowd? She said to herself, however, that as he had a key to the performers' door, he must be a member of the troupe, and she felt a strong suspicion that he was this very Zig-Zag whose name was in everybody's mouth, and who was so surprisingly late.

Still, she began to feel ashamed of being seen in a *négligée* toilet that had already attracted the attention of her neighbours, and to wonder if it would not have been wiser for her to remain with her father, whom she had left lying upon the floor, and who, perhaps, had not yet recovered from his fall; in fact, with the impulsiveness that was the greatest fault of her character, she resolved to return home without delay. Turning to see if she would have any difficulty in making her way back to the door, she saw that the young gentleman who had paid for her admission had taken a seat with his friend, on the second row of benches, directly behind her, and she heard these words exchanged in a low tone: "She's remarkably handsome. There's no question about it."

"I don't deny it, but she looks to me very much as if she were a street walker."

When Camille heard this she blushed in confusion, and relinquishing her intention of going away, she sat down again to try and recover herself. Just then a clown appeared upon the stage, and, bowing awkwardly, opened his mouth which reached from ear to ear, and said: "Ladies and gentlemen, we are about to continue the exercises by a new feat of Monsieur Zig-Zag's, the greatest tumbler and acrobat in both hemispheres. This great artist, who has been unavoidably detained by urgent business, is now about to appear—"

"What business detained him?" cried several voices.

"He went to take a drink," replied the clown, with the utmost gravity, and thereupon he vanished, amid the jeering of the spectators.

"This Zig-Zag can't be the man I am looking for," thought Camille. "The thief wouldn't have had time to change his clothes. Still, I will see."

Almost instantly Zig-Zag shot across the stage executing a series of somersaults with lightning rapidity, whilst the spangles on his costume flashed brightly.

"It is he!" murmured the young girl. "It was the spangles on his costume that gleamed through the darkness, and that tore my fingers when I tried to seize hold of him."

Camille still had some tiny fragments of the spangles under her nails.

She could therefore no longer doubt. She waited, however, for she wanted to see the fellow's hands, feeling sure that she could identify him by the unusual length and peculiar shape of his thumb. And on asking herself once again how the scoundrel could have dressed so quickly, she recollected that he had worn a long waterproof overcoat, which he had only had to cast aside to appear upon the stage in a costume suited to his part. Thus, there was no other course left for Camille but to cry out as soon as he had ceased his somersaults : "It is he who robbed my father!" and she did not shrink from the scandal and the danger that such an unexpected interruption would be sure to create.

Zig-Zag paused at last, right in front of her and close to the row of lamps that served as footlights in this rude theatre. She then perceived that he was masked like the Harlequin of the old Italian comedies. A tiny black silk mask concealed the upper part of his face, leaving visible his smiling mouth, his white teeth, smoothly shaven chin, well rounded neck, and a bit of a flesh tinted jersey, thickly spangled with silver. His eyes gleamed brightly through the holes in the mask, and Camille fancied they were fixed upon her.

But it was not the acrobat's face that interested her. She was looking for his hands, and she discovered, with no slight amazement, that the illustrious tumbler was imprisoned from his feet to his shoulders, in a linen bag spangled like his tights. This secured his arms tightly to his sides and concealed not only his hands, but also his shoes, which must have been splashed with mud during of his flight along the Boulevard Voltaire. Had he arrayed himself in this fashion to circumvent his pursuer? No; she soon saw that this garb was indispensable to Zig-Zag in the execution of his great feat, which consisted in leaping high in the air, in coming down perpendicularly, but on the top of his head; and in righting himself with a spring, to repeat the same performance a dozen times in quick succession. The sack prevented him from making any use of his hands, and in this consisted the chief difficulty of this perilous exercise, invented, it is said, by the Aïssaoua, the savage Arabs, who devour scorpions, glass, and the leaves of thorny cactus plants. Any ordinary man would have broken his neck in attempting to execute such a feat, but Zig-Zag escaped without any injury to his back-bone, and bowed gracefully to the spectators, who applauded in the most frantic manner—so frantically, indeed, that it was evident he would be obliged to repeat the performance.

Camille hesitated for an instant. This famous acrobat must have more than one feat among his accomplishments, and before the close of the performance he would doubtless re-appear in a costume that would disclose his face and hands to view. However, she had no time to lose; her poor father might be seriously injured, and he certainly must be greatly alarmed by her prolonged absence. She must join him again as speedily as possible, and so without further hesitation, she sprung up and cried, pointing to the acrobat who had paused to take breath : "Arrest him. He is a thief!"

This was sufficient to arouse a tempest. The audience unanimously espoused the cause of their favourite artist, and from every part of the hall resounded yells of "Silence!" "Put her out!" "Make her apologize!" "She is a liar!" "No; she's mad!" "Take her to Charenton then!"

The acrobat's more enthusiastic champions even rose and shook their fists at Camille, who surveyed them with lofty scorn. She was very pale, but she was not afraid; and she continued, in a clear ringing voice: "I tell you that man has just stolen twenty thousand francs from my father. Search him, and the money will be found upon him."

This denunciation brought another shower of insults upon her. "Turn the liar out!" "Your father hasn't a penny, nor you either!" "Zig-Zag is richer than you are!" "Send for the police to take her to Saint-Lazare!"

However Zig-Zag took no part in the disturbance. He could not cross his arms, as they were not free, but he assumed his most disdainful attitude, and shrugged his shoulders scornfully.

The tumult soon became so deafening that the fairy in the short skirts, whom Camille had seen on the platform outside, came in, and after addressing a questioning nod to the clown, instantly disappeared, only to make her appearance a few moments afterwards with a policeman, to whom she pointed out the woman who had been the cause of the disturbance. The affair was becoming serious, and poor Camille now perceived, when it was too late, that she had placed herself in a very dangerous position. She had left her father's house in a toilet that would not impress any one in her favour, and she was now in imminent danger of being ignominiously expelled from the place, and even of being taken to the station-house. To whom could she turn for help in her dire extremity? Her eyes met those of the young man who had paid for her admission. He was watching her with more curiosity than kindliness, still he had a good-natured face, and she thought she might appeal to him. "Sir," she said, in a tone of deep emotion, "you doubtless think very ill of me after the scene I have just made; but when you know who I am, I am sure that you will not refuse to undertake my defence. I swear that I have only spoken the truth in accusing that man."

Camille's appeal was interrupted by the policeman who laid his hand upon her arm. "Do not touch me," said the girl, indignantly pushing him aside.

"Take her out!" yelled the spectators, applauding vociferously.

Zig-Zag, who had been watching the proceedings from the platform, did not await the result, but making a low bow, executed a double somersault which carried him off the stage.

"I am ready to follow you," said Camille, turning quietly to the policeman. "But do not presume to touch me."

Impressed, no doubt, by the quiet dignity of her manner, the young gentleman, whose protection she had asked for, decided to interfere. "I will accompany you, mademoiselle," he said in a low tone.

His companion smiled sneeringly, being evidently of the opinion that his friend's conduct was absurd in the highest degree; but he would not desert him, so they both acted as escorts to Camille, who was following the policeman out of the place. As they stepped on to the Place du Trône, she turned to her protector and said: "I reside near here, at the house of my father, Monsieur Monistrol, and I should consider it a great favour if you would see me home."

"Monistrol!" ejaculated the young man. "Jacques Monistrol, the engineer."

"Yes, sir," replied Camille. "I am Monsieur Monistrol's daughter. Are you acquainted with him?"

"I can not say that I know him much," replied the young man, "but I shall soon be brought into frequent contact with him, for my father entered into partnership with him a few days ago."

" Indeed ! Then you must be—"

"Julien Gémozac, mademoiselle, and I bless the lucky chance that enables me to be of some service to you."

Camille, surprised and delighted, scrutinized her improvised champion more attentively, and noticed for the first time that M. Julien was really a very handsome young man. This son of the wealthy iron manufacturer looked not unlike a young English nobleman, with his regular features, fair curling hair, long silky moustache, white skin, large blue eyes, and rather proud mouth, and his very aristocratic countenance wore an expression of mingled frankness and good hamour. Julien, in his turn, greatly admired the more severe beauty of Camille, and reproached himself for having momentarily mistaken her for an adventuress, though he was certainly excusable for his mistake under the circumstances.

The friend who listened to the explanation said nothing, but his rather mocking smile indicated strong doubts as to the innocence of the young woman who had left her father's roof in a dressing-gown to run after an acrobat. However, the policeman had not the same reasons for remaining neutral, and so he interposed with unmistakable rudeness. "That can't be allowed," he exclaimed. "You disturbed the performance, so you will have to go with me to the station-house, and explain your conduct to the corporal there."

"To the station-house !" repeated Camille, pressing close to her protector.

The moment had come for Julien to interfere. He felt satisfied that Camille was telling the truth, and he could not desert the daughter of his father's new partner. He might perhaps have hesitated, had she been unprepossessing in appearance, but beauty is the best of credentials for a woman, and so he resolved to see her safely out of the scrape. "I will be responsible for mademoiselle," said he.

"That is all very well, but I don't know you," growled the policeman.

"You probably know my father by name and reputation—Pierre Gémozac."

"The owner of the large iron works on the Quai de Jemmapes? I should think I did know him. My brother works there."

"Well, I live there. Here is my card, and if you will call there and ask for me to-morrow, you will find me there between the hours of twelve and two."

"With mademoiselle ?" asked the policeman who liked his little joke.

"I reside with my father," retorted Camille. "If it were daylight, you could see the house from here, and if you do not believe me, you can accompany me to my door and see for yourself. But you would do much better to arrest the man who has just stolen twenty thousand francs from us. You will find him there in that place—"

"Very well, we will see about that to-morrow. The company won't leave before the close of the fair. I shall report the case to my sergeant, and give him this gentleman's card."

" All right, my worthy friend. You can tell him that I am at his service at any time. Besides, there is nothing to prevent him from making inquiries at Monsieur Monistrol's house, as well, if he chooses," said Julien.

"At No. 292 Boulevard Voltaire," added Camille, who had regained all her wonted composure. "But do not detain me. My father was roughly handled by that scoundrel, and even if he is not seriously injured, he must be very anxious about me."

"After all, you haven't been guilty of any very grave offence," muttered the officer, "so you may return home, mademoiselle ; but be careful not to get yourself in such a scrape again."

"Thanks, my good fellow," said Gémozac. "I shall be glad to prove my gratitude to you by promoting your brother if he is a good workman. Take my arm, mademoiselle."

Camille needed no urging. She fully realized the danger she had incurred, and only thought of going to reassure her father. The loafers who had been looking on now strolled away, the policeman did the same, and Camille at once turned to walk away with her protector. However, as she did so, Julien's friend followed them, and, stepping up, said cautiously : "It is doubtless very delightful to play the part of Don Quixote with such a pretty girl, but don't forget that we have an appointment at the Café Anglais at midnight."

Julien stopped short, confronted his friend, and said by way of response : "Mademoiselle, this is Monsieur Alfred de Fresnay, who requests me to introduce him to you, and who places himself, like I do, entirely at your disposal."

Camille bowed, and so did Alfred ; though the latter found it somewhat difficult to hide his discomfiture, for he had but little taste for romantic adventures and persecuted damsels.

"Pray let us walk on," murmured the young girl.

Julien complied with her request, and had the good taste not to start a conversation that certainly would not interest Mademoiselle Monistrol at such a moment. In some cases politeness consists in remaining silent. Meanwhile Alfred walked along behind them with rather a crestfallen air. He was annoyed at all this as he wanted to go and sup with some gay companions at the Café Anglais. However, some four or five minutes afterwards all three of them reached the fence which the acrobat had cleared at a single bound. Camille had been obliged to open the gate to pursue him, and she had not tarried to close it behind her. So she was not surprised to find it open as she had left it ; still she vaguely hoped to see some signs of her father, who would hardly have waited patiently at his fireside for her return from the dangerous expedition upon which she had embarked. However, she not only saw no signs of Monistrol, but there was no light in the windows of the modest dwelling.

"He must have gone out in search of me," said Camille to herself, making a futile attempt to overcome her misgivings.

"Is it here that you reside, mademoiselle?" inquired Julien.

"Yes ; come in," she replied, stepping ahead of him.

She darted straight to the door, which had been left open like the gate, and entered the hall. A death-like silence pervaded the house, and oppressed by a grim presentiment of approaching misfortune, she paused, afraid to go any further alone.

"Father !" she cried, huskily, "come here. It is I—Camille."

No one responded to her call. However, Gémozac and his friend were close behind her, and suddenly turning, she seized the former convulsively by the arm. "I am afraid," she whispered.

"And I myself feel by no means easy in mind," muttered Alfred. "This house looks to me very like a regular cut-throats' den."

Julien, being an inveterate smoker, was never without some matches, so he now drew a box from his pocket, and on striking a light, he espied a candle standing on a small table in the hall. "I will go first, mademoiselle," he said, taking up the candlestick.

"No, let me show you the way," replied Camille.

"But, mademoiselle, the thief may have had an accomplice, and as there might be some danger in that case, you had better allow me to go first."

However, she had already darted into the little dining-room whither the two friends closely followed her. The curtains had fallen, thus concealing the little sitting-room from view.

"Father, are you there?" cried Camille.

There was no response. So Gémozac stepped forward, and on lifting the door-hanging, perceived a man lying motionless upon the floor between the table and the fire-place. Camille also saw the prostrate form, and recognised her father. "Oh, my God!" she cried wildly, "he killed him!" And before Julien could prevent it, she threw herself upon her father's body.

Her words were only too true. The unfortunate inventor gave no sign of life. Seizing hold of his hand, Camille found that it was already cold. She took him in her arms, and tried to lift him, but her strength failed her, and with a low cry, she sunk insensible upon the floor beside him.

"A murder! Well this caps the climax!" grumbled Fresnay, recoiling hastily. "You have certainly got us into a nice mess."

"Silence, man, and help me first of all to lift this poor child," said Gémozac, hastily.

"And where the devil shall we take her?"

"To her bed, of course. Her room must be on the floor above."

"And afterwards?"

"Afterwards you must run to the nearest station-house, tell them that a murder has just been committed here, and bring some officers and a commissary of police back with you."

"A nice errand you are sending me on! Catch me ever attending another gingerbread fair in your company!"

"If you desert me now, I swear that I will never have anything more to do with you as long as I live. What you just said is unworthy of you. Is it possible that you are utterly heartless? Come, take the candle, and walk on ahead, I can carry her very well alone."

Julien had knelt down beside Monistrol's daughter, trying to revive her but in vain. Fortunately he was strong. He took her round the waist and rose up, having her in his arms. Fresnay now obeyed his friend's instructions, though not without some grumbling. Camille's room was on the left of the landing, and they had no difficulty in recognising it by its little white-curtained bed. Julien laid her gently upon it, took a bottle full of water from the toilet-table and sprinkled a few drops upon her face. She opened her eyes, but closed them almost instantly, murmuring a few unintelligible words as she did so; then covering her face with her trembling hands, as if afraid of some frightful vision, she again relapsed into a state of complete unconsciousness.

Gémozac was no doctor, and he had not the slightest idea of what ought to be done in such a case. Still he was of opinion that the poor girl's brain must have sustained a severe shock. "You had better bring a physician, too," he said to his friend, who sulkily replied:

"Why don't you send me for a nurse, as well, while you are about it? Upon my word! I really believe you have lost your mind. What can induce you to insist upon mixing yourself up in an affair that doesn't interest either of us in the least?"

"Speak for yourself, if you please, Didn't you hear me say that this young girl's father became my father's partner a few days ago? He was probably killed by the scoundrel who robbed him of the money which he received from my father only this very morning."

"How do you know? This girl is evidently half crazy, and I am utterly at a loss to understand her strange chase after an acrobat."

"Enough! I won't stand here and wrangle by her bedside. Follow me."

Julien picked up the candle, went downstairs, and proceeded to examine the body of the murdered man. "You certainly won't try to deny that this man came to his death by strangling?" he said, turning to the sceptical Alfred. "The murderer's fingers have left unmistakable marks upon the unfortunate fellow's throat."

Alfred stooped, examined the body with more curiosity than emotion, straightened himself up, and then said: "Fingers! I should call them claws. It was never a man's hand that made those black marks upon both sides of the throat. It was the paw of a gorilla! And what a thumb! It has torn the skin and must have penetrated deep into the flesh."

"Say it is the work of the devil, if you like, providing you will only go for the police," replied Gémozac, pushing his reluctant friend towards the door; and Alfred yielded, though not without asking: "Why don't you go yourself?"

"Because I can't leave Mademoiselle Monistrol alone in her present condition. When we get some one else here, I shall be very willing to go off, though I shall certainly return to-morrow with my mother, who will take the poor girl under her protection. But until the police arrive, I must remain to watch over her."

At this moment a wild, heart-broken cry resounded from the room above.

"Do you hear that?" cried Julien; "I must hasten back to her at once. Go, I beg of you, but return as soon as possible. I am not anxious to spend the night alone with a murdered man and this grief-stricken girl."

Fresnay was not a bad fellow at heart, but he had the Parisian fault of never taking things seriously. Monistrol and his daughter were both strangers to him; he had an engagement to sup with some gay friends that evening, and the idea of becoming mixed up in a criminal affair was extremely distasteful to him; still, he had promised Julien that he would inform the police, and not knowing exactly where to find a station-house in that neighbourhood, he directed his steps toward the Place du Trône.

Before reaching it, however, he met two policemen, and telling them that a murder had just been committed only a short distance off, in a house which he described to them, he asked them if they would have a commissary of police warned forthwith. They were naturally enough about to ask him for further information; but, unfortunately, an empty cab was passing at the time, and the temptation proving too strong for Fresnay, he merely said, hurriedly: "You cannot make a mistake. It is on the right hand side, and only a short distance down the Boulevard. There is a fence in front of the house." Then leaping into the vehicle, he cried to the driver: "Café Anglais—Boulevard des Italiens."

"A good riddance to you, humbug!" growled the elder policeman, and his comrade responded: "It's not worth while to trouble ourselves, it's only an April Fool's Day joke." And then they continued pacing their beat.

II.

PIERRE GÉMOZAC, one of the iron kings of the day, and worth his millions, resided at only a short distance from the works where he had made his fortune, on the scarcely romantic banks of the Saint-Martin Canal. It must be admitted, however, that he had built himself a palatial residence there, and that the Quai de Jemmapes is not so very far from the heart of Paris when a man owns comfortable carriages and excellent horses. The close proximity to the noisy workshops had its inconvenience of course, but the heavy thud of the steam-hammers and the snorting of the engines were sweet music to the ears of the worthy man who had made millions by building locomotives, after beginning life as a common machinist.

He had married late in life ; and by his wife, who was much better born and younger than himself, he had only had one child, a son whom he idolized, though the young fellow caused him much more anxiety than satisfaction. Indeed, Julien Gémozac, although he had arrived at the age of twenty-eight, was still but a fashionable idler, who did not seem in the least inclined to regard life seriously, and this to the great disappointment of his father, who had dreamed of making him his successor. As it was, Julien belonged to a fashionable club, led a very gay life, played heavily, and was an enthusiastic patron of the turf. Still, he had pursued his studies at the Ecole Centrale with a fair degree of success ; and he was the fortunate possessor of a civil engineer's diploma which he had no intention whatever of using. His mother spoiled him ; and meanwhile his father said to himself by way of consolation : " He must sow his wild oats ; " still he seemed to take a long while in doing so. Pending the time when the young fellow would become reasonable, his doting parents required but two things of him—that he should sleep under the paternal roof, and that he should always be present at the family breakfast. He at least conformed to the last condition, and though it not unfrequently happened that he made his appearance with haggard features and sunken eyes, still he bore up, trying to hide the effects of a night's carousing. His father then lectured him gently, and his mother, who was anxious for him to marry, proposed one heiress after another as claimants for his consideration. He did not decline these offers, but he avoided meeting the girls in question.

As might be expected, the tragical death of Monistrol the inventor, had its effect upon the Gémozac household. Julien did not appear at breakfast the next morning, nor had he returned home at all on the previous night. His anxious parents passed a very miserable day, for it was not until six o'clock in the evening that they learned what had detained him.

Deserted by his friend Fresnay, Julien had spent the night anxiously awaiting the arrival of the authorities, and in watching over Mademoiselle Monistrol, who had passed from one nervous spasm into another, and it was not until nearly daybreak that he was able to summon some passers-by to his assistance. The police were again notified, and this time made their appearance promptly ; but Camille, when questioned, could only give incoherent answers, and Julien, knowing little or nothing about the circumstances, could not enlighten the commissary to any great extent, for the scene at the performance was no conclusive evidence against the acrobat.

However, Madame Gémozac hastened to the orphan's abode as soon as she was apprised of the tragedy, and found that brain fever had set in, and that the physician who had been sent for, declined to answer for the poor girl's life. It was necessary to bury her father without her knowledge, but Pierre Gémozac and his son followed the unfortunate inventor to the grave as chief mourners, duly escorted by their workmen. A week passed by before there was any decided change in the situation; for Camille, though now convalescent, seemed plunged in a sort of stupor that paralyzed all her faculties. The detectives were diligently seeking the culprit, but they had so far discovered nothing which would serve as a clue. Madame Gémozac had placed a woman whom she could trust, and also a sister of charity in charge of the sick girl, and not only visited her frequently, but thought of assuring her future welfare.

As for Julien, the unfortunate girl had excited a deep interest in his heart, and he had not yet forgiven Alfred de Fresnay for his selfish desertion. Still, he was gradually resuming his former habits. The orphan's terrible bereavement recurred less frequently in his mind, and he did not at all think of trying to discover Monistrol's mysterious murderer.

However, on the eighth day after the catastrophe, he inquired at the breakfast-table as to how Camille was progressing, and learnt that she had left her bed for the first time a couple of days previously.

"We shall soon receive a call from her," replied Madame Gémozac, "for she insists upon coming here to thank us."

"I shall be delighted to see her," replied M. Gémozac, "not only be· cause I want to tell her how deeply I sympathise with her in her bereave· ment, but because I also have some good news for her. Monistrol's inven· tion will yield a fortune. If the matter continues prospering as well as everything seems to indicate, his daughter will be very rich, and on my side, I shall make a great deal of money out of my interest in the patent. She can already begin to live in much better style, if she chooses; for by the end of the year I shall owe her a good round sum, and in the meantime I will advance her any money she may need."

"That will help to console her," remarked Julien.

"I doubt if she will ever be consoled," replied Madame Gémozac. "I have been studying her a little during her convalesence, and now I think I understand her. She is a character, this girl of twenty. She does not seem in the least anxious about herself, or as to what is likely to become of her. She only talks of her father, and of avenging his death."

"I am afraid she will never succeed in that," said Julien. "The investi· gation is still in progress, but no definite information about the murderer has yet been secured. The acrobat, who was accused, was examined on the day before yesterday, but he succeeded in establishing an *alibi*. He will be confronted with her, undoubtedly, as soon as she is in a condition to give evidence, but I am almost certain that she won't be able to identify him."

"There is very little chance of it, I must admit; for she told me that she only saw the murderer's hand," replied Madame Gémozac.

"Ah, yes, the hand! That seems to haunt her incessantly," said Julien. "During her first nervous attack, she kept crying: 'Oh, that hand—it is coming nearer! It threatens my father! Drive it away!' She was delirious, you know. It is true that the doctor said at the post-mortem examination that her father had been strangled by an enormous hand; and, I myself, realised that when I first examined the body. Still that is no clue after all, for nearly all murderers have enormous hands. Don't you recollect that some while ago nothing was talked of but the extraordinary size of Tropmann's thumb?"

Just then a footman entered the breakfast-room, a very unusual occurrence, by the way, as M. Gémozac insisted upon breakfasting alone with his wife and son, and the servants had orders never to come in unless they were summoned: "What is it, Jean?" asked M. Gémozac, frowning.

"Mademoiselle Monistrol wishes to see you and madame, sir. I told her that you were at breakfast."

"No matter. Show her in," replied his master, promptly.

When Camille, who had been waiting in the hall, was ushered into the room, Julien scarcely recognised her. He had only seen her in the costume she had worn on the evening of their first meeting. He had left her in the height of a violent fever, with her clothes in disorder, her hair unbound, and her features distorted by suffering; whereas, she now appeared under an entirely different aspect; plainly dressed in black, with her hair arranged in a fashion that admirably suited her style of face, and pallid with suffering; however, this pallor only enhanced her beauty, and lent her a charm which impressed young Gémozac deeply. The father, who now saw her for the first time, gazed at her in speechless admiration, but Madame Gémozac rose up, took her affectionately by the hand, and seated her near her husband, who scarcely knew what to say although he felt most kindly disposed towards her.

Camille relieved him of his embarrassment, by quietly remarking: "I have been impatiently waiting for an opportunity to thank you, sir. My father was indebted to you for the happiness that brightened the last day of his life; however, it is not to you alone that I must ever feel grateful."

These last words applied to the son and to the mother, who took it upon herself to answer for all.

"My dear child," she said, kindly, "you are now almost one of our family, and we have only done our duty; Julien in assisting you in a most trying moment, and I in caring for you afterwards. My husband will do his in watching over your financial interests and managing your property. But you did very wrong to venture out to-day. It was extremely imprudent in your present state of health."

"The doctor gave me permission to do so, madame. I am quite well again. As proof of it, I underwent a long examination yesterday without feeling any ill effects."

"What! the magistrate did not fear to subject you to such a painful trial? I think he might have waited at least a few days longer."

"I called upon him unsolicited, and begged him to grant me a hearing. I made a great mistake, however, for he attached no importance to my evidence. He takes me for a lunatic, or rather, he thinks I only dreamed what I told him. Perhaps, he even suspects me of being the murderer's accomplice. He did not say so, but I thought I saw it in his eyes."

"Then he must be an idiot," exclaimed Julien, hotly.

"He blamed me for having abandoned my father to run after the wretch who had just killed him."

"But you did not know that your father was seriously injured. I was with you when you first found him lying lifeless upon the floor, and I said as much to the magistrate."

"He pretends that the murderer must have been informed by some one that my father had been paid a large sum of money that day."

"I hope he is not so stupid as to suppose that you were the person who informed him. It would be much more sensible on his part to arrest all the acrobats who performed at the fair and search for the murderer among them."

"He has released the man I accused. And now, perhaps, he will send me to prison," said Camille, bitterly.

"Ah!" exclaimed M. Gémozac. "In that case I would willingly testify that you have always been the most devoted and affectionate of daughters. I knew Monistrol for a long time, and he always spoke of you in the highest terms, and often told me how nobly you had helped and encouraged him in the many trying ordeals through which he had passed. You were his only comfort, for your mother died in bringing you into the world. You had never been separated from him, and it was chiefly for your sake that he wanted to make a fortune. By dint of perseverance and industry he succeeded at last; but he did not live to enjoy his success. I am here, however, to look after you, and your future shall be my care. I shall deserve no credit for it, however, for you are rich, very rich. Your share in the profits of the partnership I formed with Monistrol will yield you, this very year, at least fifty thousand francs, and I shall immediately make such arrangements as will enable you to live in a style befitting my partner's daughter and heiress."

"I thank you, sir, but I prefer not to make any change in my mode of life. I have always been poor, and I am perfectly content with my lot."

"But I shall be obliged to pay you this money, even against your will, for I can not keep what doesn't belong to me. Besides, how can you do without money? Your father left you nothing besides his patent."

"The house in which he died belongs to me. It was my mother's only dowry on her marriage."

"But even if you let it, it would not yield you enough for your daily wants," said M. Gémozac, smiling.

"Nor can you live there alone," added his wife. "I shall endeavour to secure suitable apartments for you in this neighbourhood. It is not a very gay one, it is true, but we shall be neighbours, and so we shall be able to see each other every day. If you consent, I will also find two trusty women to serve you."

"I am very grateful to you, madame," Camille answered gently; "but I have made up my mind not to leave the house in which I have always lived. My old nurse who has been living at Montreuil, is willing to come and stay with me, so that I need not trouble you to find any other servants for me."

"But you will need money to live upon," rather brusquely replied M. Gémozac, who could not understand the young girl's persistent refusals, "and I shall be in your debt to a considerable amount before the end of the year. You surely don't want me to send you a lawyer to make you receive your dues."

"I must ask you to keep the money for me, merely paying me what I may require to defray my expenses."

"That sounds much more reasonable," said M. Gémozac, rubbing his hands. "But you must understand that my purse is at your disposal, and that you can draw upon it as you please. I will invest for you any money that you don't use, and in a year or two, mademoiselle, you will be a splendid match, with any number of suitors to choose from."

"I haven't any intention of marrying."

"But why not, my dear child?" inquired Madame Gémozac.

"Because I have a mission to fulfill."

"A mission?"

"Yes. I am resolved to avenge my father. As the authorities are powerless, I will do what they can't, or won't, do. I will ferret out the murderer, and drag him before them, and then we will see if they still refuse to listen when I say: 'Here he is!'"

"And you hope to find this scoundrel, whose face you did not even see, so my son tells me?"

"I shall find him. I feel almost positive of it. God will not allow the scamp to escape me as he escaped those who sought him so indifferently. I will pursue him to the ends of the earth, if need be. Nothing shall deter me; and if I die with my task still unfulfilled—"

"Do not talk of dying at your age," interrupted Madame Gémozac. "Time will assuage your very natural grief, and you will forget the past in thinking of the future. Nothing is eternal in this world, my dear Camille. Some day or other you will be loved by a man worthy of you, and you will love him in return. We women are born to be wives and mothers. You talk of a mission—our mission is to make our husbands happy, and to bring up our children."

"I know it, madame; but if I ever marry anyone it will be the man who brings my father's murderer to justice."

"Take care, mademoiselle," said M. Gémozac, gaily, for he had no idea that their young visitor was really in earnest. "If you persist in this resolve, you will perhaps be obliged to marry a detective."

"No," replied Camille, firmly. "A detective would only be doing his duty in finding and arresting a murderer, and I should be under no personal obligation to him. I speak of anyone who might assist me in my work merely out of regard or sympathy for me. If such a man succeeded in his efforts, I should not begrudge him his reward."

"Well, if I were a younger man I might try to win the prize," laughed the manufacturer. "Under such conditions there are many men who would be only too happy to serve you."

Julien said nothing; but his mother read in his eyes that he would not be sorry to enter the lists. And, in fact, though he was not yet exactly in love with Mademoiselle Monistrol, Julien said to himself that it would be a great feat to win the hand of his father's youthful partner. It was not her fortune that tempted him, for he had money enough for both; but Camille was very beautiful, and her originality attracted him. Besides, he was beginning to grow tired of his aimless existence, and this would be an excellent opportunity to put an end to a life of pleasure that had ceased to amuse him. The question was to know if Mademoiselle Monistrol would accept him as an ally, and though bashfulness was not his besetting sin by any means, he dared not offer his services for fear that she might decline them.

"I admire your energy, my dear Camille," now said Madame Gémozac, "but I wonder how you will set to work to accomplish your object."

"I have no idea yet. God will inspire me."

"But you will come to see us occasionally, won't you?"

"Certainly, madame; only I must beg of you to grant me entire liberty. I must be free to come and go as I like. I may even be compelled to leave Paris—for a time."

"Ah! ah! Money is called the sinews of war," interposed M. Gémozac; "and it is always necessary in travelling. So you must do me the favour to come to my office; but no—you need not take the trouble—my cashier will bring you five thousand francs now. Will that do as a beginning?"

"It is much more than I shall need, sir."

The wealthy manufacturer stepped to a speaking-tube, which was close at hand, applied his mouth and then his ear to it; and finally, turning to Camille, said:

"It is all right. When you want any more money, you have only to let me know. Now, a word in reference to your plan. I do not positively disapprove of it, but I advise you to take no decisive step until you are better informed on the subject; for I think, with my son, that there is nothing to prove that the acrobat you accuse is the culprit."

"He is the culprit. I am certain of it."

"If that be the case, he must have decamped before this time."

"Then I shall follow him up."

"It is by no means certain that he has gone off," said Julien. "The gingerbread fair is still in progress on the Place du Trône, and as the scoundrel succeeded in establishing an *alibi* when he was examined by the magistrate, he can no longer feel any fear of arrest. I will make inquiries concerning him if mademoiselle has no objections."

"I thank you, sir," replied Camille, promptly. "I shall continue my efforts on my own side, but I gladly accept the assistance you so generously offer."

"Bravo!" said the father. "Here is the fellow-labourer you were looking for, my dear child; but I advise you not to rely too much upon his co-operation. My son spends most of his time at his club, and in other even more objectionable places; however, if the interest he takes in your cause will cure him of his bad habits, I shall be under very great obligations to you. But I dare not flatter myself as yet that you have converted him."

"You shall see," said Julien, a little hurt by this lack of confidence.

Madame Gémozac refrained from taking any part in the discussion. She thought, like her husband, that Julien would do right to abandon the life he was leading, but she also considered that this new undertaking might involve him in serious danger. She liked Camille, undoubtedly, but the independent theories which the young girl had just advanced shocked her a little; and she did not care to see her son act as the ally of so bold a young person. Besides, foreseeing that such an association would almost inevitably result in a marriage, the prudent mother did not feel inclined to encourage it, thinking, rightly enough, that Julien might do much better in the social circles in which his parents moved; and this although Mademoiselle Monistrol might ultimately become very rich.

Just then the cashier entered the room with five rolls of gold in one hand and in the other a receipt, which Camille promptly signed; she had no occasion to blush at accepting this advance upon the inheritance which her unfortunate father had bequeathed to her.

"Do you know, mademoiselle," continued Gémozac, "that I feel very uneasy when I think of your living alone in that isolated house where your father was robbed and killed? Why do you insist upon remaining there? You must have a trusty body guard, at all events. Suppose I send you, every night, one of my employés, an old soldier, a regular Hercules, who is quite capable of keeping a whole band of brigands at bay? You must, surely, have a garret you could lodge him in?"

"Thanks, sir, but I have Brigitte."

"And who is Brigitte?"

"My nurse, sir. She is as strong as a man, and afraid of nothing. She will suffice to protect me."

"If I were in your place, I would not depend upon her too much. Besides, she is not yet at her post."

"Excuse me, sir; she has been with me since yesterday. I went to Montreuil for her, and she left everything to accompany me home. She is waiting for me now, so you must allow me to take leave of you."

Gémozac rose up. His wife was already on her feet, for she did not care to prolong the interview, although she intended to pay Mademoiselle Monistrol a visit on the following day, and to have a long and serious talk with her. She kissed the young girl affectionately on both cheeks, and accompanied her as far as the stairs, while the father and son contented themselves with shaking hands with her.

The brave girl had said all she had to say, and went off with money enough to defray not only her personal expenses, but those of her campaign for several months. She also knew that she now had a warm friend in the person of Julien Gémozac. Still, she depended chiefly upon her own efforts for success, and she resolved not to lose a moment in beginning operations.

She had come to the Quai de Jemmapes in a cab, and she now ordered the driver to take her straight to the Place du Trône. She passed her home on the way, and even saw Brigitte at the window, but she did not alight. She even reproached herself for not having previously examined the booths of the fair, and she felt impatient to find out whether the company to which Zig-Zag belonged was still performing there.

A fair, like a theatre, is always at a stand-still in the morning. The place is deserted, and silence reigns everywhere. There is no bustle, no excitement, merely a few urchins hanging around, or playing at hide-and-seek among the booths and stalls which are not yet open. Here and there one sees a toy or fruit dealer arranging his wares, or a tight-rope dancer wrapped in an old plaid shawl and perched upon a stool mending a shabby tunic, or a professional wrestler, returning from market in a thread-bare overcoat with a basket upon his arm. It is the time when the artists whom the public applaud in the evening become very commonplace and approachable mortals, ever ready to take a social glass on the zinc counters of the wine shops.

Camille was well aware of this fact, and she resolved to profit by it. She even hoped that chance might bring her face to face with the celebrated Zig-Zag, and so give her an opportunity to see his hands. He concealed them in performing his famous feats, but off the stage they must certainly be visible, and they could not be mistaken for those of any other acrobat on account of the enormous thumb which the magistrate refused to believe in, being evidently of the opinion that the girl's terror had magnified the object, and impaired her sense of vision.

She took care to alight from the cab at a short distance from the Place du Trône, in order not to attract attention, and she found nearly all the stalls and places of amusement closed, as the performances did not begin until four o'clock in the afternoon; still there were some signs of life around a few of them. The one where Zig-Zag had performed seemed to be deserted, however. No sound came from it, nor did any smoke rise up from the stove-pipe that projected above the roof of the long, red travelling waggon in which the members of the troupe slept at night.

This strange vehicle, a sort of Noah's ark—a "maringotte" in the language of mountebanks—stood behind the shanty. The two bony horses that dragged it about were now unharnessed, and tied to one of the wheels, they were grazing on the scanty turf of the public highway. A man in a pilot jacket and a cocked hat was sitting, with his arms folded, on the pole of the vehicle, with a short black cutty in his mouth. This fellow had a large, florid face, adorned with an enormous pug nose, and a mouth that extended almost from ear to ear.

Camille did not recognise him at first, on account of the change in his attire ; but, on looking at him more closely, she recollected that she had seen him before, for he was the very clown who had announced Zig-Zag's speedy appearance to the impatient audience. However, his jovial sarcastic air had vanished, his eyes were as glassy as those of a blind beggar, and his face wore an expression of the deepest despondency. Some misfortune had certainly befallen him ; and this furnished Camille with a pretext for entering into conversation with him. She boldly approached him, and interrupted his reverie by tapping him on the shoulder. He had not noticed her approach, and he now gazed at her with an air of bewilderment that rendered his appearance still more grotesque.

Camille knew how to deal with poor fellows of his class. "Ah, well, my worthy friend, things don't seem to be going on to suit you to-day," she said, pleasantly.

"No, when a fellow hasn't even money enough to buy a little tobacco," growled the man, taking his pipe from his mouth, and shaking the empty bowl.

"If it were only that !"

"It's quite enough, I think. It's very easy to talk, but I'd like to see how you would stand it if you hadn't had anything to eat for twenty-four hours, and had no tobacco to keep hunger away. Besides, what business is it of yours ? I never saw you before, and I don't feel in the humour for talking."

"I am surprised that you don't recognise me. You were present on the night when I was turned out of your place because they said I interrupted the performance. Don't you recollect that the policeman threatened to take me to the station-house ?"

"Oh ! indeed ! Yes, I know you now ; but if you hadn't spoken to me, I should never have guessed you were the person in question. Besides you are quite stylishly dressed now ; there's nothing like dress to change a woman. Well, so it was you then who pretended that Zig-Zag had robbed you. You must have made a mistake, for the magistrate who examined him could find no proofs against him. Is it true that several thousand frances were stolen from you ? "

"Not from me, but from my father—and the thief killed him."

"Then it wasn't Zig-Zag. He's a scoundrel, but he wouldn't have the courage to kill a man, or even cheek enough to mislead the magistrate. Besides, the officers came here and searched us and our trunks ; it was the deuce of a stir ! However, they found nothing, and Zig-Zag proved that he hadn't been out of the building during the performance. But you can congratulate yourself upon having done us plenty of injury, my little lady."

"Why, is one of your other comrades accused ?" asked Camille, quickly. "Bring me face to face with him, and I will testify that I do not recognise him."

"Oh, no one is accused, but the troupe is in disgrace ; and we have been obliged to close up since we don't earn a penny. The manager has made himself scarce, and for two whole days I haven't had a decent meal."

"You shall have one to-day, my friend," said the girl, drawing a twenty franc piece from her purse.

The man pocketed it without any ceremony. "That's capital! Good luck to you!" he exclaimed. "You have a kind heart. The little chap will have something to eat now." And two big tears rolled down his florid cheeks.

"Have you a child!" inquired Camille, with interest.

"Yes, a little shaver who is getting on for thirteen, and who works first rate. You must have seen him the other night. Ah, if I only had myself to feed, I could get along very well, for I am used to feeling hungry—but poor Georget—it goes hard with him."

"And your wife?"

"My wife!" sneered the unfortunate clown, "why she has run away with that scoundrel Zig-Zag."

"What!" exclaimed Camille, "Zig-Zag, the acrobat I pursued to the door of the show; he has run away, you say?"

"He decamped on the day before last, and took Amanda with him," was the doleful response. "A good-for-nothing hussy whom I picked up when she was begging on the public highway. She owes everything to me. I taught her to dance and perform on the tight-rope, and was fool enough to marry her : and only three years afterwards she leaves me for a rascal who isn't worth the rope to hang him."

"But how can she have made up her mind to desert her child?"

"Oh, Georget isn't her child. Thank God! I have been married twice, and if my boy's mother was alive, I shouldn't be where I am. She fell, and was killed, while performing at Guibray fair. She was a good wife to me, and took good care of the little chap, too. Ah! he won't regret Amanda, I can tell you. She was always scolding and abusing him, and I was coward enough not to put a stop to it! Besides, when I saw Zig-Zag hanging about her, I never once suspected that there was anything wrong. What a fool I was! Now she has gone off with him, and taken all my money with her,—three hundred francs that I had saved up penny by penny. It serves me right though for being such a fool."

The poor devil was actually weeping. His sincere sorrow touched Mademoiselle Monistrol, but it did not make her forget Zig-Zag. This was an excellent opportunity to obtain some information in regard to the scamp, and the idea of making the injured husband her auxiliary at once occurred to her. "I pity you with all my heart," she said, "and I will gladly assist you in discovering the culprits—for I suppose you are not going to leave them in peace. I, also, have an account to settle with Zig-Zag, you will remember."

"Yes," growled the clown, "now I think of it, it may be that he did kill your father, for after all he is capable of anything. Nothing would please me better than to see him mount the steps of the guillotine. But magistrates are such fools. They have let him go once, and they would let him go again, even if I succeeded in finding him, and I shall have no such good luck."

"You can search for him, however."

"And how shall we live in the meantime? My boy can't live upon air, nor can I, for that matter. Our employer has shut up shop. He owes money to everybody. The waggon and the scenery and the costumes have all been attached, and I must try to get hold of another engagement for Georget and myself, but it will be a hard thing to manage, for the fair closes on the day after to-morrow."

"What is your name?" Camille asked, suddenly.

"Jean Courapied, aged forty-five, born on the road between Paris and Amiens."

"Are you anxious to continue in your present calling?"

"I don't know any other way of earning my living. My father was a juggler, and my mother a circus rider, so you see I am a child of the ring."

"But if you and your son were sure of a comfortable and less laborious existence, what then?"

"I should jump at the chance, especially if I could send the little chap to school. But unfortunately I haven't yet discovered any wealthy person anxious to adopt me and give me an income."

"I will attend to that."

"You, my little lady? Your proposal suites me to a T, but what do you want me to do? I am only a clown, and I have no right to be too particular; and yet if you want me to commit any piece of rascality, I should refuse, if only on Georget's account."

"I hope so, indeed. If I had not taken you for an honest man, I shouldn't have spoken to you."

"Then what do you want me to do?"

"Can't you guess? My father has been murdered, and I have sworn to avenge him. The authorities have let his murderer escape. I only caught a glimpse of him, but you know him—"

"Zig-Zag, you mean? I should think I did know him! We have been travelling together for eighteen months. But how do you know that it was he who—"

"I am certain of it. After the crime, I pursued him, and saw him enter your place by the back door."

"It is true that he did have a key to it, but he declared upon oath that he did not leave the building during the performance. I knew he was lying, but I thought that he had merely gone to take a drink, so I didn't want to get him into trouble. Ah! if I had suspected that he was going to steal Amanda from me!"

"Well, if you agree to my offer, we will catch him again, and when we have him I will prove him guilty both of the robbery and the murder. Do you accept?"

"Certainly, certainly; but I can't promise to catch him. He is terribly sharp, and if he has all that money in his possession, he will have lost no time in getting out of Paris."

"Listen to me," replied Camille. "I am rich, and I shall spare no expense to find him. You and your child must begin by changing your clothes. You must be respectably clad, and in such a style that people will take you for a countryman who has just arrived from the provinces with his son. You must then hire rooms in some modest hotel, and take up your abode there with a respectable amount of luggage. You had better purchase your clothes and your trunks to-day. I reside near here, in a house which I will point out to you, but it would be better for you to select a part of Paris where you will be less likely to be recognised. You must come and see me as soon as you are installed in your new quarters, and you can then begin your search without a moment's delay. I will defray all the expenses, of course, and will pay you three hundred francs a month for your services, until we have succeeded. After that, I will obtain a situation for you, and send your son to a school where they will make a man of him."

Courapied was again weeping, but this time it was with joy. "Ah, madame," he began in a broken voice, "I—"

"Call me mademoiselle," interrupted Camille. "I am not married, and as my father is dead, I am sole mistress of my actions, nor is there any one to call me to account for the use I make of my money. Now what I desire of you is, first, some information about this scoundrel. What is his real name?"

"I never knew. Amanda knows, perhaps; and yet, I don't believe that he ever confided it to her."

"But he must have told some of his comrades."

"He had no comrades. He wasn't one of us—or, rather, he adopted the profession by chance—and he must have followed several other callings before he turned acrobat."

"How did he happen to become a member of your company, then?"

"It was by the merest chance. Early last year we were on a trip through the south of France, and our head gymnast went off into Spain without so much as saying good-bye. The manager tried to find some one to take his place, but couldn't. One evening, while we were encamped in a field on the edge of a strip of woods, a tall, strapping fellow, dressed like a gentleman, in a black suit—only it was terribly threadbare—came up to us. What had he been doing there in the wood? Probably lying in wait for some passer-by, to rob him. This did not prevent him from offering us his services, however. Our manager laughed in his face. But what did the fellow do but throw off his coat, slip his hands under his waistband and then perform his wonderful feat, right there on the grass, without the slightest preparation. We were amazed. One would have sworn that he had been born in the sawdust, our expression for 'in a circus.' But no, not at all, only an amateur it seemed, a gentleman's son."

"A gentleman's son!" repeated Mademoiselle Monistrol, in great surprise.

"Yes," said Courapied, nodding his head. "He told the manager that he had got into a scrape, that his father had cut off his allowance, and that he should like to try a roving life for a time. It was all a parcel of lies, I am sure, but that made no difference, for there were not three gymnasts in France who could do what he had done; perhaps he had worked abroad, at all events our manager engaged him, and he never had cause to repent of it, for Zig-Zag brought him in more money than all the rest of us put together."

"And didn't you ever discover who he really was during all the months that he spent with you? Did no one ever recognise him?"

"There was no danger of that, for he never appeared before an audience without a mask."

"But you must have seen his face."

"Of course; and I must admit that he had just the face to please a woman. Besides, he had what they call a distinguished air. But I never could bear the sight of him, with his papier-maché complexion and his greenish grey eyes—regular cat's eyes—and his bad disposition. He was always growling! No one liked him, at least no one but that good-for-nothing hussy, Amanda, and even she concealed her fondness for him. She even quarrelled with him sometimes, and I really thought she hated him. But I understand now. It was only because she was jealous when he made eyes at the fine ladies who applauded him."

"Still, they could only see the lower part of his face."

"That was enough. He has splendid teeth, and he is exceedingly well built—tall and slender as a reed, lithe as an eel and as strong as Samson. He had a bout with our Hercules once, and threw him without the slightest difficulty."

"That is not astonishing with hands like his."

"Yes, real pincers, they never let go their hold on what they once seize upon."

"Why does he always conceal them on the stage?"

"Oh, that is a part of the performance. Besides, our fine gentleman is afraid of spoiling them. Would you believe it, he always wears gloves when he takes a walk?"

Camille was now satisfied, and she deemed it unnecessary to make any further inquiries in regard to the shape and dimensions of Zig-Zag's hands. "Where do you suppose he went on leaving here?" she inquired.

"The deuce take me if I have the slightest idea!"

"Do you think he has joined some other troupe?"

"He's no such fool! All the companies visit the same fairs. We should be sure to meet him at Neuilly or at St. Cloud, and he can't have any wish to meet our manager or me. Besides, Amanda has got very tired of the business."

"Then what can have become of them? Have they left the country?"

"No; Amanda is too fond of Paris. I have an idea that they will both try to get a footing in fashionable society, She'll go to the bad, and he'll glide in among a lot of well-dressed intriguers—that is, if he has got money enough. How much did he steal from you?"

"Twenty thousand francs."

"That is twenty times more than he needs to enable him to change his skin. And it wouldn't take him long. Two or three days at the most."

"But in the meantime?"

"Oh! in the meantime it wouldn't surprise me if they have gone to some furnished rooms in the neighbourhood of Clichy or on the Route de la Révolte. Amanda knows plenty of good places. You see they will want to conceal themselves until they get a new outfit, and they'll have no difficulty in procuring it in that neighbourhood, of old Rigolo for instance. He can dress a man from head to foot for you in less than a quarter of an hour."

"Very well, we will search for Zig-Zag wherever you think best."

"You, mademoiselle! Oh, no, you must not think of such a thing. It's as much as I dare to attempt myself. And I sha'n't take Georget with me, you may rest assured of that. But talk of the devil—you know the saying. Here's the little chap now."

Camille turned and perceived the boy, who was really a handsome little fellow, with his rosy cheeks, fair curly hair, and large blue eyes. He was evidently greatly surprised to see this fine lady talking with his father, for he opened his eyes wide and did not venture to approach. However Camille smiled at him encouragingly, and Courapied called out: "Don't be afraid, little chap. Come here. What have you got?"

"Your breakfast, father," replied Georget, timidly. "I have picked up all the scraps I could find round about the ginger-bread booths, and I must have at least two pounds' weight."

"There, isn't he a sharp little chap?" proudly exclaimed the father, dashing away a tear. "He knew I was hungry, and went off, without saying a word, to find something for me. Gingerbread isn't a very satisfactory diet, especially when it has been trampled in the dust, but it keeps one alive all the same, don't it, Georget?"

Touched by this abject poverty, Camille took the little fellow by the hand and stooped to kiss him. He made no resistance, but he dared not lift his eyes to hers, though he was not naturally timid. He took part in the performance every evening with remarkable assurance, but he was not accustomed to being fondled by a well-dressed lady.

"Do you know how to read?" inquired Mademoiselle Monistrol.

"Yes, madame, and how to write, too," replied the lad.

"You have been to school, then?"

"No, madame, it was my mother who taught me."

"That is true," interposed Courapied. "My poor wife was much better educated than I am."

"Ah, well," said Camille, kindly, "I will take your mother's place. You loved her very much, did you not?"

"Yes, madame, and I am sure that I shall love you, too."

The little chap was already reassured, and he now stood gazing at the handsome young lady in evident admiration.

"I am going to send you and your father to a comfortable place, where you will both be well treated, well lodged, and well fed," added Camille.

"But what have we got to do then?"

"Assist me in finding a man who has wronged us all—a man and a woman."

"Zig-Zag and—I know."

The care with which he avoided mentioning Amanda's name in his father's presence convinced Camille that this child, with his evidently precocious mind, would prove a valuable auxiliary.

"It won't be easy," continued the boy. "Ah, if they had only left Vigoureux here! But they took good care not to do that."

"Vigoureux?" questioned Camille.

"Yes; Zig-Zag's dog. He would soon find his master for us."

Georget had scarcely uttered these words when a big bull dog dashed past the child, grazing his legs, and nearly throwing him down.

"There's the brute now!" exclaimed Courapied. "Zig-Zag can't be far off."

Camille, pale with excitement, glanced around her looking for the acrobat, but saw no sign of him. The dog, without pausing, rushed to the building, went straight to a place where the boards did not quite reach the ground, dug away the earth with his paws and then forced his way through the opening.

"Quick, Georget; a rope and a strap!" cried Courapied.

The boy did not ask his father why he wanted these articles; he understood the situation at once, and running to the horses which were grazing near by, he took a knife from his pocket, severed the rope that bound them, slipped off a strap, and immediately stationed himself, on his knees, near the hole through which the dog had gained admission into the shanty. Mademoiselle Monistrol watched these proceedings in silent astonishment, for she did not understand the object of Courapied's strange orders. In response to her inquiring look, however, the clown rubbed his hands complacently and said, "We are in luck."

"How so?" stammered Camille.

"Vigoureux will help us to find Zig-Zag."

"What! that bull-dog?"

"Yes. He hasn't his equal for following a scent. If he was taken ten leagues away, he would have no difficulty in finding his way home. The fact that he has come straight here, no doubt from the other end of Paris, is sufficient proof of that."

"But if he loved his master so much he wouldn't leave him."

"Don't you believe that, mademoiselle. He has been trained to do errands. Every morning Zig-Zag used to send him to the butcher's with a basket, and some money inside. As soon as he was waited on, he let the butcher take the money and then he would bring the meat back without touching it. It was that hussy, Amanda, who taught him."

"And what of it?" inquired Camille, who was still in the dark.

"Why, I shouldn't mind betting anything you like that Zig-Zag has left something—something that he is anxious to get hold of—behind him, and that he has sent the dog for it."

"Father," whispered Georget, "I hear him. He is tearing up the flooring with his teeth and paws."

"Oh! what he was sent for is no doubt concealed under the floor. Let him alone. He will come out with it presently. That will be the time to catch him. Keep your eyes open, little one."

The warning was superfluous, for crouching close to the shanty, like a terrier watching for a rat, the child waited, ready to slip the strap around the jaws of the beast, at the imminent risk of having his fingers snapped off in the attempt. Mademoiselle Monistrol, more and more astonished, was on the point of questioning the clown still further, but Courapied motioned her to be silent. The decisive moment was fast approaching, and it would not do to frighten Vigoureux, who on hearing a noise might make his escape by the other side of the building. But Vigoureux did not seem to consider any ruse necessary; he had recognised Courapied and Georget, and Zig-Zag had no doubt taught him that they were of little account. So he determined to get out by the way he had gone in, though this was no easy matter, for between his teeth he carried a long flat box with a steel handle. He pushed with all his strength, however, trying to get out of the shanty.

"See! what did I tell you?" exclaimed Courapied. "Isn't he a knowing beast? Look out, Georget; now's your time. Take care not to let him bite you."

Georget performed his rather difficult task with no little skill. He dexterously slipped the strap round the dog's jaws, gave it three or four turns, and then buckled it firmly. The whole thing was done in the twinkling of an eye. Vigoureux would gladly have used his teeth; but to bite, he must have dropped the box, and he was faithful to his trust. When he found himself thus muzzled he tried to retreat into the building, but Georget had his rope ready, and without losing a second, he slipped it through the ring of a collar which the dog wore about his neck, and began to pull with all his might. Vigoureux on his side began to pull in the opposite direction, and as he was much stronger than this twelve-year-old boy, the father darted forward. Between them they soon succeeded in pulling the animal out of the shanty; whereupon Vigoureux rising upon his hind paws sprung upon Georget, and felled him to the ground. However the lad was soon on his feet again and helped his father to master the dog. The latter still carried the box and Camille silently wondered what this receptacle could contain.

"Now, mademoiselle, we have our man," remarked Courapied with a triumphant air, "or at least, we can have him whenever we like. With a guide like this dog here, I am sure of finding Zig-Zag, and I shall start in pursuit of him this very evening."

"I should like to know what the box contains," murmured Camille after a short pause.

"I don't believe there is any money in it," was Courapied's reply. "When Zig-Zag has any cash he makes it fly, and it is not likely that he left what he stole from your father, here. See, every time that Vigoureux shakes the box, one hears a rattling like that of old iron; it isn't the ring of coin."

"The money Zig-Zag took was in bank-notes," remarked the young girl.

"The deuce of it is that there is no way of opening the box, or even of getting hold of it," remarked Courapied. "Vigoureux can not open his jaws, and if I unmuzzled him he would tear us to pieces. I shall have to take him off as he is; only, dash it all, what shall I do with him until night time?"

"Take him to my house," replied Camille. "I live alone with my old nurse only a few steps from here. You can accompany me home, fasten the dog up in the kitchen, and then leave your son with me while you go and purchase some clothes for yourself and him. When you have bought what you want you must come back and dine with me, and to-morrow you can look about for proper lodgings."

"Then your offer still holds good, mademoiselle," said Courapied timidly.

"More than ever; but come, we have no time to lose."

"I hope we sha'n't have to drag the dog along. See, he is pulling me in the direction of the Boulevard Voltaire," said the mountebank, at this moment.

"That is the very direction in which we are going," exclaimed Camille.

"So much the better then. Come along, Georget, you won't have to go hungry any more. Thank the young lady, and serve her faithfully, for if she had not offered us a helping hand, there would have been nothing left for us but to drown ourselves."

"I should prefer to go through fire for her," replied the youngster, who now had tears in his eyes.

III.

EASTER came very late that year. The ginger-bread fair was still in progress, and the open air concerts in the Champs-Elysées were beginning their season. In Paris this last is a sure sign that spring has indeed come. Those who make it the business of their lives to enjoy themselves, are not obliged to consult the calendar to change their amusements; and instead of shutting themselves up in theatres, they gladly avail themselves of the opportunity to go to places where they are sure to find women in light spring toilets, and where they can dine to the sound of music.

At least Julien Gémozac and Alfred de Fresnay did so on the evening of the day when Camille Monistrol first presented herself at the house of her father's partner. Julien had not yet quite forgiven his friend for the shabby trick he had played him by deserting him after their adventure near the Place du Trône. He indeed often reproached him for it, but a communion of tastes in many things had made them as inseparable as ever. They had met, as usual, at the club, between the hours of five and seven, and a

successful game of cards having put them both in good humour, they had
mutually agreed to spend the evening at the Café des Ambassadeurs.

They had taken their seats on the terrace overlooking the concert and
dined there, surrounded by a number of people. The cream of fast society
was there, all the tables were besieged, and they were fortunate in securing
a good place near the middle of the restaurant, and close to the balustrade.
They had come to enjoy themselves, and they did enjoy themselves, though
they were not in the same mood by any means.

Fresnay, in the wildest of spirits, exchanged smiling salutations and jokes
with his numerous acquaintances of either sex, and ridiculed the singers
shouting and screeching on the stage, though all this did not prevent him
from eating and drinking enough for four. Indeed, Bacchus appeared to
have a special charm for him that evening, and it seemed as though he
would end by becoming intoxicated.

Julien, being of a less exuberant nature, found his enjoyment in thinking of a host of things in no way connected with the gay scene around him.
He was beginning to find that even the most luxurious existence becomes
monotonous when it is aimless. He recollected, too, that he was nearing
his thirtieth year, and that domestic life has its charms. And above all,
he was thinking of Camille Monistrol, the beautiful and thoughtful girl
whom he had seen that morning, and who was such a striking contrast to
the gay moths around him. Their tricks disgusted him and it affected his
nerves when he heard their shallow laughter at the stale jokes of their
chance acquaintances. He even asked himself if he would not do as well
to lead a respectable life without delay.

To do this, he had only to adopt the course which Mademoiselle Monistrol had indicated, and which had many charms for him by reason of its
very difficulties. To seek adventures and brave dangers so as to win the
hand of a virtuous girl would be more pleasant and more novel than to
keep adventuresses or allow himself to be quietly married to some rich
heiress by his parents.

These sage reflections clashed with the grimaces and contortions of a
would-be comic actor who was now on the stage and they annoyed Fresnay,
who at last exclaimed: "What is the matter with you? You are as grave as
an owl. This is our third bottle of Brut Impérial, and you haven't opened
your lips except to drink. By the time I began the second, I was as gay
as a lark ; and now I begin to feel inclined for some act of folly."

"I don't," replied Julien, laconically.

"Will you bet me a hundred francs that I won't mount the platform
and sing a love song?" inquired Fresnay, unmoved by his comrade's reply.

"You are quite capable of doing so, no doubt, but you would be taken
to the station-house ; and I should let you go without interfering, if only
to pay you out for treating me so shamefully as you did the other night."

"What ! are you still angry with me about that? Why, you ought to
thank me. I left you alone with a young lady whom you evidently admired very much."

"And with a murdered man."

"My dear fellow, I had invited two very charming young women to
supper, and—"

"Oh, be quiet ! You will never be anything but a 'masher' I'm afraid,"
was Julien's sarcastic retort.

"So you think I have no romance in my soul. You are very much mistaken, my dear fellow. On the contrary, I am longing for all sorts of

chivalrous adventures. I thirst for the unknown. Yes, I, Alfred de Fresnay, a nobleman by birth, and a sceptic by profession, I dream of an ideal. The only trouble is that I can't find her. Still, there are times when I feel a wild desire to sacrifice myself for a woman, some woman of the kind one never meets. Show me one that is worth the trouble, and I will declare myself ready to defend her against the whole world. You shrug your shoulders, and you evidently think I am jesting. That is because you don't know me. I have romantic tendencies—so much the worse for you if you have not discovered them—latent tendencies—"

"That only appear when you are intoxicated," said Julien, drily.

"And when I have won at baccarat, eh! You are incredulous, I see, my dear fellow. However, you have only to put me to the test."

"Well, look! there is your ideal now," replied Gémozac, who was becoming tired of all this nonsense.

"What! that woman who has just come in? Well, I can't contradict you. She is certainly superb, and her style of beauty is wonderfully strange."

The ideal referred to was a tall creature with a fine figure, utterly unlike those of her own sex, at the tables on the terrace. They—whether blondes or brunettes—were all cast in the same mould, and attired in the same fashion, whereas the new-comer wore a showy costume, to which no fashionable dressmaker would have pleaded guilty, and which must have been devised by herself expressly to attract notice. Her hair was of that rich chestnut hue, over which the painters of the sixteenth century went wild; and her eyes sparkled like two black diamonds, but her lips did not part in the inane smile affected by most demoiselles. With her broad-brimmed hat adorned with long curling plumes, and her low-cut dress, she looked like a Velasquez that had just stepped out of its frame.

Her arrival had evidently caused a sensation. Some mashers smiled sneeringly, and their feminine companions giggled. The new-comer was evidently a stranger, though she could hardly be freshly out as she did not seem at all timid, but stood surveying the crowd rather scornfully, jostled every now and then by the waiters, who were hurrying to and fro from the restaurant to the terrace.

Fresnay did not neglect this opportunity to convince his friend that daring adventures had no terrors for him, for he rose up, walked straight to the new-comer, and said to her without any preamble whatever : "You are looking for a seat, madame. There is one at our table."

"No indeed, I am looking for a friend," the new-comer remarked coldly, at the same time eyeing Fresnay with marked assurance.

"A friend who has failed to keep his appointment, as he is not here. Pray dine with us."

"I have dined, but I will take a seat."

Thereupon Fresnay gallantly offered the fair stranger his arm, and conducted her to the chair which he had just vacated, and which she took possession of without any urging.

Gémozac would gladly have dispensed with the society that his companion thus forced upon him, and yet his curiosity was aroused. "Where have I seen that face before?" he said to himself.

But closely as he examined the features of this beauty with chestnut hair and black eyes, he did not succeed in recollecting under what circumstances he had seen her previously. Perhaps he was even deceived by some chance resemblance. He fancied he could recall her figure, features and complexion, but there was something about her that puzzled him.

B

Fresnay, elated by his discovery, already began to assume a triumphant air. He stuck his thumbs in the arm-holes of his waistcoat, and lounged back, ogling this fantastic being. He seemed to be saying: "This is my conquest, I wish you all equal luck." However, the new-comer did not return his glances, or even open her mouth. In fact, she did not appear conscious that she was sitting at table with two gentlemen who were well worthy of any woman's notice, for Gémozac was decidedly handsome, and Fresnay was at least a tip-top swell. On the contrary, she seemed to be entirely engrossed by the gay appearance of the stage. Indeed, it absorbed her to such an extent, that she remained wholly oblivious of her neighbour's admiring glances.

"Confess that you came to see Chaillié, the little bunch-back," said Fresnay. "All the women are raving about him, though, really, I don't see why."

"I never even heard of that person before," replied the new comer, disdainfully.

"Then is this really your first visit to the Café des Ambassadeurs?" inquired Alfred.

"Yes. What are those girls sitting there on the stage for? Are they going to sing?"

"Oh! dear no. They are simply 'supers.'"

"Why are they dressed, one in blue, another in red, another in yellow, and another in green? They look like so many parrots."

"That's it, exactly. You are probably a dramatic, or perhaps a lyric artist, madame?"

"Nothing of the kind. I am a foreigner."

"Ah! that does not surprise me. French women don't have eyes and hair like yours. You must be a Spaniard," said Fresnay, in a questioning tone.

"No, a Hungarian."

"It comes to the same. Your nationality won't prevent you from accepting a glass of champagne, perhaps?"

"Willingly. I am thirsty."

Fresnay was about to fill a small glass, but the woman interposed. "No," said she, "not in that. I would rather have a cup glass."

"I will ask the waiter to bring one."

"Oh! it isn't worth the trouble. This will do."

And taking a champagne cup, which stood, full, in front of Julien, she emptied it at a single draught.

This was taking a liberty, but Julien showed no resentment. In fact, he made a slight bow, as if to thank the foreign beauty for the unexpected honour she had done him, and she, on her side, favoured him with an engaging smile. Her manners puzzled Gémozac more and more, and he tried harder than ever to recollect where he had previously met her, but, being still unsuccessful, he finally ventured on this question: "May I ask, madame, how long have you been in Paris? I have never been in Hungary, and yet I can not help fancying that your face is not unknown to me."

"That is quite possible," was the foreigner's quiet reply. "I only arrived in Paris last week, but I have been almost everywhere already, for I, not unnaturally, want to see everything that there is to be seen."

"Have you been doing Paris alone?" inquired Fresnay, with evident curiosity.

"Yes, sir," answered the Magyar beauty, and with a remarkable assumption of dignity, she added : "I can dispense with a protector, for I am not afraid of anything or anybody."

"Then you are not married?"

"I do not need a husband."

"What am I to understand from that, pray?"

"That I wish to do as I please ; and just now, it pleases me to pry into every nook and corner of this strange city. It isn't the monuments that most interest me. I want to see the Paris I have read so much about in French novels—the drinking dens, the gambling places, the—"

"And so you began the evening with a café concert in the Champs Elysées. That is right, madame. But there are many places of greater interest, and if you will accept me as a guide, I can assure you that you could not find a better one."

"Thanks ; but I have one already."

"Oh, some interpreter furnished by the hotel at which you are stopping. No doubt he will take you to the mint, the markets, and the slaughter-houses, but an old Parisian like myself could show you places that foreigners never see."

"You are mistaken, sir," said the beautiful Magyar, and once more, she assumed an air of dignity. "My guide is no hireling, but one of my compatriots, who has resided in this country for ten years or so, and who was a friend of my father's. He has placed himself at my disposal, and we go out sight-seeing together. I expected to find him here this evening. He told me he should dine here."

"And he has failed to keep his word. That is unpardonable, but I will do my best to take his place. Where would you like to go, when the concert is over ? Speak, don't hesitate. Would you like to see Father Lunette's drinking den; or 'The City of the Sun,' commonly known as Little Mazas ? Or would you prefer to sup at the 'Rabbit's Grave?' the rag-picker's favourite haunt."

"Those places must be very interesting, but my pet ambition is to witness the pursuit of a criminal or a murderer—some of the scenes described in the books of your great novelist, Gaboriau."

"The woman must be mad," thought Julien, who was beginning to look terribly bored.

"I can readily understand such a desire on your part," replied the imperturbable Fresnay. "But, unfortunately, there is no particular day appointed for such expeditions. Besides, as you seem to be so familiar with our language, you must know the proverb : 'To make hare soup, you must, first, have a hare,' and murderers, fortunately, are even more un-common than hares."

"One would not think so from the newspapers. Hardly a day passes without mention being made of some new crime. Why, on the very day after my arrival, all Paris was talking of a murder on the Boulevard—I forget the name. Oh, yes, the Boulevard Voltaire."

"Yes, indeed, that murder was of quite recent occurrence, and a very strange affair it was, too."

Julien here gave Fresnay a warning kick under the table; but the young baron, ignoring it entirely, continued : "And I shall doubtless surprise you very much, my dear madame, when I tell you that I and my friend here were both mixed up in the affair."

"You, sir ?" exclaimed the foreign beauty, with a questioning glance at Gémozac, who felt a strong desire to pommel his companion for his indiscretion

Fresnay answered for him, however. "Yes," he cried, "my friend, Julien Gémozac, whom I have the honour to introduce to you, first discovered the body. By the merest chance we happened to be near the scene of the crime. But the strangest thing of it all is that Julien is well acquainted with the murdered man's daughter."

"True, the papers did mention that he had a daughter. I remember reading so," murmured the stranger.

"And a very pretty girl she is, too, and quite young," added Fresnay with alacrity.

"Ah! how I pity her. I know what it is to be left an orphan just as one is entering life. I was sixteen when I lost my father, but fortunately I came into possession of a large fortune at his death, whereas this poor child probably finds herself reduced to poverty."

"You need not trouble yourself on that point, my dear madame," was Alfred's remark.

"Indeed?" exclaimed the foreign beauty, with an eagerness that surprised young Gémozac.

"Yes," replied Fresnay, "she will be very rich, though her father hadn't a penny. It seems, however, that he had invented some improvement to be applied to steam engines, and that the invention will yield his daughter an enormous amount of money. Julien here can explain all this to you much better than I can, for his father was associated with the murdered man, and is now in partnership with the daughter."

"Will you never have done talking about this uninteresting matter?" exclaimed Julien, now thoroughly exasperated with his half-intoxicated companion, who seemed to take a sly pleasure in making these indiscreet disclosures to an unknown woman.

"Excuse me, sir," said the Hungarian beauty, gently. "I have offended you, though unintentionally, I assure you, by questioning you friend about a person in whom you seem to take an interest. I regret it exceedingly. I also did very wrong to seat myself at your table, for you must have formed a very poor opinion of me. It is all the fault of my training, and of the education I received, however. I have always been in the habit of acting without the slighest constraint, and without stopping to consider the consequences of my words and actions. But I trust that you will not mistake me for an adventuress. I am the widow of the Count de Janos, and I am staying at the Grand Hotel until I can find more suitable quarters. If you will call and see me, I think you will change your opinion as regards me, and I will then introduce you to my compatriot, Monsieur Tergowitz, whom I expected to find here this evening."

"I really hope that you won't close your doors against *me*?" now exclaimed Fresnay.

"No, sir, but I trust that you will be kind enough to tell me your name," was Madame de Janos's dignified reply.

"I presented my friend Gémozac, but as he does not seem inclined to return the favour, I shall be compelled to introduce myself. Alfred, Baron de Fresnay, at your service, madame; twenty-nine years of age, an orphan, likewise a bachelor, and a land-owner in Anjou. Julien and myself represent respectively the aristocracy and the third estate, but I would gladly exchange the revenues of my barony for Monsieur Gémozac's millions, which will descend to his only son some day or other."

"It is enough for me to know that I have to deal with two gentlemen," said the countess, graciously. "I should be delighted to see you again, but I doubt if you will retain any recollection of this chance meeting."

"I will convince you to the contrary, and very soon," protested Fresnay, with another killing glance. He was becoming more and more infatuated with the chestnut-haired beauty from wild Hungary.

Julien on his side did not speak a word. In fact he did not believe the assertions of this beautiful stranger, who impressed him as being a mere adventuress. He was even beginning to suspect that she had her reasons for endeavouring to become acquainted with them, and he secretly anathematized Alfred for his imprudent indiscretiou as regards Mademoiselle Monistrol.

"Not only do we hope to see you again," now remarked Fresnay, "but I trust that we shall be able to take you on an interesting excursion this very evening. If you are willing we will show you a strange corner of Paris when the concert is over."

"Meanwhile," said the stranger, without rejecting or refusing the offer, "pray let me enjoy this novel sight here. Won't there be any more singing? The gaily-dressed damsels have disappeared, I see, and the stage is empty."

"They will return by and by, after a performance on the trapeze, which isn't likely to interest you much," said Fresnay, imagining that he was acquainted with the countess's tastes.

"Excuse me," she retorted, "but I enjoy the feats of gymnasts exceedingly, and am very anxious to see if these French performers excel ours in skill."

"Gymnasts," repeated Gémozac, mentally, "she uses the right word, and speaks French very correctly. Where can she have come from? She will never make me believe that she is really a woman of rank. She is some ex-governess, probably, as that fool of an Alfred will find out, no doubt, without my having to trouble myself about the matter."

Alfred continued drinking champagne to excite himself, while the foreign countess sat watching, with marked attention, the performance of two artists in flesh-coloured tights and silver fringed boots, who were executing some extraordinary feats on the horizontal bar. She was a judge, unquestionably, for she soon greeted a successful leap with an approving nod of the head, and the next minute made a contemptuous grimace when she noted the rather clumsy execution of another feat. The chair which the gallant Fresnay had relinquished to her was close to the balustrade, upon which—as though irresistibly attracted by the interesting performance—she finally leaned both elbows, without troubling herself in the least degree about the two young men sitting near her. Julien could now only see her profile, and Alfred was even less fortunate, for she turned her back upon him. The diners of both sexes who thronged the terrace paid no attention to this ill-assorted trio, but the two friends exchanged signs which the Hungarian, seated as she was, could not perceive.

"Let us decamp as soon as possible," said Julien in quick pantomime. "I don't want to be bored with this foolish woman all the evening."

"I like her," responded his friend Alfred, in the same way. "You can go off, if you like, but for my own part I shall remain and see the end of the adventure."

So no one moved, although Julien, in his secret heart, was fuming. He would have been glad to make his escape; but he felt sure that if he rose to do so, Alfred would at once protest, the woman interfere, and that he would then have to explain his reasons for this hasty departure. And he could give no good motive, for his friend knew very well that he had nothing whatever to do that evening. While Julien reluctantly sat there, facing the balustrade, like the stranger, he suddenly noticed, in the crowd below him, a gentleman who stood gazing up at the terrace as if seeking some one among the diners.

This gentleman was young, good-looking, well-dressed, and well-gloved; so it was not at all surprising that he should be eyeing the pretty girls seated at the tables above; but Julien soon perceived that his attention was bestowed exclusively upon the pretended countess, and that he must know her, for he made a gesture which could only be addressed to her, and which seemed to signify: "Very well. I understand. All right." Julien had seen only the close of the pantomime, which had no doubt lasted some minutes, but the discovery increased his distrust.

"Farewell! ye acrobats!" now exclaimed Fresnay. "They have finished at last. Now we shall have some more singing from vociferous sopranos and squeaky tenors. Is Madame la Comtesse particularly anxious to hear them?"

"By no means," replied the lady. "My friend does not make his appearance, I see, and it seems useless for me to wait for him, for I begin to think that he must really have forgotten his appointment. And I thought he would be so punctual!"

"It really is very bad form; but, fortunately, I am at hand to serve you, my dear madame, and I promise to show you a novel sight if you will trust yourself to my guidance."

"I shall not refuse if your friend will consent to be of the party," was the gracious reply.

"Pray do not rely upon me," replied Julien Gémozac, somewhat more hastily than the ordinary rules of polite society admitted.

"Oh! you must come," remarked Fresnay, "for I am going to take you to a place where you will stand a very good chance of meeting Monsieur Monistrol's murderer, and you know that you promised Mademoiselle Monistrol to assist her in finding the scoundrel."

"Who is Mademoiselle Monistrol?" quietly inquired the so-called Countess de Janos.

"She is the daughter of the inventor I was speaking of just now. I have only seen her once, and I am by no means sure that I should know her again, but my friend Gémozac is destined to see a good deal of her, and he is greatly interested in her."

"Pray do hold your tongue," interrupted Julien, angrily. He could barely control himself.

"Don't be ashamed of a sentiment that certainly does you honour, sir," remarked the noble foreigner. "That young girl is alone in the world, I believe, and it is only natural that you should become her champion; and if she really thinks of avenging her father—"

"She thinks of nothing else," exclaimed Fresnay. And as Julien turned sternly upon him to silence him, the incorrigible chatterer added: "You told me so yourself. You also told me that she had sworn to marry the man who ferrets out the murderer, and her hand is no mean prize, as her father's invention will yield her millions. I should, perhaps, have entered the field myself, but she must have a sort of grudge against me; besides, I can employ my time better."

As he spoke, he bestowed an ardent glance upon the beautiful

Hungarian, who for the first time responded to his advances by an encouraging smile.

Julien felt disgusted, and he was no doubt about to make a scene, when a waiter who had come upstairs approached the table, and asked : "Am I to hand madame a card which a gentleman requested me to deliver to the Countess de Janos ? "

"Yes," replied the foreign beauty, stretching out her hand for the card, and she had no sooner glanced at the name inscribed upon it than she exclaimed : "Ah ! I knew that Monsieur Tergowitz would not disappoint me. He is here ; he has seen me and requests me to join him." Then turning to the waiter, she added : "Tell the gentleman I am coming."

"What ! you are going to leave us ? " replied Fresnay, affecting amazement and despair.

"To my very great regret, sir ; but it is absolutely necessary. I have an engagement with this gentleman, as I remarked before," said the Hungarian beauty.

"Introduce us to him, and let all four of us finish the evening together," pleaded Alfred.

"It would be delightful, but I think it would be better to defer the introduction until some future time, at my place, for instance, when I have the pleasure of receiving a call from you."

"Is your compatriot also stopping at the Grand Hotel ? " asked Fresnay somewhat sarcastically.

"No, sir, I am alone there, and time often hangs heavy on my hands. Monsieur Tergowitz knows it, and comes almost every day to see me. So out of gratitude I must join him now. Until we meet again, gentlemen— or farewell," the stranger added, rising with such a determined air that Fresnay stood aside to let her pass, and made no further attempt to detain her.

She crossed the terrace without looking at any one, and turned into the passage leading to the stairs.

Meanwhile, Gémozac scarcely waited for her to be out of hearing before he gave vent to his indignation. "Are you determined to anger me beyond endurance ? " he exclaimed hotly, at the same time darting a fierce glance at his friend.

"What do you mean?" retorted Alfred, coldly. "Are you angry merely because I tried to ingratiate myself with a very pretty woman ?—for she is pretty, you can't deny it."

"Make love to her as much as you like then, that is nothing to me ; but don't tell her my affairs or those of my friends, if you please. It's altogether too bad !"

"So you are offended because I spoke of you and Mademoiselle Monistrol. What's the harm, pray ? That woman doesn't know you, and it isn't likely that she will ever meet the young lady in whom you are so deeply interested. The countess came to Paris to enjoy herself, and not to meddle with matters that don't concern her."

"Then you think she is a genuine countess? You really are stupid, my dear boy," remarked Julien with an air of superiority.

"Not so stupid as you suppose. I care very little about her noble origin, but I think her a very charming person, and I am looking forward to a very agreeable acquaintance. Besides, I like foreign beauties."

"Take care that she does not lead you further than you want to go. In my opinion, that creature is an adventuress of the worst kind ; and her friend, Monsieur Tergowitz, is probably no better than she is. I saw him making signs to her from below while you were billing and cooing, I have no doubt but what they understand each other perfectly. You'll get yourself into a pretty mess if you pursue the acquaintance any further. Still, it makes no difference to me. Put your head into the noose if you like, but never mention my name again before these people."

"Nor that of Mademoiselle Monistrol. Very well. It's understood; but I expect that the countess has forgotten both names by this time; and it is quite certain that she never expects to see you again, for you put on your bearish air and said nothing but disagreeable things to her all the while she was with us."

"I didn't say half as many disagreeable things to her as I wanted to," was Julien's sharp retort. "I dislike the woman as much as you seem to like her, and that is saying a good deal. Besides, I have a presentiment that she will cause me some trouble or other."

"How can she possibly harm you? You have evidently decided not to call upon her, so it is not at all probable that you will ever see her again. Besides, what possible object could she have in doing you and me any injury? You were not very polite to her; still, that is no reason why she should declare war upon you."

"What if I should tell you that I am almost certain I have seen her somewhere else, and in an entirely different costume? Besides, I can't get it out of my head that she came here expressly to enter into conversation with us, and to induce us to tell her things she is interested in knowing. In that case you served her well, for you gave her any amount of information that she did not even ask for."

"Only about Mademoiselle Monistrol. You have mounted your hobby again, I see," now said Fresnay, beginning to laugh.

"Try at least to atone for your folly by helping me to discover whom we have had to deal with. It will be an easy matter for you to obtain some clue when you call on her, for she must have a maid, and a louis or two will induce the servant to tell you all you want to know about her mistress."

Fresnay looked at his friend in amazement. "So now you want me to play the spy! Such a part does not suit me at all; still, if only to cure you of your prejudice against this poor countess— There, I see her now! She is talking with a gentleman over yonder in the corner."

"Yes," growled Julien, "with the same fellow who was making signs to her a few moments ago. I saw them, you know, and I recognise him perfectly."

"It is Monsieur Tergowitz, the Hungarian nobleman, of course," said Fresnay.

"He is neither a Hungarian nor a nobleman, I can vouch for that."

"He is very good-looking, at all events, though after all he does seem more of a Parisian than a foreigner. Ah! ah! they seem to be carrying on a very animated conversation. Just look, they have seated themselves, side by side, in two arm-chairs. It is a pity we can not hear what they are saying. You would know what to think—and so should I."

There was more truth in Fresnay's words than he supposed, for the conversation which had just begun between the foreigner and her escort would have removed all doubts as to their character and connection.

"We had better not remain here," said the man called Tergowitz. "Those two young fools whom you were with just now can see us from up there."

"I know it," his companion replied, "but I told them I was going to join you here. If we went off immediately, it would look very much as though we were running away. To play my part properly, I must remain here for a time quietly talking with you."

"Then the bait took," said the man, rubbing his hands. "What did you tell them?"

"That I was the Countess de Janos—that I had come to Paris to amuse myself, and that I had no acquaintance in the city except a compatriot, a Hungarian nobleman named Tergowitz. You, of course, are Tergowitz."

"And they swallowed the yarn?" asked the beauty's companion half incredulously.

"They pretended to swallow it, and that is all I care about for the present."

"They did not recognise you, then?"

"Oh! no : I am sure of that."

"Good! Now, what are those two fellows as regards social standing, and so on?"

"The short one is named Alfred de Fresnay. He is a baron, and seems only to think of enjoying himself. He took a great fancy to me, evidently, and I am certain that he'll run after me. He isn't dangerous, but I am afraid of the other one—the tall fair-haired fellow. He didn't say much, but he never once took his eyes off me."

"Did you find out his name?"

"I took good care to do that, and I can give you full particulars about him. He is Julien Gémozac, the son of Monsieur Gémozac."

"The Gémozac who owns some iron works on the Quai de Jemmapes? He must be worth his millions, then," said the man, and at the thought of such great wealth a flash darted from his eyes.

"Yes, and what is more, the young fellow's father was the partner of the girl's father. How strange, isn't it? And more than that, this young man happened to be at the fair on the very evening of the affair. Still the strangest thing about it all is that the Monistrol girl is rich. Her father invented something or other, and the invention is going to yield a great deal of money."

"That is something worth knowing," said the man in a pensive tone.

"Wait a bit, I haven't finished. The fair maiden has sworn to avenge her father it seems, and she offers her hand as a reward to the person who discovers the perpetrator of the crime. And Julien Gémozac is half inclined to win the prize ; I feel certain of that, so we are warned."

"I am not afraid of them," said the spurious Hungarian's companion with a sneering smile which showed his white teeth.

"Nor am I. They won't be more cunning than the magistrate was surely. Still there is that brute Conrapied. He will certainly recognise us if he meets us, and you may rest assured that he must be looking for us. Perhaps it would be well for us to spend two or three months in England."

"Nonsense, my dear! That would only be a waste of money, dawdling about and doing nothing, whereas we are sure of success if we remain in Paris. You remember the programme, don't you?"

"Perfectly. Each of us is to work on his own side, and we are to share the profits. But to begin with it will cost us pretty stiff."

"I know that. Ten thousand francs for our outfits at the least. You told them that you were staying at the Grand Hotel, didn't you?"

"Yes, and I am almost certain that Fresnay will pay me a visit there to-morrow," remarked Madame de Janos with a self satisfied air.

"Then you must take up your quarters there to-morrow morning with your maid and luggage. The trunks are waiting for you at the Eastern Railway Station, where I deposited them in your name. You will only have to call for them, and this evening I will bring you your maid. You know her, however."

"Olga, the fortune-teller? Yes, she's a sharp one, and if she can only be trusted—"

"Oh! I feel as sure of her as I do of you. Besides, she is at my mercy. If she attempts to rebel, I have the means of sending her to prison for ten years. But, let me tell you, I don't feel inclined to assume this character of a Hungarian nobleman which you have invented for me. I should only be in your way, and it would be better for me not to figure in the comedy you are going to play. I shall take up my abode somewhere else, and not under the name of Tergowitz."

"As you choose, providing I see you every day, or rather every evening."

"Very well; we can meet at our place on the plain of Saint-Denis, unless something happens to prevent it. However, everywhere else we must pretend to be perfect strangers to each other. So mind you are careful."

"That wouldn't do! those idiots dining up there have now seen me with you, remember."

"I shall keep out of their way in future. Besides, I don't want you to go too far with that swell you have just captivated. You are to receive him, and let him make love to you, but merely so as to keep informed as to the movements of his friend, Gémozac, who is probably going to turn detective so as to please the girl. I will attend to her."

"Very well," said the fair Hungarian, "but mind, no foolishness, my dear. If you think of entering the field as a rival of Gémozac's, you'll be sorry for it. I shouldn't hesitate to denounce you in that case. I've no intention of playing second fiddle to any other woman, I can tell you."

"You need have no fears of that. We are bound together, and when we have retired from business, with our fortunes made, we will go abroad, and marry. But just see, those fellows are leaving their table, and they are quite capable of coming down to take a look at me. It is time for us to go."

"Where to?"

"Why, to the Red Barn of course. It's the last night we shall have to spend there, but as you know I must go there after Vigoureux. He must have returned long ago, and we shall probably find him asleep on the box I sent him for."

"You had much better have left the box where it was. What can you want it for? Vigoureux is no doubt a very clever dog, but all the same some one might have followed him."

"Who? The old shanty is empty now, since the manager has made off; besides, I had no desire to leave the contents of my box for the first person who came along. Our forgetting it in our hasty flight has caused me worry enough already. When I get hold of it again, I shall have no further cause for fear."

The worthy couple left the garden by the gate opening on the Place de la Concorde just as Alfred and Julien entered it by way of the restaurant.

They had decided to go down to take a closer look at the countess and her escort, but they were too late. The birds had already flown.

"Never mind," said Fresnay, who always took things cheerfully, "there is nothing lost after all. To-morrow I will give you a full account of this Madame de Janos and Monsieur Tergowitz as well."

IV.

WHILE Julien Gémozac and his friend Fresnay were looking for the mysterious Madame de Janos, who had just disappeared with her equally mysterious escort, Camille Monistrol and her auxiliaries were preparing to start out upon their chase. The clock had just struck ten when they assembled in the kitchen of the little house on the Boulevard Voltaire—all three in full battle array.

Courapied had executed Camille's orders with intelligence and dispatch. A ready made clothes-shop had not only provided him with an outfit, but furnished him with a costume for Georget, and one for Mademoiselle Monistrol also. She had duly provided the clown with funds, not merely for these purchases, but so that he might have some money to go on with. In fact, she had already expended one of the five rolls of gold handed to her by M. Gémozac.

The clown now wore the garb of a plain but respectable denizen of the suburbs, and appeared quite what he pretended to be; whilst Georget looked very trim in a dark blue jacket with a triple row of steel buttons, and a cap trimmed with silver lace, the livery of a restaurant page. But the most successful disguise of all was that of Camille, who was dressed as a young journeyman printer, with a long white blouse, and a cap that entirely concealed her beautiful black hair, which she had caught up on her head for the occasion. One would have supposed that she had worn masculine attire all her life, and as she was quite as tall as Courapied, no one would have taken her for a woman. Even Brigitte began to believe that the people in the street would be deceived.

Not that the old nurse approved of this nocturnal expedition in company with a professional clown and a child of the ring. On the contrary, she had endeavoured to dissuade her young mistress from the project by every means in her power; but as all her eloquence had availed her nothing, she had resigned herself to what she was powerless to prevent.

The old nurse was a robust woman, as strong and as sunburnt as a peasant, as brave as an old soldier, and as faithful as a poodle dog. She had treated Courapied rather ungraciously at first, but she was fond of children, and Georget soon won her heart to such a degree that she exerted herself to the utmost to prepare a good dinner, to which both the father and son did ample justice.

Brigitte would even have fed Vigoureux, but he could not eat without being unmuzzled, and Courapied was strongly opposed to her doing that. He knew the animal, and declared that he would devour any one as soon as he could make use of his jaws. As it was, they had already had trouble enough to master him, and even if privation were to drive the brute mad, it was better not to unmuzzle him. Vigoureux was now lying in one corner of the kitchen securely tied to a large table, with the box still between his teeth, and foam about his snout, growling sullenly, and rolling his blood-shot eyes. It was evident that he realised his defeat, and it was also plain that he was waiting for an opportunity to secure his revenge. Had he been loose, he would have made but one bite of poor little Georget.

"We are ready," said Camille to her companions. "It is time to start."

"You had much better remain at home," growled Brigitte, shrugging her shoulders.

"Particularly as Georget and I can perform our task very well without you, mademoiselle. Indeed, I should much prefer to go alone," said Courapied.

"No, father," interposed Georget, eagerly, "mademoiselle told me I might go, and I am going."

"We will all three go," replied Mademoiselle Monistrol, firmly. "If there is any danger, I wish to share it."

"Danger, mademoiselle!" repeated Courapied, "I am sure there can be no danger, as we are merely going to try and find Zig-Zag's hiding-place. If we thought of arresting him it would be an entirely different matter, for the scoundrel would defend himself, and we should probably have a hard time of it."

"All I want this evening is to get a glimpse of him," said Camille. "When I have once seen him, I shall know what to do next."

"I am afraid it won't be an easy matter to see him without his seeing us. You may rest assured that he won't show himself in any public place. And if he's staying in some low lodging place, we can hardly go up to call on him."

"The main thing is to find out where he is, and if the dog takes us there, as you think he will—"

"Oh, I can answer for that, mademoiselle—that is, unless Vigoureux gets away from us on the road, and he can hardly do so, for the rope is strong, and I have a good grip. He will take us straight to his master's hiding-place, I'm sure of it. But it's when we get there, that our troubles will really begin. All the same I can't bear the idea of letting the box go; if I could only smash it with a hammer we might see what's inside it."

"We might kill Vigoureux and then force open the box. But as for breaking it with a hammer, it's in steel," said Georget.

"That idea is very pleasing to you because the dog has bitten you so often, and I shouldn't mind putting an end to him myself. Only without his assistance we should never succeed in finding Zig-Zag; though if we managed to open the box, we should probably find his papers."

"And something else, father," urged Georget. "If it contained nothing but papers, it wouldn't make such a noise whenever Vigoureux shakes it."

"There are some skeleton keys in it, perhaps, or a dirk. I have known for a long time that he had one, though I never knew where he secreted it."

Camille listened to this conversation between the father and the son with a slight frown. "You seem to be afraid of this man," she said, coldly.

"We have good reason to be, mademoiselle," muttered Courapied in reply.

"Very well, then, I will go alone," cried the young girl impulsively. "The dog will guide me all right, and I am strong enough to hold him."

"As if I would allow such a thing! I should be a coward, indeed! What I said just now was only because I couldn't bear the idea of giving up the box. But there will be some way to avoid that, perhaps. When we have once found out where Zig-Zag is stopping, we can bring Vigoureux back with us ; and then, as we shall have no further need of him, I will give myself the pleasure of hanging him."

As Courapied spoke he gave the dog a kick that made him spring to his feet with a stifled growl. At the same time, Georget untied the rope that bound him to the table leg, and handed the end of it to his father. A struggle ensued between the man and the animal ; but Vigoureux, being securely muzzled, did not prove a very formidable antagonist. He sprang on to his hind legs, trying to throw himself upon Courapied, but all in vain. Finally, he began to tug hard at the rope to reach the door.

"See how anxious he is to go," said Courapied. "We have only to follow him, and he will take us to that rascal Zig-Zag at a smart pace.'

Camille kissed Brigitte affectionately, and said to her, with all the coolness of an old soldier going into battle : "If I am not at home before morning, go and inform Monsieur Gémozac, at No. 124 Quai de Jemmapes. Tell him what has occurred here this evening. He will take the necessary steps to find me if need be."

"Oh, mademoiselle, no harm can possibly befall you," exclaimed Courapied. "Remember there are three of us ; and Zig-Zag won't be able to juggle us away as if he were playing the three card trick. Ah ! he's a clever fellow at that game, and might have made his fortune at it ! However, never mind all that—if there should be a bullet for any one of us, it shall be for me, for I have no fear of death now. I know that you will take care of the little chap."

"I will never desert him, whatever happens," said Camille ; "but I do not want you to endanger your life, and you won't endanger it, to-night, for we will content ourselves with a mere reconnoissance. Besides, if we should be obliged to defend ourselves, I have a revolver under my blouse, and I shall not hesitate to make use of it."

Brigitte raised her clasped hands to Heaven on hearing this startling announcement. The worthy woman knew that Camille was not afraid of anything, but she had not imagined that her young mistress would ever venture to handle a loaded firearm.

"Mademoiselle," resumed Courapied, "it's time to be off. The longer we delay, the worse the chances will be against us. Zig-Zag can't be staying in any decent neighbourhood, and if by chance he has pitched his tent any where near the fortifications, it won't be pleasant walking there after midnight."

On hearing this Mademoiselle Monistrol again kissed her old nurse who was crying in silence ; and then went off followed by her new friends. She walked ahead, but it soon became necessary to alter this arrangement. Vigoureux was needed as a guide, so that he must pass first with Courapied. This was arranged as soon as they reached the Boulevard Voltaire, and, in fact, the ex-clown went several yards ahead so as to break up the little party and thus furnish no grounds for attracting attention.

Vigoureux did not hesitate, but went down the Boulevard swiftly, and Courapied needed all his strength to prevent the impetuous animal from breaking away. Meanwhile, Camille and Georget quickly followed exchanging remarks.

"The dog knows where he is going," murmured Georget, as he watched his father and Vigoureux.

"I think so, too," replied Camille, "and judging by his eagerness his master can not be far off."

"I am not so sure about that, mademoiselle. If Zig-Zag were at Ver-

sailles, Vigoureux would pull just as hard at the rope. Last year, while
we were travelling through Picardy, the dog was locked up in a stable at
Roisel, where we had slept, and forgotten, but he broke open the door and
overtook us in the evening at Péronne, more than three leagues away.
Sometimes, Zig-Zag left him behind on purpose, just to show how easily
the dog could track us, and to astonish the folks of the towns we passed
through.   More than once he was offered two or three hundred francs
for the dog, but he would not sell him.   He knows that Vigoureux
would defend him if any officer should ever attempt to arrest him."

"Then you think he was afraid of being arrested?" inquired Camille, on
hearing this.

"Yes, indeed.   He never had any papers all the time he was travelling
with us, or if he did, no one ever caught a glimpse of them.   So it isn't at
all strange that he shunned the gendarmes.   But he is as tricky as a monkey,
and always succeeds in getting out of a scrape.   Besides," added Georget,
lowering his voice, "if ever a policeman attempted to lay hands on him,
Zig-Zag would only have to whistle for his dog.   Amanda has taught him
to leap at anybody's throat at a signal from her, though what it is no one
knows but herself.   Father says that she only has to snap her fingers and
look at the man she wants strangled.   Vigoureux understands at once."

Camille started violently.   Her father had died of strangulation, and
the word Georget had just uttered reminded her of the frightful scene.
She relapsed into silence, and the child dared not continue the conversation.

Besides, they were obliged to walk rapidly in order to keep up with
Courapied, who was dragged along by the bull-dog faster than he cared for
—indeed, at such a rapid rate that they soon reached the end of the long
boulevard, that is to say, the Place du Château-d'Eau.

There was here quite a crowd of foot passengers and vehicles, even an
omnibus office.   However, the little party did not attract much attention,
for although two or three loungers turned to look at the big dog with a box
in his mouth, it was too dark for them to see the leather strap that served
as a muzzle.   Besides, dogs carrying parcels and baskets are by no means
uncommon in Paris, and there was nothing in Courapied's appearance to
distinguish him from an ordinary citizen.

Camille and Georget, fearing to lose their leader in the crowd, quickened
their pace, and after crossing the shady esplanade in front of the barracks,
they saw the dog turn unhesitatingly into the Boulevard Magenta.

This was some indication, for the broad thoroughfare just mentioned, leads
to Montmartre, or to La Villette, according as to whether one turns to
the right or to the left, on reaching the outer boulevards.   It was proof, too,
of Courapied's acumen, for he had told Camille that he fancied Zig-Zag must
have taken refuge somewhere in that direction.

Meanwhile the dog's ardour did not seem to abate in the least.   He
tugged harder than ever at the rope, and though he occasionally paused, it
was only to growl at Courapied, who did not walk fast enough to suit him.

"You must be fatigued, mademoiselle," said little Georget, timidly.

"No," replied Camille, "I can walk all night, if need be.   But don't
call me mademoiselle any longer.   Give me a man's name, and don't fail to
use it if any one speaks to us."

"How will Jacques do?" asked the youngster, raising his eyes to
Camille's.

"As well as any other name, providing you don't forget it," she answered,
with a smile.

"Oh, there is no danger of that, mademoiselle. But I hope that nobody will speak to us."

"Because you think they would see that I am a woman? That is very possible, for I can't change my voice, and if we are questioned you must answer. Still, my disguise must be a pretty good one, for none of the passers-by have noticed me."

To tell the truth, there were very few pedestrians in the street, for late at night the Boulevard Magenta is well-nigh deserted. Still, further on there might be a crowd, as Georget, well acquainted with Paris, very rightly surmised.

In fact, on reaching the outer boulevard, Vigoureux turned to the left, in the direction leading to the Place Pigalle, which is generally crowded until two o'clock in the morning. Some incidents might therefore be expected, still none occurred, the people in the cafés not even favouring Mademoiselle Monistrol and her escort with as much as a glance.

The little party continued on their way without any interruption until they reached the open space where Marshal Moncey's statue stands. Once there, Vigoureux turned into the Avenue de Clichy, which leads to the fortifications. Courapied's predictions were steadily being realised.

Round about the Place Moncey there are numerous cafés in which the artists of the neighbourhood congregate, and restaurants where the residents of Batignolles dine in small parties. It is a noisy but respectable locality, in short. Further on, however, the avenue forks, one of the streets leading to the gate of Clichy, the other to that of Saint-Ouen. The last passes the Montmartre cemetery, and is not very popular on that account. From the other thoroughfare, however, there branch off countless streets and lanes in which dwell hosts of labourers, and not a few malefactors. The part is not yet positively dangerous, though one already perceives that its residents have nothing in common with the well-to-do citizens of the central districts. You are not yet on hostile territory, but on unknown ground.

Vigoureux chose the least lonely of these streets, to the great satisfaction of Courapied, who had no desire to pass secluded spots where foot-pads are not unfrequently lying in wait for victims. A band of these miscreants would not have hesitated about attacking a man with two lads, and as for Vigoureux, he would probably have bolted away for good with the precious box. However, Courapied's satisfaction was not unalloyed, for he knew that after passing the gate of Clichy, which was not far off, there would be nothing but waste ground, and squalid hovels.

Vigoureux tugged at the rope more furiously than ever, like a horse nearing his stable, and Courapied allowed himself to be dragged swiftly on. Camille and Georget followed more closely than before, but although they occasionally met some suspicious-looking characters, and although loud yells and curses resounded from the drinking shops they were obliged to pass, they did not heed them.

Camille could only think of her father's murderer, and her impatience to reach his place of concealment, increased every instant. She did not reflect that it would probably be impossible to gain admission into it, and that at night-time she would find it difficult to get a good look at Zig-Zag and his hands, even if she were fortunate enough to see him at all. She went on and on filled with a thirst for vengeance, and she felt firmly convinced that Providence would suggest to her a way to accomplish her object when the critical moment came.

Courapied, after passing the Clichy station of the circular railway line, and reaching the road skirting the fortifications, paused to take counsel with his employer. On the left there was the Boulevard Berthier ; on the right, the Boulevard Bessières, and in front of them, the gate of Clichy rose up.

It was a good place for a conference, for no other human being was visible, and conspirators might have assembled there to plot a tyrant's overthrow with perfect safety, just like the three Switzers in Rossini's opera of "William Tell." However, Courapied drew near the fortifications, and then summoned his companions.

"Mademoiselle," he began, "we must now decide upon our course. Beyond this gate lies one of the most dangerous parts of the suburbs, and there Vigoureux is leading us, unquestionably. One can only venture upon the Route de la Révolte at this hour of the night, at the risk of one's life."

"Why ? Because it is deserted ? " inquired Camille, half increduously.

"Quite the contrary, mademoiselle ; because it leads past lanes and alleys filled with low lodging-houses where the worst scoundrels of Paris spend their nights. If Zig-Zag is concealed in any of those places, it is not worth while to look for him, as we shouldn't find him, nor should we succeed in getting away alive."

"Let us at least go on until the dog stops in front of some house, and then we will see."

"But what if he should take us to some rents ? "

"Some rents ? " repeated Mademoiselle Monistrol, who had not the slightest idea what the clown meant.

"Yes, rents, mademoiselle, an assemblage of huts looking very like an encampment of savages. Shanties planted in the mud, and separated from each other by mire in which one sinks up to one's ankles. The ground is covered with garbage and filth, dead dogs and cats—one runs a risk of being stifled, even the police dare not show their faces there."

"But Zig-Zag, who, so you say, wishes to make an entire change in his mode of life, wouldn't be likely to take refuge in a place of that kind," urged Camille.

"Oh, not for long ; but a man stays where he can when he is waiting to step into a new skin. Besides, Amanda has acquaintances in this neighbourhood. I know it. She sent me here more than once, so that I am familiar with the entire road from Neuilly to Saint-Denis."

"Then you will be an excellent guide. Besides, what is the use of stopping here to talk when I am determined to see this through, whatever may happen ? Let us go on, you and I : Georget can wait for us here."

The brave little fellow said not a word, but he walked straight towards the gate. Courapied could not do less than follow his son's example, so he dealt out more rope to Vigoureux, whom he had had no little trouble in restraining during this short conference, and Camille walked on by his side.

They passed through the gateway, which was guarded by two custom's officials, who looked at them attentively, and would no doubt have ordered Vigoureux's box to be opened had they been entering Paris instead of leaving it. However, there is no municipal tax on liquor and similar things when you proceed outwards, and so the little party was allowed to pass.

"Are we now upon that dreaded Route de la Révolte you spoke of ? " inquired Mademoiselle Monistrol, when they had passed the gate.

"No, mademoiselle," replied Courapied, amazed at his companion's coolness, "but we shall soon reach it. It lies there before us, but this is still the Avenue de Clichy."

"And what are those huts on either side of the street?" asked the young girl.

"They serve as lodgings for the organ-grinders and the men with performing monkeys who go about the streets. There is no danger that Zig-Zag has taken refuge here. These fellows must have met our troupe again and again in their rounds, and Zig-Zag would not run such a risk of being recognised. Besides, you see that Vigoureux shows no desire to stop."

The dog was, indeed, hastening on with all his strength, and, five minutes later, the little party found themselves on the triangular space formed by the intersection of the Avenue de Clichy and the dreaded thoroughfare before-mentioned.

"Here we are now!" said Courapied, and he spoke in a subdued tone, as if afraid of being overheard, although the place seemed to be quite deserted.

There was nothing extraordinary in the appearance of the broad and dimly-lighted road which Camille Monistrol saw before her; it seemed to be an ordinary highway, and nothing more. And yet, to tell the truth, the old mountebank had not exaggerated the formidable reputation it has acquired by reason of them any crimes committed there. Its very name, which was bestowed upon it, so it is said, on account of a revolt that occurred there among the French guards, seems to have predestined it to serve as the scene of frightful events.

It begins at the Porte-Maillot, at the very spot where Louis Philippe's eldest son—the popular young Duke of Orleans—was killed on being thrown from his carriage, passes through Neuilly, and only enters the city to emerge from it again a little further on, and pass through the plain of Clichy, after intersecting the Route d'Asnières at right angles. Then it penetrates the very centre of Bohemia, passing first through the rag-pickers' own particular territory, where they virtually sleep in the open air, and eat in low cookshops, where nameless dishes and vitriolic beverages are served them. Rag-pickers, however, are, for the most part, honest men, who work all night, and sleep in the daytime; but, on nearing Clichy, the road passes under a long railway bridge, forming a sort of tunnel, in which one can waylay and murder a man with little danger of being disturbed in the operation.

On the right, there stretches an expanse of waste ground, where vagabonds and malefactors spend their nights: then come dark alleys and muddy lanes, passages which are perfect cut-throat places, and the famous "City of the Sun," so called, doubtless, because the sun's rays never gain an entrance there. And this is not all. The farther you advance, the more squalid the surroundings become, whilst the danger steadily increases. There are bandits' dens on either side. Each street recalls some criminal affair. Blood has been spilt there more than once. And yet it was in this direction that the dog still led Courapied and his companions.

"Ah, well!" muttered the poor clown, now resigned to everything, "Zig-Zag is probably hidden in the Cité Foucault. Luck is decidedly against us. Out of a hundred tenants there, eighty have been in prison."

"No matter," replied Camille resolutely, "let us go on."

And on they went, past this Cité Foucault, which Camille had never seen before, but which, as she now learnt from her companion, was the property of, and under the immediate charge of, a woman who wore masculine attire, and who did not hesitate to collar disorderly tenants, or break open their doors, and forcibly eject them, when they persistently declined to pay their rent.

The Cité is an assemblage of shanties, all built on the same pattern, and consisting of a ground floor and an upper storey, the latter being decorated with a balcony, and reached by rickety stairs outside. Everybody was asleep in the place when Camille and her escort went by, or rather everything was quiet there, and this silence was reassuring.

But opposite it, on the other side of the road, there stood a large white building, where edibles and drinkables were sold, as the enormous sign painted by an unknown artist indicated beyond any possibility of doubt. This sign, which was a real picture, represented an enormous saucepan, around which stood a priest, a beadle, an altar boy, and a grave-digger, while in the distance came a long procession of rabbits, advancing, two by two, towards the culinary utensil in which they were to be transformed into a savoury stew. Above this fantastic picture ran the words, "Le Tombeau des Lapins," an inscription which contributed not a little to the renown of the institution. Indeed, the Tombeau des Lapins, or the "Rabbit's Grave," was noted throughout the world, to such an extent, in fact, that the fashionable Alfred de Fresnay had mentioned it to the Countess de Janos as one of the curiosities of Paris.

All the residents of the neighbourhood seemed to have congregated that night on the ground floor, which was brilliantly lighted both within and without, a huge lantern swinging in the breeze above the sign. Shouting, quarrelling, and singing, could be distinctly heard, and the company must have been very large, judging by the uproar it made.

"Is that Zig-Zag's haunt?" asked Camille, seeing that Vigoureux stopped short in front of the tavern, and began to snuff.

However, after smelling about for half a minute or so, the dog again began to drag Courapied along; and the mountebank then remarked to Camille: "Old Villard, who keeps that place, doesn't lodge people. Zig-Zag couldn't find a bed there, even if he wanted one, and it is just as well. There are too many people in that den, and, if we went in, a lot of roughs would fall upon us."

Then, after some slight reflection, the ex-clown added: "All the same, it's quite possible that the rascal has been there to-night. Vigoureux must have scented him, or else he wouldn't have stopped."

"Yes, it seems likely, then, that the dog's master isn't far off," remarked Camille. "Let us get on."

"There's only the Epinette neighbourhood ahead of us, and if Zig-Zag is there," retorted Courapied, "I'm surprised that the dog didn't bring us by the St. Ouen gate. That's the shortest way."

"But he must have followed the same road as Zig-Zag," urged Camille.

"No doubt, mademoiselle. He tracks him with his scent. Oh! we are sure of not missing him; only it's a question as to how it will all end."

Mademoiselle Monistrol plainly realised by this reply that her companion was by no means tranquil in mind concerning the result of their expedition, but she felt sure that he would not desert her, and it was now too late to discuss the chances of the venture. So they closely followed Vigoureux, who seemed to become more and more eager as he approached his journey's end; and they passed several other narrow streets, dimly lighted by a few oil lamps. A little further on came some hovels scattered here and there, some built of rough boards, others of brick and stone stolen from demolished houses—huts of the most primitive kind, though built by civilized men, and two or three of which were composed almost entirely of old sardine boxes filled with earth, piled up with a certain amount of skill, and cemented together with plaster. They did not appear to be occupied, however, for not the smallest ray of light was visible.

Still, the dog steadily dragged Courapied onward, although merely a wide stretch of sterile fields was all that seemed to lie beyond.

"Can he be going to take us to Saint-Denis?" muttered Courapied. "Well, I hope he won't, for we could not get there much before morning."

All at once, however, Vigoureux made a quick spring to the left, a spring so violent that he nearly broke the rope, and after the spring, he executed a sudden turn that pulled Courapied out of the road, which, at this point, was on a level with the fields which it traversed, being separated from them merely by a ditch, not much deeper than a furrow made by a plough-share. Courapied, dragged on by the dog, crossed this ditch almost without perceiving it, and found himself in a rough field, where stones were mingled with scanty herbage.

Camille and Georget hastily followed him, and here they again held a conference in spite of the frantic struggles of Vigoureux, who nearly pulled poor Courapied's hands off by the wrists. It was necessary, first of all, to ascertain where they were, and this was no easy matter on a moonless night. To the right, on the other side of the road, the height of Montmartre loomed afar off, while behind the little party hundreds of tiny lights could be seen twinkling in the darkness, some motionless, and only a short way off apparently, others flitting about in the distance like so many will-o'-the-wisps.

"Those nearer lights are the lamps in the Cité Foucault," remarked Courapied, "and these further on are the lanterns of the rag-pickers, who are just starting out on their rounds."

"But—in front of us now?" inquired Mademoiselle Monistrol, somewhat anxiously.

"In front of us lies the Plain of Saint-Denis, and unless Zig-Zag has taken refuge in a quarry, I really don't see where the brute can be taking us."

"Father," said Georget, "it seems to me that I can see a house to the left—about a couple of hundred paces away from us."

"You must have good eyes. I don't see anything," grumbled Courapied.

"I see something," said Camille, "but I can't tell whether it is a house, or only a mound. At all events, it's evident enough that that's where the dog wants to go, so do not attempt to prevent him from doing so."

"I'm sure nothing could please me better, for I can't hold him much longer : the rope has nearly cut my fingers off. But if we follow him, heaven only knows where he will take us ! If we were only sure that there was a house, it wouldn't make so much difference, but these fields are full of holes and—"

"The dog's eyesight is far too good for him to fall in them, so he will enable us to avoid them. We shall only have to follow him in single file."

The young girl always had a reply ready for every objection, and Courapied decided, though not with a very good grace, to execute the manœuvre she had suggested. He followed Vigoureux, and it would have been difficult for him to do otherwise, unless he released the dog, for all his power of resistance was spent. Georget came behind his father and

Camille brought up the rear. This marching order was the best fitted for people bent upon surprising an enemy, for thus ranged, one behind the other, they formed a dark point scarcely visible on the far stretching plain, and the chances were that they might reach the house without their approach being signalled.

About a hundred yards from their last stopping place, they came to a large pile of stones which they had not seen before, but which was sufficiently high to shelter them from observation. It was really a house that stood a short distance ahead of them, but it was a most dilapidated one. The roof had partially fallen in, and of the two chimneys which had formerly surmounted it, but one remained. The other in its fall had strewn the surrounding ground with fragments of brick and mortar. Nevertheless, there were still some shutters to the windows, and the walls seemed sound. Perhaps they only inclosed a vacant space, however, for no fence of any kind protected the remains of a once cosy villa.

What had destroyed it? Certainly not a fire, for it was built of red bricks which still retained their original colour. Nor could it have been an enemy's cannon, for there had been no fighting hereabouts during the siege of Paris.

Courapied cared very little about knowing, however. He only wanted to ascertain if his wife and that odious Zig-Zag had taken refuge amid these ruins, and he hesitated about believing it, although Vigoureux persisted in taking him there, in spite of his resistance. At all events, the guilty couple could only have sought a temporary refuge there, and whoever came to disturb them might expect a warm reception.

"Well, what are you waiting for?" inquired Mademoiselle Monistrol at last.

"I am not waiting for anything," replied Courapied. "I think there is nothing left for us to do but to turn back, for it would be folly for us to enter the house to-night. I've no objection to trying it in the day-time—"

"By to-morrow the wretch may have fled. I want to finish the business. Besides, there is nothing to prove that he is there now. I am going to satisfy myself on that point, however," said Camille, stepping aside from the pile of stones that sheltered her, and walking resolutely towards the house.

Georget sprung forward and passed her in the twinkling of an eye, and Courapied, ashamed to hesitate under such circumstances, yielded to the efforts of Vigoureux, and let himself be dragged along.

They had only some fifty yards to walk to reach the mysterious building, and once in front of it they again paused, as if by mutual consent, for even Camille realised the necessity of examining the place before going any further.

There could no longer be the shadow of a doubt but that Zig-Zag was there, for the dog was standing on his hind paws, making the most frantic efforts to break the rope that bound him. He also tried to bark, and as the strap that served as a muzzle had become slightly loosened, he succeeded in uttering growls which could be heard from a little distance. But where was Zig-Zag hiding? Behind those walls, or in a cellar below? And how was he to be reached?

There was a gape in the front wall of the house, the entrance to a gloomy hall, the outer door of which had disappeared; however, the prospect of entering this dark passage was not inviting.

"Let us walk round the house, mademoiselle," whispered Courapied. "We shall find a better place, perhaps."

"There's a light, father," whispered Georget at this moment; and as he spoke he pointed to one of the windows.

Camille looked, and saw a slender ray of light shining through the imperfectly fitting shutters. Consequently, Zig-Zag had installed himself in a habitable room. She had found him at last, and there was now nothing to prevent her from compelling him to show himself. She would be able to see his face and hands if he came to the window with his light, and after that, she would rush up to the assault, revolver in hand, and compel him to allow himself to be bound by Courapied and Georget.

All this was extravagant and absurd, but Camille had lost the power to reason calmly. Her blood was rising to her head and she was frantic with excitement. So, without hesitation, and without even warning Courapied, she drew her revolver from her pocket, picked up a handful of gravel, and threw it against the shutter. The light within was instantly extinguished, and Camille then realised for the first time that there was not a particle of common sense in her plan; for, even admitting that Zig-Zag did come to the window instead of making his escape, she would not be able to see his hands in the dark.

"Let us run, mademoiselle," said Courapied; "there may be a number of them here; and, in that case, they will certainly kill us. I sha'n't be able to defend you, for I have worn myself out in holding Vigoureux, and I shall have to let him go, I fear."

"I would rather die here than fly at the moment of finding my father's murderer," replied Camille, in a tone of indignation.

Just then the shutters were opened softly. "Who is there?" asked a woman's voice.

Mademoiselle Monistrol was overcome with astonishment. She was looking for Zig-Zag, and by throwing the gravel she had drawn a woman to the window. And yet Vigoureux leaped about so frantically that he must have recognised the voice of the speaker.

Courapied, also, had recognised it, for he exclaimed: "That's Amanda!"

Unfortunately, he spoke loud enough to be heard in the house, and the effect of his imprudent exclamation was almost instantaneous. Both shutters were thrown wide open, and a white-robed figure appeared.

Camille and her auxiliaries remained grouped under the window where the apparition stood, and the night was not sufficiently dark to conceal them effectually.

"Ah, you wretch," exclaimed Courapied, overcome with anger, "so I have found you at last! You shall pay dearly for the way you have treated me!"

"What, idiot, is it you?" was the insolent retort. "What have you come here for?"

"I came in search of you, hussy."

"In search of me!" was the scornful response. "Well, that is good, and no mistake! Do you imagine for one moment that I am going to run about again, from fair to fair with you? I have had enough of your company, and the tight-rope, too! You can call again another day."

"I shall do nothing of the kind," Courapied declared. "I've found you now, and you won't get away from me as easily as you did the other day."

"Come and take me then. The door is open."

" Yes, and Zig-Zag is lying in wait for me in the passage, I've no doubt of it."

" You are very much mistaken," retorted Amanda, disdainfully. " I am alone, and you are a coward if you are afraid to venture in. I am only a woman, but I wouldn't be such a chicken-hearted creature as you are for the world."

" You lie ! Zig-Zag is with you."

" Zig-Zag ! Why, your watch is slow. He went off at the same time as I did, because the manager wouldn't pay us our dues. But he is not hanging about Paris. He secured an engagement in London, and he must be far off by now."

" It is false ! " shouted Courapied. " But even if it were true, he would be arrested all the same and brought back here to be guillotined."

" On account of that affair on the Boulevard Voltaire ? Nonsense ! He doesn't care a fig about that. The magistrate released him, as you know precious well, and that's proof enough that they had no evidence against him. But you seem to belong to the police now. How much have they promised you for hunting down your comrade ? A nice business you are in ! Still, if you were sharp, you might earn a living by it ; but you are too stupid. You'll never find any one and you'll precious soon lose your berth. Who did you bring with you, some officers ? "

" No, but I am going for some," retorted Courapied, sharply, for his blood was up by this time. " There is a station-house not far from here."

" Yes, go ; I will wait for them. Come, make haste while you are about it ! There are three of you, so two can stand guard here while you do your errand. Who are your companions ? There is one tall fellow and a short one. I wouldn't mind betting that the small one is that little toad, Georget."

The child was strongly tempted to reply in the affirmative, but his father hastily placed his hand over his mouth. Camille fairly trembled with impatience as she listened to this strange dialogue, and she considered it high time to proceed from words to deeds, for she felt almost certain that Zig-Zag was there—at the back of the room, no doubt—and she longed to devise some means of compelling him to show himself. It was now no longer a question of seeing his hands and face ; but one of capturing him, and to prevent his flight she would not have hesitated to fire upon him.

" Yes," continued Amanda, " I am sure that it is that little imp of a Georget. So he, too, is trying to get me into trouble ? All right ! I'll pay him for it. But where did you pick up your other friend, the one in the white blouse ? Is he some one who has been enticed into the troupe to take Zig-Zag's place ? "

As she uttered these concluding words, she cautiously retired from the window, and Courapied fancied that she was preparing to make her escape by the other side of the house. He was mistaken, however, for after retiring for a moment, Amanda suddenly reappeared, and threw out an object that described a luminous curve, like a shooting star, and then falling almost at Camille's feet, suddenly blazed up, and diffused a blinding light around. It was one of those Bengal lights with which sojourners at Norman watering-places often illuminate the beach by way of amusement.

Mademoiselle Monistrol, surprised and dazzled, recoiled, disclosing her face, which was only partially concealed by her cap.

" Oh, I see ! " sneered Amanda in her shrill voice. " It is the princess I turned out of the show the other night on the Place du Trône. You must be in her employment now, as you have brought her here. She is hunting after Zig-Zag, because she thinks that Zig-Zag killed her father, eh? Fie! mademoiselle, I wouldn't play the detective if I were you! This isn't the Boulevard Voltaire, and upon my word! I have a great mind to punish you as you deserve."

But Camille did not even hear these threats. By the glare of the Bengal light she had dimly distinguished a man's form at the further end of the room, and this vision, though seen but for an instant, engrossed her every thought.

"And so you have stolen Vigoureux, you old scoundrel!" continued Amanda. "I now understand how you found your way here with that youngster and the wench. I sent him for my jewellery box, which I forgot, and you must have caught him on the sly, for if you had attacked him openly, he would have devoured you. He has found his way back, the brave fellow, and he has brought the box. You didn't dare to take it from him, you big coward? And you've muzzled him, I see! Fastened him with a cord! You had better release him, and instantly. If you don't, you will be sorry for it."

Courapied did not obey the order, but he was greatly in doubt as to what course he ought to pursue. He did not care to follow Vigoureux into this ruined house, which looked very much like the den of a band of cut-throats; but to set the dog at liberty was to lose the entire fruit of a long and arduous expedition. On the other hand, to beat a retreat with the terrible beast was an utter impossibility, as it would be necessary to drag him away by main force, and Courapied was nearly exhausted. Besides, the enemy would hardly fail to come to the dog's rescue. The poor clown looked inquiringly at Camille, but the Bengal light was going out, and their eyes did not meet.

"So you won't release him!" cried Zig-Zag's accomplice. "Ah, well, we will see!" And a moment afterwards a sharp whistle broke upon the silence of the night.

Vigoureux, who recognised the signal at once, gave such a furious bound that he dragged Courapied to the entrance of the dark passage in spite of his struggles. "Help, Georget!" cried Amanda's unfortunate husband.

Georget ran forward and seized the rope with both hands, but the dog gave it a final jerk that severed it just as the father and son disappeared in the passage. Camille heard two cries of distress, then a hollow thud, and finally—nothing.

The first impulse is always the best one, so some people claim, and Mademoiselle Monistrol rushed forward to the assistance of her friends. The doorway was not far off. She reached it with three bounds, and was about to cross it and fall into the same trap as Courapied and Georget, but she stumbled just as she reached the threshold, and paused, for an instant, to regain her equilibrium. This slight mishap really saved her life. She inhaled a strong whiff of cool damp air, and her eyes, which had now become accustomed to the darkness, perceived a deep, yawning space instead of the floor she had expected to see.

She then understood the truth. The father and son, dragged along by Vigoureux, had found a void beneath their feet, and they had both fallen into the open trap, while the terrible animal, aware of the existence of the treacherous chasm, had cleared it at a bound, and gone to rejoin his owner, concealed in the house.

Camille feared that her unfortunate allies must have been killed in their fall, for they made no appeal for help, and although she listened attentively, she heard nothing, not even a moan. They had no doubt been killed instantaneously. And this frightful death had evidently been planned for them by Amanda, who had hoped to make away with Mademoiselle Monistrol at the same time. A fortress is protected by a moat, and this dilapidated building was sheltered from attack by a gaping cellar into which all assailants who were not forewarned were destined to fall. When Amanda had summoned the dog, she had known what would ensue ; her whistle had been equivalent to murder.

All this flashed through Camille's mind in less time than it takes us to record it ; but to come to a realising sense of the situation was not every thing. It was necessary to decide upon her course, and to decide at once, for the vile creature who had just freed herself of her unfortunate husband by means of a crime, would certainly not be content with that. The opportunity to destroy all Zig-Zag's enemies at one fell swoop would prove too tempting, even supposing that she, Amanda, was alone in the place.

Thus Camille was bound to expect a sortie and she began by preparing to receive her assailants with her revolver. She even had the presence of mind to realise that the attack would not come by way of the hall, for her enemies could not spring over the gaping void of the cellar as Vigoureux had done. However, nothing prevented them, no doubt, from leaving the house on the other side and thus cutting off the poor girl's retreat.

And yet despite all this she remained, lingering over the black cavity and hesitating as to whether she ought to abandon her allies. She repeatedly called little Georget, but no answer came. It was better to go in search of help, and besides, there was not a moment to lose if she wished to escape the peril that threatened her. And what a peril ! She might fall into the hands of that monster with a woman's face who was capable of inventing some refined form of torture ! She might be torn to pieces by that ferocious bull dog ; indeed, Amanda would no doubt excite the animal against her.

The imprudent expedition upon which the poor girl had embarked had cost her friends dear, and there was now no other way of repairing the injury she had done them than by hastening to the nearest police station and summoning the officers to the aid of Amanda's victims.

Just as she had made up her mind to do this and retreat, she heard two persons talking in the interior of the house. Amanda's voice, which she instantly recognised, and a deeper voice. Camille could not distinguish a word at first, but as the dialogue progressed, the key in which it was carried on became higher and higher, as is usually the case when people are quarrelling, and thus the young girl soon gained a pretty clear idea of the subject of the conversation. It was evident that one of the wretches wanted to dispatch her, then and there, and that the other was inclined to let her make her escape.

Naturally the young girl did not wait for the conclusion of the discussion, but fled, taking care not to pass in front of the open window. However, when she reached the pile of stones, she turned for a moment to make sure that she was not being pursued. She perceived no one, but the night was so dark that she could not see far ; however, she heard the dog bark. His owners had evidently unmuzzled him, and he was expressing his delight. The sound came from the house, but the animal might be sent after her, and Camille, only partially reassured, again started off at the top of her speed towards the Route de la Révolte. It seemed to her that she would be safer there than on this lonely plain, besides, she said to herself that this road, bad as was its reputation, led, after all, to one of the city gates.

Her masculine costume did not impede her progress, and moreover, she had nimble limbs, so that in less than five minutes she found herself upon the macadamized highway, where she paused to take breath, and also to decide upon the direction she should next take.

She knew she would reach the Porte de Clichy if she returned by the same road she had just traversed with Courapied, but she would be obliged to pass in front of the "Tombeau des Lapins," where all the disorderly people of the neighbourhood seemed to have assembled that evening. It was only by great good luck that she and her companions had met with no mishap when passing there the first time, and she might not be so fortunate now that she was alone; besides, the army of rag-pickers was just starting out. The countless lights of their lanterns were still visible in the distance, and Camille was anxious to avoid them, in which she made a great mistake, however, for rag-pickers, in general, are honest fellows, and their company would probably have saved her from any more unfortunate encounter.

However, she finally started in the opposite direction, without reflecting that this would take her further and further from the fortifications, though she ought to have remembered that poor Courapied had said to her: "This beast of a dog will finally take us to Saint-Denis, I do believe." It was no doubt written that Mademoiselle Monistrol should meet with yet another adventure that same night.

She hastened on at a rapid pace, taking care to walk in the middle of the road to avoid anyone placed in ambush, and she proceeded in this way for fully a quarter of an hour, glancing keenly to right and left and holding her revolver in her hand. She could still see the height of Montmartre rising up on her right hand side, but straight ahead there stretched a seemingly unlimited plain and not a light was visible. She then began to ask herself if she were not turning her back upon Paris, and finally she paused, but just as she did so, two figures suddenly arose out of a slight hollow at the side of the road. Mademoiselle Monistrol, engaged in seeking her way, failed to notice the fact, and after a moment's hesitation, she again walked on, though much more slowly. There was a slight rise here and she hoped that a little further on she would be able to see what she was in search of. She had only taken a few steps, however, when a slight sound made her start. It seemed to her that she heard some footsteps on the road behind her, and she quickly turned to confront the persons who were following her. She had not time to assume the defensive, however, for two men instantly sprung upon her, one seizing her by the throat, and the other around the body, and she heard these words: "Hold him fast, I'll slip the collar on him, and when I've hoisted him up on my back, just you search his pockets."

As Camille struggled with her assailants, she almost mechanically pressed the trigger of her revolver, but the bullet was lost in space.

"What, the 'mug' means mischief! He mustn't try that on!" exclaimed one of the thieves. "Wait a minute until I relieve him of that little plaything."

As he spoke, he struck the revolver a vigorous blow with a stick he held in his hand, and the weapon fell from the poor girl's grasp, whilst the ruffian's accomplice pressed so hard at her throat that she was almost stifled. She uttered a cry, but only one. She felt that a strap was being fastened round her neck, and she thought she was about to die, like her father, of strangulation. The idea that one of her assailants was Zig-Zag flashed across her mind, but she soou perceived that all these men wanted was her money. The fellow who held in one hand the two ends of the strap whilst in the other he carried a cudgel, quickly turned round and lifted Camille off her feet, so that she remained suspended like a bundle on his shoulder, whilst his companion began to search her. She still retained consciousness as the strap pressed against the nape of her neck instead of against her throat. In the latter case she would inevitably have been killed, as often happens to the victims of this class of Parisian thieves who act on what they call the "portage" system. However, Camille, still retaining her senses in a measure, felt a pair of big hands fumbling in her pockets whilst the following dialogue fell upon her ears:

"We have made a good haul this time. Here's some gold iu his breech poke, and a peter in his waistcoat. A droll apprentice this fellow is. He must be some tip-top mug who disguised himself as a workman to go and see a wench! Why, his hands are as soft as a girl's! And, dear me, it is a girl!" he added, suddenly. The cap Camille wore had just fallen off, and her long hair, becoming unfastened, fell dowu about her shoulders.

"A girl? Come, that's bosh!"

"Yes, she's a girl I tell you, and not a bad looking one, either," retorted the searcher.

"Hurry up, then; and as soon as we've divided the plunder, let's take her over there."

"But she'll cry out," urged the other scamp.

"Oh! never mind. The peelers are all asleep just now, and the ragmen of the "City of the Sun" don't pass this way."

"All the same, I shall muzzle her." And thereupon one of the rascals, taking off the greasy scarf, which served him as a neck-tie, passed it over the poor girl's mouth and wound it round her head so that she was effectually gagged.

"It's done! Let go of the strap," said the ruffian.

The other one complied with his companion's instructions, and Mademoiselle Monistrol fell all of a heap upon the road.

"She's settled. Take her by the shoulders and I'll take her by the feet."

"Wait a bit; let's settle accounts first, old man."

"What! do you think I want to cheat you?"

"I don't know, but I haven't got eyes at the back of my head, and I couldn't see you while you were searching her. Now then, show up and let's divide."

"All right— There were fourteen louis in the waistcoat pocket, with a peter, and a slang in gold. Also two five-franc pieces and nine francs in change in the breeches."

"Then hand over a hundred and fifty francs and the peter. You can keep the rest."

"Oh! come now, that won't do! I should be done. Why, they'd lend a hundred francs on the peter alone at the pawnshop. I shall keep it and give you two hundred francs in all; that's your share."

"All right. It isn't worth while quarrelling about. We'll settle up for good to-morrow."

The ruffian who had searched Camille then couuted out ten twenty-franc pieces to his companion, who pocketed the coins, saying: "Hurry up! we'll take her to old Alexandre's hut which is quite deserted now, since he has been copped."

Camille, still lying on the road, had now regained her senses, and guessed the terrible fate that the scoundrels were reserving for her. She was re-solved not to submit to it, but her only means of escape was to compel them to kill her. Her hands were now free, and she suddenly made use of them to pull away the scarf which had been placed before her mouth, and ere the scamps had time to silence her, she cried out at the top of her voice: "Help, help! Murder!"

She did not expect that any one would come to her assistance. She only hoped her assailants would dispatch her to silence her. And they did ex-claim, savagely: "If you keep on howling like that, we'll beat your brains out."

One of the thieves then took her up by the shoulders, and the other by the feet, as agreed upon, and they had already carried her across the ditch on the other side of the road, when the one holding her by the shoulders, remarked to his companion: "Look out. It seems to me I hear somebody coming up on the run. I don't want to get lagged."

"Oh, it's only some rag-picker starting out on his round, and running because he is late. You know precious well that the peelers never run when they are going their rounds."

Camille had also heard the hurried footsteps, and wondered whether they were those of a friend or an enemy. Fortunately for her, this ques-tion was soon answered.

The two scoundrels abruptly released her. She again fell to the ground, and while she was trying to rise, a man, of whom she caught but a glimpse, attacked her assailants, with a stick which he held in his hand. He used it to such good purpose that both the scoundrels recoiled. The one who also was provided with a stick, attempted to defend himself, but a heavy blow disarmed him, and this was followed by a shower of others imparti-ally distributed upon both footpads. The scoundrel who had rifled Camille's pockets received a severe cut across the face, and fled, howling with pain; the other, struck upon the head, merely had time to follow his companion so as to avoid being stunned.

Thus the stranger who had so opportunely made his appearance, was left master of the field. A few seconds had sufficed for the dispersal of the cowardly rascals, and he scorned to give them chase. He knew that they would not repeat the attack, and as he saw that their victim was in great need of succour, he approached to offer Camille a helping hand.

"Ah, well, my lad," he said, cheerfully, and naturally taking the young girl for a youth, "there is no great harm done, I hope. Still, it was a for-tunate thing that I came to your help—and it was a lucky idea of mine when I thought of returning to Paris by this road. But what the devil are you doing here, at this time of night? If you came to spend your earnings in the wineshops you must be nicely disappointed, for those rascals must have robbed you of your money, and I am surprised that they did not mur-der you into the bargain. You must have been frightened to death, eh? Lean on me; you don't seem able to stand."

"Oh, sir, you have saved my life," faltered Camille, as she gently freed herself from her protector's supporting arm.

The feminine ring of her voice evidently astonished the stranger, for he recoiled a step or two, and gazed searchingly at this apprentice who spoke so much like a young lady; then, seeing the long tresses that fell in disorder over Camille's blouse, his tone and manner underwent a sudden change.

"Excuse me, madame," said he; "I had no idea that this costume concealed—"

"A young girl," Mademoiselle Monistrol concluded. "I will explain why I assumed this disguise; but first of all, let me entreat you, sir, to assist me in succouring some friends."

"Some friends! You were not alone then?"

"No. I came here in company with a man and a child."

"Well, what has become of them?"

"A snare was set for them, an open trap-door. They fell into a cellar, and I fear they have not survived their fall."

"What! here on this plain?" asked the stranger, with an incredulous smile.

"No, in a tumble-down house, near by."

"Tumble-down, but probably inhabited, as you say the trap was set for your friends."

"Yes, by some scoundrels I was searching for, in the hope of being able to hand them over to justice—a murderer and his accomplice."

Her preserver evinced no surprise, though he probably thought that Camille was mad. "How did it happen that you were spared?" he enquired, with mingled pity and interest.

"Because I fled. I could do nothing to help them, and I wished to live to avenge them," responded Camille.

"And the scamps pursued you to this place?"

"No, sir, the scoundrels from whom you just delivered me were thieves, whom I never saw before; they attacked me as they would have attacked any other passer-by."

"But do you know anything about the persons in the house you speak of?"

"One of them killed my father."

"In that case you should have secured the assistance of the police," remarked the strange gentleman, coldly.

"I had reasons which I will explain for dispensing with their assistance. But, in Heaven's name, don't let us waste any more time here. Two unfortunate fellow-beings have sacrificed themselves for my sake, and if I abandoned them I could never forgive myself."

"Excuse me, mademoiselle, but you just told me that they must have been killed by falling into a cellar, so you will only imperil your life uselessly by returning to the scene of the catastrophe. It is scarcely likely that the guilty parties have yet left the place, and we two should prove no match for them, I fear. I, for my part, do not feel like risking it, though I am no coward, as I think I have proved to you."

"Certainly," responded Camille. "I hardly know how to express my gratitude to you. But must I leave my defenders at the mercy of those wretches?"

"The first thing to be done is to take you to a place of safety, and you will not be safe until you are back in Paris. If we remain here, we shall certainly be attacked by some other night prowlers, and the next time I may not be as fortunate with my opponents."

"Of course, I should be unwilling to expose you to further danger," said Mademoiselle Monistrol, quickly.

"Then you must allow me to escort you home, and to-morrow, with your permission, I will communicate the facts to Monsieur Macé, the chief of the detective police."

"No, that would do no good," murmured Camille, who had felt but little confidence either in the intelligence or good-will of the detective service since Zig-Zag had been released.

"Would you prefer that I should act upon my own responsibility?" asked the obliging stranger. "I am entirely at your service in that case. What, as I have just explained to you, would be wholly impracticable to-night, I would willingly attempt by daylight, and I assure you that I will soon procure you information, not only concerning the fate of your friends, but also as regards the movements of your enemies. Take my arm, mademoiselle, and let us get away from here as soon as possible, I beg."

Just then the distant barking of a dog made Camille tremble. "That dog! that terrible dog!" she murmured. "They have set him on my track. He might spring upon us and tear us to pieces. Let us go at once."

She took the proffered arm of her protector, who seemed anxious to leave the place. He led her in the same direction as she had been going when the robbers attacked her; but after proceeding a short way, he turned into a cross-road passing at some little distance from the houses of the Epinette neighbourhood and leading straight to the Porte de Saint-Ouen. The obliging stranger thought of everything, for before starting he had picked up Camille's cap and she had caught her hair together whilst walking, and having now resumed her head gear, might again pass for a youth and thus avoid attracting attention.

Vigoureux had again ceased barking, or at least they no longer heard him. Mademoiselle Monistrol was gradually regaining her composure, and, though she could not entirely overcome her remorse on thinking of her friends, she began to bestow more attention upon this brave defender whom kind Providence had sent so suddenly to her relief at the very moment when her position was most desperate. The night was too dark for her to distinguish his features, and she was anxious to reach the city gate where the gas-light would enable her to distinctly see the man to whom she was indebted for her safety. They had walked on rapidly, without exchanging a word, and Camille was grateful to her new friend for his consideration and reserve.

The street-lamps became more numerous as they neared the Porte de Saint-Ouen, and as Camille glanced askance she saw that her preserver was tall, slight, and extremely elegant in appearance. She saw, too, that he was dressed like a fashionable gentleman, in a well-fitting overcoat, tall hat, and kid gloves. The stick he had used with such telling effect was a bamboo of medium size, surmounted by a silver knob. No one would have supposed that this handsomely dressed gentleman had just been engaged in such a lively conflict. His toilet was intact, even to the buttons on his gloves.

But what could this gentleman, who seemed to belong to the best society, have been doing on the plain of Saint-Denis at such an hour of the night? As Mademoiselle Monistrol asked herself this question again and again, it occurred to her that their meeting had perhaps been planned by this carefully attired gentleman. But what could have been his object? Besides, her champion could not have known that she was there, and he certainly had no acquaintance with the roving acrobat or the foul mouthed tight-rope dancer who had just disposed of poor Georget and Conrapied so summarily.

Camille might almost have believed that the stranger could read her thoughts, for when they were only a hundred paces or so from the city gate, he broke the silence which he had hitherto preserved so discreetly and remarked : " You must have been surprised to meet me on the Route de la Révolte at such an unheard-of hour, mademoiselle. Pray don't think that I choose that notorious highway for my daily promenade. But I dined this evening with some old friends of mine who have a villa near Saint-Ouen, and instead of driving back to Paris, the fancy seized me to take a stroll through this strange part, which furnishes so many exciting items for the daily press. I was actuated, probably, by a vague hope of meeting with some adventure ; and I congratulate myself upon the very agreeable one that has befallen me. But remember," he added, gaily, " that I have reason to be equally surprised to find you roaming about a place where young ladies seldom if ever venture."

" I have already told you what took me there, sir," murmured Mademoiselle Monistrol who was considerably embarrassed by this remark.

" Oh, I do not presume to ask you for any further explanation. But will you allow me to tell you who I am ? My name is George de Menestreau. I am thirty years old, I own a little property, and I am the last of my race. I have lately travelled a good deal in the East, after residing for a long while in Paris where I returned about a week ago with the intention of living permanently ; I think I have wandered about the world enough, and would like to settle down. But my private history doesn't interest you much, I fear ; so I won't dwell any longer upon it. Now I must ask you to let go of my arm. Here we are at the gate and the custom's employés are dreadfully inquisitive. They might think it strange if they saw me in a black coat and a silk hat giving my arm to a young workman in a blouse. They might perhaps think we were smuggling something into Paris, and if they ventured to search you and ascertained that you were a young lady in disguise, the predicament might be annoying."

" I will take care to avoid it," responded Camille, stepping aside. " I will go forward and you can join me again when we are inside the city."

This course was followed. Camille's protector had somewhat exaggerated the difficulties, for the employés were half asleep and did not disturb themselves to scrutinize the young girl.

She walked rapidly down the Avenue de St. Ouen, and at a couple of hundred yards' distance from the city gate, she stopped near a street lamp, the light of which would enable her to distinguish the features of this M. George de Menestreau whose name she had just learnt, but whose face she had so far barely espied.

He did not keep her waiting long, and as soon as he had reached her, he resumed the conversation by courteously saying : " Here we are in Paris, mademoiselle, and I am quite at your orders. Shall I see you home or do you prefer to go home without me ? In the latter case I shall leave you as soon as we meet a cab. But, now I think of it, the scoundrels who assaulted you perhaps robbed you of all the money you had about you ? "

" They took both my money and my watch," replied Camille, " but that doesn't matter, I can pay the driver when I reach home."

As she spoke, she took another furtive look at the stranger, and perceived, with no little satisfaction, that he had a handsome and genial face. He was very dark : his eyes were clear and bright, his smiling lips were adorned with a silky, black moustache, and he did not look as old as he claimed to be.

Mademoiselle Monistrol was a woman, and consequently the idea of being saved by a handsome and distinguished-looking young man was much more agreeable than that of being under obligations to an unprepossessing rustic. Just then, a belated cab, which was returning into Paris after a suburban trip, came in sight, still she could not thus part from a man who had risked his life to save her, and so she said to him : "I prefer to return home alone, sir, but I hope to see you again to-morrow. I reside at No. 292 Boulevard Voltaire. Camille Monistrol is my name ; and if you do not object to going such a long distance—"

"You need have no fears of that," replied the young man, quickly. "But it seems to me that your name is familiar to me."

"You have probably seen it in the papers, in connection with my father's murder."

"What ! Can it be that you are—?'

"The daughter of Jean Monistrol, who was killed before my very eyes and whom I have sworn to avenge !"

"Oh then, I understand now why I found you on that lonely plain. You were seeking your father's murderer, and he escaped you by committing another crime, and ridding himself of the friends who were helping you. Well, I will take their place, and the scoundrels will not get rid of me so easily. Say the word, mademoiselle, and I will start out in pursuit of them to-morrow. I can find the house, if you will kindly describe it to me ; I will force my way into it, and—"

"It is built of red brick—but—stop, driver ! "

"All right ! " replied the cabman, checking his horse. "To what part do you want to go ? "

"To the Place du Trône."

"That suits me. I am on my way back to the Avenue Parmentier, where my stables are. Get in."

"Good-bye, then, until to-morrow," said Camille to her protector, with an emotion which she could not wholly conceal.

M. de Menestreau pressed her proffered hand respectfully, assisted her into the vehicle, and gave the driver the exact address, which he had duly remembered.

Mademoiselle Monistrol seemed likely to have a much more valuable ally than Julien Gémozac in the person of this young nobleman, and certainly one who pleased her better.

V.

On losing sight of the Countess de Janos at the Café des Ambassadeurs, Alfred de Fresnay had feigned an indifference he did not feel, for in his secret heart he was not a little annoyed to find that he would be obliged to wait until the next day to see the chestnut-haired beauty again. Now, when he was in a bad humour, he usually endeavoured to set himself right by no matter what kind of amusement. So, to begin with, he first tried to drag his friend Gémozac off to the Café Americain, where fast fellows of their kind always find a gay set, to help them in whiling away a few hours.

However, Julien did not care for the café ; as he was not sleepy, he preferred to go to the club, where a high game of baccarat must now be in progress. In point of fact, the young fellow was annoyed, excited, and preoccupied, and with anxious lovers, gambling acts like a sovereign calming draught. Fresnay did not need much urging to follow his friend to the club, and, in fact, he rather liked the prospect of winning a few hundred louis before daybreak, for he was of opinion, that to succeed in making the conquest of the Hungarian beauty, he must be in funds. Julien, on his side, did not go to win ; he only needed excitement, and, so that it might be all the keener, he would have even preferred to lose.

But men propose, and fortune disposes. The fate that befell Julien and Alfred was just the reverse of their wishes. Julien profited by a fine series, and filled his pockets, whilst Alfred, on the other side of the table, lost steadily all through.

Towards two in the morning, he found himself quite " broke," and as he did not care to owe money to the club cash box, he borrowed a couple of hundred francs from Gémozac who was still winning, and then quietly went off alone to sup at Peters's, by way of consoling himself. There is nothing like a loss at cards, to give a man an appetite, and the young baron really felt famished.

When he reached the restaurant, he found the common room crowded with the usual sort of people who frequent establishments of this kind after midnight. There were several young fellows more or less intoxicated, and repeating stale jokes out of last week's newspapers, with now and then a real good thing overheard in one of the taverns decorated in Gothic or Renaissance style, which the literary and artistic fraternities of Paris now-a-days mainly patronise. However, Fresnay did not care for jests, even if they were really witty, and he was asking himself where he should take a seat, when he noticed, seated alone at a table in a corner of the restaurant, a rather peculiar-looking young woman whom he had never seen there before, and who was quite unlike such other members of her sex as were present. She was modestly supping upon a slice of ham and a half bottle of common Médoc, though one instinctively realised that she would have infinitely preferred truffles, expensive fruit, and iced champagne.

There was one vacant seat beside this person, and Fresnay lost no time in taking possession of it. The young woman was not particularly pretty, nor was she tastefully dressed, but she had the complexion of a gipsy, and a toilet to match, and no more was needed to excite the curiosity of a *blasé* man of the world in quest of new adventures. He did not resort to any circumlocution in opening the conversation. "That isn't particularly savory, what you are eating," he remarked, glancing at the ham, "and what you are drinking can't be much better."

"That is quite possible ; still, I do not see that it is any business of yours," was the young woman's prompt response. "Did you sit down here to make fun of my supper ? "

"Oh ! dear no ! my dark-eyed angel," answered Alfred, gaily. " I came to offer you a better one."

"Then you can remain."

"On condition that you will order what you like," was the gallant retort.

"With pleasure. A roast chicken, a salad, some strawberries, and some old Burgundy. Champagne does not agree with me."

Fresnay called the waiter and repeated the order. Then as he glanced round the room he saw that the other guests were enjoying themselves hugely at his expense ; the women especially were dying of jealousy, and trying to deride his conquest. At this sight, he instantly resolved to get even with them, and began by pretending to treat his companion with the most profound respect.

"Excuse me, my dear madame, for speaking to you so familiarly," he said, in the same tone as he would have used in addressing a lady of the highest rank. "You must think me very impertinent."

"No, I think you very funny," replied the brunette, without the slightest embarrassment; "and I like eccentric people. Only you know we shall part after supper. I'm not one of those creatures who are looking at me as though I were a wild beast."

"The fact is, I have never seen you here before, and yet, I am a frequenter of the place," remarked Fresnay. "This is, no doubt, the first time you ever set foot in it?"

"Yes, and it will probably be the last. I arrived in Paris this evening, feeling terribly hungry, and so I dropped into the first restaurant I came to. But to-morrow all my fun will be over, as I must set to work again to earn my living."

"In what way?" inquired Fresnay.

"You seem to be very inquisitive."

"No, I am interested in you, that is all. Have you a lucrative profession, by the way?"

"I am a somnambulist," replied the brunette, drawing herself up right proudly.

"A somnambulist!" rejoined Fresnay. "But that isn't a profession. It's an ailment. And so you walk about with your eyes open while you are asleep. Dear me! how curious! By any chance are you in a somnambulistic condition this evening—"

"No, my fine fellow," said the brunette, laughing, "I'm not asleep, indeed, I'm precious wide-awake. You must come from the country not to know that a clairvoyant can earn her living."

"Ah! ah, I understand now. You tell fortunes?"

"Yes, I can tell fortunes with cards if any one wishes me to, and I read mysteries in coffee grounds; but my specialty is to foretell future events, to relate what has happened in the past, and to find missing articles."

"You know everything that pertains to your calling, I see."

"Yes, and I have never yet found my match."

' How fortunate! I have always wanted to know how I should turn out, and if you can tell me—"

"That is no difficult matter. You will come to a bad end," said the young woman, laughing gaily. "But I don't give consultations in a restaurant, mind."

"Then give me your address."

"Impossible. I have none just at present."

"No address—how's that?"

"Oh! I don't sleep in the open air. But never mind. I say, this Burgundy isn't bad."

"It comes from Musigny," replied Fresnay, adding: "By the way, you will at least tell me your name?"

"My name is Olga."

"Olga! That is a very pretty name; but Olga what?" asked the young baron, inquisitively.

"Must I show you my papers—my certificate of birth and certificate of marriage? You are presuming, I must say," retorted the brunette.

"You are married, then?"

"What difference can that possibly make to you? This roast fowl is tender, but there are not enough truffles. Why don't you eat some of it?"

"I don't like white meats."

"Nor women with dark complexions, eh?"

"On the contrary, I worship them," replied Fresnay, with remarkable alacrity.

"Oh, pray don't try to make me believe that you have fallen in love with me. I assure you that I am not sufficiently verdant to believe in that."

"Allow me! allow me! You are charming. The sun has gilded you as it were—"

"Come, no compliments, I don't believe in them. But I say, you are rich, are you not?"

"My wealth is beyond computation; only this evening I haven't a penny, unfortunately."

"I certainly hope you have enough to pay for the supper," said Olga, quickly. "I shouldn't care to be left here in pawn."

"What do you take me for?" asked the baron, with affected indignation. "I have enough, and more than enough, money in my pocket to settle the bill. Besides, I am well known here, and they would trust me, if I wished them to."

Olga again turned her attention to her supper, though not in a very tranquil state of mind, for it was evident that she feared she had fallen in with a practical joker, who was likely to leave her with the bill to pay; and this bill threatened to be no paltry one, for just then the waiter, who knew the baron's tastes, placed upon the table a lobster, a large slice of fatted goose's liver, and a bottle of Moët's Brut Impérial champagne. Fresnay, as he did ample justice to this tempting *menu*, furtively watched his guest, who was beginning to amuse him very much. He was not so astonished to learn that she was a sorceress, for she had just the right look for such a calling, and to judge by her lively talk, she must be up to all the pranks of her trade. He was already thinking how he might turn this chance acquaintanceship to account. No doubt Madame de Janos would be delighted to go and see a somnambulist in his company, in which case he would tell the brunette what she was to repeat to the Hungarian countess, paying her well beforehand. But to do this he must arrange to see her again, and so he adopted new tactics.

"I see that you either cannot, or will not, give me your address," he said suddenly; "but there is nothing to prevent me from giving you mine."

"I am sure I have no objections," tranquilly responded the dark-eyed Olga, when she had drained her glass of Burgundy with evident relish.

On hearing this, Alfred drew one of his visiting cards from his pocket, and laid it on the table in front of his guest, who, as she glanced at it, exclaimed: "What! you are a baron! How charming! I like aristocratic people, I do; and I flatter myself that they usually take to me. I have told the fortunes of more than one countess and marchioness, I can tell you."

"I will bring another to see you some day, if you like, and you can charge her whatever you please. I will pay the charges," said Fresnay, thinking of the chesnut-haired Hungarian. "Keep my card, and let me know when you will be ready to receive us."

"Oh, I see, you want me to speak a good word for you. You are a smart fellow, and to think that, first of all, I half took you for a counter-jumper."

"Thanks, my princess!"

"Oh! don't get angry. I'm really glad to have met you. I half fancied, at first, that I should be pestered by a lot of fools here; but I'm happy that I have come across a good fellow."

"Then I may hope to see you again?"

"Yes, only I trust that you will not tell any one that I took supper here with you this evening. If you did it might injure my business immensely."

"Who the deuce do you think I am likely to make my confidant in this matter?" asked Fresnay, wondering at this remark.

"Why the lady you are going to bring to see me. I suppose you are fond of her; and if she knew that I had supped here with you, she might be jealous, besides placing uo faith in my predictions."

"You need not have the slightest fear of that. I shall be as silent as the grave," said the baron "But tell me something about yourself. You have not always been a clairvoyant I presume?"

"No, I have travelled."

"But you have practised here in Paris?"

"Yes, here as elsewhere. But I haven't made my fortune at it, yet, alas! A rolling stone gathers no moss you know, and I have roamed about a good deal."

"Wealth will come in time, never fear. I'll give you a helping hand. But as you don't like champagne, though I don't know why, what do you say to a second bottle of Musigny? You only have a dead man there, I see."

"Do you imagine you can get me intoxicated," inquired the brunette sarcastically. "No, don't think of that. The supper would cost you too dear. I wish you would tell me what time it is, instead."

"Nearly four o'clock," replied Fresnay, pulling out his watch and glancing at it.

"Four o'clock!" repeated his companion. "Good heavens! I shall not get there in time," and as she spoke, she threw her napkin upon the table, and prepared to rise.

"What can possess you?" expostulated Fresnay. "You haven't finished your salad yet, and the waiter will be bringing you the strawberries."

"That makes no difference. I cannot wait for him. I'm expected elsewhere."

"You surely can't be going to see your sweetheart at this hour?"

"My sweetheart? Why, if I had one he would pay my bill, whereas you are going to settle it."

"Well, you surely don't think I shall believe that you are going to give a consultation?"

"Believe what you like, I must be off."

"But where are you going in such haste?"

"To the Eastern Railway Station, if you really must know," replied Olga.

"Ah! I thought so! you are going to meet your sweetheart at the station."

"But I haven't got a sweetheart, I tell you. Now I've taken your card, and if you want me to write to you, let me go."

"Won't you allow me to accompany you to the station?" insinuated the gallant Fresnay.

"By no means. There are plenty of cabs at the door of the restaurant, and I'm not afraid to drive about alone. Finish your supper in peace, my friend, and you shall soon hear from me—if you keep your promise."

Olga had already risen to her feet, and Alfred was obliged to yield to her will. She favoured him with an energetic shake of the hand, and then left the room with a deliberate step, careless as to the glances of the other people, who were sneering at her. In fact, her demeanour was so proud, that you would have taken her for a queen of tragedy crossing the stage.

Fresnay, who did not know what to think of this strange creature, now beckoned to the head waiter, in the hope of obtaining some information from him. "I will settle both bills," he said. "Do you know that person?"

"No, sir," replied the waiter, "I never saw her before, and I feel quite sure that this is the first time she has ever been here."

"Had she been here long when I came in?" the baron inquisitively asked.

"Nearly an hour, I should say. The landlord was unwilling to serve her, on account of her peculiar dress and appearance, but I suggested to him that she was probably a foreigner."

"She speaks French too well for that," retorted Fresnay. "Bring me some coffee and some Martell."

He was no longer either hungry nor thirsty, but he was still unwilling to go home; and to take the place of the fortune-teller, he could think of nothing better than some old brandy. His adventure interested him, as it was not in the least commonplace. One does not meet clairvoyants every day at the Café Américain. Where had that one come from, and why had she rushed away before four o'clock, like Cinderella, at the first stroke of midnight? Alfred endeavoured to solve this mystery, and in view of doing so more easily he called in the assistance of the Martell brandy but it failed to help him; on the contrary, his ideas became more and more muddled, and when some acquaintances arriving at the restaurant tried to rouse him, he told them rather roughly to go about their business. At last, indeed, he fell asleep, and when he awoke the place was almost empty. He then decided to go to bed, returned home in a cab, retired to rest and did not open his eyes until nearly noon, on the following day, when he had no little difficulty in recalling the events of the night. The most disagreeable point was certainly the loss of two hundred and sixty louis at cards, but he had been winning a good deal for some time past, so he consoled himself with the thought that his good luck would soon return to him.

His recollection of Olga had become rather indistinct, but the image of the chestnut-haired beauty was indelibly engraved upon his heart, and the first idea that occurred to him was to pay her the call which he had promised on the evening before.

So he breakfasted, made a very careful toilet, and between the hours of two and three repaired to the Grand Hôtel, where he inquired for the Countess de Janos. The clerk could not find the name upon the register at first, but after making some inquiries, he announced that the lady in question had arrived that morning, that her apartments were on the third floor, and that she was indoors.

"That is strange," said Fresnay, to himself, as he went upstairs. "She gave me this address yesterday, and yet she apparently only arrived here early this morning. It is all the stranger, as I saw her with her friend

Tergowitz, at the concert, and I begin to expect that she isn't of much account."

He was not at the end of his surprises, for on the first landing he met a gentleman who was going away, and who, on perceiving him, averted his head, and applied his handkerchief to his nose in such a way as to effectually conceal his face; however his figure and general appearance forcibly reminded Fresnay of the Hungarian friend whom Madame de Janos had joined on the evening before at the Café des Ambassadeurs.

"Good!" thought Fresnay, "I am just in time. A quarter of an hour sooner, I should have found my place taken. Now it is vacant, and I shall amuse myself a little by chaffing the countess on the assiduous attentions of her compatriot. Heaven grant that she will consent to receive me. She must have finished her toilet by this time; and besides, I am vain enough to believe that she is expecting a visit from me."

He continued climbing, and was quite out of breath when he reached the third floor, where he spent some time hunting for the countess's number. He found it at last, and saw that the key was in the lock of the door outside. However, he resisted the idea of surprising the countess, and gave a discreet knock. He soon heard a light footfall, and then the door was set ajar, and a woman's face appeared.

Two exclamations of surprise resounded at the same instant. The woman recognised him, and he, on his side, recognised her. It was Olga, the clairvoyant of the Café Américain, who stood before him. She had changed her gypsy-like costume for the trim attire of the typical soubrette, and this garb became her well.

Instead of admitting Fresnay immediately, the shrewd creature at once stepped back, closed an inner door, and then opening the outer one wide, advanced, so as to bar the way to this unexpected visitor.

"What, goodness gracious, is this you? What on earth has brought you here?" she exclaimed, with unaffected astonishment.

"I called to see the lady whom I promised to bring to you to have her fortune told," replied Fresnay, laughing; "but as I find you here—"

"Don't speak so loud, pray don't. If she were only to overhear you—"

"So you are her maid?" asked Fresnay.

"As you see."

"And it was to meet her at the Eastern Railway Station, that you left me so abruptly this morning?" continued the inquisitive baron.

"Yes, indeed. So you know her?"

"Certainly I do!" was the retort. "She is even expecting a visit from me. Ask her if she isn't. Shall I give you my card? No, that is unnecessary, for I gave you one at the restaurant, and I feel sure that you have not lost it, and that you know the name by heart."

At this moment a bell rang in the next room. "Come," said the baron, "your mistress is growing impatient. Make haste and announce me."

"I suppose I must," retorted Olga. "But not a word, promise me. If madame knew you had met me before, she might dismiss me."

"And then you would be reduced to fortune-telling again," said Fresnay, ironically. "Very well, I will say nothing, on conditions that you will give me some information from time to time, respecting this same Countess de Janos, and the life she is leading in Paris."

Olga lacked the time to reply, for at this moment Madame de Janos, losing all patience, opened the inner door herself, and paused in evident astonishment at seeing her maid engaged in conversation with a gentleman, whom she did not at first recognise.

Fresnay lost no time in averting the questions which were evidently upon the lady's lips. "Excuse me, madame," he said, removing his hat, "your maid, who does not know me, refused me admission; but I insisted upon being received. Did I do wrong?"

"No," replied the countess, after an instant's hesitation. "I was just going out, but as you have taken the trouble to climb so many stairs—"

"A thousand thanks. I will promise not to detain you long."

Thereupon Olga stepped aside to allow the baron to pass into the countess's apartments, which consisted of three communicating rooms, the first of them being crowded with some immense trunks which did not seem to have done much travelling as, to all appearance, they were quite new.

"You see I am scarcely settled yet," remarked Madame de Janos. "I don't expect to make a very long stay at the hotel, and that is the reason why I have not yet opened my innumerable boxes. But I have a sitting-room where we can chat more comfortably. Come, sir." Then, turning to her maid, she added:

"I am not at home to any one."

Alfred followed the countess into the stiffly furnished sitting-room and took a seat upon a sofa of the kind which upholsterers call a tête-à-tête. She had closed the door on entering, so that Olga who was left among the trunks might not inconvenience them.

"I must confess that I did not expect to see you again," began Madame de Janos. "I felt sure that you had entirely forgotten our chance meeting at the café concert, by this time."

"Then you are offended with me for having ventured to call?" asked Fresnay, quickly.

"No; but I am afraid that I was rash in promising to receive you. We are of the same social rank, it is true, and I must confess that your conversation last evening entertained me greatly, but unfortunately Frenchmen are so exacting."

"Perhaps, but you are free to refuse my petitions, and in the meanwhile, what harm can a little innocent conversation do to either of us? But, by the way, what have you done with Monsieur Tergowitz?"

"What a memory you have for names!" said Madame de Janos, with a keen glance at her companion.

"And for faces, too. I just met that gentleman on the stairs, and recognised him instantly."

"He did just leave me. You don't presume to censure me for receiving his visits, I suppose?" asked the countess, quickly.

"Oh, no. I have plenty of faults, but I am not jealous," replied Fresnay, with affected gravity.

"Jealous!" repeated the countess, bursting into a laugh. "What right have you to be jealous in this case, pray?"

"It would be rather presumptuous, that's a fact," answered the baron, meekly. "Besides, your Hungarian friend is a very gentlemanly looking fellow, and I hope that after the concert, he showed you some interesting parts of this strange city with which you are so anxious to become acquainted."

"On the contrary, he only escorted me to the Café Napolitain to take an ice, and then saw me back to this hotel before midnight. I was terribly tired, and slept, oh so soundly!"

"I didn't. I thought of you all night, and I did not go to bed until five o'clock this morning. I can not sleep when I am in love."

"In love, you!" said Madame de Janos, with a pretty pout. "Come, confess the truth. You spent the night at the card-table, or in supping with your friends."

"I don't deny it. That is my way of curing my heart-aches. This time the remedy did not prove effectual, however. I lost a great deal of money, and I admire you more than ever."

"Oh! indeed—well your admiration will soon pass off, no doubt. However, the pecuniary loss is a more serious matter, and if it be a large one—"

"Oh, it will not inconvenience me. I have money enough to indulge in a few expensive whims now and then if I like. There is one I should like to gratify, but I doubt whether it will succeed? It depends entirely upon you."

"Upon me?" said Madame de Janos, lifting her eyebrows in genuine surprise.

"Yes," replied Fresnay, "I inherited, last year, the property of an uncle, who bequeathed to me, among other things, a very pretty little house in the Rue Mozart, at Passy. I have not succeeded in letting it, and I never could make up my mind to live in it. It is too far off. I prefer my rooms in the Rue de l'Arcade."

"Ah! you live in the Rue de l'Arcade?" said the countess, making a mental note of the address.

"Yes, at No 19. I forgot to tell you yesterday that I have very cozy bachelor quarters there. But I have just taken it into my head to let my house on the Rue Mozart to a pretty woman. Oh! I should be very accommodating as to terms. If my tenant allowed me to visit her, I should never present any rent bills. Come, as you say you want comfortable quarters, why shouldn't you become the tenant I am looking for?"

"You must have lost your senses!"

"By no means. The house isn't furnished, but my upholsterer could attend to that in a fortnight's time. You need sign no lease, and you will be at liberty to leave the house at any time; but during your stay in Paris, you would be infinitely more comfortable there than in a hotel, so I don't see why you should not accept my proposal."

"Because it isn't serious," said the countess, looking Fresnay full in the face.

Madame de Janos seemed especially charming that day, and her attire suited her. Her eyes sparkled with a strange lustre, and her dressing-gown set off her sculptural figure to advantage. Fresnay felt "hit" and he resumed, earnestly: "Come, pray don't think that I am joking. What shall I do to prove to you that I am in earnest? Will you come to Passy with me. I will show you over the house, and then we will go and call on my upholsterer."

"Ah! you are talking business," interrupted Madame de Janos, "whereas I came to Paris to enjoy myself."

"It won't be my fault if you don't. I promise you that. Will you accept my offer?"

"Can you suppose that I can answer yes or no just as if it were only a question of taking a drive in the Bois de Boulogne? What a strange opinion you must have formed of me. What would you think if I answered 'yes'?"

"I should think you were a superior woman above petty prejudice, and besides, if you accepted, it would be a proof that I don't displease you."

"Oh! I never said that you did."

"Well then, the arrangement I propose is a very sensible one, it seems to me. You told me yesterday that you were looking for suitable quarters. I offer you my house. Give me the preference. That is all I ask."

"I must have time for reflection," said the countess, laughing.

"In other words, you wish to consult Monsieur Tergowitz."

"I never consult anything but my own inclination. You are quite mistaken in regard to the nature of my connection with that gentleman. He was one of my father's best friends."

"Indeed! He looks very young for that."

"He is a little older than I am. I should have said that he was my father's ward. We were brought up together. You will not be likely to meet him, however, for he just called to inform me that he expects to leave Paris this evening. Important business matters oblige him to return to Hungary."

"That suits me!" exclaimed Fresnay. "Then it's agreed?"

"Not at all! not at all! I have by no means made up my mind as yet," retorted the countess.

"Oh! you'll soon come to a decision, and in the meanwhile, I'll order the furniture."

"How impulsive you are! You barely know me, and yet you talk like that. You must have been guilty of no end of follies in your time, and you need a mentor. You ought to take the advice of that quiet friend of yours whom you introduced me to yesterday evening—Monsieur Gémozac. Just ask him what he thinks of this fine scheme of yours."

"I don't think he would even take the trouble to express an opinion," replied Fresnay, disdainfully. "Mademoiselle Camille Monistrol engrosses all his thoughts, and he has ceased to take any interest in my affairs. He has been seized with a desire to discover the late Monsieur Monistrol's murderer, and if he isn't speedily cured of his folly, it won't surprise me to learn that he has become a member of the detective force."

"I can not find it in my heart to blame him," said Madame de Janos, gently. "Indeed, I should be very grateful to you if you would keep me informed of your generous friend's efforts to help that young girl in avenging her father."

Fresnay did not recollect his friend's advice given on the night before, but responded impulsively: "I will not fail to do so, and I thank you for thus giving me an assurance that I shall see you often. You shall have a full report every day, if you wish it, while you continue staying here at the Grand Hôtel, and when you have moved into the Rue Mozart—"

"Excuse me, I did not say that I consented."

"Oh! it amounts to the same. I will call for you to-morrow at noon, so as to go and select some furniture. I'm off now, for you told me you wanted to go out. You see that I'm discreet, and know how to behave myself. By the way, you will keep your maid, I suppose?"

"But, I assure you—"

"Come, come! it's all understood. You will want two other servants, and as there are no stables to the house, I will hire you a good brougham from a first-rate job-master."

Madame de Janos was not wanting in bounce, but Alfred possessed even a larger supply of that commodity than she did, and he had already gained the upper hand to such a point that she did not know how to put a stop to his boldness. Printing a kiss upon her hand he exclaimed: "Till we meet again, my dear countess ; I shall dream of you to-night."

And thereupon he left the room so hastily that he nearly overturned Olga, who was listening at the door. He shook his finger at her, and as she showed him out of the apartment he found an opportunity to slip a one hundred franc-note into her hand, and whisper : "You see I am willing to pay liberally. Serve me faithfully, and you will make more money than you ever did by fortune-telling. Not a word to your mistress, mind. You know where I live. Call and see me occasionally, between ten and eleven in the morning. I shall have a lot of things to ask you, and I sha'n't haggle over the price of your information."

Olga looked at him in astonishment, but without waiting for her reply, Fresnay bounded down the staircase. He was delighted with his visit and said to himself : "Ah ! ah ! so we are going to have some fun. If that maid is faithful to me, I shall soon know what to think about her mistress's pretended noble birth ! It will cost me a set of furniture, but no matter ! After a time my upholsterer will take it back, at a loss to me of course. As for the house, I didn't hope to let it till next year ; and, at all events, I shall amuse myself better than that baby Gémozac who is such dreadful spoons on that orphan girl of the Boulevard Voltaire. As for myself, I infinitely prefer the widow of the Grand Hôtel."

On arriving at this conclusion, Fresnay lighted a cigar, and set out on foot for his club, where he expected to find his friend Julien.

VI.

CAMILLE MONISTROL, overcome with fatigue and emotion, did not rise until very late on the morning following the eventful night which had so nearly been her last. Brigitte, whom she had aroused at about two o'clock in the morning to pay and dismiss the cabman, had refrained from questioning her respecting her adventures, and even from asking her why Courapied and Georget had not returned with her.

The old nurse did not regret their absence by any means, and she especially congratulated herself upon being well rid of Vigoureux, that terrible brute which had seemed inclined to devour everything and everybody that came in its way. She hoped, too, that her young mistress had renounced her chimerical schemes of revenge, and would give up running about the streets at night-time with people of questionable morality. When Camille woke up she did not take the trouble to undeceive Brigitte who could not personally assist her, or even advise her in the embarrassment in which she now found herself. Still less could she confess to her old nurse that a young man who was almost a stranger to her now engrossed her thoughts, and that she was even impatiently awaiting his coming.

That was the real state of things, however. She longed to see the brave defender who had rescued her, at the peril of his life, from the hands of two vile scoundrels. She owed more than existence to him, and she had scarcely had time to express her gratitude. Indeed, he had evaded her thanks with a modesty that greatly enhanced the value of the service rendered.

He had promised to call and see her on the Boulevard Voltaire, but would he keep his promise ? Camille almost doubted it. She said to herself that a man of society would feel it his duty to succour a young girl assailed by scoundrels in a lonely spot, but that he would not consider it incumbent upon him to continue an acquaintance thus formed by chance; and her rescuer was evidently a man of the world—one who must, indeed, move in the very best society. The name he bore, his personal appearance, his attire and his distinguished manners, all indicated, beyond any possibility of doubt, that he belonged by birth to the aristocracy.

Why, then, should he give any further thought to a singular adventure, which was evidently in no way connected with his ordinary life? The little that Camille had said to him about her personal situation, and her expedition in search of a murderer, was not calculated to induce a fashionable gentleman to grant her his protection, much less to second her in her efforts. Men willing to become detectives to oblige a woman, are but very seldom met with.

And yet, Mademoiselle Monistrol could only appeal to this young man for assistance in her attempt to find not merely Zig-Zag, but also and especially Courapied and his son, who had paid so dearly for their devotion. Were they dead, or had they survived their terrible fall? However that might be, Camille could not abandon them. Indeed, she already began to reproach herself bitterly for having followed the advice of M. de Menestreau, who had urged her to return home, and not incur a risk of sharing the fate of her unfortunate auxiliaries by again repairing to that lonely house.

He had probably done quite right in thus preventing her from endangering her life, but this certainly need not deter her from making the attempt under more favourable conditions : that is to say, by daylight, and with more formidable weapons than a pocket pistol, and, above all, accompanied by a brave and sensible friend who would not shrink from danger, but who would run no unnecessary risk.

And that friend could be only this same M. de Menestreau. Camille could think of no other person who was in a position to attempt this perilous task. If he failed to keep his promise, there would be nothing left for her but to apply to the police, though she had lost all confidence in them since her father's death.

On rising, she resumed her mourning garments, and then Brigitte served her her breakfast, but without succeeding in ridding her of her gloomy thoughts. Camille counted each minute as it slipped by, and at last, in view of trying to quiet her impatience, she went out into what she called her garden, that is to say, into the inclosure that surrounded the house. There were here some beds where she had sown a few seeds which were just beginning to spring up, and she never failed to water them morning and evening. She was about to do so now, when the sound of a vehicle stopping on the boulevard just in front of the house made her start.

She turned quickly, but instead of the person she was expecting, she saw Madame Gémozac and her son alighting from a handsome brougham. They could not have come at a more inopportune moment ; but it was too late to avoid them, so that Camille stepped forward to meet them. Julien bowed, and Madame Gémozac, kissing the young girl upon both cheeks, said, in a most affectionate tone : "I have come to fetch you, my dear child, as you didn't come to see us. We only talk of you at home, and my husband would have accompanied me if his time was not so entirely engrossed by business. Julien, who is differently situated, insisted upon coming with me."

Camille stammered a few words of thanks, but it was very evident that her thoughts were elsewhere. In fact, they were wandering across the plain of St. Denis in company with George de Menestreau.

"How did you spend the day yesterday, after you left us?" continued Madame Gémozac. "I have done very wrong to leave you alone in this house, which must be so full of harrowing associations; and I really must insist upon your leaving it as soon as possible. We are all very fond of you, and I hope that you will consider yourself quite one of our family. Do not grieve us by living so much aloof from us."

"I am very grateful to you, madame," replied the girl, without any display of feeling, however, "but I explained to you why I desire to remain where I am. I have a duty to perform; and, until I succeed in finding my father's murderer—"

"What! you still persist in that scheme, my dear Camille?" asked Madame Gémozac. "Why, it is folly—generous folly, I admit—"

"Possibly, madame, but I shall not abandon it."

"Then allow me to remind you that you have accepted my help," interposed Julien.

"I know that, sir, and I do not repent of it. But I, also, must act in the matter; and I now have reasons to believe that I shall discover the culprit. I at least know that he has renounced his former calling, and also that he is still in Paris."

"In that case it will be impossible for him to escape a well-organised search. He can easily be identified by the remarkable shape and size of his hands, and I shall begin by giving the agents I mean to employ a full description of them. I shall also join them, if necessary, in ferreting out the scoundrel."

"I am deeply grateful to you, sir, for your kindly intentions," replied Camille, but all the while she was thinking: "It isn't you who will find Zig-Zag, and the only man who is capable of finding him does not come."

Madame Gémozac did not think it advisable to oppose her son just then; but she resolved to make him listen to reason as soon as she was again alone with him. The prudent mother's visit to Mademoiselle Monistrol was not due solely to the interest she felt in the orphan. It had an object. Madame Gémozac had perceived that her son was deeply interested in Camille; and that very morning she had extorted from Julien a confession that he was seriously and deeply in love with the young lady.

Now, although Madame Gémozac did not positively oppose this plan of a marriage with the wealthy heiress of the inventor, she, nevertheless, felt it her duty to become better acquainted with the young girl before giving her consent to the match.

Camille was a very charming girl, but, in point of fact, the Gémozacs knew almost nothing about her. They had never seen her until after her father's death, and were entirely ignorant of her habits, and of her true character. Lovers seldom trouble themselves about such paltry details, but mothers feel very differently. Thus, Madame Gémozac had called in quest of information, and if she had brought her son with her, it was because she feared he might call without her, and carry matters too far in the first tête-à-tête interview. Now, she did not care for him to declare his love without her consent, and she also hoped to prevent him from engaging in a dangerous and absurd undertaking merely to please a foolish young girl. Pending the opportunity to lecture him as he deserved, she realised the necessity of changing the subject, and so she hastily remarked: "And this is the house you refuse to leave! How can you be so fond of it?"

"I have always lived here, madame, and my father died here," replied Mademoiselle Monistrol, rather drily.

"But it is not a suitable home for a young girl."

"And why not, madame?" asked Camille, with some show of astonishment.

"Because it is too lonely. However, the woman you spoke about yesterday is with you, I hope?"

"Brigitte? Yes, madame. She is here. Would you like to see her? I will call her if you like."

"No, it is not at all necessary," replied Madame Gémozac. "Show us over the house rather. I am anxious to see the room where your father was killed. My son has told me all that occurred during that terrible night."

"I have not forgotten what he did for me," murmured Camille.

"But what I did, mademoiselle, is nothing in comparison with what I mean to do," said Julien, eagerly. "I need only a word from you to act."

"Let us visit the house," interrupted Madame Gémozac, anxious to curtail her son's offers of service.

"Are you really so desirous of going indoors?" asked Mademoiselle Monistrol.

"Well, I hardly suppose that you intend to receive us in this yard where every passer-by on the boulevard can see us," replied Madame Gémozac, considerably piqued.

"I am used to it, and as I have nothing to conceal, it makes no difference to me whether people watch me or not," replied Camille coldly.

"Very well, mademoiselle. I understand that you do not desire our company, so there is nothing left for us but to withdraw."

"You misunderstand me entirely, madame," protested Camille. "The only reason I do not invite you in is that it is always very painful to me to enter the room where my father was so cruelly murdered. However, we need not go into it."

"Oh! we had still better stay here. After all, it is a matter of no consequence, especially as I have but little time at my disposal this morning," was the cold answer. "I will therefore take leave of you. When you feel any inclination to come and see us, you will be very cordially received, and my husband bade me remind you that his purse was at your disposal."

Camille, cut to the quick, made a deprecating gesture, which did not escape Julien's keen eyes.

"That is hardly a correct statement of the case," he interposed, quickly. "You are my father's partner, mademoiselle, and any money you may require is, of course, at your disposal. I will gladly serve you personally, and I beg that you will tell me all you know about the scoundrel you are looking for. You say that he is still in Paris."

"Yes, at least he was last night."

"Did you see him?"

"No, but I am sure of what I say."

"Then you have already entered upon your campaign, I suppose?" said Madame Gémozac, ironically.

"Yes, madame," was the girl's unhesitating reply.

"You have lost no time, I see, and it seems to me that you can easily dispense with Julien's assistance."

"I did not solicit it, and I only accepted it because I am already under such deep obligations to your son that the idea of being still more indebted to him was not distasteful to me. But I should be sorry if he exposed himself to any danger on my account, and imperilled his life by helping me to find my father's murderer."

"I am quite ready to do so!" exclaimed Julien, earnestly.

On hearing this enthusiastic response, Madame Gémozac quite lost her temper. "You are mad," she said, angrily, to her son. "I will not have you transform yourself into a detective merely to please this young lady."

"I am master of my own actions, mother," replied Julien, coldly, "and I must call your attention to that fact. Besides, this is hardly the place to discuss such a delicate subject."

"That is true. Let us go, for I trust you will not grieve me by letting me go alone."

"Certainly not, mother," retorted Julien, "but I hope that Mademoiselle Monistrol will kindly permit me to call again at an early day."

Camille made no reply. She was suffering terribly, and Madame Gémozac's maternal zeal tried her patience to its utmost limits. She did not wish to offend the mother or wound the son, but she was determined not to yield, even if she were obliged to alienate the wife of her father's generous partner, and refuse the help of the young man who seemed so eager to serve her.

"Farewell, mademoiselle," said Madame Gémozac, with marked coldness. "I am extremely sorry to have disturbed you. You are expecting some visitor, no doubt, and it is high time that we made room for him."

"You are altogether mistaken, madame," faltered Camille, blushing deeply.

"Oh dear no!" was the retort, "I am not mistaken. See, a vehicle has just driven up to your gate."

A cab had indeed stopped in front of the house, and at its window there appeared a face which Mademoiselle Monistrol instantly recognised, but which was speedily withdrawn.

"We should be in the gentleman's way," remarked Madame Gémozac. "Come, my son, we have no further business here."

This time Julien followed his mother without a word, and Camille, deeply humiliated, saw them re-enter their brougham. The visitor who had put them to flight had now hastily pulled up the window, and drawn back into a corner of his cab.

"It is he!" murmured Camille, "and he fears to displease me by showing himself. Ah! in him I shall have a more serious and able defender than that young man who pretends that he loves me and who still relies on the police to find Zig-Zag."

Madame Gémozac's brougham now rapidly drove away and Camille thought she saw Julien lean out to try and catch a glimpse of the person hiding in the cab.

She felt some little remorse at having wounded the son and irritated the mother when she could have mentioned the name of her visitor, and even have introduced him to them without blushing. But to explain his visit it would have been necessary to divulge the events of the previous night, and she instinctively felt that the Gémozacs would disapprove of her conduct. Moreover, she felt that it would be worse than useless to speak of an expedition which had proved so unfortunate as regards Courapied and poor little Georget.

Then, too, she was overcome with joy at the sight of her preserver. He, perhaps, brought her some tidings of her unfortunate friends, and she had so many things to say to him.

He waited until the brougham was some distance off and then alighted. Mademoiselle Monistrol had advanced half way to meet him, and as he approached her, hat in hand, she could better appreciate his personal attractions than she had been able to do in the dimly-lighted Avenue de Clichy.   He seemed to her now much handsomer than on the evening before.   His sympathetic and pleasing face wore a grave and even affectionate expression, and he seemed to be trying to read the thoughts of the young girl whose eyes met his so frankly.

"Excuse my tardiness, mademoiselle," he said gently.   "I did not call this morning for fear of disturbing you, for I knew that you would be in very great need of rest.   And, indeed, even now, I fear, I came too soon, for I disturbed you—you were not alone."

"Madame Gémozac and her son were with me.   My father, only the day before his death, became a partner with Monsieur Gémozac in working a patent of which he was the inventor, and the young man you just saw came to my assistance on the evening of the murder.   But I am talking of matters you know nothing about, for last night I could not tell you my story."

"You merely told me that you were hunting for your father's murderer," replied M. George de Menestreau softly.

"My story is very short and simple," resumed Camille.   "A scoundrel crept into our house one evening.   He sprung upon my father, strangled him and then fled.   I pursued him as far as the Place du Trône, where I saw him enter a building in which a company of acrobats were performing.   I went in and tried to secure his arrest, but no one would listen to me, and I very narrowly escaped being arrested myself.   Monsieur Julien Gémozac happened to be present, and he protected me although he did not know me at the time.   When I returned here in company with him, I found my father dead."

"That was terrible!" remarked M. George de Menestreau.   "Why didn't you denounce the murderer without loss of time, mademoiselle?"

"I remained for several days between life and death, and when I was able to take any action in the matter, it was too late.   The acrobat I accused had been questioned and released.   It was not until yesterday that I succeeded in finding any trace of him—and you know the result of the expedition I attempted—"

"Upon the advice of some persons who accompanied you, I believe; was not that the case?"

"Yes," replied Camille, "upon the advice of a man who formerly belonged to the same acrobatic company as this Zig-Zag."

"What a singular name!"

"That is how the murderer was known to the public, at all events; but he has another name, of course, though I have not succeeded in discovering it.   The scoundrel fled with the wife of one of his comrades—the same man who furnished me with my information.   This poor fellow had a son, about twelve years of age, whom we took with us, and who disappeared with his father.   But excuse me, sir, I have neglected to invite you indoors."

She forthwith turned towards the house, M. de Menestreau accompanying her.   At the doorway they met Brigitte, who seemed considerably surprised to see her young mistress in the company of this handsome young stranger.   She might also have felt some astonishment at seeing Camille usher this gentleman into the very apartments which she had refused to show to Madame Gémozac ; however, she had not witnessed the interview with the ironmaster's wife and son, and, besides, she understood very little about polite usages. Camille began by conducting her preserver straight to the dining-room, where she had not eaten a morsel since the murder.

"It was here that the murderer concealed himself," she remarked, in a low voice.

"But how did he gain an entrance?" inquired M. George de Menestreau. "Had your servant foolishly neglected to lock the street door?"

"We had no servant at the time. The person you just saw has only been with me a few days. My father took no precautions against thieves, as we possessed nothing that would be likely to tempt them. But, unfortunately, on that very day, we had received twenty thousand francs from Monsieur Gémozac. How the murderer became aware of this fact, I do not know, but he certainly was aware of it. The terrible deed was committed in this way : My father was seated at the table, completing a drawing which he was to take to his partner. I was seated in that corner doing some needlework. The curtains near which you are standing were closed as they are now. Suddenly I saw a hand appear between the two hangings and part them."

"Like this," said M. de Menestreau, stepping forward.

As he spoke he removed his gloves and parted the curtains with his bare right hand, a slender white hand—an aristocratic hand with tapering fingers and almond-shaped nails, the exact opposite of the frightful claw-like hand that had so often haunted Camille in her dreams.

"Yes," replied Mademoiselle Monistrol, "and that hand was all I could see of the murderer's person."

"What! you would not be able to recognise his face if you saw it again?" asked M. de Menestreau.

"No, as he sprung upon my father he overturned the lamp. It went out, and—"

"Then how can you possibly hope to find him?"

"He had the hands of a gorilla," replied Camille, "and I should only have to see them to be able to say with certainty : That is the man!"

"Yes, that is, indeed, a peculiarity which may ultimately prove of service to us—that is, if we are fortunate enough to find the culprit."

"You doubt it, then?"

"I fear that the expedition you made last night may have induced him to decamp—that is, if he really was an occupant of the old house you spoke of."

"No matter ; my friends are there and I can not abandon them," replied Camille, eagerly.

"I have come to take you there. I should have gone alone, but I did not know exactly where to look for the house. You must show me the way to it, and we will talk the matter over, and see what it is best to do."

"Thanks. I expected no less from you, and I am ready to accompany you," said Camille.

"Then the same cab that brought me here can take us to the Saint-Ouen gate. Once there we will proceed on foot, and you shall show me the way, mademoiselle."

"The way?" repeated Camille. "Yes, I hope I shall find it, and yet, yesterday I didn't leave Paris by the Saint-Ouen gate."

"No matter, mademoiselle," replied George de Menestreau, "I will undertake to conduct you to the spot where I met you last night. You must point the house out to me. It can not be far from there."

"A few hundred yards at the most."

"Very well, then. It will be an easy matter. I am rejoiced to see that you have enough confidence in me to accept me as a companion."

"I do so gladly. How could I possibly doubt one who saved my life?"

"And you feel quite sure that no one will reproach you for the step you are taking?" inquired M. de Menestreau, in a tone of friendly solicitude.

"Who would venture to do that? Now that I have lost my father, I am alone in the world, and no one has any right to control my actions."

"What, have you no guardian?"

"No ; if I had, it would be Monsieur Gémozac, my poor father's partner. He is my guardian to all intents and purposes—if not officially—for my entire property is in his hands. He is to furnish the necessary money for working the patent which is my sole inheritance, and he will take charge of my income for me."

"All this makes it the more necessary that your position should be legally defined. You are not of age yet, so that you require a guardian to watch over your interests. But excuse me, mademoiselle, for thus meddling with your affairs. The interest I feel in you is my only excuse. And, besides, I have experience which you lack, and if I can ever be of use to you, pray believe that my services are quite at your disposal. For the moment, however, it is a question of beginning our campaign, and I must ask your permission to define the object of our expedition. Your first object is to find that acrobat whom you accuse, and who bears such a strange nickname—"

"Zig-Zag— He is the murderer, I'm sure of it," replied Camille.

"I presume so, since you tell it me. Still, I hardly fancy that he has waited for us in the house where you fruitlessly tried to surprise him last night. The attempt you made must have alarmed him, and he has, no doubt, changed his quarters. All that we can reasonably hope is that he may have left some traces of his sojourn in that house—traces which may enable us to follow up the pursuit."

"Oh ! quite so," muttered Camille.

"However," resumed M. de Menestreau, "you are also anxious to find your two allies, whom you were forced to abandon so as to avoid sharing their fate."

"Yes, sir. I particularly wish to find them. They sacrificed themselves for me, and I have greatly delayed in going to their help."

"Oh ! there is no reason to regret the loss of time. One of two things has happened. Either that bandit has shut them up in the cellar into which they fell, so you told me, and in that case we will deliver them, for they must still be there—people don't die of hunger in eighteen hours—or else they are dead, Zig-Zag either having murdered them, or their terrible fall having killed them. And I won't hide from you that this last supposition seems to me to be the more likely of the two."

"They must, at least, have been hurt by the fall."

"If they are only hurt we shall be able to remove them from the cellar, and take them home, without letting anyone into the secret. But if they are dead, are we to leave their bodies there?"

"No, certainly not. It would be too horrible," said Camille warmly.

"Then, in that case, we must make a declaration to the commissary of police, relate your nocturnal adventure in detail, explain to him why and how you entered into a connection with these people who were mountebanks, comrades of the murderer. It may be that the veracity of the narrative will be questioned; if not, the authorities will take the matter up. You will be set on one side, and you will not be able to continue your search."

"It would be a great blow to me if I had to renounce it; but it would also pain me to be accused of telling a falsehood. However, I am ready to suffer anything rather than leave the bodies of my unfortunate friends unburied."

"I approve your views, mademoiselle," said M. de Menestreau, warmly; "and whatever may happen, I shall be there to advise you and help you. Now that we have agreed upon our course, we had better start."

"Yes," replied Camille, "pray go and wait for me in the cab. I will be with you in half a minute."

Mademoiselle Monistrol's champion bowed and left the house, whilst Camille went upstairs to make a hasty toilet. A few moments later, Brigitte, in consternation, saw her pass the kitchen door, and did not dare to raise a single objection to such a hurried departure, or even to ask her where she was going, escorted by that good-looking young man. However, it was just as well that the old nurse remained silent, for Camille was not disposed to answer any questions. She at once took her seat beside M. de Menestreau, and the driver, who had already received his orders, whipped up his horse in a style which meant business.

As the young girl took her seat in the vehicle, she noticed a large parcel on the floor at her feet. "I am prepared for any emergency, you see," remarked her new friend. "As I may be obliged to explore the cellar, I have taken the precaution to provide myself with a rope and a few implements, which may prove of use."

"I thank you most sincerely, sir," replied Camille, "but remember that I mean to accompany you wherever you go."

"I have no objection to your doing so, providing you do not expose yourself to unnecessary danger."

"But you do not hesitate to imperil your own life, although you have no loved one to avenge."

"Well, to tell the truth, I adore adventures, and danger has always had an irresistible charm for me. Still, I must confess that it is chiefly sympathy for you that prompts me, mademoiselle. You inspire me with a feeling I can scarcely define. You would laugh at me if I told you that I fell in love with you when I met you in an apprentice's blouse on the plain of Saint-Denis; and I do not believe in love at first sight any more than you do. But profound regard may very naturally spring from circumstances like those that brought us together. You are alone in the world, and so am I. I think, too, that we are congenial in character. Hence, it is only natural that we should understand each other thoroughly, even on a short acquaintance; and it was doubtless foreordained that we should some day meet. But all this sounds very like a declaration of love. That would be premature, and I sincerely assure you that you are not to regard it in such a light."

"I see that you are one of the most frank and generous of men," said Mademoiselle Monistrol, who experienced a strange emotion.

"Still, if I should ever venture upon asking for your hand, I should have to ask it of you personally," continued George de Menestreau, gaily, "for I should not know whom else to apply to, as you have no father, mother, or guardian. For want of some one better, I should perhaps be obliged to appeal to Monsieur Gémozac, and that gentleman might think that I was after your fortune."

"I do not know whether he would impute such sentiments to you or not," interrupted Mademoiselle Monistrol, "but I am not dependent upon Monsieur Gémozac, and if I ever marry, I shall choose my husband myself. Still, before choosing him, I should like to know him thoroughly—"

"Whereas you do not know me at all. All I ask, however, is that after this expedition—whatever the result of it may be—you will not insist upon our acquaintance coming to a close."

"I should be very sorry if it did," replied Camille quickly. "You will ever be welcome at my house. Besides, how could I dispense with your assistance? It is not likely that we shall succeed in finding Zig-Zag to-day, and I have no one else to help me in discovering him."

"But Monsieur Gémozac has been informed of your plans, I presume?" said M. de Menestreau.

"Yes, but he disapproves of them."

"And he is too old to be of much service to you. But how about his son—the young man I saw in your garden when I drove up?"

"He approves of them, or at least he pretends to do so; but, unfortunately, he is incapable of rendering me any effectual help. Just now, for instance, he was advising the employment of detectives—"

"Who would do nothing at all. They had the culprit in their custody once, and they released him. They can not be depended upon, that is evident. We will do better than they have done, mademoiselle, you may rest assured of that. But, pray, give me a little information before we reach the scene of action. All you saw of Zig-Zag was his hands; however, you spoke to me of a woman whom he had eloped with. What was she like?"

"Tall and dark," replied Camille. "I saw her for a moment at the fair, and I recognised her on the night when she appeared at the window of the house where we are going."

"All right. Then you would be sure to know her again anywhere. But wasn't there a dog in question?" asked M. de Menestreau.

"Yes, Zig-Zag's dog. The worthy fellow who served me caught him on the Place du Trône at the moment when he had a box belonging to his master between his teeth. Courapied muzzled him and—"

"Courapied? Is that the husband of the woman Zig-Zag eloped with? What funny names all these people have!"

"The woman is called Amanda."

"How ridiculous! But tell me, the dog guided you, didn't he?"

"Yes, to the ruined house. He dashed inside, Courapied followed him—"

"And turned a somersault in the cellar. Now I understand everything, mademoiselle. Thank you. It is as if I had taken part in the expedition, and I know what we have got to guard against. We shall soon go into action. This cab for a wonder has a fast horse and we are approaching the St. Ouen gate."

"I wish we were there already," replied Camille.

After that the conversation dropped, and at the expiration of a quarter of an hour the cab drew up in the avenue at the very spot where Camille had conversed with her protector by the light of the street lamp. She and M. de Menestreau alighted, the latter carrying the parcel which he had brought, and they passed out of the city this time without any fear of the custom's officials.

Camille followed with her protector the route she had traversed during the night, and easily recognised the spot where he had come to her assistance. The old house rose up in the plain at a few hundred yards from the Route de la Révolte, and Mademoiselle Monistrol at once pointed it out to George de Menestreau.

"It it nearer than I thought," said he, " and I am delighted to see that there are no other houses in the vicinity. We shall be able to work at our ease. Nobody will come to disturb us."

He was right in relying upon solitude, for this neighbourhood is less frequented in the daylight than in the night-time. The prowlers who lie in ambush, or find a resting-place there, are not particularly fond of the sunshine.

"Don't let us lose time, however," said George. "We must visit the place from top to bottom. Come along, mademoiselle."

Camille required no urging. Courapied and Georget were there perhaps, buried alive under the ruins and waiting in anguish for delivery. Each minute's delay might cost them their lives. The young girl soon found herself in front of the dilapidated red house and speedily recognised the window at which Amanda had appeared and the entry of the passage which her allies had so imprudently entered. The window shutters had remained open, Zig-Zag's companion not even troubling to close them after the fall of Courapied and Georget into the cellar, and it seemed probable that she and the acrobat had speedily decamped together with their dog.

M. de Menestreau asked for a description of the scene, and when Camille had furnished it, he remarked, " If you will take my advice, mademoiselle, we will begin by examining the house on all sides. There may be another door by which the wretches made their escape, and by which we can enter the house without danger of breaking our necks."

The advice was good and Camille followed it, noticing that the other frontage was yet even more dilapidated. The wall was full of large holes, and the portions of it that were still standing seemed likely to give way at any moment. Indeed, the very bricks of which it was composed seemed to have been calcined by heat and loosened by an explosion.

"I have it!" exclaimed George. "This building was once used for the manufacture of fireworks, and one fine day some of the combustibles took fire, and blew up the whole establishment. The accident must have occurred a long time ago, for plants are growing in the crevices of the wall, and the ruins have no doubt since served as a place of refuge for all the scoundrels in the neighbourhood. I shouldn't be surprised if it had served as the abode of a gang of coiners, still it seems hard to believe that Zig-Zag and his feminine friend lived here even temporarily. Ah! here is another door, at the foot of an exceedingly unsafe-looking staircase."

"It is strong enough to hold us, however," said Camille, darting forward before her companion had time to prevent it.

He was obliged to follow her, and he reached the large empty room to which the stairs led almost at the same moment that she did. There was nothing here but four bare walls, a cracked ceiling, and groaning floor.

"The wretches have been here, evidently," said the young man, pointing to a piece of candle that was lying on the floor.

"Yes," replied Camille, "they were in this room when we reached the house. I saw the woman distinctly when she approached the window, and

I feel sure that the man was in the rear. I even thought I espied him at one moment."

"Oh! he was here. No doubt of it, mademoiselle" replied M. de Menestreau, "and the dog came here too, for here is his collar."

"Yes," said Camille, "and there is the rope which snapped in Coura-pied's hand, and the strap that served as a muzzle for the dog."

"The wretches must have taken him with them. So much the better! He will perhaps help us to find them again. What surprises me most, is that they did not pursue you after making away with your companions."

"I think they would have done so," replied Camille, "if some other bandits had not attacked me on the road. Zig-Zag and his companions must have said to themselves that those fellows would spare them the trouble of killing me."

"At all events," observed M. de Menestreau, "they don't appear to have spent the rest of the night here. The only bed is the flooring. And I don't suppose they will come back now that you know their den. They must have found more comfortable quarters."

"Unless they have taken refuge in the cellar into which my friends fell," urged Mademoiselle Monistrol.

"That is improbable. People may be scoundrels, but for all that they hardly care to sleep beside the corpses of their victims. However, the question now is to find out what has become of your friends. They are not here, so let us begin first of all by visiting the hall."

They descended the stairs together, and then perceived for the first time that the hall extended from one end of the house to the other. There was no door on either side. In exploring this dark and treacherous passage, the floor of which had given way in many places, it was natural for M. de Menestreau to go first. He even tried to prevent Mademoiselle Monistrol from following him, but in vain. She clung to his overcoat. Besides, the passage was of some width and the daylight came in at the further end, so that there was hardly any reason to fear an accident. Still they proceeded very cautiously, George testing the floor carefully at every step.

"I see the opening," he remarked, after a little while. "It is time for me to light my lantern and explore the depths of this pit."

He opened his parcel and drew from it a long rope, which he uncoiled, and also a lantern, which he proceeded to light. Then he continued slowly advancing towards the opening, still closely followed by Camille.

"Why, here is a ladder!" he exclaimed, on reaching the edge of the aperture.

There was indeed a ladder, two rungs of which projected above the floor, and the other end of which must rest upon the soil of the cellar.

"I hope you are not going down," said Camille, hastily. It was the first time she had shown any apprehension.

"I must take a look into the pit first. When I find out what there is below I shall know what it is best to do," replied the young man.

He thereupon fastened the lantern to one end of the rope, and then slowly lowered it into the opening.

"George!" called Mademoiselle Monistrol, leaning over the edge of the aperture.

There was no response.

"They are dead," she whispered, and then, with a shudder, she drew closer to her new friend.

"We have good reason to fear that they are, for the lantern has not yet touched the bottom, and I have lowered at least ten feet of rope. Ah ! it touches the bottom at last. A fall of fifteen or sixteen feet is quite enough to kill a man, to say nothing of a child. Besides, if your friends had survived the fall, they would have availed themselves of the ladder ; that is, unless Zig-Zag brought it here afterwards in order to descend and despatch them. I must go down and satisfy myself upon that point, for although I have been moving my lantern about down there, I can see nothing but dark soil."

"In that case, I will go down with you," said Camille.

"Pray do not think of such a thing, mademoiselle. You could not descend the ladder dressed as you are. Ah ! if you wore your 'prentice garments of last night it would be different. However, even if the bodies of your unfortunate friends are there, how could you endure the sight ? "

Camille could not repress a shudder at the thought.

"Moreover, we must be prepared for any possible contingency," continued M. de Menestreau. "What if Zig-Zag should be hiding somewhere about here, and should take it into his head to cut off our retreat by taking away the ladder? We should then both be caught in the trap. It would be far better for you to remain here, so that you can warn me if you hear any suspicious sounds. In that case, I will come up again at once."

"But what if the wretch should be hiding in the cellar, and should attack you as soon as you reach the bottom ? " urged Camille in distress.

"He would meet with a warm reception. I have a six-shooter in my pocket, and I would blow his brains out before he had a chance to touch me. And besides, as I shall have my lantern, he won't be able to surprise me."

As the young fellow spoke, he placed his foot on the topmost rung of the ladder, and began the descent, swinging the lantern to and fro in front of him, but without letting it fall low enough for any assailant hidden in the cellar to snatch it away.

A prey to the most poignant anxiety, Camille watched the light which grew dimmer and dimmer, in proportion as M. de Menestreau descended.

At last, the voice of the brave explorer reached her, clear and distinct. "I have reached the bottom," he cried, "and I see nothing as yet. I am going to make the tour of the cellar. Don't be alarmed if you lose sight of my lantern. I shall not be gone long.'

At the same moment the light disappeared, and although the eclipse had been announced, it increased Mademoiselle Monistrol's terror tenfold. It seemed to her that she would never again see her brave preserver, the only friend she had left her in the world.

She waited a minute—five minutes, and then, unable to endure the suspense any longer, she called M. de Menestreau by name. The call remained unanswered, however, and the light did not reappear. At last despair seized hold of her.

"He is dead," she moaned in her distress, "Zig-Zag was lying in wait for him below. Zig-Zag has killed him, strangled him. He kills all whom I love. Ah, well, let him kill me, too ! "

And without pausing to reflect, she prepared to descend into the depths from which no one seemingly ever returned. Very fortunately, however, she did not have time to carry this senseless project into execution, for she had scarcely placed her foot upon the top rung of the ladder before a friendly voice called out from below : "Here I am, mademoiselle."

Never did an Algerian trooper, lost among the wilds of the Sahara, hear the bugle of the company he had been seeking for hours, with greater delight.

Camille stepped back upon the rickety floor of the passage, and then, turning to look down, she saw M. de Menestreau slowly ascending the ladder with his lantern. She felt almost tempted to throw her arms about his neck when he reached the top, a little out of breath, but quite safe and sound.

"Well?" she asked, eagerly.

"There is no one there," replied M. de Menestreau. "I saw nothing whatever of your friends, and Zig-Zag must be a long way off by this time."

"Heaven be praised! I was terribly frightened," said Camille. "I could not see your light, and you did not answer when I called you."

"Because I did not hear you. The cellar is very large, and I wished to explore it carefully to satisfy myself that there was no other place of egress. One can only enter it and leave it by this trap-door. It has merely been used as a coal cellar apparently; there are still some piles of coal dust there."

"But what can have become of Courapied and his son?" asked Camille, anxiously. "Can it be that Zig-Zag buried them where they fell?"

"The same idea occurred to me, but I examined the ground carefully, and satisfied myself that it had not been disturbed."

"They may have made their escape by the ladder then! But no, that is impossible, for they must have been seriously, if not fatally, injured."

"No, the pile of coal dust may have broken their fall, and it would not surprise me to find out that they did make use of the ladder to escape from the cellar."

"I can not for one moment believe that the scoundrels who set this trap for them would have allowed them to make their escape," retorted Camille.

"I will tell you presently how I explain their mysterious disappearance. But there is nothing more for us to do here, so let me extinguish my lantern and suppress all proof of our visit."

So saying, he blew out his light, and seizing hold of the ladder in his strong arms, raised it slightly up and then sent it flying with such force that it passed altogether through the aperture, and fell with a low crash on to the cellar floor.

"Why have you done that?" inquired Camille in great surprise.

"I have taken my precautions so that no one may pass this way; now let us start," said M. de Menestreau, and he took up his lantern and cord, again tied up in a parcel.

Mademoiselle Monistrol made no objection. The idea of criticising her preserver's acts or refusing to follow his advice, did not once occur to her. They went round the house again before returning to the Saint-Ouen gate, by the same road that had brought them there.

Camille anxiously waited for M. de Menestreau to speak. She dared not question him.

"Mademoiselle," he said, suddenly, "I fear I shall wound you by destroying a cherished illusion. You asked me just now, what could have become of your friends? My opinion is that they have fled with Zig-Zag, and that they were in league with him to entice you to this place."

"In league with him! Impossible! Courapied loathes the cowardly scoundrel who stole his wife from him, and Georget hates the step-mother who always treated him with the utmost cruelty."

"Nevertheless, I am still of the opinion that all the scoundrels had combined against you. Your two guides threw themselves boldly into the pit, knowing full well that they would fall upon a pile of coal dust and sustain no injury. They expected that you would follow them, and, in this way, place yourself completely at their mercy."

"But they could have killed me just as easily before I reached the house," urged Camille.

"But not with impunity. Your body would have been found on the Route de la Révolte, an investigation would have been started, and suspicion would, perhaps, have fallen on your father's murderer. Now Zig-Zag did not care to have the police set upon his track a second time. That is self-evident. He would greatly have preferred to strangle you in the cellar, or to shut you up there and allow you to perish of starvation. To do this last he would only have had to draw up the ladder by which his accomplices made their escape, and close the aperture, for that house has been abandoned for years, so that no one would have thought of going there to deliver you. The scheme was a very clever one, most skilfully combined, and it is a miracle that you escaped. Do you know why they did not pursue you? Simply because they thought you had fallen into the cellar, and they hastened there first of all."

Camille hung her head, but she could not make up her mind to condemn her friends.

"Pray reflect and reason with yourself," resumed M. George de Menestreau. "It is evident that Courapied and his son did not remain in the cellar, consequently, some one must have helped them out. In that case, how does it happen that you have seen nothing of them since? Had they been true friends of yours, they would have gone straight to your house. But they have taken good care not to do that; so they must be enemies, and everything seems to indicate that they have decamped with the other bandits. There is nothing to prove that they will not repeat their efforts, however. Zig-Zag knows now that you have sworn to pursue him to the death, and he must be equally determined to get rid of you. We have seen what he is capable of. He will not accept his defeat; on the contrary, he will set other traps for you. Indeed, he may attack you at night in your lonely home, into which you were so imprudent as to admit his accomplices."

"What must I do?" asked the girl. "Advise me, sir; you to whom I am indebted for my life."

"I advise you to move immediately—to take some rooms in a more thickly populated part of Paris, and engage a trusty servant. I, myself, will attend to all these matters for you, if you desire it."

"Madame Gémozac made me the same offer—and I declined it."

"Accept it, mademoiselle, and don't quarrel with a family, the head of which holds your fortune in his hands. When you are installed in suitable quarters, abandon dangerous expeditions, and leave to me the task of ferreting out your father's murderer."

"But how can you possibly identify him?" asked Camille. "You have never even seen him."

"And you, mademoiselle, only saw his hands, which you have described to me, so that I know as much about him as you do. I also have one great advantage over you; Zig-Zag does not know me. Will you give me full authority to act in your stead? My efforts shall not prove unavailing, I promise you."

Camille was evidently in doubt as to what answer she should give, so George de Menestreau added: "Take time to reflect, mademoiselle. I do not propose to accompany you back to the Boulevard Voltaire. With your permission, I will escort you to the cab, and at four o'clock to-morrow afternoon I will do myself the honour to call upon you, and submit to you some plans that I can not, or rather dare not, propose here."

'I shall expect you, sir," replied Mademoiselle Monistrol, who was not only greatly agitated, but also exceedingly anxious to know her new friend's meaning.

VII.

A WEEK has elapsed, and there is a marked change in the situation. Camille Monistrol still thinks of avenging her father, but she also thinks a great deal about George de Menestreau, who has declared his love, and is now an avowed suitor for her hand.

Julien Gémozac has also declared his passion, in spite of his mother's counsels, but he has obtained only evasive replies from Mademoiselle Monistrol. He suspects that he has a rival, though he has never met him at the young lady's house, for he only dares to call there at such hours as she appoints, and is obliged to content himself with serving as an intermediary between his father and Camille. M. Gémozac, senior, is not so adverse to his son's courtship as he is daily acquiring proof of the vast profits which the Monistrol patent will yield.

Alfred de Fresnay has succeeded in overcoming the scruples of the Countess de Janos, who is now comfortably established in the charming little house in the Rue Mozart, speedily furnished by an able upholsterer, and the fair Magyar has a constant visitor in the person of her landlord. He is greatly amused with the countess who is a peculiar woman, now madly gay and now gloomy to excess. However, she no longer talks either of her aristocratic birth or her ancestors, and the name of Tergowitz is never mentioned.

Fresnay, indeed, is beginning to suspect that his charmer was born at Batignolles or Belleville, but these suspicions do not trouble him in the least. At least none of his friends have recognised her, though she has often been to the circus and the theatre with him, and he constantly displays himself in her company seated in an open carriage in the Champs-Elysées and the Bois de Boulogne. Olga, the whilom clairvoyant, is still in Madame de Janos's employ and serves her with exemplary zeal and fidelity. Fresnay has tried more than once to learn from her something about the past life of this pretended countess, but Olga remains as mute as a fish, and all the liberal gratuities he bestows upon her fail to loosen her tongue. Still she seems tired of the easy life she leads in the Rue Mozart, and it can be seen that she would prefer to return to her former avocation as a fortune-teller. She experiences a kind of nostalgia for Bohemianism.

The house where Fresnay has lodged her with Madame de Janos is not at all like the humble dwelling at the other end of Paris where Mademoiselle Monistrol spends long and gloomy hours, in a solitude the monotony of which is barely relieved by the visits of her two admirers. She still has no news either of Courapied or of Georget, and like M. de Menestreau, she begins to believe that they have really gone off with Zig-Zag.

The uncle, whose property Fresnay had inherited, had been a rake in his time. It ran in the blood as it were, and Alfred only followed the family traditions. Now this uncle of his had, in the last days of his life, built himself a little house which he intended should be the seat of his amours. Gout rising to the stomach carried him off however, before he could carry out his project, and the abode he had built himself was the one which his nephew had placed at the disposal of the bewitching Madame de Janos.

Situated at the corner of the Rue Mozart and the Rue de la Cure, this house did honour to its architect, who had availed himself to the best advantage of a comparatively small surface. A gable in the Flanders gothic style, with a terrace by way of garden, projected in the direction of the heights of Passy, and passers-by were at liberty to imagine that behind the almost monumental frontage there were suites upon suites of vast apartments. In reality, however, there were but three rooms on each floor ; reception rooms on the first one, bed and dressing-rooms on the second ; and under the roof, accommodation for three servants. As yet, however, Fresnay had failed to procure the promised cook and valet, and Olga, alone, waited upon her mistress.

The young baron had formed certain habits on the first day of the connection and from these he never departed. He came to fetch the countess at four o'clock every afternoon, and went with her for a drive in an elegant victoria ; he dined with her at a first-class restaurant and devoted his evening to her till it was time to go and look up his friends at the club and try his luck at the card table. Fortune, by the way, was beginning to favour him at baccarat, so that he had every reason for satisfaction.

One charming spring afternoon it chanced that he drove rather earlier than usual down the Rue Mozart towards the countess's abode, and though she usually waited for him on the terrace, he gazed at it in vain. She was not to be seen, but suddenly on raising his eyes he fancied he espied a man's face at a window on the second floor. A moment later and the apparition had vanished. This circumstance rather nettled Alfred who hastily alighted and proceeded to the front door. In his position as landlord of the house he had kept a latch key, not exactly with any bad intention but in view of being ready for any emergency, so he noiselessly slipped into the hall, where Olga as a rule came to receive him. She was not there however, but on listening it seemed to Fresnay that he heard her voice and even a burst of laughter on the floor above. "They are amusing themselves upstairs," he muttered to himself. "Supposing I found myself face to face with a gentleman? I thought I saw a man at one of the windows. I don't care to fight a duel for that beauty's sake—still all the same this is perhaps the time or never to find out what I really ought to think of her."

He then stealthily ascended the stairs, and on reaching the first floor landing he stopped again to listen ; hearing nothing however, he drew the door curtains of the drawing-room slightly aside, and beheld a sight for which he was certainly quite unprepared. The drawing-room was divided into two apartments by a moveable partition with an open doorway, which was as yet unprovided with curtains. Now in that section of the room adjoining the landing, and directly in front of Alfred, though with her back towards him, Olga was sitting at a small lacquer table strewn with cards, telling the fortune of her mistress, whom Fresnay espied only at intervals, for she suddenly appeared before him, six feet above the floor, and then instantly disappeared again, borne back by the steady swaying of a trapeze upon which she was standing, in complete acrobatic array—flesh coloured tights, a short, pink satin skirt, satin slippers, and unbound hair waving over her bare shoulders.

"She must have been a circus-performer," thought Fresnay. "I always suspected something of the kind."

And instead of going in so as to put a stop to the performance, he remained quite still enjoying the original sight. To behold one's lady-love perched upon the bar of a trapeze is a pleasure vouchsafed to but few mortals, and our eccentric friend experienced no little satisfaction as he gazed upon the vision as it swayed swiftly to and fro through the air, like a bird, or the pendulum of a clock. He took good care not to interrupt the exhibition, and the more particularly as Olga was talking very loud, and he was not sorry to have an opportunity to hear what she was saying to the countess.

"Here is the Knave of Hearts again!" exclaimed the maid. "It is a good card, but it turns up too often."

"Impossible! It can not appear too often," replied Madame de Janos, as she swung merrily to and fro.

"We have seen him to-day, and it would never do for him to meet the King of Clubs."

"I don't care a fig for the King of Clubs," rejoind the countess as she reappeared in sight.

"Clubs mean money. But here is a troublesome Queen of Diamonds. It seems likely there will be some trouble on account of a woman."

"Any one who attempts to interfere with me will have a hard time of it," replied the countess, from her airy perch. "But I don't fear any rivals."

"Why! look! here comes the Nine of Spades, the very worst card in the whole pack. I tell you that everything will end badly," retorted the maid.

"Nonsense! You bore me with your predictions. Go and prepare my bath. It is time I began to dress. The baron will be here presently."

"And he must not find himself face to face with the Knave of Hearts."

"Ah! so I am the King of Clubs," thought Fresnay to himself.

"Make haste," continued the countess, "I will be up-stairs in five minutes, and then you can come down and fetch the trapeze and the ropes. The baron would look blue if he saw them, and I don't care to part with him just yet."

Olga gathered up her cards, rose and turned toward the door, while her noble mistress executed what gymnasts call a *rétablissement* on the horizontal bar.

Fresnay had the presence of mind to conceal himself in the folds of the curtain, and he did it so skilfully that Olga passed him without seeing him. A more deeply enamoured lover would have followed her at a little distance, to satisfy himself whether the Knave of Hearts was concealed somewhere about the house; but Fresnay was not jealous, and he could not resist the temptation to play a joke upon Madame de Janos. So he stole into the room on tiptoe, and found her still on the trapeze.

"Good-morning, countess," he said, in his blandest tone.

She quickly jumped to the floor, and stood defiantly before him, with her arms folded over her breast. "How did you get in?" she asked, curtly.

"By the door; it was open," said the baron, telling a fib for once.

"I should not have imagined that you would stoop to play the spy upon me."

"I! Why, I never had any idea of doing such a thing! Nothing could have been further from my intentions. I called a little earlier than usual, to invite you to take a drive in the Bois; but I cannot say that I regret it, as I have surprised you in a costume that becomes you marvellously well, and see that you possess a talent to which you have never alluded."

"I have often told you that I was an admirer of all kinds of athletic exercise, and I have quite been deprived of any since I came to live here, for I am still waiting for the saddle horse which you promised to place at my disposal."

"That's a hit for me," said the baron gaily. "But I have my eye on a likely horse and you shall put him through his paces. We'll go out riding every morning."

"Well, if you do that I'll forgive you, but what an idea to make your appearance here without the slightest warning. Didn't your carriage come down the street?"

"Yes, it did as usual; only you were so absorbed in accomplishing wonderful feats that you didn't hear my approach. That is what comes of being too fond of gymnastics."

"It's a taste which dates from my childhood. My father gave me my first lessons when I was scarcely seven years old. By the way, did you come straight upstairs?"

"Why, yes! And I'll confess that before coming in I amused myself by glancing at you between the curtains. I admired your strength and suppleness, and laughed at the foolish things your maid was telling you."

"How is it that she didn't see you as she went off," asked Madame de Janos.

"Oh! her mind was full of her cards, and when you sent her off upstairs she brushed against me without knowing that I had arrived."

"It is as well that she should know it," retorted the countess, approaching the staircase and raising her voice.

"Did you call me, madame," asked the maid, leaning over the bannisters.

"No; but Monsieur de Fresnay has arrived, so get everything ready for me to dress."

"Is it to warn the Knave of Hearts that you call so loudly?" asked Alfred, with a smile.

"I know no Knave of Hearts, and pray don't make a scene. It would be both absurd and superfluous," retorted Madame de Janos, "And, by the way, I want to tell you that I feel very lonely here, so you must introduce me to some of your friends, beginning with the gentlemen I saw with you at the Café des Ambassadeurs."

"Gémozac!" exclaimed Fresnay; "you will find his society anything but entertaining, I assure you."

"But why?" inquired the countess. "I was very much pleased with him on the evening I met him, and I don't see why you haven't once brought him to call on me, unless, perhaps, you are jealous of him."

"On the contrary," protested Alfred, "I should be delighted to bring him; but there is no doing anything with the fellow. He is madly in love, and, what is worse, he longs to marry the object of his affections."

"With whom is he so deeply infatuated?"

"With an orphan girl—just like the hero in Monsieur d'Ennery's play— you know 'the Two Orphans'—we went to see it."

"The daughter of that inventor, I suppose, whom you spoke to me about on the evening I met you at the Café des Ambassadeurs."

"What a memory you have!"

"I never forget anything you say, you see. I am not like you, who forget everything you promise me."

"Another hit at me. You allude to the saddle horse, I suppose. You shall have it to-morrow."

"I rely on you, then," said the countess; "but talking of the promises you have failed to keep, didn't you engage to keep me posted as concerns the movements of your friend, Gémozac? and yet, since I have been living in the Rue Mozart, you have not once mentioned his name."

"Had I suspected that his love affairs would have interested you in the slightest degree, I would have told you all about them," replied Fresnay.

"How could I possibly help feeling an interest in an unfortunate girl and in your most intimate friend? It seems to me that it was only natural I should do so."

"Neither of them need your pity, I assure you. The girl will have several millions which won't cost her anything, and although she does not reciprocate Julien's passion, he has the wherewithal to console himself, for he will be even richer than she is. You may say, perhaps, that money does not give happiness, but I assure you that it contributes a great deal towards it; and you must admit that I am right."

"Then Mademoiselle Monistrol does not return this young gentleman's love?" asked the countess.

"It would seem not," was the dry reply.

"He is very good looking, however."

"Yes; but love, you know, comes, or doesn't come, as the case may be. As regards myself and you, it was a case of love at first sight."

"Don't be stupid! You imagine you like me, but as for loving me, why you are not even jealous."

"Oh, yes! I am as jealous as a tiger," protested Fresnay eagerly.

"Well, if you were, you wouldn't talk so foolishly. I see there is no means of chatting seriously with you, so I'm going to dress for our drive."

"The fact is, that although you look very charming in this costume, it isn't quite a carriage dress! What a pity! You *would* create a sensation in the Bois. That little girl of the Boulevard Voltaire couldn't show herself in such an outfit."

"How do you know?" inquired the countess.

"Why, she is much too thin—you have only to glance at her to see that."

"No matter. She greatly interests me. How is she progressing with her search for her father's murderer? If I had been in Monsieur Gémozac's place, I should have found him long before now."

"Very possibly," said Alfred. "You have experience, boldness, and tact, whereas poor Julien is not the shrewdest fellow in the world by any means. Would you believe it, he has applied to a private detective agency for assistance, and is paying large amounts to scoundrels who pretend to be searching for Zig-Zag, while they are really spending their time, drinking and carousing at my artless friend's expense? Besides, I'm convinced that this acrobat Zig-Zag is a mythical personage. People don't have such hands as his."

"What do you mean?"

"Ah, yes, you don't know, but Mademoiselle Monistrol pretends that he has a hand like an ourang-outang's paw, hooked and hairy, with long nails, and a thumb like a lobster's claw!"

"That's absurd. The poor girl must have been mistaken in her fright, and if she relies on that characteristic to find the murderer, she is greatly mistaken."

"I fear so; and yet my friend Julien does not despair. Hope on, hope ever, is his motto. In spite of all his mother's protests, he goes to the Boulevard Voltaire every day, and when his lady-love refuses to see him, he spends whole hours gazing at the house. One of these evenings he will go and play the guitar under his charmer's window, I expect. And the worst of it all is that he has a rival."

"A rival?" exclaimed Madame de Janos, in astonishment.

"Yes, whom the girl receives on the sly, but though Julien has been watching, he has not yet succeeded in getting a glimpse of him. Besides, even if he did, it wouldn't enlighten him, for he probably never saw the favoured suitor before."

"Who knows?" muttered the countess, pensively.

"Why, how deeply this seems to interest you!" added Fresnay, noting the flush and the strange expression that had suddenly appeared upon his companion's face.

"And why shouldn't it? Besides, I am naturally inquisitive, and mysteries always have a great charm for me," replied Madame de Janos. "I think I could give Mademoiselle Monistrol some good advice if I only knew her."

"She is not likely to cross your path, so forget the poor girl, and go and dress for our drive in the Bois. There must be a crowd there this fine afternoon, and all the women will be jealous of you, I'll be bound."

"Are you particularly anxious to go to the Bois?" inquired the Hungarian countess, now suddenly regaining all her wonted indifference of manner.

"No, indeed, but after all there is nowhere else to go. Besides, if we dine at—"

"It is a deal too early to think of dinner now. Why can't we pay that poor Mademoiselle Monistrol a visit instead?" asked Madame de Janos.

"Pay Mademoiselle Monistrol a visit?" repeated Fresnay, who looked at the chestnut haired beauty in amazement, wondering how such a fantastic idea could have entered her head. "And on what pretext, pray? You are not acquainted with her, and she isn't even aware of your existence."

"What difference does that make?" replied the countess, coldly. "You know her—at least so you say, and so you can surely introduce me to her."

"A fine recommendation an introduction from me would be!" retorted the baron. "I only saw her once, and then merely for a few moments; and if she hasn't forgotten me entirely, she can't have a very pleasant recollection of me, for I left her rather unceremoniously—it was the evening her father was murdered. Gémozac hasn't forgiven me for it yet, and he must have complained of me to the young lady."

"Well, then, this will be an excellent opportunity to apologise," urged Madame de Janos. "I will intercede for you, and she will forgive you, I am sure of it."

"This is absurd. There is no possible pretext for my taking the Countess de Janos to see Mademoiselle Monistrol."

"Indeed! So you consider me unworthy to be received into the society of this virtuous damsel?" asked the fair Magyar, with a sneer.

This question was so entirely unexpected that Fresnay did not know what to say in reply. As he remained silent : "So you refuse to do what I ask ?" continued the countess, angrily. "It is the first time I ask any-thing of you, and it shall be the last."

Alfred, fairly nettled, was about to make some harsh rejoinder when Olga, the maid, abruptly entered the room exclaiming : "The bath is ready, and there is no longer any one up stairs. I fancy that—"

The girl stopped short. She had just perceived the baron, and she re-gretted having spoken like this, the more so as Madame de Janos had warned her of Fresnay's arrival.

"So there had been somebody upstairs ?" sneered Fresnay.

"Oh ! no, sir ; it was a slip of the tongue," rejoined the maid, with superlative impudence.

"I'll bet it was the Knave of Hearts," resumed the baron, laughing.

"Oh ! so you heard me, sir, telling my mistress's fortune. But all that is humbug ! I myself don't believe in it, and I merely played with the cards to amuse madame."

"And you amused me also without knowing it."

"Come," said the countess, drily, "you didn't call here, I presume, to chat with my maid, and you will please do me the favour to leave me alone with her. I need her help, and I don't need you."

"Then you won't dine with me ?" inquired Fresnay.

"No, indeed, as you won't take me where I want to go."

"But I repeat that that idea of yours is a most extravagant one. Have as many whims as you please barring that—"

"Extravagant ideas delight me, and, besides, I'm bored to death here. The omnibus dépôt on the left, a convent garden on the right ! Nice sur-roundings I must say. It is no doubt a deal more pleasant on the Boule-vard Voltaire. I shall go and see for myself one of these days."

"I hope you won't take it into your head to go there without me," said Fresnay, earnestly.

"Oh ! no, I shouldn't venture on that, of course ! You talk as if I were not my own mistress."

"But you wouldn't go if I forbade it."

"I just should go in that case. I'm not a dog in a leading string."

"So I see. You belong to a race which has never put up with slavery, and I have no desire to humiliate the noble blood which flows in your veins. But I also like my freedom."

"Oh ! every one for himself, and now just stand aside if you please."

Thereupon waving Fresnay aside, the descendant of the Magyar nobles seized hold of the trapeze, climbed upon the bar, and once in position, began to perform some most dangerous and difficult feats.

"Charming !" said Alfred, laughing heartily. "You ought to come out at the summer circus."

"Don't defy me to do it," retorted the countess, making the trapeze swing.

"Well, that would be better than making stupid visits."

"Stand aside, if you don't want the bar to break your head. I won't be responsible for the damage."

"All right. So you refuse to accompany me to the Bois ?"

"Most decidedly."

"Farewell, then, until to-morrow, most adorable countess," said Fresnay, blandly. "Don't disturb yourself to leave your perch. Olga will escort me to my carriage."

"Olga! I forbid you to stir."

The poor maid found herself in a most uncomfortable position by reason of the indiscreet words she had spoken a short time previously. She hardly knew whom to obey, the baron or her mistress. Finally, however, she decided to beat a retreat into the first division of the drawing-room, and as Fresnay passed her, he managed to whisper:

"Ten louis for you, if you come to see me to-morrow morning. You can easily find time before your mistress is up."

The maid in her confusion answered neither yes nor no, and Fresnay hurried out of the house. A lover of a different stamp might have been afflicted by the countess's conduct, but such was not the case with him. As for the proposal to visit Mademoiselle Monistrol, he attached but little importance to it, and yet he considered it would be as well for him to warn Julien, so that the latter might take steps to prevent vice from forcing an entry into the abode of virtue. Accordingly, in view of meeting Gémozac as soon as possible, he told his coachman to drive him to the club.

The club to which Alfred and Julien belonged, where they often spent their evenings—one might really say their nights—was not one of the most aristocratic in Paris, nor yet was it one of those gambling-houses into which one can secure admission as readily as into an inn. There was a regular ballot for the election of members, but black-balling was seldom resorted to. Moreover, a member was at liberty to invite a friend to dine at the club, and this guest was at liberty to remain until the next morning, and even to take a hand in any of the games of cards. A dangerous practice this, and one there had been much talk of suppressing, but as no serious trouble had yet arisen, the committee had taken no action on the subject.

Consequently, Fresnay, on entering the room devoted to baccarat, was not much surprised to see two or three new faces at the table. He had not come to watch the players, however, but to find Julien Gémozac, and he failed to see him for the very good reason that Julien—who was holding the bank—was sitting with his back to the door. Alfred accordingly turned to leave the room. As he did so, he was accosted by an acquaintance with whom he had long been on familiar, though not on intimate terms. Such friendships are common in Paris. Men meet on the boulevard, at the club, at the restaurant, or at the houses of fashionable damsels, they even lend one another five-and-twenty louis for a few hours at a push, but they do not visit each other, and one of them may disappear any fine morning without the others troubling themselves in the least as to what has become of him.

"How is the game progressing?" inquired Fresnay of this acquaintance, whose name was Daubrac.

"About as usual," was the reply. "The heavy players have not put in an appearance yet, and the others have suffered so much of late that they are a little shy. Our friend Gémozac is acting as banker now in a modest way."

"Indeed! Ah! yes, I see him now. Is he winning?"

"I think so, for I hear the players grumbling."

"Then I will wait until he has finished; I don't want to spoil his luck, though I want to speak to him."

"Well, ask him why he has been looking so gloomy for the last few days. He hasn't to my knowledge met with any loss, and, besides, he is rich or will be so, some day. His father is said to be a millionaire."

"He has perhaps some heart troubles, but they'll pass off."

"Oh, yes, those kind of worries always come to an end. But talking of love, who is that splendid woman I have seen you driving about with recently? No one knows her, but she creates a sensation wherever she appears.' '

"She's a foreigner," replied Fresnay, curtly.

"Ah! indeed! People pretend that you have shut her up in an ivory tower between Anteuil and Passy. Oh! I don't blame you for doing so. The bird might fly away if you didn't keep it in a cage."

Fresnay made no answer to this remark, for he was watching a gentleman who had just approached the table and thrown a bank-note upon it, and it seemed to Alfred that this new player strongly resembled M. Ter-gowitz, the Countess de Janos's compatriot.

"Do you know that man?" he asked Daubrac.

"No, it is the first time I have ever seen him here," Daubrac replied, after a prolonged stare at the new-comer. "I think he must be the guest of some member or other. That practice ought to be abolished. Some day we shall have a sharper getting in here and going off with every one's money."

"I am anxious to know who brought this fellow here, and what his name is," said Fresnay.

"That wouldn't be a difficult matter. His name and that of his enter-tainer must be on the dinner list. I will go and see ; I don't particularly fancy his face."

"Come back and give me the benefit of your inquiries," said Fresnay, stepping up to the card-table.

He stationed himself opposite the person who so deeply interested him, and began to examine him with the closest attention. The stranger was still young, tall, dark and of elegant appearance, while his features re-sembled in a marked degree those of the Hungarian whom Fresnay had seen talking with the pretended Countess de Janos at the Café des Ambassadeurs. However at that establishment Fresnay had only caught a side view of him, whereas, now, he saw him in front, and he didn't feel certain about his identity. At all events it soon became evident that this gentleman was an extremely lucky player. He had attacked the bank with a five-hundred franc note, and meeting with success in this venture, he doubled his stakes twice in succession and soon had four thousand francs in front of him.

"I hold the amount," said Gémozac who was almost broken by this loss, for he had opened the bank with a hundred louis only, and had merely doubled that sum since he had begun playing.

"Julien had better mind what he is about," muttered Alfred. "It is all that Mademoiselle Monistrol's fault. He's playing to forget his troubles."

Julien, having lost again, had to apply to the club cash-box for a loan of fifty louis. "Dash it !" grumbled Alfred, "Gémozac doesn't know whom he has to deal with. If this man is the Countess's Hungarian, he is not to be trusted. He isn't cheating now, because he isn't dealing the cards, but just wait until he gets hold of them. I must warn that simpleton of a Julien."

Thereupon he began to manœuvre in such a way as to get nearer to his friend to whom he could not, with propriety, make signs from a distance.

Several more members had now come up attracted by the new-comer's luck, and there was some little difficulty in forcing a passage. On the way to the banker, moreover, Fresnay was stopped by Daubrac, who whispered : "That man is a Monsieur Tergowitz, and he was invited here by that Polish major with an unpronounceable name."

"Good ! I am satisfied now," growled Fresnay, and reaching Gémozac, he tapped him on the shoulder just as the Hungarian again came off victorious.

Julien turned, and on seeing his friend he rose up saying : " I will relinquish my place to any one who wants it." The players murmured a little, as they had secured but little of the plunder, nearly all of the winnings going to M. Tergowitz. However, they could not compel Gémozac to go on, so after a short silence, as some one suggested that the bank should be put up at auction, the stranger said, quietly : "I will take it at a thousand louis, gentlemen."

This was the height of assurance for a bird of passage, who was not even a member of the club ; but no protest was made, for each player hoped to retrieve his losses through this victor who risked such a large amount so carelessly.

Fresnay instantly took hold of Gémozac, and dragged him off into a corner of the room. "You are mad," said he, "to win two hundred louis with so much difficulty and then lose them in three hands ! It's absurd."

Gémozac shrugged his shoulders.

"Come," said Alfred, "you won't joke me again about my infatuation for the countess."

"I have a right to play," responded Julien, "and all kind of folly is permissible—gambling as well as spooning upon an adventuress."

"But do you know who just won your money ? " insisted Alfred de Fresnay.

"No; nor do I care. I only play to divert my mind, and I did not even look at the person who cleaned me out."

"Well, look at him now. Don't you think he looks like someone you once saw before ? "

"Well, yes," replied Julien, taking a rapid glance, "it does seem to me I have seen him somewhere before, but— "

"I'll tell you where you have seen him. Do you remember the noble foreigner you caught making signs to my Countess de Janos, the other evening, at the Café des Ambassadeurs ? "

"Ah yes ! This man does look very much like that fellow, it's a fact," replied Julien.

"I am certain that they are one and the same person. I am satisfied, too, on another point. My charmer is deceiving me with this same individual. She assured me that he had returned to Hungary. But I find him here, and I am almost sure that he was at her house a little while ago. He doesn't lose his time, see ! Since he has taken the bank he has steadily gone on winning."

"Well, don't play against him, that's all. And if I were you I would have nothing more to do with that pretended countess. I am satisfied that she is an adventuress of the very worst kind."

"I think I shall keep away from her in future," retorted Fresnay, "although I find her very amusing ; but I shall probably astonish you a great deal, my dear boy, by telling you that she takes a great interest in you— and is a most particular friend of yours."

"What do you mean ? "

"That I have just had a real quarrel with her, because she wished to compel me to introduce her to Mademoiselle Monistrol."

"That was certainly most impudent on her part," exclaimed Gémozac indignantly. "I can not conceive how she ever even heard of Mademoiselle Monistrol."

"You forget that, on the evening when we met her first, I alluded to the murder of Mademoiselle Monistrol's father. Our conversation must have made a deep impression upon her mind for she refers to it constantly, so constantly, indeed, that I am almost inclined to believe that she knows the perpetrator of the crime. If the murderer really was the acrobat who figured at the Gingerbread Fair, it would not surprise me if she had met him in her travels, for I suspect that she is a member of the same profession. I just caught her executing all sorts of dangerous feats upon a trapeze. I fancy she must have belonged to a circus troupe."

"I am glad to see that you no longer mistake her for a real countess," said Gémozac, ironically. "Still, I don't suppose that she is in any way connected with the scoundrel whom I am in search of."

"What if I should discover that this handsome Monsieur Tergowitz is none other than Zig-Zag himself?"

"Look at his hands."

"I confess that they are white, and that the hooked thumb is wanting. He uses them with wonderful dexterity, however. See how the cards slip between his fingers, and they are just what he wants, for look, he gathers up the entire stakes. The Polish major who invited him here to dinner must have favoured us with a sharper."

"Never mind those conjectures. Do me the favour to tell me what you said to the Hungarian damsel when she had the audacity to ask you to take her to see Mademoiselle Monistrol,"

"I refused, of course, and she flew into a passion; whereupon, I left her, as I am not fond of scenes. But her request furnished me with plenty of food for reflection. There is some mystery in all this, but it will be solved to-morrow morning, for the countess's maid is coming to call on me. A couple of hundred francs will loosen her tongue and induce her to tell me all I want to know about her mistress, and perhaps about Monsieur Tergowitz as well. But, by the way, how are you getting on as regards the Boulevard Voltaire?"

"Oh! matters are still at the same point. I go there every day and I am received once in every three or four visits—when the coast is clear."

"And you don't feel discouraged!" exclaimed Fresnay. "You must be smitten, and no mistake."

"I swore to myself again to-day that I wouldn't return there. But to-morrow I shall be back there again. It's beyond my control. You can't understand it, because you have never been seriously in love."

"No; but if such a misfortune befell me, I should never linger in a state of uncertainty. I should at least like to know my rival and have an explanation with him; for, let me tell you, you are really cutting a most ridiculous figure in all this. Why don't you wait for that fellow on the boulevard and boldly tackle him, since you haven't courage enough to ask Mademoiselle Monistrol who he is."

"She told me his name yesterday," replied Julien. "He is called Monsieur de Menestreau."

"The name doesn't tell one anything. How did she make his acquaintance?"

"It appears that he rendered her some service or other. She gave me to understand that he was certain of being able to find Monistrol's murderer."

"Hum! he must be some adventurer who has scented that she is rich and wants to win her good graces in view of marrying her. You ought not to let her remain at the mercy of a man who only wishes to get hold of her money. Why don't you warn your father of what is going on ? He isn't her guardian officially, but he manages her fortune, and he, at least, has the right to give her advice. He ought to go and see her and ask her to introduce him to this Monsieur de Menestreau. When you know what to think of the latter you will be able to form a plan. Marry or don't marry, that's your own look out, but at all events begin by clearing the ground.'

"You are right. I will follow your advice and speak to my father to-morrow morning. He isn't altogether opposed to my idea of marrying Mademoiselle Monistrol, though my mother won't hear the subject spoken of."

"I can understand that," rejoined Fresnay. "However, do as I tell you. I'll make some inquiries on my own side, and between us we shall soon know what to think of your rival and the origin of his acquaintance with Mademoiselle Monistrol. Hallo ! Tergowitz has left off playing and he is going away with his hands full of gold and notes, not to mention counters. I shall tell the countess about all that to-morrow. In the meanwhile come for a drive with me up the Champs Elysées. There is nothing like fresh air to improve a man's ideas ! "

VIII.

WHILST the Baron de Fresnay was leading a gay life, and George de Menestreau was paying court to Camille Monistrol, who received him most graciously, Courapied and his son were having an extremely hard time of it at some distance from the Boulevard Voltaire and further still from the Rue Mozart. They were not dead, as Camille had rather lightly imagined, nor had they gone off to join Zig-Zag as M. de Menestreau groundlessly declared.

They were living, despite themselves, in a very gloomy place, and they were at a loss to understand how they had got there, although they remembered their fall perfectly well, together with the incidents which had preceded it. After a swoon of some duration they had picked themselves up, badly bruised and cut, but with no bones broken, and they had found themselves in perfect darkness. The ground they stood upon was cold ; when they stretched out their arms, their hands encountered damp walls, whilst not the slightest ray of light reached them from above. Everything seemed to indicate that they were buried alive, and destined to perish of starvation.

The father and son, after exchanging some gloomy remarks of condolence, attempted to explore their prison. This was no easy matter without a light, but they finally discovered that this subterranean dungeon was a narrow passage, so low that Courapied could touch the ceiling by standing on tiptoe with his arm uplifted. How far did this gallery extend ? This they could not guess. Indeed, they came to a stand-still before reaching the end of it. On the other hand, they discovered that it was not empty, but lined on either side with barrels and hogsheads, and numerous other articles, the nature of which they were unable to ascertain during this first hasty examination.

Evidently this was not the place into which they had fallen on dashing into the corridor in pursuit of Vigourcux. A fall of six or seven feet would not have rendered them insensible, so they must have been brought here before they regained consciousness, and the persons who had shut—perhaps

walled them—up here must have had the amiable intention of leaving them
to die by inches.

Only Zig-Zag and his accomplice, Amanda, could have devised such
frightful torture, and if they refrained from despatching their victims, it
was only because they had felt absolutely certain that the old clown and the
lad could not escape. Courapied had certainly never heard the story of
Ugolino, who was reduced to devouring his own children, but he realised
the terrible fate that awaited him and his son, and bitterly regretted the
part he had taken in this disastrous expedition.

The sole hope that remained was that the young girl might have escaped
from the murderers lurking in the house, and that she would have the
courage to return with some members of the police force to release her unfortunate friends. However, the problematical contingency of deliverance
might be delayed, and in the meantime they must have food.

The prisoners were not hungry as yet, having had their fill at Mademoiselle Monistrol's. Brigitte had treated them to an excellent and bounti-
ful dinner just before they started out; still in a few hours' time this repast,
which seemed likely to be their last, would be digested, and hunger would
return. How should they satisfy it? For some time poverty had
familiarized them with fasting, but one can not fast indefinitely, and save
in the cases of such people as Signori Succi and Merlatti, death follows
upon long-continued abstinence.

They already suffered another torture, for to live in utter darkness is
terrible. And what darkness it was! That of the entrails of the earth;
the heavy opaque night of the tomb. It oppressed them as if they had
carried on their shoulders the weight of the ruined building which rose
above the vault of this accursed dungeon. Moreover it aggravated their
terrible situation, for they could not see where they were going, and by
walking about, haphazard, they ran a great risk of falling into another pit.

Despair took possession of Courapied's heart, and throwing himself on
the ground, and drawing his son near him, he awaited the approach of
death. At last he fell into a heavy slumber, which was more like lethargy
than sleep, and which Georget did not disturb. The brave youngster was
wide awake, and while his father slept, he racked his brain to devise a
means of escaping from their prison. At his age, one is not easily discouraged, and something whispered to him that his life was not to end thus;
so he began to review what had happened, and to weigh the chances of
salvation that remained.

In the first place, where were they? This house which had so many
subterranean passages must be the habitual resort of a band of thieves or
counterfeiters. Why had so many casks been left there, since the people
who had formerly resided in the building had long since abandoned it?
Had the vault but a single entry, or did it lead to some aperture connected
with the open country. The cellar into which they had first fallen must
be on the other side of the wall, but where was the connecting door? It
was a question of finding it, or of finding another one. They had been
brought into this dungeon, and as there was a way in, there must be a
way out of it. Moreover, had their captors intended to kill them, they
would have done so before now; so that all hope was not at an end.

However, Georget had little expectation of succour from without. Even
Mademoiselle Monistrol would be likely to think twice before repeating an
attempt that had so nearly cost her her life, even admitting too, that she
was still alive; hence, Georget would probably be obliged to depend en-

tirely upon himself, for he feared that excitement and the fall had affected his father's brain a little.

The great difficulty was the darkness and the physical suffering it caused him, for all sorts of sparks danced before his eyes, and it sometimes seemed to him that there was a crushing weight upon his eye-balls. What would he not have given for a simple candle and a box of matches?

Suddenly it occurred to him that while roaming about the Place du Trône that morning, in search of fragments of gingerbread, he had found a few matches which he had picked up to carry to his father, who had no means of lighting his pipe. The presence of Mademoiselle Monistrol had prevented him from giving them to the clown, but as he had changed his clothes since, he was not sure that he still had them about him. And even if he had transferred them from one garment to another, was it not more than likely that they had dropped out when he fell into the cellar?

He fumbled in his pockets, his heart beating all the while with indescribable anxiety, for he felt that his life depended upon finding them. Soon he raised an exclamation of delight, which failed, however, to arouse Courapied. The matches were there in his trousers pocket. As Georget drew them forth he would not have exchanged them for diamonds or pearls. However, his delight was of short duration, for, on counting them, he found that he had only nine in all.

With this slender stock he could hardly hope to discover the outlet of this dungeon; and in any case, he must hoard them with the utmost care, for so many matches burned were so many chances of salvation lost. And would they even burn, if he decided to use them? Might not the dampness of the cellar have so injured them as to prevent them from taking fire?

He passed his finger lightly over the tip of one of them, and had the pleasure of seeing a faint phosphorescent gleam. This was like the dawn of hope; still, a match only burns for a few seconds, and then leaves one again in darkness, unless one has a lamp or a candle; and Georget scarcely hoped to find either of these. Still, he said to himself that the casks he had brushed against must have been placed there by some cooper, and that the latter might have left a bit of candle there.

The chance of discovering this scrap was well worth the sacrifice of a match; but where should he scratch this match? The soil was soft, the walls were damp, and even the soles of Georget's shoes were not dry, for he had tramped a long distance in the mud before reaching the ruined house. However, he rose up and took a few steps in view of finding the casks again. He satisfied himself that the wood of the first one with which he came in contact, was not wet; and then he struck his match quickly upon a stave that seemed a little less smooth than the others. The phosphorous emitted some faint bluish sparks, followed by the fizz of the burning sulphur, and finally the wood was set alight.

Georget experienced a feeling of delight akin to that of a shipwrecked sailor who suddenly beholds a light-house shining before him, and he instantly profited by the opportunity to cast a hasty glance at the objects around him.

Happy chances like misfortunes never come singly, and the first thing upon which his eyes fell was a large lantern, standing on a hogshead near by. He feared that it was empty, but, on opening it, found that it contained a long candle, which he lost no time in lighting.

"Saved!" he murmured, and thereupon he ran to his father, and shook him violently. Courapied sprung to his feet with all the alacrity of a man who fears that his life is threatened, and he fell into fighting position with his fists raised.

"Don't be afraid, father; it is I," said Georget, softly.

"You!" exclaimed the clown, "I didn't know you. Your face is as black as a negro's."

"And so is yours. You look like a coal-heaver."

"Oh, I see how it is. We must have fallen on a pile of coal-dust."

"There is none in this passage; so we have proof that we were brought here," retorted Georget, sagaciously. "But here is a lantern which I have found and which will assist us in finding our way out." And thereupon the plucky little chap briefly told his father what he had done.

"We haven't a moment to lose, for the candle won't last long," Courapied replied. "So let's first look round, and then begin our exploration."

They were only a few steps from the wall that bordered the unencumbered side of the passage, still, although they examined it carefully, they saw no sign of any door. Courapied kicked against the wall in several places, and also sounded it with his fists, but in no spot did anything like a hollow noise resound. "I should have thought there was a door hereabouts," muttered the old clown, "but it seems there isn't, so let us go on." They started off, Georget carrying the lantern, and as they passed along they noticed that the casks that lined the other side of the passage were all methodically arranged and provided with spigots. A little further on, too, they again came to the pile over which they had stumbled in the darkness, and saw that it was composed of canvas-covered hams.

"Ah! ah!" said Courapied, "this cellar serves as a storeplace for some scamps who smuggle things into Paris. They must come here frequently, and we shall soon receive their visit unless we manage to get away before they call. At all events, it seems certain that we sha'n't die here."

"Let's get on, father," replied Georget. "The candle's burning and we've only one, remember."

They went on until they reached a point where the passage forked. Not knowing which branch to choose, they turned to the right, but soon encountered an unexpected obstacle in the shape of a deep excavation, with a perfectly vertical edge, and into which they would certainly have fallen had it not been for the lantern which Georget carried. They could not see the bottom of this pit, and the candle gave too dim a light to enable them to ascertain whether the gallery extended beyond this broad trench.

Disheartened by this discovery, they retraced their steps, and entered the other branch passage, only to find it likewise impassable, being completely closed up at the further end by a substantial stone wall.

"There is no outlet anywhere," murmured poor Courapied, disconsolately.

"Unless there be one above our heads," replied thoughtful little Georget.

They looked up, but could see no sign of daylight; and without stopping to reflect that it might be dark out of doors, they returned to the place from which they had started.

"There is one comfort," said Georget, pointing to the hams and hogsheads, "we shall not perish of hunger or thirst. But we must be careful with the light, and if you will let me I'll blow out the candle."

"Blow out the candle!" exclaimed Courapied. "Are you mad, boy? What will become of us without a light?"

"But, please remember, father, that if we let it burn," said Georget, timidly, "it will only last us about three hours, and after that—"

"We shall not be able to see, it is true," retorted the clown, "but if you put it out, how the deuce will you light it again, my lad?"

"I had nine matches in my pocket, and I now have eight left, so for eight days we can have a light for ten minutes or so at a time—just long enough for us to eat."

"A fine prospect that would be. Why, we might as well die and have done with it," said the clown, shrugging his shoulders.

"You forget, father," urged the little fellow, "that some one or other is almost sure to come down into the cellar in the course of a week's time."

"Some one! Yes. Zig-Zag, probably, to see if we are dead," retorted Courapied.

"No, father, not Zig-Zag; but the persons who stored these goods here. You said so yourself just now, so we must try to keep alive until they come."

"That is true. You are right, child. But as we have a light now, let us profit by it, and fix ourselves as comfortably as we can manage."

"Very well, father, I will begin by making our beds. There is no necessity for us to lie on the damp ground any longer."

"Make our beds! and out of what, pray?"

"Out of the hams, of course. Just see."

And Georget, attacking the huge pile of American hams, proceeded to spread them out upon the ground in such a way as to form two couches, a large and small one, and at the head of each of them he duly placed several more hams to take the place of pillows.

"The mattresses are a trifle hard," he said, with a laugh; "but it will be better than sleeping on the ground. We only lack blankets, but, after all, it isn't cold here."

"You certainly are an ingenious shaver," said the father, admiring his son's inventive talent.

"And I have taken care to select a place where we shall be near our larder," added Georget. "We shall only have to reach out our hands to take a bit of pork or to turn the tap of one of the hogsheads."

"But how about bread?"

"We must manage to dispense with that."

"But the casks are empty, perhaps."

"Oh, no; I tapped on them, and they sounded full."

"But what can they contain?" remarked Courapied. "Certainly not water. Smugglers wouldn't be likely to hoard up any of that commodity. It's to be had for nothing."

"But, father, you don't like water, so you won't be sorry if this should happen to be some wine."

"That's true," replied the clown, with a smile. "Well, try a little, just to see."

Georget turned the tap of the cask nearest him, and allowed a little of the liquid to run into the palm of his hand, which he at once raised to his mouth.

"Ugh! how strong it is!" he exclaimed, as he spat forth the fluid, not daring to swallow it.

"It is brandy," growled Courapied. "If it were good stuff, it wouldn't be so bad. But it must be some common spirit or another. We sha'n't be able to stand it long if we don't find anything else to drink."

"At all events I shall use a little of it to wash my face," replied Georget. "I don't care to remain a negro any longer."

Courapied followed his example, availing himself, of course, of the opportunity to taste the liquor, which proved to be almost pure alcohol.

"We had better let this stuff alone," he growled, as he rose to his feet again ; "Unless we are fortunate enough to find a spring, we shall soon be burned alive."

"We must be careful, too, about the light," added Georget, closing his lantern, "for a lot of the liquor has soaked into the ground while we have been making our toilet, and a spark might start quite a conflagration. Are you hungry, father?" added the thoughtful little fellow.

"No, not yet."

"No matter. I am going to cut two or three slices of ham. I have my knife in my pocket, fortunately." Suiting his actions to his words, he ripped off one of the canvas wrappers covering the hams, and this served as table-cloth and plate for the slices, which he proceeded to cut. Then, while rummaging about he found an old tin can, which he proceeded to partially fill with brandy.

"The cloth is laid, we will breakfast whenever you please, father," he remarked, as soon as these various preparations were completed.

"That won't be very soon, I think. I haven't much appetite. What time do you suppose it is ?"

"I don't know, for I haven't a watch any more than you, father. But it could not have been far from midnight when we fell into the cellar ; though I have no idea how long we remained unconscious."

"Nor have I," replied Courapied. "Did I sleep long after our first exploration? All I know is that if you had not woke me, I should be dozing still. In fact, I feel sleepy now."

"So do I, father, and there is nothing to prevent us from indulging in a nap. When we have had a good sleep we shall perhaps have a better idea as to what we ought to do."

Courapied, nothing loath, stretched himself out upon his novel couch, and was soon fast asleep.

Before following his father's example, Georget placed his eight precious matches inside the lantern, to protect them from the dampness, blew out the candle, set it beside his hastily improvised couch, and was soon peacefully slumbering.

Their sleep was a prolonged one, and yet Georget woke up before his father. Though not a little hungry, he did not care to breakfast alone ; so he sat up and waited for Courapied to give some sign of waking. Instinctively he began to listen with remarkable attention, in the hope that he might perhaps hear some sound from outside. But nothing disturbed the profound silence of the vault, not even the vibration which the constant passage of vehicles imparts to all houses in Paris. However, this was not surprising, for conveyances seldom descend the Route de la Revolte, which was a few hundred yards from the ruined house.

"Ah !" thought Georget, "if the young lady abandons us no one will come unless it be the smugglers—"

Suddenly, however, he fancied that he heard a heavy object strike the other side of the wall, still, the sound was so indistinct that Georget asked himself if he were not the victim of an acoustical illusion ; for the strongly built wall was not likely to be a very good conductor of sound.

The lad rose, however, and crawling to the place from which the noise had seemed to proceed, he applied his ear to the wall and listened with breathless attention. Hearing nothing, and without reflecting that his voice would not resound beyond the masonry, he shouted with all his might, with no other result than that of arousing his father.

How great would have been the despair of both prisoners had they known that the sound in question had been produced by the fall of the ladder which M. de Menestreau had used in exploring the cellar, and that their benefactress, Camille Monistrol, was in the passage, almost over their heads, and ready to rescue them if they were still there.

"What is it, my boy?" asked Courapied.

"Nothing, father, unfortunately," replied little Georget. "I thought some one was demolishing the wall to free us, but I was mistaken."

"There is no hope for us, my dear child, no one is thinking of us," sighed the old clown.

"Then they must have killed the young lady, for I am sure that she should not abandon us," retorted the youngster, indignantly. He had been greatly touched by Camille's kindness, and believed her to be a true friend.

"I don't see why you think so. For my part, I am awfully sorry that I got myself into this scrape on her account; and if I ever get out of here alive, I shall tell her so pretty plainly. It's disgraceful—not troubling herself any further about the people she led to death! I know nothing at all about her, for I never even saw her before she came to the fair grounds in search of me. She said that Zig-Zag killed her father, but nobody knows whether she was telling the truth or not."

"Oh, father, why should you think that she had any idea of deceiving us? She risked her own life, just as we did, and it was no fault of hers if the dog dragged us into the passage."

"I lose all patience with you when I hear you defending her," retorted Courapied. "Come, hold your tongue, and light the lantern. I want something to eat."

"So do I," muttered Georget, stooping to pick up the lantern. He had retraced his steps and reached the spot where his father lay, without much trouble. His eyes were growing accustomed to the darkness.

The first thing Georget did after lighting the candle was to measure it off into eight equal parts which he marked with his finger-nail, inserting in the first notch a large pin which he had picked up in Brigitte's kitchen.

"What are you doing that for?" asked Courapied, sullenly.

"So that we may not burn too much at a time," replied the ingenious little fellow. "If we don't go beyond these marks, we shall be sure of having a light at our disposal until the end of the week," he added, almost gaily.

"It will, perhaps, last longer than we shall," was the old clown's gloomy reply.

Georget offered his father the most appetising slice of ham, though that is not saying much, for this meat from over the sea lacked freshness. It had no doubt remained a long time in the vault since crossing the Atlantic, and, besides, it was so salt that the two prisoners' palates began to burn them. As a remedy for this, Courapied swallowed a large draught of liquor which by no means made him feel more comfortable. Georget more prudently contented himself with rinsing his mouth with the alcoholic beverage. He only swallowed the ham with difficulty, still he managed to get it down.

As for Courapied, the fiery spirits seemed to his taste, and the repast would have been a prolonged one had not the dropping of the pin warned Georget that it was time to extinguish the candle. He did so without sounding the curfew, that is, without warning his father, who gave vent to his disapprobation in several vigorous oaths, which the lad pretended not to hear. However, the brandy was rising to Courapied's head, and he fell back on his couch. He was not intoxicated, but he no longer had the full possession of his faculties.

Georget, whose lucidity of mind was perfect, now realised that he could not depend upon his parent's co-operation in effecting their escape from the cellar. The clown had grown old in a profession that demoralises even those who possess the best of principles ; and after making a fool of himself for the public, he seldom failed to go and quench his thirst at the nearest drinking-shop. In this way he had acquired a marked partiality for alcoholic beverages, and without being what one calls an habitual drunkard, he got tipsy pretty frequently, and when he was in that condition he was, of course, of no use whatever.

The lad, knowing all this, resolved to dispense with Courapied's assistance entirely, and so began to explore the dungeon without him. He gradually accustomed himself to groping about in the darkness, guiding himself by the wall and avoiding the gallery which led to the pit. Unfortunately these attempts resulted in no discovery that would favour any plan of escape.

It certainly seemed to him that there must be an opening at the end of the closed passage, for he noticed there a draught of fresh air which must come from above, but although he raised his head and strained his eyes to the utmost, he could not discern the faintest ray of light.

Then a frightful life began for him. Courapied slept all the time, waking occasionally, but only to drink again, and poor Georget, who drank nothing, suffered terribly from thirst. Time passed without his being able to form any idea of the number of hours that dragged by so monotonously, for in the inky darkness he was, of course, utterly unable to distinguish day from night. The lad only lighted his lantern to get some food for his father, who ate almost nothing, though he had no difficulty in finding the tap, filling his can and drinking even in the darkness.

This misery must inevitably result in death unless the smugglers or the dealers in stolen goods should take it into their heads to visit the cellar where their merchandise was concealed. Georget thought that if they came at all it would be by the opening, of which he suspected the existence, so he dragged himself again and again to the end of the gallery, in the vain hope of seeing them appear. But these painful efforts only fatigued and discouraged him still more.

At last on one occasion he experienced a pleasure he had ceased to expect. He heard the barking of a dog, and having been cut off from the world so long, the sound astonished him as much as the foot-print on the sand of the desert island astonished Robinson Crusoe. This sound indicated the close proximity of a living creature, and as Georget could hear it distinctly, there must be some communication—probably by means of an open shaft or well—between this passage and the surface of the earth.

The animal could not be far from the mouth of the shaft, but the thought that it might be the terrible Vigoureux lessened Georget's delight very considerably.

"Zig-Zag may have left him to guard the only place of egress, and to devour us if we should attempt to leave the cellar," this precocious boy said to himself. "Still, I would rather be devoured by him than die of hunger. But I see no opening, and even if I did, I should be unable to climb up to it."

The barking finally ceased, but Georget, after listening awhile, heard the hollow rumbling of distant thunder. A storm was coming on, for the peals became more and more distinct. The poor lad stood with his eyes uplifted, breathlessly awaiting a flash of lightning. It came at last, cutting athwart the dark sky, and by its fleeting light the youngster caught sight of a sort of chimney which extended from the roof of the passage to the surface of the plain. It seemed to him that this chimney was narrow enough for one to climb up it by clinging to the sides, as chimney-sweeps do. But it began six or seven feet above the floor of the passage, and the child could devise no way of reaching it. Still the discovery of this outlet was none the less precious, and Georget firmly resolved to overcome the obstacles that prevented him from making his escape in that direction.

He soon had another and equally agreeable surprise. He felt several big drops of rain fall upon his forehead. The clouds had broken, and the rain was falling with sufficient violence to reach the cellar by way of this shaft, which consequently could not be very deep.

This water was an inestimable blessing to Georget, who was perishing of thirst. He decided to quench it by profiting of the shower, and after at first catching a little water in the hollow of his hand—merely enough to moisten his parched lips—he thought of a more practical plan and hastened back in search of the tin can which his father filled too frequently. Having secured it he again returned to the orifice without awakening his parent. When he reached the foot of the shaft, anew, the storm had turned into a deluge, and it took him but a few minutes to fill and drain the can which held a little more than a pint. Then he filled it again, this time for his father who was still sound asleep.

The refreshing draught lent Georget new energy, and he felt ready to brave any danger to save himself and Courapied, who certainly stood in great need of assistance. However, he never did anything without due reflection, and so without stirring from the spot where he was receiving such a salutary shower bath, he tried to form a correct idea of the situation and of the chances of escape that were presented. He now understood why he had never discovered the existence of this shaft before. All his visits to the passage into which it opened, must have been made at night-time and when the stars were concealed by clouds.

He had needed a flash of lightning to see it. Still daylight must come sooner or later and then he might perhaps be able to get a better view of the shaft. He already realised that it could only be used by men as it was much too small for the passage of boxes or barrels. Consequently, the vault must have some other door which no doubt communicated with the cellar into which the father and son had first fallen. There was such a door, unquestionably, but so skilfully concealed in the wall that it seemed useless to look for it.

However, Zig-Zag knew where it was, for he had opened it to place his victims into a less accessible dungeon. Was the acrobat connected then with the people who stored their goods here, or was he merely acquainted with the place? This point was of but little importance for Georget who did not dwell upon it. He must escape by the shaft, that was evident, but how was he to manage?

The great difficulty was to reach the opening in the roof of the passage. Courapied, who was twice as tall as Georget, might have reached it by a bound or by setting his foot on some cleft in the stonework and climbing up alone. Or else he might have given his son a lift on his back and let him go on ahead. Still it was preferable to find some more practical course which might prevent the necessity of one of the two prisoners remaining behind.

After a little reflection, it occurred to Georget that he might make a rough step-ladder by piling several casks one above the other. He had noticed that three or four of them were empty, so it would be an easy matter to move them, and he resolved to perform this preparatory task alone and without delay. Courapied was in no condition to assist him, so that he need not wake him before daylight.

The clouds were passing over, and the rain had ceased to fall. Georget retraced his steps, bearing the can of water, and soon reached the place where his father was still sleeping on his couch of hams. He placed the can within the sleeper's reach; then in order to work more surely, he decided, sorely against his will, to light his candle.

He had but one match left him, and he greatly disliked sacrificing it, for if this plan of escape should fail, he would be condemned to perpetual darkness. There seemed to be no alternative but to make the venture, however. And so he burnt his ships as it were—lighting with his last match the last little bit of candle that remained.

He found the empty casks without any difficulty, and selecting the one that seemed the strongest he proceeded to roll it to the foot of the shaft. Courapied slept on, in the meanwhile, snoring sonorously. He had soon rolled the cask to the shaft and setting it on one end he climbed upon it. Then raising his eyes he fancied that the sky was already less black, and that the first grey gleam of early dawn was beginning to steal over it. In half-an-hour's time it would be light.

A week had elapsed since the youngster had seen the sunshine for the last time, and perched upon the cask he joyfully waited for it to appear. The patch of sky which he could descry above the orifice grew less dark and less perceptible, but the light from above did not yet reach the bottom of the shaft. It seemed to be in a measure screened by something or other, still, it was so far barely dawn. Georget fervently prayed that the coming day might be illuminated by a bright spring sun, for in cloudy weather he would not be able to distinguish such difficulties or facilities as might be offered during the ascent which he intended to make in view of escaping from this dreadful prison.

The brave little fellow, standing on the cask, had already measured the distance that separated him from the vault above and had ascertained that he could not reach it, however high he might try to raise his arms. Still he hoped that a spring might enable him to accomplish this feat, providing of course that his hands found something to clutch at.

To make the experiment, he waited for additional light. The dog no longer barked and all risk of danger outside seemed to be at an end, for the prowlers of the plain of Saint Denis retire into their dens at the hour when honest working men usually get up and start off to engage in their daily toil. Besides, it was the height of improbability that Zig-Zag and Amanda should be roaming about the neighbourhood at daybreak, but they could not guess that their last victims were about to resuscitate.

Georget, who already pictured himself outside, soliloquized: "Where shall we go when we get out of this dreadful place? To the young lady's —providing they haven't killed her— But who knows whether she will admit us? Will she believe us when we tell her about our being shut up here? She may accuse us of being in league with Zig-Zag; and, besides, father has a grudge against her and he's capable of saying something foolish."

At this moment he heard Courapied calling him in a husky but forcible voice which carried a good distance, for the old clown had acquired on the stage the habit of shouting under all circumstances.

"Here I am, father!" said the little fellow jumping down, and thereupon he hastened to Courapied whom he found sitting upon the hams and swearing like a trooper.

"What have you put in this?" he yelled, shaking the can.

"Water, father, I brought it to you. Drink it. I have had some already."

However, the intoxicated man threw the precious water—procured with such touching solicitude—straight in the boy's face, saying with an oath: "Take your water. I want brandy. Turn on the tap."

"But, father, you must get up now. I have found a way out of this dungeon."

"Well, be off then. I am going to stay by the cask, and as you refuse to wait on me, I will wait on myself," retorted Courapied who was fairly fuddled.

He stretched out his hand, seized hold of the tap, and as the liquid gushed out, he tried to fill his can, but as he did so he overturned the lantern with its lighted candle.

Georget sprung forward to pick it up, but he was too late. The soil being saturated with the liquid, blazed up like so much sulphur and the flames compelled the brave child to draw back. He was not injured, but Courapied, who was as thoroughly saturated as the ground, was almost instantly enveloped in flames.

The poor clown writhed and shrieked in his agony, and his son vainly attempted to drag him away by his burning garments. He would perhaps have succeeded in this generous effort, but the overheated barrel exploded, and the spirits it contained burst from it in a torrent of flame that instantly engulfed Courapied.

Georget, although he had the presence of mind to spring back, was badly burned, and had barely time to save himself. His father was lost—lost beyond all power of rescue. The flames and smoke already filled the cellar, and the other casks would soon take fire, so what good would it do for him to remain in this furnace? The instinct of self-preservation made him turn and flee, pursued by the dense smoke which nearly stifled him.

He was unable to draw breath until after he had passed the point where the passage forked, nor could he even have remained there many minutes without perishing by suffocation, for the fire was approaching with frightful rapidity. He soon reached the foot of the shaft, however, and leaped upon the cask. Looking up he now saw not only the light of day, but a number of iron bars projecting from one side of the shaft, and forming a very trustworthy ladder. Similar bars are found in all the Paris sewer-shafts to enable the sewer men to descend or climb.

The lowest of these bars was fully a yard above Georget's head, but he was as supple as an eel and as nimble as a chamois. Making a vigorous spring he seized hold of the first iron bar with one hand, and raising himself by that, high enough to reach the one above it, he continued in this way until his feet found a place of support.

The rest of the ascent would have been mere play for a boy who had practised gymnastics ever since he was four years old, but unfortunately the smoke from the cellar had now reached the shaft, and forced upward by the draught, was now ascending in dense coils which completely enveloped poor Georget. He could do longer see, and yet a bright sun shone in a cloudless sky overhead. However, he persevered, albeit he was completely blinded by the smoke, but just as he began to feel confident that the painful ascent was nearly completed, his head came in contact with an obstacle. The mouth of the shaft was covered with an iron grating.

This time Georget's courage deserted him, and he gave himself up for lost. The smoke was becoming more and more dense around him, and the heat more and more intolerable. Indeed, the poor lad found himself in much the same position as a man seated on the top of a chimney, below which a hot fire had been suddenly ignited.

He pushed against the grating with all his might, first with his head, and then bending somewhat with his shoulders, and he fancied that it yielded a little. However, just as he had summoned up all his strength for a final effort, he heard the same loud barking that had startled him before; but this time the dog's snout was so close to the grating that Georget could feel his hot breath.

"It is Vigoureux! I am lost!" he murmured.

Feeling that there was little choice between being torn in pieces by this ferocious animal, and perishing of suffocation in the vault, he was on the point of letting go his hold on the bars, when he was stunned by the noise of a frightful explosion, which, at the same instant, expelled him from the shaft with irresistible force.

Everything went up at the same time. Georget, the grating, and the dog were all lifted high in the air. Indeed, the eruption of a volcano could hardly have produced more astounding results than this outburst from the cellar, in which at least eighteen casks of brandy had exploded almost simultaneously.

The shaft by which the poor lad had just made his way to the surface of the plain was now belching forth flames and dense clouds of black smoke; the soil had trembled, and one of the walls of the old house had fallen. The rising sun looked down upon a scene of desolation, and many people, attracted by the noise, could be seen hastening to the spot.

When Georget at last regained his senses, there were several men already standing around him—some rag-pickers, a few loafers, and a couple of employés of the Paris Octroi or customs' service who had been on their way to the Saint-Ouen gate when the explosion took place.

In the distance might be seen the dog, running off at the top of his speed, though no one evinced any inclination to pursue him. Georget did not ask himself if the animal were Vigoureux or not. His only thought was of his father.

"My father! save my father!" he exclaimed, in a supplicating tone.

"Where is he?" asked an old rag-picker.

"Down there in the cellar."

"And how came he in the cellar?" asked the customs' officials.

"He fell into it when I did."

"But what on earth have you set fire to down there?" asked the rag-picker, gazing at Georget in astonishment. "You are as brown as a roasted pig."

"Some casks of brandy caught fire," stammered the poor lad. "It was an accident. But, pray, let me go to my father's assistance."

"Ah, ha!" exclaimed one of the officials. "Brandy, you say; we must look into this matter!"

He thereupon whispered a few words to his companion, who hastened off in the direction of the gendarmerie barracks recently erected on the Boulevard Bessières.

In the meantime, several other persons had come up, among them Father Villard, the landlord of the famous establishment known as the "Tombeau des Lapins," and who, on hearing the particulars, exclaimed: "This must have been going on for some time. There has been a light in the house every night for a week or more, and that meant something. But, now, the old shanty is knocked over. Well, it's a good thing this happened, as it will put a stop to all these goings on. But to think that you revenue men shouldn't have discovered all this long ago, especially as the scoundrels' store-house wasn't five hundred yards from the fortifications."

"It isn't too late now, perhaps," growled the official. And violently shaking the weeping Georget, he savagely exclaimed: "Come, you young rascal, take me to the entrance of the cellar in which you left your father."

"Yes, yes, gladly," sobbed the boy.

This was more easily said than done, however. The mouth of the still smoking shaft was close to the pile of stones where Camille and her friends had paused to deliberate before trying to force their way into the house; consequently, the subterranean passage was on the side nearest to the Route de la Révolte, and it did not extend very far. However, all trace of the entrance to the hall in which Conrapied and his son had met with their accident had been destroyed when the house-wall was demolished by the explosion.

"It was there," wailed Georget, pointing to a pile of bricks.

"Don't try to play the fool!" grumbled the official. "You must think me green and no mistake. Why don't you say that you won't tell, and have done with it? You'll have to speak out by-and-bye, though, when you find yourself in prison."

"In prison? I? Why, I have done nothing wrong."

"Oh, you will be let off after you've told us where the rest of the band are. You can't make me believe that you are not one of the gang."

"He acted as spy for the rascals, of course," said the landlord of "The Rabbit's Grave."

"Yes, yes. That was it! To prison with him! It will serve him right!" cried the others.

"I am willing to go with you wherever you wish," said Georget, exasperated; "but won't somebody go to my father's assistance? You certainly won't let a man die without trying to save him."

"If he is down there in the cellar, he must have been roasted long ago," remarked one of the by-standers, with a chuckle such as a cannibal might have given on hearing "broiled man" spoken of.

"I would willingly go down, but it isn't possible," said one of the rag-pickers looking on. He approached the opening, as he spoke, but the smoke and a sickening smell made him recoil. "Oh, oh!" added he, "it isn't a smell of brandy. The chap down there is roasting."

The boy burst into a passionate fit of sobbing. He realized that his father was dead. It mattered little what became of him now.

"Come, now. What is your name?" asked the custom-house officer, brusquely.

"Georget Conrapied."

"An odd name, upon my word. Well, what do you do for a living?"

"Oh! he's a page at a restaurant," remarked one of the by-standers.
"That is very evident. Don't you see the buttons on his jacket?"

"No, no! I'm uot a page," murmured Georget. "I belonged to a company."

"A company of what? You won't make us believe you belonged to a
theatre."

"My father and I performed at fairs."

"That may be true," said one loafer. "It seems to me that I did see
the lad at the gingerbread fair."

"Yes, and so did I; we were there," retorted the last speaker's companion.

"That is not the question, however," said the official, and again turning
to Georget, whose cheeks were wet with tears, he asked : "Where do you
live?"

"We did sleep in our employer's travelling waggon—" began Georget.

"And now?"

"We have no home left us, sir. Our manager failed, aud we did not
know what was going to become of us when we fell into the cellar."

"You are trying to deceive me, I see, you young rascal. But, never
mind, your accouut is as good as settled. I am going to walk you straight
off to the station-house. We'll see if anyone appears to claim you."

Georget had Camille Monistrol's name upon his lips, but with his youthful
shrewdness he reflected·that the young lady who had treated him so kindly
would not like to be mixed up iu such an affair, and so he remaiued silent.

Two gendarmes now came up, led by the other customs' official, and
Georget, with touching resignation, resolved to go to prison rather than
mention Mademoiselle Monistrol's name.

IX.

EVERYONE knows that the course of true love never runs smooth, and that
obstacles only increase a genuine lover's ardour. This was certainly true
in Julien Gémozac's case. He was madly in love, and the more coldly
Camille Monistrol treated him, the more passionately he adored her.
Despite everything, he persisted in paying attentions to a young lady who
not only treated them with marked indifference, but who finally refused to
even see him when he called. Now he knew that she received a certain M.
de Menestreau, and yet he lacked the energy to go and ask her for that
gentleman's address and to pick a quarrel with him, despite the fact that
he had already fought two duels aud feared uobody in the world. Camille
held him spell-bound, as it were, although she had done nothing to encourage him. In fact, she had acted all through in a contrary sense.

All Fresnay's counsels were of no avail, and the reproaches of Julien's
mother, and the remonstrances of his father proved equally futile.

The great iron manufacturer treated the matter much more coolly than
his wife did, however. Being essentially a business man, he said to himself
that, as her father's patent was yielding large sums already, Mademoiselle
Monistrol would soon be the possessor of a handsome fortune, aud consequeutly
a very desirable wife for his son, the more especially as, thanks to such a
marriage, the immense income which was sure to accrue from the invention
would thus be kept in the family. Moreover, from a social point of view,

such a marriage was quite in conformity with M. Gémozac's views. He, himself, had begun life as a workman, and he had no desire to see his son espouse an aristocratic heiress. He believed in marriages between people of similar birth.

What he feared most was that Julien, exasperated by Camille's refusals to see him, might plunge into the wildest dissipation. Indeed, he even suspected that this was already the case, for the young fellow's allowance was considerably overdrawn, and the cashier had reported to his employer that he had applied for ten thousand francs only the day before. He had, no doubt, required this sum to pay a gambling debt, for, in love as he was, he surely did not waste money over profligate women.

He no longer made his appearance at the mid-day meal, perhaps because he was sleeping after a night spent at the baccarat-table, or perhaps because he had gone out early to hang about the house of his divinity, in the hope of catching a glimpse of her. His father was unable to tell which was exactly the case. However, things had come to such a pass that he wisely concluded that it was time for him to interfere. He could not bear the idea of treating Julien like a refractory child, whom one puts on bread and water; or, in other words, to cut off his allowance, and refuse him the money he spent so recklessly; besides, he realised that paternal admonitions would have no effect upon this headstrong young fellow, and he finally decided that the best thing he could do would be to take the bull by the horns, or in other words, to appeal to the cause of all this trouble : the lady herself.

Camille had not paid a single visit to his house since the bitter words she had exchanged with his wife, so he resolved to call on her and wring a confession from her. He could not believe that she had acted badly, nor could he believe that she had taken a dislike to a young fellow so attractive in every respect as his son was. On the contrary, he imputed her apparent coldness and indifference to either shyness or coquetry. Besides, he knew that she was somewhat eccentric, and inclined to be independent; and, perhaps, also Madame Gémozac had wounded her pride in some way or other. He, for his part, felt confident of his ability to make her listen to reason.

There also were other motives that made him particularly desirous of an immediate interview. Camille was not yet of age, nor had she any near relative living. Hence it was necessary for her either to chose a guardian or take the necessary steps to secure her regal independence. M. Gémozac was strongly in favour of the latter course. Mademoiselle Monistrol would soon have important business matters to transact with her father's partner, deeds to sign, and so on; and for this reason, it would be advisable to place her in a position to manage her fortune herself. M. Gémozac wished to advise her to adopt this course, and to offer to take the necessary steps to effect such an arrangement.

Besides, would not this be the best way of proving to her that he had no intention of interfering with her future course, or of dictating to her in her choice of a husband? M. Gémozac was an honest man above all things, and he did not wish that Mademoiselle Monistrol should for one moment suppose that he was anything else.

So, one fine day, without consulting his wife, or saying anything to his son, he left the house at about the hour he usually entered his office, and drove to the little house on the Boulevard Voltaire.

He had never called upon the deceased Monistrol during the latter's lifetime. Wealthy folks do not disturb themselves for the people they assist, so that the inventor had always repaired to the Quai de Jemmapes when an interview had been necessary. Still, although Gémozac had never seen the house where his partner had met with so tragical a death, he was in a measure acquainted with it, as his wife and son had often described it to him. He was now not sorry of an opportunity to visit it, as he had never been able to explain to himself how such a crime had possibly been committed ; and, besides, he was in great doubts as to whether Mademoiselle Monistrol was safe in such a lonely place, and he intended again advising her to move into better quarters.

Ten minutes after starting from the Quai de Jemmapes, his coachman, who had already driven Madame Gémozac and Julien to the Boulevard Voltaire, stopped his horse in front of the fence which limited the enclosure. M. Gémozac alighted from the carriage, and looked around for a bell to announce his arrival, but seeing none, he tried the gate, and found it unlocked. Once inside the enclosure, he examined the house, and made a grimace on perceiving that it was little or no better than a porter's lodge. Moveover, it did not seem to be inhabited, for all the shutters were closed. However, he walked across the enclosure, thinking that the sound of his footsteps would attract the attention of a servant, but no one whatever appeared.

"This reminds me of the Palace of the Sleeping Beauty," he said to himself. "The girl has perhaps gone out. But that famous nurse, who was to guard her so faithfully, what has become of her? Perhaps her young mistress has taken her out with her, a very sensible precaution, for the child is too pretty to go about Paris alone."

He again advanced, but not knowing exactly where to find the entrance to this deserted place, he decided to walk round it and look for a door. He instinctively turned to the right, and soon discovered a portal, but was surprised to find it wide open.

"The deuce !" he murmured, "Mademoiselle Monistrol must be very careless to leave her house at the mercy of the first rascal who comes along, especially after the misfortune that lately befell her—this is really too bad."

Just then, however, it seemed to him that he heard some one talking, and on listening more attentively, he distinctly heard two voices, one of which was certainly that of a man. "Oh, ho !" M. Gémozac said to himself, "my visit seems to be rather inopportune. The gentleman I hear talking must be Julien's rival—his favoured rival, the young man whom my wife so narrowly escaped meeting on the day she called here last, and who was the cause of her quarrel with the girl. I heard that my son had never managed to see him. Matters have gone further than I supposed, and I begin to think that poor Julien would do as well to retire from the field. Still, I sha'n't be sorry to have a look at this suitor."

Accordingly, he walked boldly up the steps, taking care to make as much noise as possible, and to clear his throat two or three times. He was evidently heard, for the talkers suddenly became silent, and the noise of chairs rolling back on their castors, announced that they were rising.

Almost immediately, Mademoiselle Monistrol made her appearance, dressed as if she had just come in from a walk, for she had not taken time to remove her hat.

"It is I, my dear child," cried Gémozac. "You were not expecting to see me, I'm sure."

"No, I was not, sir," replied Camille, without the slightest embarrassment. "But, as you know very well, you are, and ever will be, welcome here."

"Then you are sure I do not disturb you? I fancy, though, that you are not alone."

"That is true," replied the young girl promptly; "but I shall be very happy to introduce you to a visitor who has just called. Pray come in, sir."

Gémozac required no urging, but immediately followed Mademoiselle Monistrol into the dining-room where he found himself face to face with a very good-looking gentleman who was standing there, hat in hand. He was able to secure a very good view of this person, as the shutters of the back window of the apartment were open.

"Monsieur George de Menestreau," said Camille, with a wave of her hand in the direction of her first visitor.

On hearing this name, Julien's father started and began to scrutinize the gentleman with rather annoying persistency. His son had informed him that Mademoiselle Monistrol was receiving the visits of a young gentleman, but he had not told him the gentleman's name, though Camille had taken no pains to conceal it.

"Excuse me, sir," said M. Gémozac, without giving the young girl time to complete the introduction, "but don't you belong to the department of the Aveyron?"

"Yes, sir. To whom have I the honour of speaking?"

"I am Pierre Gémozac, and I knew your father well. He was an iron-master in that part of the country, and he sold me excellent metal. He was one of the most honourable men that I ever knew. He is dead, I was told."

"Yes, he died several years ago."

"I was aware that he had a son, and I have always wondered why this son did not continue his business."

"I had not the slightest taste for it," replied M. George de Menestreau, "on the contrary, I was passionately fond of travelling. Having the means to gratify my taste, I left France for America, where I remained a long time. Since then, I have been in China and Japan, and only returned to France after making a trip around the world."

"You never told me that you had been such a traveller," murmured Camille.

"And I was very much misinformed," added M. Gémozac, "for, excuse my frankness, I thought that Menestreau had died a ruined man, and that his son had disappeared.".

"My father did, in fact, meet with reverses, but I inherited property from my mother—and travelling is not disappearing," replied George, drily. "I am, however, very happy to meet you, sir, the more happy from the fact that I intended to call on you very shortly."

"May I ask why?"

"Not to ask you to give me Mademoiselle Monistrol's hand in marriage, as you are neither her relative nor guardian, but to ask for your approval of the match. I certainly owe this act of deference to the generous man who came to her father's assistance, and who has since been her friend and protector."

M. Gémozac looked inquiringly at Camille, who immediately exclaimed:
"It was I, sir, who advised Monsieur de Menestreau to give you this proof of respect, and as chance has brought us together, permit me to broach a

rather delicate subject. Your son has probably spoken to you of a project he had formed, and which certainly does me infinite honour, but—"

"Oh, yes, and I did not raise the slightest objection to it. His mother was rather opposed to it, but she would soon have modified her views, and I will not conceal from you the fact that my son will be in despair when he learns that you intend to marry Monsieur de Menestreau. However, you are free, my dear Camille, and I have no right to blame you for following the dictates of your own heart. I, indeed, came here to-day for the express purpose of urging you to take such steps as will make you absolute mistress of your own actions and of your fortune. I will at once attend to the settlement of your respective interests. Your account with me shall be settled every year or every six months, as you may prefer, and you need only maintain with me and mine such a connection as you please."

"It can be only of the most affectionate nature," replied Camille, warmly, "as you approve of my choice."

"I am not called upon to approve it. Monsieur de Menestreau is the son of a very honourable man, and I have no reason to doubt but what he has inherited his father's virtues. Still, I trust he will take no offence if I make some inquiries respecting him in that part of the country where his earlier years were spent."

On hearing this announcement, which sounded not unlike a threat, George de Menestreau bit his lips, but the next instant he replied with un-ruffled calmness: "You will do quite right to make such inquiries, sir. I fear I am well-nigh forgotten in my old home, but I flatter myself that I have left no unpleasant memories there."

"I am quite sure you have not," said M. Gémozac, thinking the contrary all the while, and secretly resolving to write to one of his correspondents in the Aveyron that very day.

He recollected having heard a vague rumour that the elder Menestreau had been ruined by his son, who had turned out very badly; but so many years had elapsed since the ironmaster's death that M. Gémozac would not trust to his memory. He felt sure he should have plenty of time to make the necessary inquiries before Camille bound herself irrevocably. One can not marry in France without giving the authorities due notice of one's intentions. The formalities require a fortnight at the very least, and M. Gémozac would not need more than four or five days to obtain a reply from Rodez or Decazeville.

"I am afraid I have made you a poor return for all your kindness," now faltered poor Camille; "but I assure you that I am deeply grateful for all you have done for me. Pray, tell your son, sir, that had my heart been free—"

"Which it is not, unfortunately," interrupted M. Gémozac in a slightly ironical tone. "Julien will have to console himself as best he can, and perhaps everything will turn out for the best, after all. But it seems to me that you had sworn that you would only marry the man who succeeded in finding your father's murderer. I am well aware that Julien has not fulfilled those conditions. Monsieur de Menestreau has doubtless been more fortunate, and the murderer has been arrested or is about to be?"

"Alas! no," replied Camille sorrowfully. "And I even begin to fear that he never will be caught. Monsieur de Menestreau has done everything in his power but without success. However he saved my life."

"Indeed!" exclaimed M. Gémozac, "that being the case, I can not marvel at your desire to reward him. So your life has been in danger you say! Did the same man that killed your father try to kill you also?"

"I heard that he was hiding in an old house near the Saint-Ouen gate, and—"

"It was probably Monsieur de Menestreau who gave you this valuable information."

"No, it was a poor clown who was a member of the troupe to which Zig-Zag belonged. The story is too long a one to tell you in detail. However, I started out to find him one evening in company with this clown and his son. They never returned—"

"What! did Zig-Zag exterminate them, too? Why! he must be a regular monster."

"I do not know exactly if he killed them," replied Camille, "but they disappeared, or rather, they fell into an open trap-door in the hall of the house, and I very narrowly escaped sharing the same fate. I did escape it, however, and fled; but on the lonely plain upon which the house stands I was attacked by two of the scoundrels who haunt the suburbs of Paris, and Heaven only knows what would have become of me had not Monsieur de Menestreau rescued me from their clutches at the peril of his life."

"Monsieur de Menestreau's appearance just at the critical moment was truly providential. What a romance your adventures would make!" said the ironmaster with a touch of irony in his voice.

"They are only too real," murmured Camille.

"Oh! I haven't the slightest doubt of it, but the romance should have a fitting finish. You ought to have returned and visited this brigand's den in broad daylight."

"I did not fail to do so, sir," replied Camille, "Monsieur de Menestreau accompanied me. He very kindly explored the cellar into which my unfortunate guides had fallen, but their bodies were not there."

"Consequently they are not dead. If I were in your place, mademoiselle, I should beg Monsieur de Menestreau to call the attention of the prefect of police to the house in which such wonderful things occur. What kind of a place is it?"

"It is a brick house—a red brick house half in ruins. Everybody in that neighbourhood knows it," said Camille, who was somewhat nettled by M. Gémozac's jocular air and sarcastic language.

"A red brick house in ruins! How strange! I very rarely read the items of general news in the papers—but this morning my eyes happened to fall on a paragraph which said that yesterday a red brick house on the plain of Saint-Denis, very near the Route de la Révolte, an unoccupied place half in ruins, had been nearly demolished by an explosion. It appears that the cellar was used as a store place by a gang of scoundrels who were leagued together to defraud the revenue, and that it was full of casks of brandy that caught fire, nobody knows how."

"Good heavens!" cried Camille, "can it be—"

"There were two victims, so the paper stated," continued M. Gémozac, "a man who was burned alive in the cellar amid the flaming liquid, and a lad who escaped from the place, though not until he had sustained serious injuries."

"And what became of him?" eagerly asked Mademoiselle Monistrol who was all attention.

"The paper did not mention, but he was probably taken to a hospital—at least if he was really badly injured. Still, this story can have no con-

nection with yours, and I hardly know why I related it. If it has interested you, you will have no difficulty in learning all the particulars of
the affair. It will go the round of the press and there will be lots of information about it in to-morrow's journals. But I must leave you now.
Business matters require my attention. I only ran away from my office
for a few moments to talk with you about your affairs. We now understand each other thoroughly, and hoping to see you soon again, I will leave
you now with your betrothed. I have the honour to wish you good-
morning, sir."

M. de Menestreau bowed with marked coldness, and M. Gémozac senior
withdrew without shaking hands with Camille, who was not particularly
affected, however, by the change in his manner. Indeed she heaved a sigh
of relief as if she were delighted that the sarcastic ironmaster had at last
taken himself off.

"This puts an end to a most embarrassing situation," she remarked to
her lover. "I have never told him the plain truth in reference to my
feelings, and I am glad I never did so. But what do you think of the
strange story we just heard?"

"I don't believe a word of it," replied George de Menestreau promptly.
"It is doubtless a pure fabrication—some hoax invented by a penny-a-liner
hard up for copy as they say. But even if there should be some foundation
for it, there can be no connection between this affair and your expedition
with Zig-Zag's friends. They are probably a long way from the brick house
before this time. However I have a piece of bad news for you—at least,
bad for me. I am going away this evening."

"Going away?" exclaimed Camille in dire astonishment. She could
scarcely believe her ears.

"Yes, mademoiselle," rejoined George sorrowfully, "I am summoned
to England by a very intimate friend who requires my services in a very
important matter."

"And you deferred informing me of your intended departure until now?
That was very wrong," said Mademoiselle Monistrol, reproachfully.

"I did not know it myself yesterday. The letter I have received from
London arrived only this morning. I dared not call before the hour you
had appointed, and I was about to tell you of this annoying circumstance
when Monsieur Gémozac arrived. I did not care to announce my intentions while he was here, for I thought he might fancy that I was anxious
to leave France before his friends could enlighten him about me."

Camille was looking very sad and grieved. "What an absurd idea!"
she said.

"Didn't you notice that he went away extremely angry? Had he contented himself with venting his displeasure upon me, I should not have
cared; but he treated you coldly, even rudely, and it is my duty to warn
you that you must not place any further reliance in him. He will never
forgive you for having preferred me to his son, and he will do all he can
to injure me."

"That makes no difference to me!" exclaimed Camille, impulsively,
"my feelings will not change. Neither calumny nor absence will make
me forget that we belong to one another."

"If I were sure of that, I should go away with a much lighter heart, I
assure you," said George.

"Is it possible that you doubt me?" retorted the young girl. "What
have I done to excite such distrust on your part? and what must I do to

convince you that I will keep my promise? If the law permitted it, I would marry you to-morrow."

"But the law prevents it, and the formalities to be observed are many and tedious. Ah! I wish we were only English. Then we should only have to present ourselves before a Protestant clergyman, and to declare to him, upon oath, that there was no legal obstacle to our marriage. If we did that, he would marry us forthwith. But, unfortunately, in this country the law is different; and, before a priest and a mayor will have the right to unite us, my enemies will have time to blacken me in your eyes!"

"They will not succeed in doing that," replied Camille, "but, to reassure you, I am quite willing to go to England and marry you there, and thus avoid all annoying formalities."

"You would do that! You would brave prejudice and slander!" said George, with a glance of mingled admiration and gratitude which went straight to the young girl's heart. "You would not be afraid to offend those Gémozacs, even although the father has your fortune in his hands?"

"I would willingly sacrifice my fortune to insure my life-long happiness; but nothing can take it from me. I have found among my father's papers an act of co-partnership, signed by Monsieur Gémozac."

"That is very fortunate," remarked M. de Menestreau. "Thanks to that document, you hold him."

"Besides," replied Camille, "whatever the nature of my future relations with him and his family may be, I feel sure that Monsieur Gémozac would never intentionally defraud me of a single penny."

"And you are willing to leave France with me this evening?" urged George.

"No, my friend. Although I am very independent, I must show a certain amount of respect for public opinion. People would be sure to say that I had eloped with you, and I do not intend to give them a chance to say that. I will join you in England. Brigitte shall be my travelling companion, and when I return to France, it will be as your lawful wife. But I cannot start until I have learned all the particulars of the strange affair that Monsieur Gémozac spoke of just now."

"What, do you still believe that newspaper hoax? It's absurd."

"Well, I can't help thinking of it," said Camille. "Something tells me that the lad who was saved was the son of Zig-Zag's enemy, that very Georget of whom I have so often spoken to you. I never can bring myself to believe that he betrayed me."

"I do not share your confidence, my dear Camille, but you may be sure that if the lad saved from the explosion was your young friend, he would not have failed to come here without delay."

"But he is injured, perhaps, or, who knows? he has been cast into prison as an accomplice of the smugglers. And what will he say if he is questioned? He will speak of Zig-Zag and of me."

"Very possibly, but what can one do?"

"Why, go and see him, and ask him to tell you what happened to him. As yet I don't know where he is, but I shall know it to-day, for I am going straight to the Saint-Ouen gate, and to the brick house. I will question the custom-house people there, and the neighbours."

"Yes, and compromise yourself irretrievably. I entreat you, my dear, to abandon this project, and if you insist upon having the matter investigated, allow me to do it for you," said M. de Menestreau.

"You—when you must leave this evening."

"Everything considered, I can certainly defer my journey for twenty-four hours. I will at once warn the friend who is expecting me by a telegram."

"And I shall see you again to-morrow? Ah! well, in that case, I willingly accept your offer. Only promise me that before to-night you will do your best to bring me some news of Georget."

"Say rather of the lad who was picked up near the house," remonstrated Camille's lover. "That does not amount to the same thing, by any means. Still, I will do my very best. But let me hear you repeat that you will really join me in London. I can scarcely believe in so much happiness."

"I have promised, and I never break a promise," said Camille gravely.

George de Menestreau made a sudden movement, as if he were about to throw himself upon his knee before her, but she checked him. "I hear Brigitte's voice," she said. "I sent her out on an errand, and she must have returned. But how strange! she seems to be uttering cries of alarm."

The noise of a door banged-to followed upon the cries which Camille had heard, and an instant afterwards Brigitte darted into the room pale and breathless.

"What is the matter?" asked Camille in alarm.

"That dog, that terrible dog!" faltered the old servant with great difficulty.

"What dog?" inquired Mademoiselle Monistrol, who was immensely astonished.

"The clown's dog—the brute that was here the other night," replied Brigitte, though not without an effort.

Camille started, and even M. de Menestreau could not repress a gesture of surprise or emotion.

"Where is he?" asked the young girl, as she recovered some degree of composure.

"In the kitchen, mademoiselle, and it is fortunate that I was able to shut him up there, for he is not muzzled, and he would certainly tear us to pieces. He doesn't look as if he had eaten anything for a week."

"That's strange," said Camille. "But how did he get in? Had he been following you?"

"Why, I was entering the house, with my basket on my arm, when, just as I opened the kitchen door, something dashed past me, almost overturning me. Indeed, the beast would have knocked me flat upon the floor if I had not held fast to the door. I had scarcely time to close it; and if I had lost my senses for an instant, I am sure that the dog would have sprung at my throat and strangled me, and then have come up here and finished you. But he can't get out. The window is too high, and I took the precaution to close the shutters before going to market. But, hark! don't you hear the noise he is making?"

In fact, several heavy repeated blows proceeding from the kitchen were now distinctly audible.

"Go ahead, you vile brute," growled Brigitte. "The door is a strong one—I know that—and you will only wear yourself out. But dear, dear me! if the beast keeps on, he will break all my plates and dishes. What is to be done, mademoiselle?"

Camille, who was as much at a loss as her old nurse, now looked at George de Menestreau, and saw that her lover seemed to be considering the situation.

"If we could only succeed in muzzling him," remarked Mademoiselle Monistrol, thoughtfully, "he might enable us to find Zig-Zag again."

"What! you think of repeating the expedition of the other night!" exclaimed Brigitte, lifting her hands to the ceiling in holy horror. "And after all that happened too! You yourself reached home alive, it's true, but you need not expect to be so fortunate another time."

"It would be folly to repeat that venturesome attempt, mademoiselle," said M. de Menestreau at last. "Besides, I am satisfied in my own mind that this dog does not possess the wonderful powers which your guide ascribed to him. If he was really so much attached to his master, he would not have left him; and it can not be Zig-Zag he is searching for, as Zig-Zag isn't here, unless one can suppose that he knows all the places that Zig-Zag ever visited, and that supposition would be absurd."

Camille had listened attentively. "Then how do you explain his coming?" she asked.

"In the simplest manner possible," replied George. "Listen to me. This dog, like many others, remembers places wonderfully well. His master must have driven him away, or have lost him intentionally, probably fearing, and with good reason, that the animal might lead to his identification; for a dog can not be disguised like a man, remember, and every acrobat in the country knows this one. So Zig-Zag managed to get rid of him somehow or other, and the dog has been roaming about the streets ever since in search of food. He finally returned to the Place du Trône, where he had once stayed for some time with the acrobatic company, and while running about the Boulevard Voltaire, he no doubt passed your house, and suddenly remembered that he had once been here."

"That is quite possible," murmured Camille, though only partially convinced. "However, what is to be done? He is a dangerous animal, I know."

"Well, he can't be allowed to remain here in any case," said George de Menestreau.

"But can we drive him out?"

"Oh! we mustn't even try to do that. I should not be at all surprised if he were mad, and even if he is not, it would not be advisable to have any trouble with a dog of his size and strength."

"I'm sure I have no desire to touch him," muttered Brigitte, shuddering at recollection of the animal.

"But what shall we do with him?" inquired Camille again.

"Exactly what policemen do with dangerous stray dogs; kill him, of course," said George.

"That will be no easy matter, I assure you."

"I will attend to the matter, mademoiselle. Since my late adventure on the plain of Saint-Denis, I have always carried a revolver in my pocket."

"You must not run any risk. I won't allow it," said Camille in dire alarm.

"Oh! don't be afraid. I shall not enter the kitchen. I shall shoot him from outside. There must be an opening of some kind in the shutters, isn't there?"

"Yes, two," promptly replied Brigitte. "Monsieur's plan is an excellent one."

"Then show me the place, my good woman. Mademoiselle will remain here. It isn't advisable for her to witness such a sight."

"Oh, no, I insist upon accompanying you. If there is likely to be any danger, I am determined to share it."

"If there were any danger, I should insist upon your remaining here," retorted George, imperiously, "but there can be none, so come with us."

As they passed the kitchen door, they heard, not noisy barks, but the hoarse howls which are considered to be a characteristic symptom of hydrophobia.

"You have had a narrow escape, my dear Brigitte," remarked M. de Menestreau as he heard these howls. "If this dog had bitten you, you would certainly have died a horrible death."

"Don't speak of it, sir," groaned the old nurse. "It makes my blood run cold just to think of it. Make haste and kill him, pray. I sha'n't feel comfortable until you've done so."

They all left the house together, and Brigitte led the way to the tightly closed shutters that protected the kitchen windows.

M. de Menestreau peered through one of the small heart-shaped openings and then said : "I see him. The deuce! there is a space of at least six inches between the shutters and the window. It will be more difficult to get a good shot at him than I thought, especially as it is quite dark in there."

He had scarcely uttered these words when the crash of broken glass made him recoil.

Vigoureux having either seen or scented him, had dashed against the window with all his might. "That's capital," said M. de Menestreau. "The job will now be easier." And thereupon he got his revolver ready. The dog took another spring and this time he succeeded in getting his forepaws on to the window-sill. The glass broke and fell under the blows he dealt it and the aperture was soon large enough for his head to pass through. He cut himself badly, however, and his nose, which now appeared at the opening in the shutter, was torn and bleeding.

On beholding him, Camille and Brigitte started back in terror, as well they might; he had forced his head half way through the hole, his eyes were blood-shot, his lips covered with foam, and the ferocious howls he uttered as he pushed, were enough to freeze one's blood.

He was looking straight at M. de Menestreau, who did not move, but aimed at him with his revolver. He now fired, and it was time, for the shutters, strong as they were, were cracking under the strain to which they were subjected. The animal uttered a cry of pain, but did not retreat.

M. de Menestreau had taken good aim, and had fired at short range, still the bullet had swerved a little, and instead of piercing the dog's brain it had inflicted a wound just below one eye. Brave as a man may be, he doesn't fire upon a mad dog without feeling some emotion, and the hand of Mademoiselle Monistrol's valiant defender had no doubt trembled.

However, strange to say, Vigoureux, instead of drawing back to escape the bullets, redoubled his efforts to force his way out into the yard.

"Run away, my dear Camille," cried M. de Menestreau, again raising his revolver.

Camille did not move, however. The terrible sight fascinated her, and she could not take her eyes from it.

M. de Menestreau fired a second time, and without much better success. He hit the dog in the eye this time, but he did not kill him, and this new wound only increased the excitement of the animal, who with one frantic effort broke the hook that held the shutters. They flew open, and Vigoureux rolled out upon the gravel of the court-yard.

At this sight Brigitte fled, screaming with terror, and Menestreau sprung back to cover Mademoiselle Monistrol, who stood her ground, resolved to share the fate of the man she loved. George still had four bullets left in his revolver, but the dog was not mortally wounded, and it would now be much more difficult to get a good shot at him than when his head had appeared as a convenient target. The animal was up in an instant, and although he had sufficient strength left to spring upon his executioner, he nevertheless dragged himself slowly towards him, moaning in a pitiful fashion.

M. de Menestreau took advantage of this unexpected respite to take careful aim, and his third bullet passed through the animal's spinal column near the hips. Vigoureux sunk down, but even then, with the aid of his forepaws, he dragged himself painfully along, with his eyes still fixed upon George de Menestreau's face. It seemed almost as if the poor brute was pleading for mercy and reproaching Menestreau for treating him so cruelly. But Mademoiselle Monistrol's champion was not to be softened. A fourth bullet struck Vigoureux between the shoulders, and he fell upon his side.

He once more opened his remaining eye, gazed at his pitiless executioner, and then expired.

"At last he's dead!" muttered M. de Menestreau between his teeth. "He can not hurt any one now. But he was a tough customer. I thought once that I should not succeed in dispatching him. You must have been terribly frightened," he added, turning to Camille.

"For you, yes; and I must confess that the poor beast's suffering touched me deeply."

"I could understand that if it were any other dog. But are you sure that this one really belonged to Zig-Zag?" inquired George.

"Positive. Ask Brigitte, and she will tell you—"

"Oh! that is the very same dog," interrupted the old nurse, who had suddenly reappeared upon the scene of action. "I'm sure that there are not two animals like him in the world."

"Then there is nothing left for us to do but to get rid of his carcase," remarked M. de Menestreau. "Bring me a spade, and I will bury him in one of the flower-beds."

"Oh, no, we might catch the plague," said Brigitte in alarm. "Let me attend to that, sir. I will drag him out upon the boulevard, and the police will take him away."

"Don't fail to do so at all events," said George.

"I will see that it's done," interposed Mademoiselle Monistrol, "and now permit me to remind you that you promised to make inquiries about that poor boy."

"I am going now; first, to the ruined house, and if I can obtain no reliable information there, I shall then apply to the commissary of police of the Epinettes neighbourhood."

"Thanks," replied Camille. "I shall await your return with great impatience. So don't keep me waiting longer than you can possibly help."

"I shall take good care not to do that, as your departure for England is dependent upon this information. Indeed I even hope to be able to make my report before night. Will you be at home all day?"

"Yes, my dear George, I have not yet entirely recovered from the shock that dog caused me. The dreadful scene has upset my nerves completely. I need rest to set me right again. So go, my friend, and return soon," concluded Camille, offering both hands to her lover, who walked off at a rapid pace, after imprinting a tender kiss upon them.

Brigitte watched this affectionate leave-taking in silence, but her rather sullen air indicated that she was not very well pleased. "Do you really intend to go to England, mademoiselle?" she abruptly asked her mistress.

"Yes," replied the young girl, with some little embarrassment; "but we shall not be separated. I intend to take you there with me."

"Take me to London, never! Why, I should die of home-sickness in two days in that heathenish country! I am like an old tree, I can't bear transplanting; and besides England is a deal too far from Montreuil. And what is more," added the old nurse sulkily, "if you are going to marry that handsome young man, you will make a great mistake, and one you will repent of all your life. There, I've told you now! I had it on my conscience and I couldn't keep quiet any longer. Of course I know that it is no business of mine, but I can't help worrying about it, and I wish your poor father were alive to hear me. He would not let you follow a man you do not know from Adam—"

"You forget that he saved my life!" interrupted Camille in a firm voice.

"Bah!" retorted the old servant. "I shouldn't be so surprised to learn that he was in league with the rascals who attacked you. That young fellow is only after your money, I'm sure of it. Why didn't you take the other, the light-complexioned one? We know something about him, and he loves you for yourself."

"Enough," said Camille, imperiously, the more irritated by these remarks from the fact that she realised the justice of them, at least to a certain extent.

X.

OUR light-hearted friend Alfred, Baron de Fresnay, did not take his quarrel with the beautiful Hungarian very deeply to heart. In a couple of hours' time he felt quite consoled for having been turned out of the house in the Rue Mozart. A drive in the Bois with his friend Julien, an excellent dinner at the Café Anglais, and a visit to the Summer Circus which had just opened in the Champs Elysées—such was the treatment he resorted to; and without troubling himself any further about the capricious fair one, he returned to the club about midnight, intending to try his luck again at the card-table, if only to verify the saying: "Unlucky in love, lucky at cards."

M. Tergowitz was no longer there. After dinner he had prudently taken his departure, laden with the spoils of a dozen members whose funds he had exhausted. Gémozac had left his friend after the circus without telling him where he was going, but Alfred surmised that he was anxious to curse his more fortunate rival, and brood over Mademoiselle Monistrol's indifference.

Alfred, on his side, took the bank at baccarat, was twice broke, and finally succeeded in regaining all he had lost. He returned home at about five o'clock in the morning, well satisfied with his night's work, and not at all uneasy about the morrow. He went to bed, fell asleep, and began dreaming the most delightful dreams. He imagined indeed that he was winning all M. Tergowitz's money, and that the Hungarian countess had given up all connection with her compatriot, and was now desperately in love with himself, Fresnay. He even dreamed that he had discovered Monistrol's murderer, and that the beautiful Camille, touched by such a proof of his prowess and devotion, had offered him her hand and fortune.

Unfortunately, he was aroused from these blissful dreams at about nine o'clock by his valet, who had orders never to enter his room before noon. Alfred opened his eyes languidly, glanced at the clock, and then hurled a volley of vigorous oaths at his over zealous servant. He called him a brute, and if he did not call him a knave, as they do at the Comédie Française, it was only because Jean would not have understood him. However, Jean, accustomed to these ebullitions of temper, did not flinch.

"There is a lady here who particularly wishes to see you, sir," he said, tranquilly.

"Tell her to go to the devil!"

"She assures me that Monsieur le Baron made an appointment with her," rejoined Jean with unruffled composure.

"That is false! I never make appointments with any one for such hours. Is she pretty?" Then seeing the valet hesitate, he added: "What a fool I am to ask the question. No pretty women are abroad so early in the morning. Just show her out."

"I tried to do so, sir; but she won't go."

"That's strange," said Fresnay, musing; and half fancying that his visitor might be the countess, he added: "Did you ask her name?"

"She says her name is Olga."

"Olga!" ejaculated Fresnay. "Why, that is a fact! I remember now that I did tell her to call this morning, and if I had foreseen that she would come at daybreak, I would have thought twice before summoning her. Where have you left her?"

"In the smoking-room, sir."

"Very well; go and tell her I'll be there presently," rejoined the young baron.

Jean vanished at once, and Fresnay, after a deal of growling and swearing, finally concluded to get up. After making a hasty toilet, and lighting a cigar to freshen his clouded brain, he dragged himself to the smoking-room, which was near his sleeping apartment.

"So here you are!" he said to his visitor, who was arrayed in one of her mistress's dresses. "You must have been a sutler girl to get up so early in the morning. You no doubt used to serve out matutinal drams to linesmen or artillerymen."

"I knew I should disturb you," said Olga, "but—"

"But you did not want to lose the ten louis I promised you. You shall have them; that is, providing you earn them. What have you to tell me?"

"It depends upon what you want to know?"

"Well, first of all, who was upstairs yesterday when I called on the countess—a lover of hers, eh?"

"Yes, on the second floor. You could have surprised him had you only chosen," replied Olga, promptly.

"Oh! I didn't care to do that," said Fresnay, with an air of disdain, "but just tell me who is this fellow."

"An old friend of madame's. A handsome chap whom she has known for a long time."

"His name is Tergowitz, is it not?"

"How do you know that?"

"I know a great deal more than that," said Fresnay winking. "He pretends to be a Hungarian, but he is no more a Hungarian than I am!"

"No, I don't think he is," replied Olga, frankly; "but I am unable to say exactly what he is."

"And the pretended countess was born in a doorkeeper's hovel at Montmartre, was she not?"

"Oh! no, indeed! Her parants were very respectable people, indeed, and she was educated to become a school teacher; but she preferred a more lively life. I see I can safely tell monsieur everything. The fact is, she has had splendid opportunities, but she has not profited by them. She gave up everything to run about, and she has had her ups and downs— more downs than ups, I fancy. Now that she has met with a real gentleman, it is a pity for her to lose him, and it will end in that way if you don't choose to shut your eyes."

"Why? Is she so deeply infatuated with that fellow, Tergowitz?" asked Alfred.

"Yes; there's a bit of that, and besides, they are old cronies, and have been mixed up together in ever so many affairs that I know nothing about. Still, although they haven't really quarrelled, things haven't been going on as smoothly as they might have done for two or three days past."

"Why? Is Tergowitz jealous?"

"Oh! dear no," said Olga, "it is madame, who is jealous—dreadfully jealous, I can tell you. She fancies he is paying court to a very rich young girl, and she is furious, for she has taken it into her head to marry this Monsieur Tergowitz herself; and this whim is all the more absurd on her part, from the fact that she is already married."

"Indeed, you can't mean it. Who is she married to?" asked Fresnay, eagerly.

"To a good-for-nothing fellow she married because she was dying of hunger. I know nothing about him, for I never saw madame while she was living with him. But I did not come and disturb monsieur merely to tell him things he knows already; I came because something new has happened."

"Something new?" said Alfred. "How's that? Has she got hold of a third admirer?"

"Oh no!" replied Olga. "She wants to leave off leading the life she does."

"Pooh! has she come into a fortune then since yesterday?"

"Oh no! After your visit she was in a dreadful bad humour, and there was no approaching her—"

"I'm aware of that," retorted Fresnay. "She nearly knocked me over with her trapeze. But go on."

"Well, in the evening, she wouldn't have any dinner, but sent me off to the summer circus. When I came back I let myself in, and as I went up I heard her talking—disputing frightfully—"

"With whom, pray?" asked Fresnay.

"Why, with Monsieur Tergowitz, who had come back! He used frightful language, and, at one moment, I really thought he was going to beat madame."

"That Hungarian doesn't seem to be very well bred," remarked Fresnay. "But go on; what next?"

"Well, they finally seemed to become reconciled, and Tergowitz went off. This morning madame rang very early for her chocolate and the newspapers. While she was reading them she suddenly gave a cry, and started up so suddenly that she overturned her cup. I asked her what the matter was? She didn't answer, but sprung up out of bed, and began to walk up and down the room, gesticulating excitedly, and talking to herself. I thought she was going mad. Suddenly she began to throw on her clothes, calling to me to bring her boots, her mantle, and her hat. And she kept on scolding me for not being quick enough. It usually takes her two hours and a half to dress, but this time it didn't take her ten minutes. I ventured to inquire if I should fetch her a cab. 'No—hold your tongue.' was the only thanks I received. 'Would madame be back to breakfast?' 'She really did not know.' 'And if Monsieur de Fresnay should call before madame returns?' 'Shut the door in his face.' I hope monsieur will not be angry with me for repeating these words."

"On the contrary, I am infinitely obliged to you," replied Alfred. "Now what do you think of all this? Do you think she intends to take French leave of us?"

"I'm afraid so, and, to tell the truth, you have behaved too generously with her, and too kindly. She just likes that Monsieur Tergowitz because he's so harsh."

"Dear me! That's a pretty revelation. The idea of her being so sweet on a fellow who is nothing more than a card-sharper, I'll be bound. He went to my club yesterday, and won everybody's money."

"That doesn't surprise me," said Olga.

"What, does he really cheat!"

"He might, for I know that he can do anything he likes with his hands."

"Dear me, that's worth knowing;" said Fresnay; "I shall be on the look out in future whenever he holds the cards. But to return to your mistress, has she really gone off for good?"

"Well, I noticed that she took all her money with her. Still, she left all her clothing and jewels. Wouldn't it be well for monsieur to come over to the house and see if everything is all right there? And then, if madame should take it into her head to come back, you could have a talk with her."

"That wouldn't be a bad idea, but I can't go yet, for I haven't breakfasted."

"You might breakfast there, sir; I am a capital cook."

"Then why shouldn't I?" exclaimed Fresnay. "You shall prepare breakfast for me, and tell my fortune while I partake of it. If the countess returns, I shall be glad to see what kind of a face she makes when she finds us seated at the table together."

"She might dismiss me," said Olga; "still, I don't care for that, for I feel sure that you will see me safely out of the scrape."

"I will give you enough money to open a consulting office, and I'll send all the idiots of my acquaintance to you to have their fortunes told," rejoined Fresnay, laughing heartily. "You can make enough in six months to retire from business. In the meantime, here are your ten louis to begin with. Put the money in your pocket, go for a cab, get into it and wait for me at the door. I will be ready in twenty minutes."

Olga slipped the bank-notes in her bosom without more ado, and hastened off in search of a cab.

Fresnay thereupon turned his attention to his toilet. This chat with the maid had altogether roused him, and as he was fond of a joke he decided that he would spend the morning pestering the countess, for he felt certain that she would return to the Rue Mozart, having left her jewellery and dresses there. It even occurred to him that he might draw her out concerning this man Tergowitz, whose mysterious conduct aroused his curiosity. He felt convinced that this so-called foreigner was an adventurer of the worst class, and that the fair countess herself belonged to the same species. That being the case, he determined to try and find out what game this interesting couple was playing, and what its precise object was, in view of putting respectable folks on their guard if need were. He was not afraid of Tergowitz in the slightest degree, and as for the so-called Countess de Janos, he did not care what became of her. A woman could always be replaced in his opinion, and he was already consoled for the loss of the fair Hungarian.

However, it was a question of striking the iron whilst it was hot, and so he dressed as rapidly as possible, and after telling his valet that he should not return home during the day, he hurried downstairs and joined Olga, whom he found waiting in the cab which she had procured in accordance with his instructions.

He asked her numerous questions as they bowled along towards Auteuil, but he now found her less inclined to give him confidential information about her mistress. She probably considered that she had already given him two hundred francs' worth of private news. Perhaps, too, she was already beginning to repent of having in some degree betrayed Madame de Janos.

"Come now, my girl, where does this Tergowitz live?" Alfred inquired at last. "He must have some place of residence surely."

"Yes, no doubt," replied Olga, "but I don't know where it is."

"That's nonsense, I am sure! You must have known him before you entered the service of the countess," urged the young baron.

"Very slightly. I seldom saw him."

"Did they reside in Paris when they lived together?"

"I think not. They have both travelled about a good deal," replied the maid.

"That doesn't surprise me. The countess must have been a circus performer," said Fresnay.

"What an idea, sir!" ejaculated Olga.

"An idea that would instantly occur to any one who saw her upon the trapeze. She is a star of the first magnitude, too. It is a very rare accomplishment with young ladies of respectable birth, however. Not that I think any the worse of her for having danced upon the tight-rope. I have always had a fondness for artistes. But tell me how old is she?"

"Monsieur knows very well that a woman is always of the age she looks to be," replied Olga, sagaciously.

"She looks young, I admit it. But be frank now, doesn't she dye her hair? I saw a lot of bottles on her dressing table the other day."

"All women dye their hair now-a-days."

"I don't blame her, I am sure," said the baron, shrugging his shoulders, "After all, that Venetian chestnut suits her to perfection. But what colour was her hair before she dyed it?"

"Black or dark brown, I think. I am almost sure that she was a brunette."

"Very possibly, for she has a pale skin, and jet-black hair. If she should take it into her head to change her nationality, she would have no difficulty in passing herself off for a Spaniard, or even for a South American. However, she is a Frenchwoman, I suppose?"

"Yes, a pure-blooded Parisian," replied Olga, "besides that can be seen easily enough. But it would be useless for you to ask me her real name, for I can't tell you, as she has always concealed it from me—on account of her family—you understand."

"She's a Montmorency, probably," replied Fresnay.

Olga did not seem to notice the joke. In fact, it may be surmised that she had never heard of the first barons of Christendom. However, these remarks, and others of a similar nature, occupied the time until they reached Auteuil, but on alighting at the door of the house on the Rue Mozart, Fresnay was not much wiser than before.

"If you don't need me for a moment, sir, I will go to market," said Olga. "It is only a few steps from here, and you can have breakfast in half-an-hour."

Fresnay thereupon gave the maid a louis and entered the house, while the ex-fortune teller ran into the kitchen to fetch her basket.

There had not been the slightest change in the drawing-room since the evening before. The ropes that supported the trapeze were still dangling from the ceiling. However, judging by the maid's account, it was not likely that Madame de Janos had indulged in her favourite pastime that morning.

On the floor above, there was every indication of a hasty departure. The dressing-room and bed-room were both in the utmost disorder. The chairs were strewn with dresses, the floor with silk stockings. Several flowers had been pulled from a jardiniere and lay about amid fragments of letters. Several jewel cases, moreover, were open on a side table, while on the bed there was a long and narrow box strongly resembling a pistol-case.

An open newspaper lay on the pedestal beside the bed. It had apparently been thrown there impatiently, and it at once occurred to Fresnay that it was in this paper that Madame de Janos must have read the news that had so greatly excited her ; so he picked it up and glanced over it, in the hope of finding the paragraph which had no doubt done all the harm. "What can it have been?" he soliloquised as he looked at the first page. "There is a dull leader, it couldn't have been that. Then the report of the sittings at the Chamber and the Senate. But no, she doesn't bother about politics. News from Tonquin—she takes no interest in that. Well, let us see the second page." Here he found a long list of carriage accidents, thefts, fires, sudden deaths, and other items of a local Parisian character, but nothing that could have the slightest connection with either Madame de Janos or her friend M. Tergowitz. However, he finally noticed that a paragraph had been cut from the last column on the second page, and this was doubtless the work of the countess. Moreover, if she had taken the trouble to do this in her haste and exasperation, it must have been in order that she might be able to show Tergowitz something that concerned either him or herself. She had evidently gone to see her lover or confederate.

"I will soon find out what the paragraph was about," thought Fresnay. "I shall only have to send Olga to the nearest newspaper shop, to purchase another copy of this same paper."

Thereupon, while waiting to solve this mystery, he began to look around him for some more significant clue. He saw that the jewellery was all in the various cases lying about, including some handsome diamond pendants, and several rings and bracelets. Why had the countess left all these

E

things at the discretion of her maid? This was another mystery which he could not solve for the time being. Finally he picked up the flat box which was lying on the bed, fully expecting to find it locked. To his very great surprise, however, he had only to lift the cover to open it, and his astonishment increased when he beheld its contents, which proved to be a pair of dark steel gauntlets which might have formed a part of the armour of a knight of mediæval times. Fresnay could hardly believe his eyes, and he was obliged to take up the gauntlets and turn them over and over in his hands before he could make up his mind that he was not mistaken.

Whence came these curious articles? The ancestors of this pretended Madame de Janos had certainly not figured among the Crusaders, and consequently these gauntlets could not be a family relic. Had she stolen them from a museum? And why had she preserved them so carefully? This also was mysterious, most mysterious.

On examining them more closely, Fresnay perceived that they were certainly of modern make. The steel was shiny, and they were lined with a soft kid that had become slightly discoloured by use, particularly at the points that corresponded with the fingers joints. This seemed to indicate that they had been worn, but by whom, and under what circumstances? Perhaps by some actor in a grand spectacular drama. But how had they come into Madame de Janos's possession? Did they belong to Tergowitz? That pretended Hungarian's life had doubtless been full of strange vicissitudes, and it was not unlikely that he had been an actor in his day.

Finally Fresnay tried the gauntlets on, and found them very comfortable. It was only necessary to press a spring to fasten them on, and once secured, they did not impede the movements of his hands in the least. On the contrary, they seemed to increase his grasping powers, to hold a sword or a sabre for example.

"They are perhaps fencing gloves of a new design," Alfred said to himself. "I have a great mind to take them and show them to my fencing master."

And then hearing Olga's step on the stairs, he slipped them into the pocket of his overcoat.

"Breakfast is served," said the maid, from the doorway, dropping a low courtsey.

"What do you think of all this?" asked Fresnay, pointing to the dresses and jewel cases.

"Oh, I told you, sir, that madame went off as though she were mad. She knows very well though that I should never touch her jewels, still I prefer not to enter the room. The breakfast will be cold if you don't come down."

Fresnay considered that he had plenty of time to question the girl about the gauntlets, so he followed her down the stairs. The table was laid in the dining-room. Upon a cloth of dazzling whiteness, there were some delicate pink shrimps and rosy radishes flanking a dish upon which some poached eggs cooked with truffles were displayed. As a substantial element, there was a dish of cold meat of various kinds; and for dessert, a basket of superb strawberries. Moreover, in a cut glass decanter there gleamed some wine of the clearest topaz hue.

"Ah, you are quick!" exclaimed Fresnay. "It would have taken my valet an hour to prepare such a breakfast."

The maid courtesied, and replied: "I truly hope that monsieur will find everything to his liking. As for the wine, it is some of the choice Sauterne that monsieur sent to madame."

"I did not expect to drink it, but as it is drawn, fill my glass, my dear," said Alfred, attacking the eggs.

Olga filled the glass, and remained standing, with one hand resting upon her hip, in the traditional pose of a stage sutler girl. To complete the resemblance, she only needed the customary little barrel secured to a strap slung over her shoulders.

"You look very pretty in that attitude," continued Fresnay, "and your poached eggs are a great success."

"Monsieur is a flatterer."

"No, upon my word! You have a very piquant way about you, really. Come, sit down, and let us have a chat," added the baron.

No very great amount of urging was required to induce Olga to take a seat at the table. Besides, she had already supped with Fresnay one night at the Café Americain. As regards the present situation, it was very evident that she no longer felt any fear of being surprised by her mistress or of losing her employment. She plainly realised that the young baron was fairly tired of Madame de Janos. Possibly she even flattered herself that she might take her mistress's place in M. de Fresnay's affections, and Alfred's compliments perhaps heightened this illusion.

"Ah, madame must have lost her head completely to act as she has done," she remarked, with a sigh. "I wonder what monsieur will do about this new escapade."

"That depends," replied Fresnay, as he helped himself to a second glass of Sauterne. "I think, however, that I shall forgive her if she confesses how wrongfully she has acted and tells me the truth about Tergowitz."

"Monsieur seems to feel a great interest in that man," remarked Olga, demurely.

"The same interest as one always feels in the achievements of a clever rascal. To tell the truth, I am curious to know who he is, and how the part he is playing is likely to end."

"If it ends badly for him, it won't end well for madame. They quarrelled last night, it is true, but up till now they had been on the best possible terms, and they have been working together in perfect harmony."

"Working together is good!" said Fresnay. "Do you mean to say that they have been leagued together trying to extort money out of idiots?"

"I should answer yes, if I did not fear to offend you, sir," was Olga's reply.

"Oh, I will cheerfully acknowledge myself to be one of the dupes, and I shall not be in the least offended if you prove to me that this amiable couple have really been amusing themselves with me. On the contrary, I shall be infinitely obliged if you will give me full information in regard to them. If you would only tell me their true story and their real names, I could not do enough to prove my gratitude." And with these words Fresnay darted a killing glance at Olga.

"Monsieur is jesting," murmured the fortune-teller, blushing with delight.

"No, I am really in earnest, upon my honour, I am! I begin to believe that these two people have some crime upon their conscience. In union there is strength; you have heard of that proverb no doubt, and perhaps you are also acquainted with the saying, that, when thieves fall out, honest folks get their dues. Well, now that these two are at loggerheads, they will very likely denounce each other, and as you may suppose, I feel no desire to be mixed up, even indirectly, in an affair that is likely to come before the Court of Assizes. You can very well understand that."

"Oh, it won't go as far as that," remarked Olga.

"Ah, ah! I see very well that you haven't told me everything you are acquainted with. Now, go on, and tell me all you do know about them. I swear that you shall not repent of it. I will make your fortune."

"If I were sure, sir, that you wouldn't tell madame how you obtained your information, I would gladly tell you all I know," said Olga whose tongue was itching to speak.

"I will not tell her, I promise you that. Come, go on. If you like, I will give you a start in business. On the night I met you at the Café Americain, you told me you were going to meet some one who was waiting for you at the Eastern Railway Station. It was a falsehood, was it not?"

"No," replied Olga, "by all I hold sacred, madame arrived by the five o'clock express."

"That is to say, she pretended to arrive then. For I met her at the Café des Ambassadeurs on the evening before."

"I knew you must have met her before, as you called at the Grand Hôtel to see her," resumed the maid. "I was greatly surprised, though, that she had invited you there, for she might have known very well that the hotel people would tell you that she had only arrived that morning."

"One can not think of everything. But come, just tell me, where did she come from."

"From Paris. M. Tergowitz had proposed to me to become her maid, and offered me good wages."

"Well, how did you become acquainted with this estimable couple?"

"I met them frequently at fairs when I was a somnambulist, and as business was bad, I accepted Tergowitz's proposal, on conditions that he wouldn't mix me up in any of his nasty affairs."

"I understand your scruples," said Alfred ironically. "However, come to the point. You met them at fairs, you say; was the countess in your line then—"

"Oh! dear, no, sir; but she performed on her side; and my place often happened to be next to theirs."

"I was right, then, when I said that the countess had been a circus-performer."

"Yes, she hadn't her equal as a tight-rope dancer a few years ago, but since she grew stout she has figured chiefly in the show at the door."

"She must have drawn a crowd with those eyes of hers. But in what capacity did the Hungarian nobleman appear? As the clown?"

"Oh, no; Amanda's husband was the clown."

"So her real name is Amanda. She did well to change it. She calls herself Stephana nowadays. That is much more aristocratic. But what was Monsieur Tergowitz's specialty?"

"He was an acrobat, sir," replied Olga, "and one of the cleverest I ever saw. He could earn a handsome living anywhere just with one feat that he calls 'head-first.' There isn't an acrobat at the Champs Elysées circus that could be compared with him. I saw that for myself only the other night."

"Head-first!" repeated Fresnay, striking his forehead as if appealing to his memory. "Wait a second. It seems to me I have heard of that fcat before. Under what name was Tergowitz in the habit of appearing at the fairs ? "

"Zig-Zag was his stage name."

"Good heavens! Zig-Zag! Do you say Zig-Zag?" cried Fresnay, springing to his feet so hastily that he overturned the basket of strawberries.

"Good heavens! what is the matter with you, sir?" exclaimed Olga, also springing up in alarm.

"Come, tell me, were not Zig-Zag and Amanda performing together, about three weeks ago, at the fair on the Place du Trône?" inquired Fresnay, eagerly.

"It is very possible, or even probable, for their employer never missed one of the fairs there. Still, I cannot swear to it, for I was not in Paris at the time," replied Olga.

"Where were you, then?"

"At Beauvais, where I did not make a penny. Some creditors seized my horse and conveyance, and I had barely enough money left me to buy a third-class ticket back to Paris. I hoped to find some way to earn a living here, and I was lucky for once, for I had not been here an hour, when I met Zig-Zag in the street—Zig-Zag arrayed like a prince. It was easy to see that he was doing well, and I didn't hesitate to speak to him, but asked him if he couldn't do something to help an old friend, and thereupon right away he proposed that I should enter Amanda's service."

"Didn't you ask him how he had made such a fortune?" inquired the young Baron de Fresnay.

"Of course I did, and he replied that he had recently inherited a fortune from an uncle. This did not surprise me much, as I had always understood that his family was a wealthy one, and that he had run off to lead a vagabond kind of life. He also told me that he had had enough of the circus business, and that he was going to make a fresh start in life. It was evident that he had plenty of money, and that he must have shared it with madame, for she had plenty of clothes and a little good jewellery."

"I know where they got the cash," muttered Fresnay. "Now give me the scoundrel's address."

"I swear to you that I do not know it. I swear it by the ashes of my mother," replied Olga earnestly.

"Where have he and Amanda been in the habit of meeting one another recently?" resumed Alfred.

"Here, as I have already told you, sir; though when madame went out, it was to see him, I am sure. But she never talked to me about her affairs, and I never ventured to follow her, as you can understand very well."

"But you will do so now, if I pay you for it, will you not?" asked Fresnay.

Olga had expected something different, and she pouted with disappointment. "I am no spy," was her rather curt reply. "I have told you this about madame, because I thought you ought to know it. But why do you want me to follow her? Do you really think then that Zig-Zag has been guilty of robbery or murder?"

Fresnay was about to reply in the affirmative, but suddenly he changed his mind. It was very evident that this woman knew little or nothing about these persons' immediate antecedents. Indeed, it was doubtful if she had even heard of the murder on the Boulevard Voltaire, and certainly her mistress had not taken her into her confidence. Thus it would be far better for him to keep what he knew to himself, for Olga, better informed in regard to what had transpired, might take her mistress's part and warn her of her danger. After all, neither of the two women were worth much; creatures of this kind willingly stand by each other and make war upon honest folks. So Fresnay decided to change his tactics.

"Come," said he, "you are a good girl and I only ask one thing of you, not to take sides against me. You will understand very well, that after all this I can't have anything further to do with the countess. However, I don't intend to make a row, we shall separate peaceably. If I went into a passion just now, it was because I had seen that fellow Zig-Zag performing at the fair, and wonderfully clever that 'head-first' feat of his was. However, it annoyed me that I should have my nose put out of joint by a mountebank, and for that reason I fired up."

"You have met Monsieur Tergowitz several times, you say," resumed Olga after a short pause. "But in that case how does it happen, then, that you failed to notice that he and Zig-Zag were one and the same person?"

"I had only seen Zig-Zag with a mask over his face," replied the Baron de Fresnay.

"That is true. I forgot that he always appeared before the public masked," muttered Olga. "But you must have seen Amanda, too."

"Yes," said Alfred, "and now I think of it, I don't understand why I failed to recognise her when I met her in the guise of a countess. It is true that she had already dyed her hair, and that changes her greatly, of course."

"Yes, so greatly, that I, myself, scarcely recognised her when I met her again," replied the maid. "But I hope that when she returns home, you won't tell her to her face all that I have told you about her and her friend Tergowitz."

"I shall take very good care not to do that, for she would tear my eyes out, and I don't want a scene. There shall be an amiable parting, that's all. I sha'n't venture on any reproaches, nor shall I ask her any embarrassing questions. But she is not here yet, and I should like to do proper justice to this breakfast prepared by your white hands—they are very white—so do me the favour to resume your seat and keep me company. I can not bear to eat alone."

Olga, nothing loath, reseated herself, and proceeded to re-fill the glass of the baron, who said: "I dislike drinking alone even more, so pour yourself out some Sauterne, my dear, and let us chink glasses."

"No, no," simpered the fortune-teller. "I am only a poor servant-girl."

"That makes no difference. You'll soon have a rise in the world, I promise you. Come, no ceremony. Hold your glass, I'll fill it myself."

Olga obeyed, and Fresnay poured her out some wine, thinking to himself: "You fancy you hold me, you hussy, do you! But you are greatly mistaken, it's I who hold your mistress. To think that I shall be the captor of old Monistrol's murderer, and that if I like I shall be able to summon Mademoiselle Camille to give me the promised reward—her fortune and her hand."

The maid now leant towards Alfred to chink her glass against his, but at this very moment a sharp voice called out: "You are enjoying yourselves, I see. It is quite evident that you were not expecting me!"

This voice, which they both recognised, rang in poor Olga's ear like the trump of doom. She rose up and darted to the end of the room so as to be out of the reach of her mistress's anger. However, Fresnay was neither alarmed nor surprised. He had almost expected this theatrical interruption, and was glad it had taken place. So he remained quietly in his seat and drained his glass to the very last drop.

The countess dropped the door curtains, and slowly advanced to the table, surveying Alfred with eyes that positively blazed with anger.

"Will you be kind enough to inform me what gives you the right to make yourself so much at home here!" she asked

"But it seems to me that I am at home, at least to some extent," replied Fresnay, smiling.

"I know that this house belongs to you, but I am occupying it, and I forbid you to set foot in it again as long as I remain here. As for you, hussy," added Madame de Janos, turning to Olga, "you are dismissed. Leave the house immediately!"

"Madame will be sorry for this," replied the fortune-teller, manœuvring all the while to reach the door.

"No threats, if you please! Behave yourself, and don't let me hear of you again, or I will save you the necessity of seeking lodgings elsewhere, by sending you to the penitentiary. You will be properly cared for there."

"It would seem that Mademoiselle Olga hasn't a clear conscience herself," thought Fresnay. "Can it be that she, too, was implicated in old Monistrol's murder? That would really be strange. But no—it isn't possible."

"Very well. I am going off," rejoined Olga, but in a much less insolent tone.

She glanced at the baron, in the hope that he would interfere, and take her part, but Fresnay said not a word, so Olga departed, secretly vowing vengeance upon both of them.

"It is our turn now, sir," said Madame de Janos, sternly.

"Why these tragic airs, my dear?" asked Fresnay, coolly. "A scene about poached eggs is simply ridiculous, for I don't suppose jealousy can be the cause, as I certainly must have better taste than to prefer your maid to yourself. However, in your absence, I thought it wouldn't do any harm to order breakfast, as I was dying of hunger."

"You did not come here to get your breakfast; you came to play the spy."

"Oh! come my dear, don't accuse me of that," replied the baron. "I came to speak to you about that saddle horse, you know. I have just left Tattersalls!"

"I don't care either for your horse or for you."

"Good heavens, you surely don't mean to put a stop to our friendship?"

"I am about to leave France, and shall never set eyes on you again, thank Heaven!"

"Oh! that is too dreadful. You are leaving France for Hungary, I suppose?"

"Probably."

"In company with your old friend, Monsieur Tergowitz?" resumed Fresnay.

"What business is that of yours, pray?" snappishly inquired the countess, drawing herself up with a dignified air.

"None whatever. Only it seems to me that I saw him yesterday at my club."

"You know him, then?"

"Yes, indeed. Why, I saw him with you at the Café des Ambassadeurs, you remember, and I met him on the staircase of the Grand Hôtel on the day I first called upon you. Besides, the Pole who brought him to our club registered him under the name of Tergowitz, which is by no means a common patronymic, so there couldn't be any mistake. I can even tell you some news that will doubtless prove of a very pleasing nature, as you are such a very particular friend of his. He has just won a very large sum of money at play."

"What do you call a large sum?"

"Oh, everything is comparative, fifteen or twenty, or perhaps even thirty thousand francs. I didn't count what he had about him, so I can not say exactly what the amount was; I am not on speaking terms with him you know, and I don't suppose that he even knows me by sight."

"Do you think he will revisit the club?"

"I really can not say. Why do you ask the question?"

"Because I am looking for him."

"You are looking for him? Don't you know where he lives, then?"

"Yes. I went to his place this morning, but I could not find him, nor could any one tell me when he would return; and yet I must see him to-day."

"To decide with him upon the hour of departure? I can understand that," remarked the baron. "Shall I send him to you if I happen to meet him?"

The countess started. She perceived at last that Fresnay was ridiculing her. Anger had blinded her at first, but her eyes were now opened, and she began to fear that Olga had betrayed the secret of her connection with the pretended Hungarian gentleman. All further subterfuges would therefore prove unavailing.

"Come," resumed the baron, "it's no use quarrelling. We both realise that we have seen enough of one another, but that is no reason why we shouldn't part good friends. In fact I am quite at your disposal if I can possibly assist you in any way."

"Are you speaking seriously?"

"Quite seriously, I assure you. Just try me and you won't feel any doubt on the matter."

"Then this is what I have to ask of you," replied the countess. "Just never to see that hussy Olga again. I presume that she has her box ready; and if she hasn't already taken herself off, I shall turn her out of the place without any ceremony."

"You will do quite right."

"Well, I see that you are a gentleman," resumed the countess, "and before we part for good, I am going to ask one last favour of you."

"It is granted, whatever it may be," replied the Baron de Fresnay, graciously.

"Oh, I shall not take too great an advantage of your kindness," replied the countess. "It is simply a request that you will accompany me—"

"Where? Not to Hungary surely?"

"Not nearly so far. I only wish you to come with me to witness an execution, right here in Paris."

"Very good, I am willing," replied Fresnay who thought he could divine the truth.

"All right, then; come, I have a cab at the door. Give me time to dismiss that hussy Olga, and we will start."

XI.

AFTER the explosion that saved his life, poor little Georget passed several days and nights that were almost as wretched as those spent in the cellar of the ruined house.

He had been dragged before a commissary of police, and that functionary had subjected him to a searching examination. A man charged with a capital offence could not have been treated more harshly ; and the youngster was only guilty of having been blown up in the air. However, he was strongly suspected by the officials of being in the employ of the gang of frauders that had made the cellar of the deserted dwelling their store-place, and the magistrate tried to compel him to denounce them.

But Georget could not do that as he did not know them, and he defended himself, as well as he could, by telling pretty nearly the truth. He declared that while in pursuit of a stray dog, his father and himself had lost their way on the plain of Saint-Denis, and, night coming on, they had taken refuge in a ruined house, where they had fallen through an open trap-door into a very deep cellar from which they were unable to escape. There they had remained at least seven days and nights among piles of hams and casks of brandy, to which his father had accidentally set fire.

After listening to this not altogether unplausible explanation, the commissary visited the scene of the catastrophe in company with Georget. The gendarmes were already there, and the cellar had been partially explored by several workmen engaged for the purpose. Of course all the debris could not be cleared away in so short a space of time ; however the charred remains of Courapied were discovered. The wall that had divided the cellar had been injured by the explosion, but as it was still standing, a careful examination showed that several large stones in the middle of it had been cleverly arranged to turn upon themselves when pressure was applied to a certain spot. This then was the secret outlet to the vault—the "open sesame" which both the father and the son had failed to discover, and when it was shown to Georget he could not help shedding tears at the thought that, better informed, they might both have made their escape in safety.

His later story did not correspond in all respects with what he had said to the by-standers immediately after the catastrophe, but the commissary did not attach much importance to any slight discrepancies ; nor did he think for an instant of accusing the lad of having set fire to the casks of brandy in the hope of getting rid of his father.

He insisted, however, upon knowing the name, residence, and profession of the deceased ; but Georget, fearful lest he might implicate Mademoiselle Monistrol, confined himself to saying that his father was so poor he had no home, and that most of the time they had roved about, earning their bread as best they could. He made no further mention of their profession as acrobats, fearing that this might bring the crime on the Boulevard Voltaire to the fore once more.

Now vagrancy is not a very grave offence, and Georget would probably have been released forthwith, had it not been for the clothing he wore. It will be remembered that he was attired as a restaurant page and the costume had been greatly injured by his sojourn in the vault, not to speak of the damage caused by the explosion, while he was ascending the shaft. His cap had been blown away and his jacket and trousers were both badly torn. However, the commissary suspected him of having stolen this outfit, and all the youngster's protestations to the contrary were powerless to convince the official who held his fate in his hand. So the commissary, instead of setting him at liberty, sent him to the Dépôt until further information could be obtained respecting him.

Georget made no protest. He knew that they would become tired of keeping him, sooner or later, and that he would then be free again. The worst was being shut up in companionship with all sorts of rascals. However, he was patient, and contrived to avoid associating with the loafers and pick-pockets among whom he now found himself. The brave lad really grieved over but one thing : that he was not able to attend the funeral of his father, who had been duly buried. He vowed vengeance on Zig-Zag and Amanda, who had made him an orphan ; and he secretly resolved to resume the hunt that had resulted so disastrously, to track them to their hiding-place, and finally to deliver them up to justice, and thus avenge both his own father and Camille's at one and the same time. What Courapied had failed to effect, he, Georget, would accomplish. He wasn't a drunkard, and he did not know what discouragement meant; so that he seemed bound to succeed.

Pending his release from the Dépôt, which might happen at any time, he carefully prepared his plan of action. He felt sure that Zig-Zag and his companion were still in Paris, and that it was not at fairs he must look for them, but in places of fashionable amusement. He said to himself : "I will earn my living by calling carriages, and opening doors for theatre-goers. It will take time, but I shall find them all right sooner or later."

Such were his plans, when one morning, after forty-eight hours' detention, which had seemed terribly long, one of the assistant jailers called him. The boy's heart throbbed loud and fast at first; for, knowing nothing about the customs of the prison, he fancied for a minute or two that he was about to be cast in a gloomy dungeon, to perish there.

He did not care to question the official, and was most agreeably surprised when the man opened a massive door and pushed him out, saying as he did so : "Clear off, you young scamp, and see that you don't get back here again."

He found himself in the yard near the Sainte Chapelle, and at the first glance, seeing no place of egress, he began to doubt whether he was really at liberty or not. However, he mechanically walked across the yard, and chance led him at last to a passage conducting to the Quai des Orfèvres. So he was free again ! He was in the open air, and he experienced keen delight in gazing at the blue sky, which he had only espied through the prison bars for the last forty-eight hours, besides having it quite shut out from his view whilst in the dungeon vault of the Plain of St. Denis. Leaning on the parapet of the quay, he tried to collect himself and decide what he should first do. Freedom is not everything. One must have food, and he was penniless, and he knew that no one would trust him for a single copper's worth. At his age emotion does not interfere with appetite, and he was hungry, almost as hungry as he had been that day in the vault, when he had discovered the American hams. There, at least, he had been fed, badly, it is true, but at all events gratis, whereas in Paris one must pay for one's sustenance.

He certainly knew a place where he might obtain an excellent meal, besides obtaining accommodation for the night. In fact, he had only to present himself at Mademoiselle Monistrol's abode to be received with open arms, but he did not wish to be seen entering the house on the Boulevard Voltaire ; for, though he was as brave as a lion, he was also as prudent as a serpent, and he greatly feared that he would be followed by some member of the detective force.

He had taken it into his head that he might have been released by the officers of the prison in order that they might find out where he would go on leaving the Dépôt, for he had read several of Gaboriau's novels, and had learned through them that the police sometimes resort to this expedient when they have failed to establish the identity of a recalcitrant prisoner. He forgot that novelists do not always pride themselves on a strict adherence to the truth ; besides, he greatly exaggerated his own importance.

At all events he resolved not to go straight to Mademoiselle Monistrol's residence, but to approach it by the most roundabout way and to examine the outside of the house carefully before venturing in. After satisfying himself that no suspicious character was dogging his steps along the quay, he walked leisurely towards the Ile Saint-Louis, which he traversed from end to end ; and then crossed to the right bank of the river by the Pont Henri IV.

Before reaching the Place de la Bastille, he turned more than once to see if any one was following him, and, reassured at last on this point, he had about made up his mind to approach the Boulevard Voltaire by the Rue de la Roquette, when, on passing a station from which several lines of omnibuses started, he saw a woman whom he fancied he knew, alighting from one of the vehicles.

Her face seemed familiar to him, but he could not exactly recollect where he had met her, for she was handsomely dressed, and Georget's acquaintance with richly clad ladies was extremely limited. She, also, had paused on seeing him, and now stood watching him with strange intentness. On her side, she was evidently asking herself where she had seen him before.

At last she approached him and asked in a low tone: "Aren't you Georget, Courapied's son ? "

"Yes, madame," replied the lad, though not very promptly, for he wondered who this person could be. "But I don't know who you are."

"All the same, you have climbed into my waggon often enough, and no longer ago, too, than last year, at the Saint-Cloud Fair, don't you remember?"

"Oh, I know you now, madame," exclaimed the youngster. "It was you who told fortunes and had such a big horn."

"Exactly, but I'm not following that business now."

"That is very evident. You have retired with a fortune, I judge," replied Georget, gazing admiringly at Olga's attire.

"I can hardly say as much for you, my lad. You look dreadfully seedy. Where did you get that rig-out? Are you a page boy now ? " asked the fortune-teller.

"No, but I am trying to earn my own living."

"Isn't your father with you ? "

"My father is dead ! "

"Is it possible!" exclaimed the fortune teller, raising her hands in astonishment. "Why, the last time I saw him he looked as hale and hearty as could be. He was always as gay as a lark, poor Courapied. He drank too much, though, at times, and I suppose it was liquor that carried him off at last."

"No, madame, he was killed."

"What's that you tell me! Who could have killed him?"

"Zig-Zag."

"Nonsense! In that case Zig-Zag would have been arrested, and I saw him only yesterday. And your step-mother, what has become of her?" added the fortune-teller, anxious to ascertain how far Georget's information went.

"Amanda? Oh! she ran away with Zig-Zag, and she helped him to kill papa. If you know where they are, pray tell me. I am looking for them."

"What for?"

"In order to have them both sent to the guillotine," replied the youngster, savagely.

"Just hear the boy! But how, in the name of fortune, did they kill Courapied?"

"Why, father was trying to find them. He wanted to get his wife back. They enticed him into a house near the Route de la Révolte. I was with him at the time. We fell into a cellar through a trap-door that they had left open expressly for us. They afterwards shut us up in this cellar, and we should have starved, if there had not been lots of hams and casks of brandy. The brandy caught fire, however, and father was burned to death. What I am telling you is quite true. It was in all the papers." Georget had heard this from a fellow prisoner during his detention at the Prefecture Dépôt.

Olga, who had been strongly inclined to doubt the lad's statements at first, was struck by this last assertion, for she recollected that that very day, her mistress, the pretended Countess de Janos, had rushed out of the house like a madwoman after a hasty glance at her morning paper. She, Olga, had just left the house in the Rue Mozart, vowing vengeance upon her former mistress, so that these disclosures were most gratifying to her. She considered her meeting with Georget, who had such serious reasons to complain of Amanda, to be exceedingly well-timed; and she immediately determined to turn the opportunity to good account.

"I begin to think you are telling the truth," she exclaimed. "I have no love for the good-for-nothing creatures, so I shouldn't be sorry to see them come to grief. But you are very much mistaken, my boy, if you think that what you have just told me will cost them their heads. Persons are not guillotined for shutting a man and a boy up in a cellar. They would get only six-months' imprisonment, at the very longest."

Olga was well informed on legal matters, having been "in trouble" on various previous occasions.

"But they have done something much worse," promptly replied Georget, forgetting for the moment that this disclosure might lead him further than he wished to go.

"What did they do, then?" asked the fortune-teller, with great eagerness. "Did they steal the manager's money before they ran away?"

"Oh," replied Georget, with alacrity. "The manager hadn't any money. The concern is all broken up, and father and I didn't get as much as a penny. We found ourselves in the streets."

"Then where, in the name of fortune, did they get the money they are living on now? For I know very well that they are rolling in gold."

"From a man that Zig-Zag murdered."

"Nonsense!"

"It is the truth," replied the youngster, gravely. "That affair, too, was in the papers.'

"I very seldom read them. When did it occur?" asked Olga, all aglow with curiosity.

"About three weeks ago."

"I was not here then. I was at Beauvais, where business was so dreadfully bad that I came to Paris almost without a penny. But are you sure that Zig-Zag and Amanda were guilty of this crime?"

"Well, I am not sure that Amanda had any hand in it," said Georget, "but she must have profited by it, as she ran away with Zig-Zag just afterwards."

"Yes, that is as plain as daylight," said the maid, as she reflected; and after a short pause, she resumed: "Well, you are anxious to find them, you say?"

"Oh, yes, yes!"

"In order to denounce them?"

"Certainly," replied Georget, with remarkable promptitude. "I would show them no mercy, if I could only lay my hands on them. They have done me no end of harm, not to speak of the people who were kind to me."

"Yes, that hussy Amanda did treat you shamefully; there is no doubt about it. And if it were her fault that your poor father was roasted alive, I can understand that you have a grudge against her. But how will you manage to set hands on her?"

"Oh! you need only tell me where she is."

"Well, to tell you that I must know it myself. And, besides, just let me tell you she's not easy to deal with, nor Zig-Zag either. They are neither of them worth a curse, I know that, having associated with them, worse luck—and yet I shouldn't like them to learn that I betrayed them."

"Oh! you may be sure that I won't mention you," said Georget, promptly.

"Is that true?"

"Quite true. I'll swear it."

"Then come with me."

"Are you going to take me where they are?"

"Listen to me," answered Olga, "I saw Amanda this morning—only an hour ago, in fact. She did not tell me where she was going, for she is a sharp one, and distrusts everybody; but, just as I left her, she stepped into a cab, and I heard the address she gave the driver. I even noticed the number of the vehicle, and if we should find it in front of a certain door, it will be proof positive that she is in the house."

"Let us be off then," said Georget, eagerly.

"All right; but I warn you that I sha'n't go in. I don't want to see her."

"Very well; I shall go in by myself."

"You can do as you please, of course," said the fortune-teller, "but I shall go about my business, and you will have it out with her alone."

"That suits me, right enough," rejoined Georget. "Is it far from here?"

"Not very far. We shall be there in twenty minutes or so. But I would rather you did not walk along beside me. We might meet Zig-Zag, you know."

This remark proved that Olga was a prudent woman. Having some little matters on her conscience, she did not at all care to meet the ex-acrobat, who would now have readily denounced her had occasion offered.

"I will follow you at a little distance," said Georget.

"Let us start, then. Try not to lose sight of me."

"There is no danger of that," was the youngster's response. "I have sharp eyes and good legs."

Olga took up the line of march, and Georget followed her some fifteen steps in the rear. The maid was delighted. She had the best of reasons for keeping in the background as much as possible, for she feared fatal reprisals, but chance had furnished her with an unexpected opportunity to avenge her wrongs upon the spurious Madame de Janos and the so-called Tergowitz without compromising herself in the least.

Georget, on his side, was equally jubilant, for he flattered himself that his father's murderer was already in his power, and as he would hardly have known how to find him unassisted, he congratulated himself most heartily upon his meeting with Olga. He was not a little surprised to see the fortune-teller turn into the Rue de la Roquette as if she had had the same intention as himself of going to Mademoiselle Monistrol's house, and his astonishment increased as he saw her, when half-way up this dingy narrow thoroughfare, which leads to the place of execution, turn to the right, into the spacious bustling Boulevard Voltaire.

Where could she be going? And how had that odious Amanda summoned up the requisite assurance to repair to the very neighbourhood where her lover had committed such a terrible crime?

However, Olga hastened on, and Georget soon caught sight of the little house in which he had dined with his father before starting out upon their unfortunate expedition. At all events, thought he, he might take a peep in as he passed by, and then decide as to whether he should return there after finding out Amanda's retreat and leaving Olga.

He was walking on, following the curb of the broad shady footway, and carrying his head erect with his eyes all attention so as not to lose sight of the fortune-teller, when he suddenly stumbled over something that was lying right in his path. It proved to be the body of a dead dog, and Georget, on glancing at it, uttered such a sharp cry that Olga turned and retraced her steps, startled by the youngster's signs of agitation and terror.

"What is the matter?" she asked, gazing at the little fellow in astonishment.

"It is Vigoureux, Zig-Zag's dog. You must remember him," faltered the lad, who looked extremely perplexed.

"Why, yes, you are right," said Olga, stooping to examine the dog's bloody carcase. "It is that hateful beast that was always snapping at everybody. One day at Beaugency fair he tore a brand-new dress in pieces for me with those fangs of his. Thank heaven! he can't bite any one now."

"He has been shot," murmured Georget. "It certainly wasn't Zig-Zag who did that. He thought too much of his dog. But how did the brute come here? That's what I can't understand."

"How do I know?" returned Olga. "His master used to perform on the Place du Trône. Vigoureux was looking for him, perhaps, and some passer-by shot him. Besides, look at the foam round about his mouth. He must have gone mad. You surely don't pity such an animal."

"No, but I'm afraid Zig-Zag cannot be far off."

"Bah! he won't eat you if he is. If he had you in a house, he might make things lively for you, but he won't dare to molest you in the street. Still I can't say that I'm particularly anxious to meet him. Leave that carcase and follow me as far as that cab you see standing over there. It looks very much like the one I saw Amanda get into."

"What! over there in front of that fence?" asked Georget in amazement.

"Yes," replied the maid. "Is there anything very astonishing about that? You seem to have lost your wits."

"Why it is the very house where Zig-Zag strangled the man he robbed."

"Nonsense! You must be mistaken!"

"Oh! I'm not mistaken," retorted Georget, shaking his head. "I know the house; I went there once with my father."

"And is the house occupied now?" asked the maid, whose curiosity was again aroused.

"Yes. The daughter of the man that Zig-Zag killed, still lives there. At least, unless she has left since I saw her last, ten or eleven days ago."

"Did she live alone?"

"No, she had an old servant with her."

"And Amanda has gone to pay her a visit? How strange!" said the fortune-teller, beginning to reflect, and then as she remembered how jealous the spurious Countess de Janos had been of her so-called compatriot, Tergowitz, the truth began to dawn upon her mind.

"Who knows but what she intends to kill the young lady, too," murmured Georget, shuddering at the thought that his benefactress might be in mortal peril.

"You need have no fears of that, child," retorted the fortune-teller. "Amanda has some one with her—a regular gentleman, not a scoundrel like Zig-Zag. But the deuce take me if I can imagine what induced her to bring him here. This matter is worth looking into, really; so wait here for a moment while I go and take a glance at the cab."

Georget, now greatly excited, and trembling for Camille's sake, despite all that Olga had told him, watched the maid as she approached the vehicle and glanced at the number painted upon its lamps.

"It is the very same cab," she remarked, when she had returned to the lad's side. "That hussy Amanda is in the house, undoubtedly, so that if you miss her, it will be entirely your own fault."

"No, it won't, for she may leave in the cab, and in that case, I sha'n't be able to follow her on foot," replied the sagacious little fellow.

"That's all very pretty reasoning, but you need not wait for her to come out. The gate of the enclosure isn't locked. Walk straight in upon her. I should like to see the hussy's face when she catches sight of you. She dresses like a fine lady, now in silk and satin, and she sports all sorts of jewellery, and she has dyed her hair red as well, still you will recognize her all the same. Call her by her right name, and ask her when she last heard from Zig-Zag—just for fun. You'll get the best of her—never fear. And you needn't be at all afraid of the gentleman who is with her. He will take your part, I assure you."

"Oh! I'm not afraid of him,' replied Georget, who had listened attentively to these instructions. "I'm not afraid of anything, except of troubling the person who lives there."

"What, the daughter of the man that Zig-Zag killed? Why, on the contrary, she will thank you, I'll be bound, for she must be as anxious to avenge her father as you are to avenge yours. Besides, I'm almost sure that Amanda is plotting some mischief against her. At all events, it's your own concern, and I must leave you to manage the affair as best you can. I have put you on the right track, and you have only to bag your game. And now good-bye, I am going off, and I trust you won't forget your

promise not to mention my name, whatever the result may be. I shall
leave Paris immediately, in order to be out of reach in case of any scandal.
I shall come back, perhaps some day when both Zig-Zag and Amanda are
safe in jail, but remember, if you ever meet me, that you have never seen
or heard of me before. Do you understand? And now by-bye, and good
luck to you."

With this rather unceremonious leave-taking, the prudent Olga crossed
the boulevard, and walked rapidly towards the Place du Trône. She had
fired the train, and did not care to stay and witness the explosion which
she felt might prove fatal to herself. She was pretty certain however,
that she would speedily learn the upshot of the affair.

She certainly left poor Georget in a very embarrassing position. Great
as was the lad's desire to unmask Amanda, and capture Zig-Zag, he
nevertheless hesitated to intrude upon Mademoiselle Monistrol without
giving her some warning. He did not know what was her present position
in reference to this affair; and besides, he feared disturbing her repose,
and causing her undesirable emotion, by creating a scene with Amanda, in
her presence. Moreover, what should he say in the presence of the strange
gentleman, who was escorting Amanda, and who might be an enemy of
Mademoiselle Monistrol's, despite what Olga had said to the contrary.
However, it was necessary to come to a decision, and Georget at first resolved to try and effect a quiet entrance into the enclosure. Gliding past
the fence, he perceived that the cab-driver was fast asleep on his box,
whereupon he slipped into the garden, without even daring to raise his
eyes to the window of the sitting-room, where Mademoiselle Monistrol
spent most of her time when at home. Moreover, he especially feared
being seen by Brigitte, who would be likely to receive him ungraciously.

Fortunately, the servant did not make her appearance, and conveniently
enough, Georget's eyes happened to fall upon a tiny out-house in which M.
Monistrol had been wont to keep his hoe, rake, watering-pots, and other
gardening implements. Zig-Zag had, perhaps, hidden there on the night of
the murder; at all events, Georget now slipped inside, and crouched down
behind a door which he would only need to push open to appear upon the
scene. From this convenient corner, through the badly joined planks, he
could plainly see anyone who entered or left the house, and he decided not
to let Amanda make off, but to bar the way as soon as she approached.
Motionless and all but holding his breath, he anxiously awaited the proper
moment to appear.

XII.

AFTER M. George de Menestreau's departure in search of news respecting
the explosion at the ruined house, Camille relapsed into a most despondent
mood. Life again seemed to have lost all charm for her, and the future
appeared even more desolate and gloomy than on the day immediately
following her unfortunate father's death.

Since that terrible catastrophe, everything appeared to have conspired
against her. The murderer—the terrible Zig-Zag, the man with the monstrous hands—was still at large. If the papers could be believed, one of
those who had tried to assist her in capturing him, had met with a most
tragical fate, and Georget, poor little fellow, was in prison. All her former
friends had deserted her. The Gémozacs were now, to all appearance,

hopelessly estranged from her: the mother would have nothing more to do with her, since she had retired in high dudgeon after the scene in the enclosure; the father also had left her, deeply offended by her engagement to M. de Menestreau, and his return seemed very doubtful, whilst the son, her disconsolate lover, whose pride had necessarily been deeply wounded by the preference she had shown for George, seemed about to yield his place to a rival. Even Brigitte did not hesitate to express her disapproval of her young lady's choice, and flatly refused to accompany her to England.

To compensate for this widespread defection, Camille had George de Menestreau's devotion—that is to say, the devotion of a man whom she scarcely knew, and with whom she had fallen in love much after the fashion of a school girl, who knows literally nothing of life.

She had fallen in love with him in a moment of chivalric exaltation, and she persisted in regarding this love as really serious, and in attaching undue importance to her fancy; still, she was beginning to vaguely realize that she was, perhaps, doing wrong to unite her destiny irretrievably with that of a handsome young man, whose principal claim upon her favour consisted in having put two scoundrels to flight.

However, despite these promptings of her heart, she persisted in her determination, and was ready to keep her imprudent promise to join George de Menestreau in England and marry him there. Her sole condition, and that was hardly worthy of the name, had been that he should bring her some news of Georget, or rather of the victims of the explosion on the plain of St. Denis.

She was not obliged to wait long for this. In less than two hours after shooting Vigoureux, M. de Menestreau returned to the Boulevard Voltaire, and found Camille alone in the little sitting-room where her father had met with a violent death at the hands of a murderer. He came in unannounced; for Brigitte, after a scene with Mademoiselle Monistrol, had taken up her basket and gone off to buy the dinner.

Camille received him with less warmth than usual, for she felt strangely depressed in spirits. She at once inquired after Courapied and his son.

"It seems that one can place very little reliance upon newspaper reports in this case, as in many others," M. de Menestreau remarked, rather carelessly. "An accident, similar to the one described, certainly did take place on the plain of Saint-Denis; but the victims were two poor scamps, a man and a boy, both of them tatterdemalions, who were sleeping there for want of a better refuge, and who were in no way connected with the parties in whom you take such an interest. It is quite certain that we were deceived by a mere coincidence. These two were surprised there by the explosion, but, in proof of how mistaken you were, they were both identified before they were buried. Their name was Dubois—father and son—and they were rag-pickers by profession."

"So the boy is dead, too?" murmured Camille, in a tone of profound grief.

"He survived the accident a few hours," replied George, "but his injuries were so serious that he did not live the day out. He was buried this morning. I learned all these particulars from the commissary of police who drew up the report on the affair."

"Dead! Both of them dead for me!" sadly repeated the young girl, her eyes filling with tears, and she sank down upon the sofa near her.

"What! Do you still believe that they were so devoted to your interests? How can I convince you that the scamps you are so strangely interested in have rejoined their accomplice, Zig-Zag? Remember that they were no longer in the cellar on the day of our expedition to the plain of Saint-Denis. I feel quite certain in my own mind that they had taken themselves off with your father's murderer, and are now leading a gay life on their share of the plunder."

"Do not try to convince me that they betrayed me. If my faith in them is only a delusion, do not take it from me. It would grieve me deeply to lose it," replied Camille, who was now in a most dejected state.

"Heaven preserve me from wounding your feelings, mademoiselle!" exclaimed George on hearing this. "I will never speak of them again. But permit me to allude to myself, as I have only a few moments more to spend with you. As I told you before I left just now, I hoped to be able to defer my departure until to-morrow. But I have just received a telegram from London which makes it absolutely necessary for me to leave this evening,—it is almost a question of life or death for my friend—and— shall I confess it?—I have no hope of ever seeing you again."

"No hope of seeing me again—what! don't you mean to return, George?"

"Most certainly I do—but shall I then find you unchanged—will you receive me—will you be mine?"

"How can you ask me that? Have I not pledged you my word?" retorted Camille warmly.

"Yes, mademoiselle; and I do not doubt your intention of keeping it. But what will happen after my departure? You will be surrounded by persons who hate me from low envious motives, and who will not fail to traduce me, I am sure of it."

"To what persons do you refer?"

"First and foremost to Monsieur Gémozac," was George's answer. "He wants to keep you for his son, on account of your fortune. Oh! you shake your head, but I feel certain of it, and what will prevent him from telling you that he has received the worst possible reports concerning me. He will be the better able to do so as I shall not be here to defend myself, and—"

"But Monsieur Gémozac is an honourable man, and he is utterly incapable of misrepresentation or falsehood, I am sure," replied Camille. "I informed him in your presence of my intention to marry you. I have solemnly promised to be your wife. What more can you exact?"

"Nothing; I have no right to exact anything whatever. But I entreat you to leave Paris with me."

"You know perfectly well that it is an impossibility," replied Camille firmly.

"Why should it be impossible? You need not consider Monsieur Gémozac's wishes, as you are in possession of the deed of partnership that insures your independence."

Camille started with surprise. This commingling of impassioned protestations of love and questions of a financial import struck her most unpleasantly. Was this suitor really more in love with her money than with herself, as Brigette had affirmed to be the case? M. de Menestreau perceived the frown which rested for a moment on the young girl's brow, and he realised that it was time to have recourse to his strongest means of persuasion.

"Come with me. I beseech you on my knees," he pleaded, falling at Camille's feet with a grace that the greatest of actors might well have envied.

But is not that simile a faulty one? Was not George sincere? His tones of voice, his attitude, his gesture, all bespoke the truest, warmest passion.

Mademoiselle Monistrol, surprised and frightened, drew back, but he had time to seize hold of her hands, which he began to cover with burning kisses.

"Let me go," she cried, trying to release her hands.

But George held them firmly, and all at once springing to his feet, he passed his arm round Camille's waist, and so great, perhaps, was the impulse of his passion that he drew her to his heart in spite of her frantic efforts to free herself. At the same moment, however, a hand was laid upon M. de Menestreau's shoulder, and a voice cried out: "Turn your face to the audience, you scoundrel!"

George's grasp promptly relaxed, and he turned, furious with rage, while Camille sunk, half fainting, back upon the sofa. She had caught a glimpse of a woman's face, and she thought she must be dreaming.

But George had already recognised the intruder, and—his handsome features distorted by an expression of fiendish frenzy—he sprung upon her, saying with an oath: "So you have betrayed me! Ah, well, you shall die. I'll wring your neck for you!"

"Not here, at all events, Monsieur Tergowitz," quietly replied the Baron de Fresnay, suddenly emerging from the dining-room, where he had been hiding behind the door curtains which once before had screened M. Monistrol's murderer.

"Madame de Janos told me you were here," resumed the baron, with astonishing composure, "and insisted upon my acting as her escort. She feels the need of an explanation with you."

The scene now presented would have furnished an admirable study for an artist. M. de Menestreau and the feminine intruder darting glances of hate at one another; Camille in utter dismay, and M. de Fresnay as if he were chatting with some friends at the club fireside.

However, promptly advancing, hat in hand, towards Camille, who lacked the power either to move or speak, the baron gently said: "Pray excuse this most unceremonious intrusion into your home, mademoiselle. I flatter myself, however, that you will thank me by-and-by, for having presented myself here without your permission. Besides, I have already had the honour of meeting you under circumstances which I am sure you have not forgotten. I was with my most intimate friend, Julien Gémozac, on a certain eventful evening, you recollect."

Camille made no reply, nor did she move. She as yet failed to understand the full import of Alfred's words. However, that chivalrous champion of beauty in distress, the handsome, amorous George de Menestreau turned as pale as death.

"I will now give Madame de Janos a chance to speak," Fresnay continued, turning to Camille's lover. "You know her very well, it seems, sir, and she must think a great deal of you, as she has come here in search of you."

"Enough, sir!" replied M. de Menestreau, haughtily. "Stand aside, and let me pass. I don't know you any more than I know the woman who has come here with you."

However, Fresnay did not evince the slightest intention of obeying this peremptory order, and as for the spurious Madame de Janos, shaking her clenched fist at the speaker, she cried vehemently: "You dare to deny me, you scoundrel! Tell me to my face that you have not been my lover, I defy you to do it."

"You shall answer to me for this scene, sir," said George de Mcnestreau, who was white with rage, as he turned to the Baron de Fresnay. "You are the sole cause of it, and—"

"Silence, you scoundrel!" cried the spurious countess, stepping forward. "A gentleman does not fight with a villain like you. It is not by the hand of a baron that you will meet your death. Oh, you need not scowl at me! I know what it may cost me to denounce you, but that makes no difference to me. The game is played, and however fine a hand you may have held, you were greatly mistaken if you imagined you would win. You deserved to lose, and you have lost. What! you think of deserting me just when it becomes in your power to marry me, for I have been a widow since yesterday, let me tell you. Ah! well, you shall perish on the guillotine, you thief, you murderer! Yes, murderer, that's the long and short of it!"

"What do you say?" cried Fresnay, in pretended astonishment. He knew very well what to think on the subject, and had been in momentary expectation of this outburst.

"You don't know all," continued Madame de Janos, passionately. "You think him only an adventurer, but I—I will tell you what he is. He began by robbing his poor father, who died of grief and mortification. Yes, he brought his father's white hairs in sorrow to the grave. And then he became a gambler—a sharper—and after cheating at cards, again and again, and living by his wits as best he could, he became an acrobat, and was only too glad to join our strolling company in order to escape from the gendarmes, who were in pursuit of him for trying to rob a farmhouse. Oh! I remember very well how he stepped out of a wood on the roadside and joined us. And then he began making eyes at me, and I was fool enough to fall in love with him—worse luck too! I had much better have hanged myself, for I shouldn't have had to end my days in the penitentiary as I shall now— And if that were all he had done! But the rest, can't you guess it? If you and your friend Gémozac hadn't been so blind, Zig-Zag would have been in prison a fortnight ago."

"Zig-Zag!" repeated Mademoiselle Monistrol, turning inquiringly to George de Menestreau.

But the latter, by a great effort, had managed to regain a semblance of composure, while Amanda was shouting out her narrative, and with a scornful shrug of the shoulders he now replied: "That woman is raving mad!"

"Villain!" shrieked the pretended countess, who was now nearly frantic with rage, "we will see if I am mad! Look at me, mademoiselle. You do not recognise me, because I have dyed my hair, but you have seen me before. You saw me on the evening your father was killed—you saw me on the Place du Trône, in the acrobat's booth. It was I who went for the police and who had you turned out of the show which you had entered while pursuing your father's murderer."

Camille uttered a wild cry, and looked at Menestreau, with her eyes dilated by horror.

"And as for that fellow, do you recognise him now?" impetuously continued Amanda, who had quite lost all power of self-control.

"No, no! It can not be! It is impossible!" murmured the poor girl in dismay. She could not bring herself to believe that the courageous champion who had saved her from death and outrage on the Route de la Révolte, the handsome cavalier, whom she had admired and loved, on whose assistance she had relied in her pious mission, was actually the very villain who had so treacherously despoiled and murdered her poor father on that tempestuous April night, the memory of which was ever present in her mind.

However, Amanda, as if meeting all Camille's objections, now resumed: "You will not believe me because the scoundrel rescued you from two scamps on the plain of Saint-Denis. That's your reason, eh? Oh! he knew what he was doing. He had made inquiries and had learned that you were rich. In fact, it was my fault, for I told him so. That very night, he began to deceive me. I ought to have foreseen it. I was with him in the ruined house when that brute Courapied fell into the cellar with his brat, and you made your escape. Guess what he told me before he started out after you. He said that he was going to murder you on the highway, and I was fool enough to believe him. But that wasn't his little game. Oh! dear no! He had very different plans, the hypocrite! He hoped that you would be attacked, and so you were, and he appeared upon the scene just in time to rescue you. Your gratitude was so great that you fell in love with him on the spot, and if I had not come here to warn you to-day, you would have married him before the end of the week. But I am here, and you shall not fall into his clutches. You have never done me any harm. It is upon him that I wish to wreak my vengeance, not upon you. Come, baron, there must be a servant somewhere about the house. Just call her, and send her for two policemen to arrest Zig-Zag and me."

There came a pause. Amanda had done so much talking, and had shouted so loudly that she was panting as much from loss of breath as from excitement. Camille sat with one hand screening her eyes, as if to hide the terrible scene from her view, and indulge in the despairing belief that it was not true, but all a dream—some terrible but deceptive nightmare. As for the poor girl's lover, he preserved a look of mingled haughtiness and hatred. Forcible and circumstantial as were Amanda's charges, it was evident that he was not yet cowed. M. de Fresnay, on his side, seemed embarrassed, and evinced no eagerness to follow the countess's instructions to send for the police. In point of fact, he had not foreseen that matters would come to a climax so quickly, and he began to repent of having subjected Mademoiselle Monistrol to such a trying scene. Although the poor girl looked as though she were about to faint, George de Menestreau at length had the audacity to turn to her, and say: "You must understand, mademoiselle, that I scorn to defend myself; for you know as well as I do that I am not Zig-Zag. You have seen him, or rather you saw his hands. I remember that you told me so."

"Yes," faltered Camille, and, hope suddenly returning to her, she added: "Yes, I saw his hands—monstrous hands with fingers like claws, which I shall never, never forget—but yours—"

"His hands!" interrupted the spurious countess, with a spiteful laugh. "They are white and slender, but if you imagine that they are not strong enough to strangle a man, you are very much mistaken. You don't know Zig-Zag. He has the strength of four ordinary men. He fought with our Hercules once at the Neuilly fair, and conquered him with those same small hands of his."

"No, no! his are not the hands of the murderer!" exclaimed Camille, again roused to some slight energy by the very horror of the charge. "The assassin's hands were of enormous size. I shall never forget them as

I just told you. And then that crooked thumb—those fingers, hooked like claws!"

"Would you recognise them if you saw them again, mademoiselle?" inquired Fresnay.

"Yes, at once," answered Camille, without the slightest hesitation.

"Well, I will show them to you." And with these words the baron drew from his overcoat pocket the steel gauntlets which he had found in the house in the Rue Mozart.

Mademoiselle Monistrol recoiled in horror, and closed her eyes to shut out the sight of the instruments of death by which her father had been strangled. As for M. de Menestreau, he turned yet a shade paler than before, and savagely clenched his fists.

"I see, now, why you set such store by your box!" cried Amanda. "Ah! you scamp! I never knew how you had managed. Well, you see your appliances haven't brought you any luck. If you had not sent Vigoureux to fetch the box, we should never have been caught. Now your doom is sealed, and mine, too. We both have a through ticket for Mazas, old fellow!"

Menestrean—Zig-Zag—made no reply, but bounding forward, he struck his accomplice a heavy blow with his fist, pushed Fresnay aside, and darted out of the room.

"You shall not escape me," cried the tight-rope dancer, starting off in hot pursuit of her faithless lover.

Fresnay hastened to the assistance of Mademoiselle Monistrol, who had fallen back fainting, for he was not at all anxious to overtake the interesting couple. He was only too glad to get rid of the Countess de Janos.

Both she and Zig-Zag might possibly have made their escape, for Brigitte had not yet returned from the market, if Georget had not been watching from the shanty in which he had concealed himself.

When he saw Amanda and her lover emerge from the house, he at once sprung out of his hiding-place and seized Zig-Zag by the leg, crying, "Help! help! Murder! murder!"

In the meanwhile, Amanda, wild with rage, had overtaken her accomplice, and throwing herself upon him, she held fast to his overcoat collar, despite all his efforts to shake her off.

Just then, attracted by Georget's cries, two police-agents, who had been pacing their beat on the Boulevard Voltaire, hastened up, and the cab-driver who had brought Amanda and Fresnay to the house, jumped from his box and rushed into the enclosure.

Zig-Zag, seeing the officers approaching, at last realised that he was lost. But he did not bother about bewailing his fate. He was pre-eminently a man of action, gifted with exceptionally strong nerves. He knew that in a desperate situation he must apply a desperate remedy. So he freed himself with a sudden jerk which sent Georget reeling to the ground, and drew his ever-present revolver from his pocket. He was evidently determined not to be taken alive. But, before turning his weapon upon himself, sufficient time remained to him to wreak vengeance upon the woman whose treachery had wrought the failure of his artful scheme.

"Kill me, villain!" cried the maddened Amanda, boldly confronting him. "I prefer that to ending my days in gaol, and, as for you, it will only increase your chance of ending your life upon the guillotine."

Zig-Zag fired, and the unfortunate woman fell, shot through the heart. He fired again, and this time the bullet hit Georget in the shoulder, just as the youngster was staggering to his feet. Then with a third bullet this accomplished scoundrel blew his own brains out, without the slightest faltering, so fully was he determined upon death.

It thus happened that the policemen on their entrance found two life-less bodies and an unconscious child stretched out upon the grass, and the cab-driver raised his hands in alarm on perceiving that one of the victims was the lady whom he had brought from the Rue Mozart. He, perhaps, feared that he might lose his fare.

The driver was not alone in reaching the scene of bloodshed, however, for Julien Gémozac, who as usual was in the neighbourhood, had heard the shots. He had come to see if what his father had told him concerning Mademoiselle Monistrol's engagement with M. de Menestreau was indeed true; and he had intended to slap his preferred rival in the face at the risk of mortally offending the young girl whom he still adored despite every-thing. It will readily be understood, however, that the situation having so completely changed, he wasted no time in deploring the fate of Zig-Zag, but darted into the house where he feared he should find Camille also a corpse.

As he fairly flew up the steps, three at a time, he fell into the arms of his friend Fresnay, who, attracted by the reports, was coming out to view the scene of carnage, and who quietly remarked : "Your lady-love is in doors. Go and console her."

Julien did not stop to ask for any further explanation, but hastened into the sitting-room, where he found Mademoiselle Monistrol reclining in an arm-chair, her lips parted, her eyes dilated with horror, and her arms hanging inertly at her sides.

"Are you hurt, mademoiselle?" he cried, anxiously, seizing hold of her cold white hands.

She shook her head, but no sound came from her parched lips. It seemed indeed as though she had lost all power of speech.

"The scoundrel tried to kill you, I am sure," continued Gémozac. "Who saved you?" Then, seeing her silent, he added : "I can guess. It was Fresnay. But you need have no fear now. The villain is dead."

"He killed himself, did he not?"

"I don't know," was Julien's answer. "There is a woman and a man and a little boy, all lying in a pool of blood in the enclosure."

"A little boy! Take me to him." And so saying, Mademoiselle Monistrol tried to rise, but Julien checked her.

"Spare yourself the frightful sight," he said. "I don't know who the child is, but I recognised the woman. A creature who had bewitched my friend Fresnay."

"She was the accomplice," murmured Camille.

"As for the man—"

"He was my father's murderer."

"What? You cannot mean it!"

"It is the truth," answered poor Camille, with a shudder. "And I thought I loved him—I had promised to marry him! Ah, why did he not kill me too?" And the poor girl burst into heart-rending sobs.

Julien, utterly bewildered, knew not what to say in reply.

"You wish to die," he at last murmured, reproachfully. "No, live, I beseech you. Live, and let me make you happy! Have you forgotten that I love you?"

"Do not say that. I am not worthy of you," replied Camille, drying her eyes.

Julien was about to protest, when Fresnay entered abruptly, and exclaimed : "It is all over ! Zig-Zag has inflicted punishment upon himself,
after sending Amanda into the other world. The child is coming round all
right, though the deuce take me, if I know where he belongs to. He is
dressed like a restaurant page, and— "

"Georget ! it is poor little Georget ! I must see him !" cried Mademoiselle Monistrol, with emotion.

"You will see him quite soon enough. The police are coming to question you. Let me answer them for you. But before they come, I must
say a word to both of you. You, Julien, my friend, are passionately in
love with Mademoiselle Monistrol, and to marry her is the one desire of
your life. It is no fault of yours, if you did not capture Zig-Zag, and
it was purely by chance that I succeeded in winning the prize that mademoiselle offered, and I will not wrong her by claiming it. Good for nothing
fellows like myself make wretched husbands, so I very willingly relinquish
my claim to you."

Julien held out his hand to his friend, and gave Camille a pleading
glance.

"You, mademoiselle," resumed M. de Fresnay, "made a great mistake,
as not unfrequently happens, but you were born to make my friend happy,
so pray give me your hand."

Camille, who was deeply moved, did as she was bid, and the baron forthwith placed her hand in Julien's.

"Now," said he with comical gravity, "that is as it should be. You
are betrothed, engaged, call it whatever you like. But when will the
wedding come off? I invite myself to it, remember. Now let me usher in
the officers. I hear them coming up the steps."

So saying, Fresnay hurried out of the room and met the two policemen
in the hall. He prepared to answer their questions in person, for he
rightly understood that Camille was in no condition to do so ; while, as
for Julien, the latter was ignorant of the various incidents which had preceded this appalling tragedy.

"What is the cause of all this?" asked the elder of the two officers,
"I have sent for the commissary, but in the meanwhile a doctor will be
wanted ; for the little fellow who is lying on the grass is in a bad way.
The man and the woman seem to be quite dead."

"Yes, they are," said Alfred. "But there is a servant here who will
fetch a doctor to attend to the little boy.—Here ! Madame Brigitte !"
he added, going to the street door and calling to the old nurse, who had
just returned with her market basket on her arm, and who stood, a picture
of consternation, at the little gate of the enclosure.

She was extremely frightened, and it was only after repeated calls, and
detailed instructions that she decided to go for a medical man. Little
Georget was picked up by the policemen and laid upon the sofa in the
sitting room, where Camille, despite her emotion, carefully tended him,
pending the arrival of the practitioner.

As might be expected, a crowd of inquisitive sightseers had speedily
gathered upon the boulevard and the police had no little difficulty in
preventing an invasion of the premises. Fortunately, the commissary of
police was not long in coming, and as he was accompanied by reinforce-
ments, the throng was speedily driven back. The side walk being cleared,
the dead bodies were duly laid upon stretchers, which had been brought
for that purpose, the messenger having briefly acquainted the commissary

with the nature of the affair. George de Menestreau was almost past recognition, for the bullet with which he had shot himself, had inflicted frightful injuries; however, the spurious Countess de Janos lay there in all her beauty, with her features barely contracted, and the young Baron de Fresnay could not help giving her a pitying glance.

After a brief examination, the commissary, who was an expeditious man, turned to an inspector, who accompanied him, and said : " Those two bodies must be taken to the Morgue at once. There is no need for the doctor to examine them, here. The cause of death is patent, and as for the circumstances, I shall at once question the people in the house. Later on they will be summoned before an investigating magistrate. You, sir," he added, turning to the baron, "must be able to tell me all about this. We will go indoors."

Fresnay preceded the functionary up the steps, and into the sitting-room where Camille, with young Gémozac's assistance, was binding up Georget's wound.

" What, another victim !" exclaimed the commissary at this sight. " I was not aware that any one else was injured. This is a serious business. Were all three shots fired by the man who committed suicide? The revolver which I have picked up, was lying close beside him."

" Yes," said Fresnay. "That man, sir, was an impostor and a murderer. Some time ago he murdered the father of the young lady who lives in this house. Monistrol, her name is; and the murderer was then performing as an acrobat on the Place du Trône hard-by."

" Ah! I remember that affair very well," said the commissary ; "I made some inquiries about it, but there was no proof against the acrobat, who was suspected, and the investigating magistrate discharged him. Has anything fresh come to light?"

" Yes," replied Fresnay. " With the money this fellow stole from Mademoiselle Monistrol's father, he slipped into another skin as it were, and lived in style. He was acquainted with the woman, whom he just killed, and she through jealousy denounced him to Mademoiselle Monistrol, whom he wished to marry as she has a large fortune. That little boy there also knew him, and the rascal finding himself exposed, preferred death at his own hands, to punishment, such as he deserved, at those of the law."

" What was his name ? "

" He lately called himself George de Menestreau, and I really believe that was his real name. He had previously been going under all sorts of aliases. He was called Zig-Zag in the acrobatic world."

" Menestreau ? " said the commissary. " It seems to me that I have heard that name before. What part of France did this man come from ? "

" I am sure that I can't tell you," rejoined M. de Fresnay ; " but, perhaps, this young lady can do so."

Mademoiselle Monistrol looked up from the sofa on which she was seated beside little Georget, and faltered with emotion : " I heard that he came from the department of the Aveyron."

" Ah! then I was not mistaken," said the commissary of police. " I myself belong to that part of France, and I remember that the Menestreau family were ironmasters there. Old Monsieur de Menestreau was a very upright worthy man, but he was ruined by his son, who forged his father's name to acceptances for a large amount. The poor old gentleman died of grief and the young scamp made off. There was a search made for him at the time, but it never proved successful. No doubt the authorities hardly believed that a young man of noble birth and good education could have become an acrobat; and yet, I remember now, young Menestreau was the captain of the gymnastic club of Rodcz, his native town; and one of his earliest feats was to embezzle a sum of money belonging to the society. The affair was hushed up at the time, his father paying for him, but after the great crash the matter was often mentioned. Well, this fellow has richly deserved his fate, and it would have even been better had he met with his death upon the guillotine. However, it is most unfortunate that he should have been able to wreak vengeance upon that poor woman outside—a beautiful creature she is, I must say—before he died."

"Oh! she hardly deserves any pity," interrupted Julien Gémozac. "I am convinced that she was his accomplice in the murder of Monsieur Monistrol. The only one worthy of compassion is this poor little fellow here."

"Yes," said the commissary, "he seems to be suffering badly. What a while the doctor is in coming."

At this moment the door opened, and a stately old gentleman appeared upon the threshold flanked by Brigitte. He walked at once to the sofa, and after a glance at Georget's wound, he declared that it was not serious. The only thing was to stop the flow of blood, and for that he would apply proper remedies. The bullet was not lodged in the flesh, it had merely grazed the shoulder, and would, no doubt, be found somewhere in the yard— perhaps, indeed, it had lodged itself in the wall of the house. "However," added the medical man, "it will be best to send this little fellow to the hospital. If a cab can be procured, I will take him there myself."

"No! no!" exclaimed Camille. "He risked his life for my sake, and I will attend to him—it cannot be very difficult, as you say, sir, that the wound is not a serious one."

"Well, mademoiselle," replied the doctor, "if you are willing to undertake the task, there is no reason why I should prevent your doing so. Have you a bed available? If so, the youngster had better be undressed and—"

"I will attend to that, sir," said Brigitte, who had now recovered her composure.

"And we two will carry him upstairs," said Fresnay, referring to himself and Julien.

The doctor's suggestion was at once acted upon, and the commissary of police being left alone, occupied himself for a few minutes in taking some notes to enable him to draw up his report. As soon as Julien and Alfred came down stairs again he remarked, "I think that I now understand the matter, thanks to what you and the police agents have told me. But of course there will be a formal inquiry conducted by an investigating magistrate. You, gentlemen, must give me your names and addresses, and hold yourselves in readiness to appear and give evidence whenever called upon to do so."

The two young men complied with the functionary's request; and, at that moment, the arrangements for the removal of the dead bodies to the Morgue having been completed, the commissary decided to take his leave.

The Baron de Fresnay was also anxious to go off, for he suspected that he might be in the way of Julien and Camille, who no doubt had a number of things to say to one another. However, to his surprise, Gémozac exclaimed: "Come with me to my father's, Alfred. I must tell him all about this at once."

Just then Camille came downstairs again; Brigitte and the doctor had remained with the little patient in the bed-room.

"We are going to my father's," said Julien turning to his betrothed. "And if you will allow it, mademoiselle, I will send my mother to you."

"Pray do so," replied the young girl. "We did not part on the best of terms, the last time we saw each other, but I am sorry if I gave her any cause for offence. I regret too that I was so utterly misled."

She could say no more ; the sobs rising in her throat, choked her powers of utterance.

"Come, come, mademoiselle," interposed Fresnay, "let us forget the past, and remember the old saying : 'All's well that ends well.' "

The young girl silently offered her hand to Julien, who printed a respectful kiss upon it, and then the two friends left the house whilst Mademoiselle Monistrol returned to the bedroom to see how little Georget was progressing. The cab was still waiting outside, and when Alfred approached it, the driver felt delighted, realising that he should not lose his fare, as he had for one moment feared. The two young fellows drove off to the Quai de Jemmapes, Alfred still thinking of the erratic countess, and Julien silently enjoying the happiness which had so suddenly and so unexpectedly come upon him. He regretted that it had been prefaced by such a terrible tragedy ; but the fact remained that Camille, fully enlightened as to the unworthiness of her other lover, had now tacitly consented to become his, Julien's wife ; and that was blissful compensation for all the despondency and anxiety through which he had passed, since the rainy night when that rascal Zig-Zag had committed his first murder with the aid of his formidable gauntlets.

The affair created a great deal of talk, but everything was satisfactorily cleared up, and the tragedy has, by no means, marred the happiness of the newly married pair. For Julien and Camille are married. M. Gémozac, senior, willingly gave his consent to the match, and though his wife had once made a show of demurring, she was softened by her son's pleadings, and now, she and Camille are the very best of friends. Julien and his wife are travelling in Italy, and their honeymoon is one of unclouded bliss. Camille only feels sad when she thinks of her poor father.

As for our gay friend Fresnay, he has resumed his old habits, but he is no more successful in amusing himself than formerly. There are times when he even thinks with regret of Amanda, Countess de Janos.

Olga has gone to tell fortunes in the South of France, and contrives to steer clear of all infringements of the law. Whatever may have been her earlier misdeeds which gave Zig-Zag a hold upon her, she scarcely fears that they will be raked up now-a-days, since the acrobat and Amanda are both dead. Georget is at present a clerk in M. Gémozac's offices, and as he gives proof of remarkable intelligence, he has a bright future before him. The little house on the Boulevard Voltaire is to be pulled down, and one of those stately seven-floored mansions so common in Paris is to be erected on the site covering the whole extent of the enclosure. When the great ginger-bread fair comes round again with its shows and booths, and pistol galleries, it is scarcely likely to be signalised by such a crime as that which cost poor Monistrol his life, and led his daughter through such strange adventures.

THE LOST HEAD.

I.

IN those days—it was the good time—Algeria had no deputies, nor prefects, nor railway lines ; and I had not yet reached my twenty-fifth birthday. I was an assistant paymaster at the treasury of the African army, and my duties mainly consisted in watching over the money which the paymaster-general despatched from Algiers to the inland stations.

Two or three hundred thousand francs, in five-franc pieces, were loaded upon mules, each animal carrying two cases, containing ten thousand francs apiece, and being escorted by a private of the commissariat service on foot. We were provided, too, with an escort of mounted chasseurs—the whole party comprising a dozen foot-soldiers and a dozen mounted troopers, including myself.

This was but a scanty escort for such large sums of money, and I have often wondered why the Arabs let us pass. A hundred marauders would have speedily conquered us, and, upon sharing the spoils, there would have been a handsome amount for each of them. Fortunately, they were badly informed as to our movements, and as the money was not despatched on fixed days, there were never any accidents.

It was lucky that we had to deal with barbarians. In a civilized country a joint-stock company would have been started to "work" these silver deposits which periodically crossed the deserts ; or else some cunning Fra Diavolo would have found a means of becoming a millionaire in six months' time.

For my own part, I never troubled myself about mischances. In fact, I always looked forward with delight to these expeditions, which were perfect shooting outings, for on the road I brought down any number of partridges with my gun, whilst as for hares, they were so plentiful, and so wanting in agility, that I could have killed them by scores with a stick. Every evening, when we bivouacked, there was plenty to eat ; and whenever we reached a district paymaster's station, we could rely upon a first-rate supper and comfortable sleeping accommodation. On the road one inhaled the fresh mountain air, and there was often an opportunity for a nice little canter.

The worry for me, as a rule, was that I had no one to talk to. The commander of the escort was usually a non-commissioned officer, more conversant with the rules of discipline than posted as regards general knowledge, besides being scarcely inclined to make friends with a paymaster, who was looked upon as but half a soldier, albeit he wore a uniform and a képi with three stripes, besides carrying a sabre.

However, on one occasion, it chanced that I fell in with a quartermaster, who had nothing of the old "growler" about him. He was a tall fellow, with light moustaches, and I at once set him down as a man of good birth, who had joined the army on account of some youthful freaks. He seemed, however, to have adopted the profession of arms in earnest, for he looked after his men in a proper way, and his brown complexion, the result of sunburns, showed that he had made more than one campaign.

We were going from Blidah to Milaniah—two long marches, somewhat wearisome on account of the road. You have to follow a series of stony ravines, and ford, at least a score of times, a winding stream called the Oued Djer. I thus had to remain in the quartermaster's company for a couple of days; and, naturally enough, I wished to find out what he had in him, as the saying goes.

We had exchanged a few words of politeness, but he did not seem inclined to keep up a conversation, and I fancied I could notice that he was study-ing me; whilst, on my side, I stealthily examined both his manners and his features. I soon remarked that he had quite an aristocratic profile, white hands, and curly hair, and that he did not carry himself in the saddle in that stiff style which is usually inculcated in military riding schools. He must have learnt how to ride at home when he was young. I tried to renew the conversation with him, but my efforts proved fruitless; he gave but brief answers to the few common-place questions which I asked of him, and then stationed himself at the head of his chasseurs.

Having renounced trying to make such a taciturn fellow sociable, I con-soled myself by firing at the game which flew out of the cover at each step taken by my escort. It is not easy to aim when one is on horseback, so that I often missed, and at times I espied a derisive smile on the lips of the quartermaster, who frequently turned round to look at me. He evidently felt some contempt for my shooting performance, and, annoyed by his mute raillery, I decided that I would not speak to him again unless it were to give any necessary orders.

However, it was ordained that we should become better acquainted. We found ourselves in great embarrassment when we had to cross the Oued Djer for the third time. It was the end of November, the weather was superb, but the rain had fallen heavily some days before, and the stream, greatly swollen, had now become quite a torrent. Whilst we were fording it, one of the mules, stumbling, was carried away by the water with the government's twenty thousand francs upon its back. The quartermaster tried to stop the animal, but in the attempt his own horse stumbled against a rock, with the result that the rider took a complete bath. Fortunately, I was near at hand, and whilst the men were darting in pursuit of the mule, I helped the quartermaster into his saddle again.

He was drenched from head to foot, and, instead of thanking me as I ex-pected, he indulged in a variety of oaths.

"It serves me right," he said at last, "I ought not to have ruined myself for Cyprienne."

On hearing this remark, I could not help bursting into a laugh, whereupon he eyed me rather savagely; but realising, no doubt, that it would be ridiculous on his part to start a quarrel, he eventually laughed in his turn, and exclaimed: "Excuse me, sir. But it's a recollection that always comes back to me whenever I find myself in a mess."

Then, having hurriedly felt a bag secured to his saddle, he added fervently: "Thank heavens, the cord hasn't broken. I should prefer to be drowned rather than lose that bag."

"The deuce!" said I, "is it full of gold or diamonds, then?"

"No; only if I had lost it in the stream, I should have blown my brains out."

"And then Cyprienne would have had an additional misfortune upon her conscience," said I. "I have remembered the name you just mentioned for the simple reason that I, myself, have had reason to complain of a certain Mademoiselle Cyprienne."

"It's perhaps the same one," said the quartermaster.

"Well, mine is an actress in Paris, at the Folies Dramatiques theatre! was my reply.

"That's it!" exclaimed the quartermaster. "Well, as you know her, you are aware that it's worth a man's while to make a fool of himself for her sake. Now and then it puts me in a rage and yet, to tell the truth, I haven't any spite against her."

The ice was now broken; the men had fished the mule out of the stream, and we had all reached the opposite bank. The quartermaster and I then began one of these conversations in which one anecdote leads up to another. He had squandered his fortune by acting upon the advice of what is called "Luther's Song," though Robert-the-Devil sings it in Meyerbeer's well-known opera:

> "Who loves not woman, wine, and song,
> He is a fool his whole life long."

The quartermaster, however, had parted with his patrimony in a provincial town; for Cyprienne had paced the boards in the country before showing herself before the footlights of a third-rate theatre in Paris; and at the period when my quartermaster became her lover, she had been playing the part of the heroine, at the theatre of the locality where he was wasting both his money and his time.

The affair was a vulgar one, no doubt, but as for the quartermaster there was nothing common about him. He had a peculiar way of telling things, and he combined bitter with humorous remarks in the most surprising style. He pretended not to regret anything of his former life, and yet he sighed whenever he looked at a little dog which ran on briskly before his horse; and on one occasion I actually heard him mutter:

"Poor little beast! He's all that I have of her remaining to me."

This dog, which he called Brusquet, and more familiarly Quéquet, was a cross between a griffon and a poodle, with straggling hair and frightfully dirty; however, it never lagged behind, and no obstacle frightened it: in fact, it took to the water and swam across all the streams like a genuine Newfoundland. It could easily be realised that it had once followed a company of strolling players.

The quartermaster had only stayed in Paris now and then, for a short time; still it chanced that he was acquainted with several persons whom I I knew, and after telling him my name I naturally asked him his.

"My comrades call me Bogue," he answered, "but that's only a nickname. My real one is that of a tree."

"Pommier then or Poirier*?" said I.

"No, no. There's a 'de' before my name."

"The fact is, I have never heard of a Monsieur 'de' Poirier," I retorted.

"Nor of a Monsieur de Prunier, I suppose? Well, try and guess. I'll stop you when you have proved successful."

---

* *Pommier* means apple tree and *Poirier* pear tree. They are tolerably common surnames in France, but without a prefix as stated by M. du Boisgobey further on.—*Trans.*

The riddle seemed a funny one to me, and I began to call to mind all the names of trees that I could think of, but without hitting upon the quarter-master's real cognomen. He laughed heartily at my various suggestions, and I amused myself by addressing him by the name of some fresh tree or plant each time that I spoke to him. Naturally enough I chose the strangest I could think of, calling him Monsieur de Peuplier (Poplar) and Monsieur de Tulipier (Tulip), &c. I ended by thinking of Coignassier (Quince tree), and considering that funny enough, I stood to it, not calling the quartermaster otherwise throughout our trip. We had now become the best friends in the world, and during the rest of the march we chatted gaily about "deeds of love and war," as Coconnas puts it in Alexandre Dumas's novel *La Reine Margot*. Moreover, the quartermaster—now freed from his "blues" —actually began to deride the wayward Cyprienne, although he had once loved her so dearly, in every sense of the word.

II,

It had been arranged that we should bivouac near one of those little dome-like structures, which the French improperly call "marabouts;" and in the distance we could already descry the cupola or quobba, dedicated to Sidi-Abdel-Kader-Bou-Medfà, when a ragged Arab suddenly stepped out of the brushwood and started a conversation with our men, in that vernacular, half French, half Arab, which reminds one of Molière's, spurious "Turk" in the *Bourgeois Gentilhomme*.

This Arab looked the picture of a footpad, but his only weapon was a stick, and we did not pay any attention to him.

However, some five hundred paces further on, we met three other natives, as wretchedly clad as the first one, and to all appearance as inoffensive. Our men asked no better than to chat and chaff them, so that all four of these fellows walked on with our party. I would have willingly dispensed with their company on account of the three hundred thousand francs which we had with us; and, accordingly, preparatory to a decision upon the sub-ject, I asked them where they were going.

"Hallo!" said the quartermaster, at once turning to me, "so you have learnt the Arab tongue, I see. What a funny idea of yours."

I was certainly not a first-rate scholar in the language of Mahomet, still I knew it well enough to question these fellows and even to understand what they said to one another. They told me that they were going to the market, at Milianah, and they begged of me to let them spend the night near our bivouac fires. I answered neither yes nor no, but consulted the quarter-master, who declared that we need not be alarmed by their presence, as he would undertake to transpierce all four of them with his trusty blade if they gave us the slightest trouble.

The permission having been granted, the dirtiest of the band took hold of one of Coignassier's boots and reverently kissed his knee. This effusive respect and the quartermaster's efforts to rid himself of the supplicant, afforded me great amusement; and yet it seemed to me that whilst kissing the sub-officer's boot the dirty Arab had, with his left hand, felt the bag, hanging from the saddle.

However, on reflection it occurred to me that I must have been mistaken, for if these fellows wanted to steal anything it certainly could not be the oats which this bag undoubtedly contained. I also fancied that I could

hear the fellow in the ragged bumous mutter in Arab to his compatriots :
"It's there ; " but I attached the less importance to this remark as I was
not positive that I had rightly understood it.

Half-an-hour later, we reached the "quobba" which rose up on a verdant
hillock.   Our bivouac ground was calculated to delight the eye, and, at the
same time, everything that we needed was obtainable there.   Some lovely
mountains extended on all sides ; the water was as clear as crystal, and
there was plenty of wood at hand, which blazed brightly as soon as it was
lighted.

The horses were duly picketted by Coignassier's orders, and the tents
were put up.   Mine was a large one, and as soon as it was ready, the men
deposited inside it the money chests which were to serve me as a mattress,
whilst my rug did duty as a blanket and my saddle as a pillow.   The fires
were soon alight, and the cauldrons began singing.   During the march I
had shot three hares and five brace of partridges.   There was enough for
every one.   I had also provided myself before starting with a turreen of
foie gras, six bottles of Bordeaux claret and three of old brandy.   My
orderly knew how to cook fairly well, so I invited Coignassier to share my
repast, which proved an excellent one, and my new friend was soon in high
spirits.   He had brought his dog with him into my tent, together with the
bag which had hung from his holster, and which must certainly contain
something precious, at least I thought so, for he never let it out of his sight ;
and, as an additional precaution, he now ordered his dog to lie upon it.

The Arabs whom we had met on the road were squatting upon their
hams near the fires, and our men were amusing themselves by throwing
them every now and then a bone to pick, or a biscuit and some bacon,
which latter the Mahommedans, like the Jews, hold in the utmost horror.

A glass or two of brandy soon dispelled the despondency of Mademoiselle
Cyprienne's whilom admirer, who no longer talked of the past, but began to
speak of his hopes of promotion.   He did not hide from me the fact that he
had once been lowered to the ranks on account of some extravagant freaks,
but he hoped that he would become chief quartermaster very soon, as he
was now charged with a highly important mission.   What this mission was,
however, remained a mystery, for he did not evince any disposition to
enlighten me respecting it.

At last we left the tent to have a smoke in the open air, and I was then
not a little surprised to see Coignassier draw from his red sash a clarionet, a
real blind beggar's clarionet, which he at once carried to his lips, beginning
to play the celebrated "Tartar March" from "Lodoïska," an opera by the
departed and forgotten Kreutzer, who was all the rage when our great-
grandmothers were young.   I held my sides, laughing to my heart's
content, and the strange music drew around us not merely the chasseurs
who were acquainted with their sub-officer's tastes, but also the Arab
prowlers, who certainly took him for a madman.   In fact, they treated him
with all the respect which men of their persuasion invariably show for
lunatics, and, a few hours later, he probably owed his life to the strange
mistake they had made in this respect.

Having finished the air, he put up his clarionet, dismissed the troopers
and the Arabs with a majestic gesture, and turning to me, he exclaimed :
"It can't be helped.   That's my style, you know.   I'm fond of the ' Tartar
March ; ' and there's no accounting for tastes.   Besides, on an expedition
a man plays whatever instrument he can.   I should prefer a piano, no
doubt, but the natives have forgotten to provide one.   And now good

night. I shall have the reveillé sounded at daybreak, so I am going to bed at once, and I advise you to do the same."

With these words he shook hands with me, fetched his bag from my tent, and repaired to his own, accompanied by Brusquet, who followed him like his shadow.

As I did not care to sit and watch alone, I went and stretched myself out on my three hundred thousand francs, which did not provide anything like so comfortable a shake-down as a good spring mattress would have been. I was rather tired by the ride, and yet I had some trouble in getting to sleep. I reflected as to the Arabs whom we had imprudently allowed to bivouac with us, and as to my new friend, Coignassier, who puzzled me as much as if he had been a riddle. I wondered what part of France he came from, and what family he belonged to. His bag also was a mystery, just like the mission with which he pretended he was entrusted. He might have one, of course, still I had not the slightest idea what it could be. At last, after an hour's reflection, I ended by closing my eyes, and then I fell sound asleep.

III.

I WAS aroused all of a sudden by the report of a fire-arm. In an instant I sprang to my feet, and as I had not undressed I immediately darted out of my tent.

The day was just breaking, and I could see the quartermaster crawling on all fours out of his canvas shelter, and five or six chasseurs hurrying right and left. What had happened? I could not understand. Had we been attacked? By whom? And what had become of our assailants? I called Coignassier, but instead of replying, he darted after his men, shouting at the top of his voice, "Ah! the brigand has stolen it!"

Brusquet was running after his master, and I finally followed the dog, overtaking the whole party just as they had gathered round the naked body of a man, who lay upon his stomach with his arms outstretched. Coignassier at once turned him over with a kick; and I saw that the fellow was one of the Arabs who had accosted us on the road—the very one who had kissed the quartermaster on the knee. I recognised him at once by a small blue tattoo mark between his eyebrows. He was quite dead.

Coignassier was raising his foot to kick the corpse in the face, but I restrained him, and asked him why this poor devil had been killed. The quartermaster did not answer me, however; he was shouting out, what to me at least proved utterly unintelligible words: "Stole it! he stole it! And yet I had hidden it under my saddle! My account is settled this time. I shall be accused of having sold it to the Bedouins—I shall be summoned before a court-martial, and then I shall be shot without any ceremony!"

"But, dash it all," said I, "what has he stolen from you?"

"My bag!" cried the quartermaster in a rage.

"Well, he can't have carried it far; since he was killed at fifty paces from our encampment."

"He must have passed it on to one of his accomplices," replied Coignassier. "I am done for, I tell you; I shall receive a volley in the breast."

Despairing of obtaining any enlightenment from the maddened quartermaster, I decided to question the men. They told me that they had been

F

awakened by their leader's shouts, and that one of them, quicker than the others, had fired upon a man who was running off, and had brought him down. They showed me that this man, after completely divesting himself of his garments, had rubbed himself all over with oil. Arabs frequently employ this system when they wish to purloin something from an occupied tent at night-time. If the occupant perceives the thief he is unable to arrest him, as the fellow's greasy, naked body, slips between his fingers.

This had been the case with the quartermaster and the dead Arab. However, whilst Coignassier continued belching forth the most frightful oaths, I heard the cur barking behind me ; and on turning round, I saw it dive in among some bushes, and finally reappear dragging something heavy. "Ah ! ah !" said I to the quartermaster, "don't swear any more. Your dog has found your treasure for you."

Coignassier sprang upon his bag, quickly untied the strings which secured it, opened it and exclaimed : "It's there. Thank God ! Thank *you* Quéquet ! Cyprienne, I forgive you."

This last remark almost made me laugh despite the fact that a corpse was lying at my feet. The exclamation addressed to Cyprienne, the actress, was indeed so amusing that I could barely restrain myself. However, in- quisitiveness soon gained the upper hand, and interrupting Coignassier who was now jumping with delight, I asked him, "What is there in that precious bag of yours?"

"Ben Allal's head, my dear fellow," he replied. "I'm saved, and I shall be promoted when I return to Algiers." So saying, he drew from his bag, by the ears, a human head, livid and hideous, which had been emptied and filled with tow and embalmed by the Gannal process.

"How horrible !" said I.   "But why have you that head with you ?"

"What, don't you know, my dear fellow, that Ben Allal was the most powerful Arab chief of all Algeria after Abd-el-Kader, whose first lieu- tenant he was? However, General Tempoure's column routed his horsemen near the Morocco frontier, and he then lost his life. Do you see that cut across his skull ? Well, it was inflicted by a sergeant of the Oran spahis— Siquot—a Parisian like yourself. He is to have the cross of the Legion of Honour for that."

I at once remembered the story then of recent date, and, with some re- pugnance, I examined the wound. It was really a fine sabre stroke such as some Knight Templar might have dealt a Saracen in the days of the Crusades. The blade had cut through the burnous and the triple "chachia,' split the bone and laid the brains bare.

"All the same," resumed Coignassier, "before the scamp was killed by Siquot he had slain a couple of chasseurs of the Second Legion, and un- horsed Captain Cassaignoles. And he only had one eye—see for yourself. It was by that, that he was recognised when he was on the ground."

I knew that the great chief had valiantly defended himself before he was overpowered ; and so I could not help exclaiming : "But why do you carry his head about in a bag like this? I think it disgraceful. We are not savages, dash it !"

"Ah ! you don't know the Arabs," replied Coignassier. "They would never have believed that Ben Allal was dead ; so, as he was for a long while Khalifa of Milianah, the governor general is sending his head there. It's market day there, to-morrow. The head will be exhibited on the great square, and the Arabs whom Ben Allal used to command will see it.   Do you now understand why I was afraid of being court martialed and shot, and why I shall now obtain promotion? I have been trusted with a confidential mission, and my orders were, not to tell anyone what I had with me. It was feared that I might be attacked on the road, and for that reason I was sent with your party. To all appearance I was escorting your money-chests and nothing more. I can't imagine how those rascals, whom we met yesterday, had learnt that their Khalifa's head was in my bag; but at all events, it's sure enough that I've had a close escape."

I began to believe that the quartermaster was right and that our ragged companions had been emissaries of the Emir. One of them had lost his life in making the audacious attempt to regain possession of Ben Allal's head; and although the others had made off from the encampment, they were no doubt within a short distance. This part of Algeria is covered with underbrush which furnishes a secure hiding-place for bands of Arab prowlers; just like the "maquis" in Corsica serves as a refuge for the brigands. It was important that we should not allow the fugitives enough time to recruit a party of adherents, so we determined to start at once, and proceed as rapidly as was possible with the mules, laden with the weighty chests of silver.

The remainder of our journey was accomplished without any mishap, but we no longer chatted, Coignassier and I. We each had our share of responsibility and we kept our eyes and ears open, attentive to everything around us. In the depth of my heart I could not help admiring the courage and devotion of that ragged Arab who had sacrificed his life to spare his compatriots a sad humiliation, and who, when mortally wounded, had retained sufficient presence of mind to fling the bag containing the head into the bushes, where we should certainly never have found it, had it not been for Brusquet's keen scent.

At two o'clock in the afternoon we reached Milianah. The quartermaster at once repaired to the commander's residence to hand over Ben Allal's head; while on my side I rode with my chests to the paymaster's where I was received with open arms. In the evening a copious repast with some good wine set me quite right after all my emotion, and I went to sleep in a comfortable bed, without any further thought of my eccentric friend Coignassier, who had duly obtained accommodation at the Chasseurs' barracks.

However, on the morrow, after breakfast, I repaired to the market-place which overlooks the endless plain of the Chéliff. The sky was beautifully blue, and on the clear horizon there uprose the massive mountains of the Ouarensenis, o'ertopped by a snowy peak which the Arabs proudly call "the eye of the world."

There was a crowd on the market-place, and in the centre, a detachment of horse gendarmes mounted guard over the head of Ben Allal which was fixed to the summit of a pole. The Arabs passed by, looked at it, and went off in silence, but hatred of the Gaiour visibly gleamed in their eyes. I fancied that I espied one of our ragged companions among them, but I did not care to start an inquiry. On the contrary, I was anxious to return to Algiers as soon as possible, and I resolved to cover the eighteen leagues which separate Milianah from Blidah at one march. So I left the mules with the paymaster, and at three o'clock in the morning I started off with an escort of six spahis.

At breakfast time we halted on the grass, close to the quobba where we had had such an alarm the day before. The Arab's corpse was no longer visible, but while scouring the brushwood to try and raise a hare, I espied

Brusquet's carcase hanging from a branch.   The Arabs had, no doubt, stolen the dog at Milianah, and had executed him on the very spot, where, to their great grief, he had discovered the head of their favourite leader, Ben Allal.

In all probability, Cyprienne never heard of the untimely fate of the animal which she had given to her friend the quartermaster.   Coignassier, as I have called him in this story, left the army, after securing a commission ; he married, had several children, led a respectable life and died not long ago.   What was his real name, you may ask ?   Well, I learnt it at Algiers, and it was really the name of a tree—a tree which grows throughout France, and the fruit of which provides sustenance for the peasants of five or six of the central departments.   I cannot even yet understand why I did not guess it at once ; however, it seems to me useless to print it here.

Inquisitive people, who are anxious to learn it, may make inquiries of Cyprienne, providing they can only find her.   She must now be a broken-down old doorkeeper, somewhere in the neighbourhood of Vaugirard.

THE GENDARME'S WIFE.

By JULES CLARETIE.

I.

The sergeant, astride on a straw-seated chair, was smoking his pipe outside the gendarmerie of Pierrebuffière. The smoke slowly ascended, looking like bluish breath, and forming a swelling coil which twined and finally evaporated in the warm air of the July evening.

Martial Tharaud had in his time seen many a coil of smoke thus ascend and evaporate above the mouths of cannon. Nowadays the father of a family, with stripes on his arm, he took his rest in his garden and no longer asked for anything in the world, not even for promotion to the rank of quartermaster; for then he would perhaps have had to move to Eymoutiers, to St. Léonard or to Limoges, and he was fond of his little nook at Pierrebuffière, of the roses which he himself had grafted, and of the creeper which climbed up the white walls of the house, forming festoons round about the tricolour flag in painted zinc which was displayed over the door.

The sergeant smoked his pipe, watching some urchins who were playing on a mound a little distance off, throwing long dart-like nails which lodged themselves in the ground as if they had been arrows; and, from time to time, he called out to them: "Eh! youngsters take care! Mind you don't hurt yourselves; you might pierce your feet!"

And then he turned his head, glancing over his shoulder and looking at a woman, still young, dark and pretty, who was hurrying to and fro in the kitchen where the copper saucepans glittered like ruddy gold: he smiled at her, and said, between two pulls at his pipe: "How mad the little ones are for a game!"

Thereupon, the woman, with her arms bare, plump white arms, partially covered with flour, advanced, and leant upon the window sill, turning towards the urchins her face which was at once energetic and gay, and to which the kitchen fire had imparted a rosy glow. Then looking at the little ones as they threw their iron missiles with all the force of their arms, she said:

"Bah! there's no danger! And, besides, it makes them skilful and brave."

"And it will give them a good appetite for your ' clafoutis,' Catissou!" rejoined the sergeant.

The ' clafoutis,' a Limousin dish, as massive as the thick cabbage soup of the province, was already cooking in the oven, with its black cherries embedded in dough, looking just like bricks surrounded by mortar.

"By the way, is the 'clafoutis' getting on all right?" added the sergeant; and thereupon Catissou shrugged her shoulders as if to say: "Is
your housekeeper in the habit of spoiling her pastry? What a stupid you
are, my dear."

II.

"A GOOD wife," said Martial Tharaud to me as I passed by just then and
wished him good day. He was in the humour for a chat.

"Yes, yes," he added—he became loquacious whenever he spoke of
Catissou—"my wife's a good wife—there are few women to equal her. No
one would believe it, eh? when they see her wiping the children's noses for
them—we have three youngsters, you know, all three boys, you can see
them playing over there—but no one would believe it, I say, when they
see her cooking the dinner that she used to be a mountebank and went
about from fair to fair. And yet it's true. It's quite a story. I'll just
tell it you."

The sergeant took another pull at his pipe, cleared his throat and then
resumed : "It was ten years ago. I had just left the hussars and joined
the gendarmerie at Limoges. It suited me as I belong to the part, and the
adjutant said to me one morning that there was a fine capture to be made.
A worthy old man, named Coussac, a master mason, had been murdered in
his house in the Faubourg Montmailler, and no one could tell who had
done the deed. It was September, and we were to make our rounds and
keep our eyes open on account of the sportsmen who were about, without
shooting permits. Well, the adjutant, that's Monsieur Boudet, who's now
our captain, told the quartermaster, who's been promoted paymaster's
adjutant with the cross if you please—told the quartermaster, I say, that
the sergeants and men were all to be extra vigilant ; and that if under the
chestnut trees or at the roadside they met any suspicious looking fellows—
anything doubtful you know—they were to apprehend them at once, and
take them before the proper parties.

"Well, the whole district was warned. Orders had been sent to Châ-
teauneuf, to Ambazac, to St. Sulpice, Laurière, everywhere in fact, even to
Rochechouart and Bellac. In one word the whole department was on foot.
Good !

"But it's all very well you know for a man to say to you like that—
'You must arrest all disreputable-looking people.' There's no certainty
about disreputable looks. There are people of the kind who are really very
worthy fellows. Why, I knew a party who would at least have been
guillotined, or at all events sent to the galleys, merely on the strength of
his looks. But he was a chap, who under other circumstances, would have
received the Montyon prize for virtue and good conduct, and have deserved
it too. He cared for a lot of people, and gave all he had to the poor. A
saint, upon my honour, a saint with a convict's head. Whereas there are
other people, you know, to whom the priests would give absolution without
confessing them—they don't look as if they had ever had the slightest
peccadillo on their conscience, and yet if they were served aright they
would have a pair of handcuffs clapped on their wrists at once.

"But no matter. We were told to arrest the suspicious folks ; and we
did so. We collared some of those Lorrainers you know, who come to
Sauviat and St. Yrieix to buy china ; we collared some pedlars too, some
old chaps, and some beggars as tanned as their leather bags, and even some

idiots who were roaming about without knowing it. Not a single one of them, however, was capable of hurting old Coussac.

"Meanwhile time was getting on, and the real murderer of the Faubourg Montmailler couldn't be found. The fact is, it wasn't easy to tell who had killed the master mason. There weren't many clues, and it looked as though the matter would never be cleared up. However, one day I was at the gendarmerie rubbing down my horse, when a fine girl with dark eyes like blackberries, and red lips like cherries, comes up to me and says, right plump 'Well, after all, is there any news of the murderer? I'm Leonard Coussac's daughter!'

"It made me feel queer to hear her talk like that. She had spoken with such energy, dash it, and there was such anger blazing in those eyes of hers, that I felt almost ashamed that I hadn't yet laid my hands on the scoundrel who had killed her father! So, by way of apologising, I tried to explain to her that it wasn't our fault, that we hadn't much information about the murderer, and so on; but all the while she looked so fixedly, right into my eyes, that I began to feel confused, and suddenly I said to her:

"'Well, mam'selle, to make it short, even if I had to lose an arm or a leg in collaring that scoundrel for you, I'd do my best to capture him all the same. I'd risk anything,' I added; and that was quite true; only it wasn't so much duty that influenced me, but rather those big black eyes of hers which blazed and blazed away at me all the while.

"'However,' said I, 'I should want a clue—'

"'A clue,' she answered; and she shrugged her shoulders. 'Well, isn't the hand a clue?'

"'The hand? What hand?' I asked.

"Thereupon Catherine Coussac—her name was Catherine, Catissou in our dialect—began to tell me a story, the story of the crime, a story which I confess made a shiver run down my back. It was on a September evening, as warm as summer, when that poor fellow Coussac was killed. He had with him at his house in the Faubourg Montmailler some money which had been left with him by Monsieur Sabourdy, the contractor, who employed him, and who had just started for Guéret. There was about ten thousand francs in all. Coussac was to pay the men, and settle two heavy bills; one the mortar merchant's, and the other the wood merchant's, bills which would fall due three or four days later—on the Monday, so to say. Well, the Saturday came, the workmen were paid, and Coussac returned home well pleased, and with the appetite of a horse who had earned his oats. Well, he had eaten his cabbage soup, his 'bréjeaude,' as they called it, and some 'gogues'—a kind of black pudding, you know—and, after the meal, Madame Coussac, the grandmother, who felt rather tired, went up to bed, while Leonard and his daughter, Catissou, stayed downstairs, seated near the wardrobe, where the money was kept, he reading the *Limousin Almanack*, which had just been published, and she knitting a woollen stocking.

"I must tell you that Coussac's place overlooked a garden at the back of the house. There was a window, with shutters, but as it was rather warm that night, it had been left slightly open. The shutters, too. Well, Coussac was reading by the light of a little lamp, with a shade, and Catissou could hear him turning the leaves of the almanack over and over. She has often told me since, that while she sat working there, mechanically, the continuous rustling of the leaves, and the ticking of the clock, made her feel rather drowsy. However, suddenly, just as with a yawn, she was raising

her eyes from her work to see if it wasn't yet time to go to bed, she perceived—she thought at first that she was mistaken, that she was dreaming,
that she had the nightmare—she perceived, I say, between the shutters, a
big hand, softly gliding *—it was an astonishing hand, broad and thick,
with something frightful about it, something which Catissou remarked at
once. All four fingers, which were almost as thick as my thumb, were
equal, all of the same length ; they all ended as if they had been cut at the
tips in a straight line. But they hadn't been cut, mind you, they had nails
like other fingers, only, as I said before, they were all of the same length ;
and they were spatulated, as Dr. Bouteilloux told me afterwards ; yes, that
was the doctor's word—spatulated.

" Well, that hand slipped between the shutters—that frightful hand, looking just like a big spider with its legs, and it was evidently trying to push
the shutters back without making a noise. For a moment, too, it even
remained there quite motionless, as if the man it belonged to had guessed
or could see that Catissou was looking.

" For one moment she fancied that she was dazed, that the lamplight
had affected her eyes, and made her see red and black spots, as is the case
when you have looked at the sun. However, she kept her eyes wide open,
feeling very frightened, and the hand advanced, sliding along the wood-
work with its huge fingers, all of equal length. Then, as Catissou couldn't
doubt any longer, she wanted to cry out, but she felt a grip at her throat
as if the hand had been strangling her. Try what she would, not a
sound came from her throat. But she managed to rise up, and, stretching
out her arms towards her father, she shook him by the sleeve, and pointed
at the window—at the terrible hand, which seemed to grow bigger and
bigger, and which was steadily coming nearer and nearer. However, just
as old Coussac, turning round, was about to catch sight of the hand, the
shutter was rapidly pushed back, and the window as speedily opened ; the
sudden draught, at the same moment, made the door at the end of the
room open—it had not been properly closed—and then the breeze swept in,
and the lamp, after projecting its flame and smoke towards the ceiling, went
out, leaving Catherine and her father quite in the dark.

" Hearing the thud of someone jumping into the room, Coussac tried to
find a knife in the drawer of the table, at which he had been reading—a
knife to defend himself, especially to defend Catissou and Monsieur
Sabourdy's money ; but before he could open the drawer, he was caught at
the throat, and he felt something cold enter him there —near the shoulder—
and the point reached his heart. Catissou was calling out ; she saw nothing, but she guessed it all. However, a blow, as heavy as if it had been
dealt with a hammer, fell upon her skull, and stretched her upon the floor.
The scoundrel must have had cat's eyes. He could distinguish everything,
and he aimed well.

" If Catissou escaped death, it was because the blade of the knife which

* The reader having previously perused M. du Boisgobey's story, " Thieving Fingers,"
will note the similarity between the opening of that tale and the present one. It is right
to add, however, that the incident of the murderer having a monstrous hand is based upon
the reports of a well-known French " celebrated case," so that there is no plagiarism to be
imputed either to M. du Boisgobey or to M. Claretie. The two stories have a similar point
of departure, founded upon fact, and we have brought them together in the present volume,
so that the reader may note and appreciate the different manner in which the writers have
dealt with their subject, whilst working upon much the same basis. M. du Boisgobey's
tale is, of course, more developed, and it is more imaginative ; M. Claretie's narrative,
which is but a sketch, keeping nearer to the actual truth.—*Trans.*

had pierced her father's heart had broken in the wound. Besides, the assailant didn't need any other weapon than his fist. The poor girl fainted away, she couldn't tell for how long, and when she returned to her senses, she found herself in the same low room, which smelt of the lamp, that had gone out, of oil and blood combined ; and old grandmother Coussac, in her nightdress, and whiter than the linen, was trying to revive poor Leonard, whose mouth was full of blood, and who feebly pointed to his heart, as if to say : ' It touched me there. There's no remedy.'

"I needn't tell you that the wardrobe where Coussac had placed the money had been broken open, and that the bank notes had fled. Ah ! what a terrible night it was ! The Faubourg Montmailler will recollect it for years to come. The neighbours were roused. A search was made in the garden. Houses were surrounded and scoured from top to bottom. Footprints left by shoes with big nails were found on the flower-beds, and measured. People were advised not to touch them. Lanterns were lighted. Folks hurried here and there searching ; and in the meanwhile poor Coussac was dying, and his old mother like a fury, repeated : ' If I only held the rascal who killed him, I'd shove my fingers into his mouth, and pull out his tongue.'

" And while all this was going on, Catherine, half crazy, could still see that hand, that frightful hand with its four fingers of equal length crawling along the oaken shutter like a spider or a crab.

III.

"As you can no doubt imagine, one did everything one could to find the scoundrel who had sent the poor fellow to ' Louyat.' That's how they call the cemetery at Limoges. The word comes from ' Hallelujah ! ' so the priest told me. Yes, one did everything one could. But, I repeat it, how about the clues ? There were no clues ! Of course there was that hand which Catissou had told me about at the barracks, but nobody in the district was known to have a hand like that. All the masons who had worked with old Coussac were questioned, one after another ; but no, they didn't know of any journeyman in their line with a paw of that kind. They themselves were above suspicion, all worthy chaps, extremely well known ; a bit fond perhaps of washing down their chestnuts with a few glasses of raw wine; but a glass more or less, that isn't a crime. Besides, they had none of them known that Monsieur Sabourdy had left any money with Coussac, beyond what was necessary for their pay. So who could be the man with a paw like the one which Catissou had perceived?

" One day, a butcher who worked in the Rue Aigueperse came to tell us at the gendarmerie that some time before, having had a quarrel with a tall chap, with an evil look, the fellow had drawn his knife, a big Montron dagger knife, and the butcher remembered very well that he had noticed, when the fellow took this knife from his pocket, that he had a very funny hand, a big hairy hand, with four fingers of the same length. A phenomenon, that's what you call it I think. Well the knife with which poor Coussac had been killed precisely happened to be a Montron dagger knife. Only, the butcher didn't know where the fellow he spoke about had come from, or where he had gone, and no one else in Limoges had ever seen him. In fact, it seemed as though the butcher was making fun of us !

"However, the search went on. We hunted among the bushes as if we were beating up game, and always came home without having found any-thing. I was in a rage for my part, yes, in a rage, for I had said to Catissou, looking her straight in the face :

"'Come, demoiselle Catissou, answer me frankly. What would you give to the man who brought you your father's murderer, by the neck ?'

"Catissou hadn't replied, but she had become as white as a china plate, and you should have seen her eyes, her beautiful black eyes, they wept and wept, and they promised too. Only all that didn't help me to find the murderer.

"Then, at the very end, seeing that not a man of the twelfth legion, from the colonel down to the last gendarme, could set hands upon the rascal, Catherine said : ' All right; as you men can't find him, well I, my-self, will do so.'

"She still had her grandmother all that time, old widow Coussac—a true woman she was, who since the murder of the master-mason had become as taciturn as a fish, and as fierce as a dog about to go mad. She only re-peated one phrase : 'What ! won't anyone find that rascal who killed my son, so that I may see him on the guillotine ?'

"However, Catherine gave up her work as a dressmaker, and to every-one's surprise she asked the prefect of police for a permit to do the mounte-bank business at fairs. It astonished me, it astonished us all, but me especially, when at the fête of St. Loup, or the fête of St Martial, at Limoges, and all through the district, we came upon a shanty with a big painting on canvas, a painting which was Catherine Coussac's portrait in pink tights, a red velvet jacket and copper spangles ; while up above, in big letters, were painted the words, ' The Silurus Woman.'

"'The Silurus Woman !' what a funny name ! It was already a singular idea on Catissou's part, to join the mountebanks at fairs, though I must tell you that those folks are often as good as others, and some are even better than others—poor people they are, too, always on the road, feeding and sleeping at the wayside, dislocating themselves to amuse us, and nibbling at misery just as the skinny horses which drag them and their houses about, nibble at the grass, beside the highways. Yes, it was already a funny idea for her to make herself a stroller as they put it. But ' the Silurus Woman,' that was more comical still. ' The Silurus Woman.' Do you know what that is? It's to be a torpedo woman, and a torpedo woman, that means an electrical one. No one can touch you without feeling an electric shock. The silurus is a fish which numbs your arm when you touch it ; a fish with a kind of electric battery in its inside. And so, Catherine Coussac sent a shock through your arm, when-ever she touched it. Yes, the Silurus Woman, that's it !

"But I didn't need to touch her to be electrified ; I only had to look at her. She's twenty-eight years of age now ; and she's got rather fat ; and yet she's mightily pretty all the same. Well, ten years ago, when she wore on her black hair, the lace cap which the women of our part have foolishly set aside to wear hats and bonnets like everyone else, well, I say, ten years ago the fellows who saw her, and didn't turn round to take a second look, were rank fools. And what a figure she had ! And what a complexion ! There are some pretty girls at Limoges, but upon my word, I don't say it to flatter myself, still, the prettiest of them all was Catissou !

"And so there were plenty of spectators to see the Silurus Woman ! Yes, there were. She didn't need a big orchestra like the Corvi circus to attract attention, or a lot of jokes like those which the company playing the 'Tour de Nesles,' fire off before the performances. Oh! dear no! She simply showed herself; and the fellows said, 'What a fine girl!' and then they went into her shanty.

"One day, at Magnac-Laval, it was Shrove Tuesday, I, myself, went in to see the Silurus Woman just like everyone else. She was there on a little stage, and down below her, crouching like a sorceress, sat old mother Coussac with a frown on her face, and looking at everybody, at one person after another, as if she had wanted to cast a spell on them. I stepped forward, and Catherine recognised me; and then, while I stood in front of her, telling her how well her costume suited her, with her short skirt, her tights showing her calves, and her boots, which looked no longer than a child's, she smiled, and said in a funny way:

"'Oh, as for you. I don't need to see *your* hand.'

"And it seemed to me that there was rage lurking in her eyes.

"Ah! then I understood what the brave girl was up to. I knew now what she wanted to find, and why she was scouring the country, disguised as a mountebank. She still remembered that hand, that frightful, ferocious hand, and she offered everyone her own, white and as soft as satin, but all the same, capable of taking a firm hold; and she hoped that among the hands extended to grasp hers she would some day recognise the one with the fingers of equal length, the one that had been stained with her father's blood!

"That was Catissou's idea! It was the only clue that existed, and she had said to herself that she would make it suffice. It is difficult to search through the world for a scoundrel; you might as well look for a needle in a bundle of straw. Still, there is always a chance that a murderer will come and prowl about the spot where he committed his crime. Upon my word, blood is like a magnet; it attracts.

"No doubt the scoundrel had left Limoges at the first moment; and yet, was that even certain? At all events, he would some day pay a visit to the Faubourg Montmailler. When he did so, the Silurus Woman would have a chance of again seeing that hand of his, that wonderful hand which never left her thoughts, which haunted her indeed to such a degree, that, as she has often told me, she could see and feel it in her dreams, the big hairy fingers pressing into her neck like pincers, during the night.

"In this way Catissou travelled about a good bit with her old grandmother. She went wherever she could. The Silurus Woman's travelling waggon was dragged, jolting, over the roads by a horse which had once belonged to us gendarmes. A discarded horse, which, no doubt, still pricked its slit ear whenever it scented a criminal. Animals are cunning, you see, and they know a great many things that we have no idea of.

"Well, by going about like that, rambling from fair to fair, the two poor women, the murdered man's mother and daughter, must have covered pretty nearly as many leagues as make up a journey round the world. They went through Auvergne, they saw Bordeaux, Toulouse, Tours, even Orleans. And a good many other parts, too, down south. Still they always came back to our department, the Haute Vienne with more confidence. It was a superstition, a presentiment, an idea they had like that, one of those things you can't account for. They said to one another:

"'That was where the murder took place, that's where the murderer will be arrested.'

"'Pon my word, women guess a number of things. I was talking of animals, just now, but women are still sharper. So it happened that one day—oh! I remember it as well as if it were only yesterday—it was the 22nd of May, and a Tuesday too—the booths and shanties of the fête of Saint Loup were creating quite a hubbub on the Place Royale at Limoges, what they call the Place de la République now-a-days.

"There was something of everything, roundabouts with wooden horses for children to ride upon; a wax-work exhibition, a theatre of performing monkeys, the Pezon menagerie, and I don't know what all. And of course there was the Silurus Woman. Catherine, as fresh as a nosegay, with new red tights, walked about the platform, pointing to the show-bills of her performances, and calling out, 'Walk up, walk up, ladies and gentlemen,' whilst old grandmother Coussac, who looked as if she were a hundred years old, poor woman, as yellow as a quince, and as skinny as a nail, coughed in the most dreadful fashion, but still rolled her piercing eyes, which seemed loaded like pistols.

"'Walk up! Walk up! Walk up!'

"I didn't wait for the summons to be repeated, I went in like everyone else; only, as I did so, I said to Catissou: 'Good afternoon, mademoiselle!'

"'Good afternoon, gendarme,' she answered.

"She knew my name very well, and yet she treated me as a stranger. To my mind, she said: 'Good afternoon, gendarme,' like that, meaning: 'Well, you may be a gendarme, but for all that you don't know how to collar the people who murder poor old men.' As it was, she had a perfect right to call me 'gendarme,' as I was wearing my uniform. And, besides, all that is of no importance.

"Well, in I went. There were a score of people in the place, men and women, and while Catissou smiled around, grandmother Coussac, crouching down, looked savagely at everyone as was her habit.

"I can see the scene now, as if I were still there. Catissou standing on the stage, with the red hangings at the back, her pretty dark face, with sequins in her hair, a rose in her dress body, her pink tights, and amid all the red and pink her round arms showing very white. And what a head, too! Enough to turn every other. Some sunrays were glinting through the canvas awning, and they made all the spangles, which she had sewn on her costume, sparkle like gold and diamonds. Ah! what a pretty girl! I'm speaking of her now as if she were a stranger. But, no matter, she was a fine girl!

"And there she stood telling the spectators all about the electrical silurus which lives in the Nile and the Senegal and which the Arabs call the thunder fish; and how this fish gives you such a shock that you would think it was lightning, and how the skin and the nerves of the silurus— But no matter; Catissou repeated that speech hundreds and thousands of times, no doubt; but it's all forgotten now. It's all over! Perhaps she doesn't remember it at present. But she had it on the tip of her tongue in those days, I can tell you. And she spoke like an advocate at the bar, and the people who were listening opened their mouths in astonishment, and gazed at the Silurus Woman with all their eyes, which was a proof that they were not wanting in taste.

"After her speech she as usual held out her hand and she said to the people: 'Here, shake hands with me, you will feel the shock. But don't be afraid, it won't hurt you!'

"There were some who laughed, and others who almost grew angry as they shook their fingers. Still they all raised their paws to Catissou's little hand to have the pleasure of touching it. All of them. And I was there, I was, and I looked on; and I almost began to feel jealous of all those people who were fingering Catherine's white hand, when quite of a sudden —ah! dash it! that was a thunderbolt—I saw the Silurus Woman turn as pale as death and spring on a hand which was held out to her, just like a dog might spring upon a piece of meat.

"Standing before her there was a tall strapping fellow, built like a Hercules, with curly red hair escaping from under a large felt hat. He wore a starched blouse over a peasant's jacket, and had very broad shoulders; he was quite a colossus, indeed. I had a side face view of him, and I saw that his under jaw projected like a pike's, and that his temples almost hid his eyes. He hadn't any beard, merely a few hairs on his pale flabby cheeks. There was altogether an evil look about him.

"Catissou had looked the fellow full in the face, and now holding his hand, a hand which seemed enormous in her little one, she clutched hold of it as if her life had depended upon her keeping a firm grasp.

"I felt a shiver run down my back, and I said to myself: 'It's the scamp! She's got hold of him at last.'

"Yes, she had got hold of him and she held him well, never you fear; and looking as pale as death she said to the big fellow who had suddenly turned as livid as herself:

"'I say, you chap, do you happen to know Leonard Coussac's murderer?'

"The man drew back and tried to free his hand from the grasp of the Silurus Woman. Ah! she didn't need to be electrified to give him a shock. He drew back his arm but without being able to free himself, and then he tried to push her away and he called out: 'Come! are you mad? Just let go of me!' He turned his head round like a wolf as he spoke and I could then see his eyes, ferocious and maddened, looking for the way out.

"'You wretched scamp!' cried Catissou, who was digging her finger-nails into his flesh. 'It was you, you who did the business. Yes, you, you!'

"And then she shook the Hercules, as if he had been a plum tree; he was quite stupefied by her anger. However, he soon recovered himself! He freed his hand from Catherine's grasp, and then I saw what a frightful hand it was, with fingers of equal length, looking just like some huge spider. But he dealt Catherine a blow on her shoulder before I could interfere and she fell down upon her knees; and then he turned round, looking like a wild boar surprised in his lair, and made for the exit.

"All the people were running off; they were every one of them frightened.

"The fellow was about to take a jump, pushing the people before him and digging them in the ribs, when I, by wheeling to the right, got straight in front of him. He had an evil look when he saw my képi and white stripes. He had perceived them before, only I wasn't then discharging my duty.

"He was a head taller than myself, but I raised my arms and caught him suddenly by the top of his blouse.

"'In the name of the law I arrest you,' said I.

"The scamp's only reply was to give me a kick with his knee in the stomach, and I should have rolled over, I think, if Catherine's presence had not trebled my strength. Oh! I didn't care for the kick with the knee! I held the fellow, and I pulled him and dragged him about. I didn't let go my hold. You would have had to cut off my hands at the wrists to make me do so. And he, he kept on giving me blows with his jaw on my head, hoping that he would stun me or break my skull. Suddenly—I still bear the mark—suddenly, he whips out a knife and gives me a thrust near the neck, just in the same part where old Coussac was mortally wounded— That thrust was habitual to the rogue, so it would seem.

"He no doubt expected that he would kill me, but the collar of my tunic saved my life, and the blade of the knife—a Montron knife with a yellow handle—merely cut my collar and made a slight gash in my neck. Then I seized hold of the arm with which he was holding the knife, and I kept it up above my head, saying to myself, 'If that knife comes down again it will be all over. I shall be done for.' I could see the knife up there in the air like the sword of that fellow they always tell you about at school—Dam—ah! Damocles, that's his name; and round the handle of the knife there were the four fingers of equal length which had enabled Catissou Coussac to recognise her father's murderer.

"I don't know how long that battle lasted, while my blood, spurting out of my wound, washed the rascal's face for him; still it must have lasted some time—a very long time, it seemed to me. I felt that I was losing my strength, that I was about to let go of the fellow's arm, and that the knife would come down on me again; when, suddenly, that blackguard gave a shriek—oh! a savage shriek—just like a pig's shriek when he's being butchered—and he then leapt up in the air, with me still clinging to him, as a matter of course. And then, as if to escape from some dog which was biting his calves, he drew back, drew back so fast, that he stumbled, and down we went on the ground, I on the top and he under me. But there was something still clinging to him, the something that had made him give that shriek, and when I took a look I saw that grandmother Coussac had taken him by the legs and was biting and eating him to make him let go his hold.

"And meanwhile we rolled about on the floor, entwined like so many worms; but fortunately it didn't last much longer. Catherine was on her feet again, and she helped me to hold the arm with the weapon; or, rather, she disarmed the rascal, and I with my right hand held him by the neck, and pressed hard enough to stifle him. And then, well, help came. Quartermaster Bugead hurried in with a comrade. The rascal was mastered, lifted up, dragged along, handcuffed, and pushed and carried through the crowd, which wanted to kill him now that he was taken, though, just before, all those worthy people had felt dreadfully afraid of him.

"It was high time that help did come, I can tell you. I couldn't bear it any longer. I was getting dizzy, so dreadfully dizzy, and—of course it was very stupid on the part of a gendarme, but the fact is—I fainted away from loss of blood. However, I could feel that a pair of white arms was supporting my head, and, instead of the Montron knife up above me, I now saw, through a fog as it were, Catherine's large black eyes, which were softly smiling at me.

IV.

"WELL, sir, that was how a knife thrust brought about a happy marriage. My wound got well again, as I scarcely need to tell you, since here I am; but it got well very soon indeed, for it was Catissou who attended upon me. The Silurus Woman became a sister of charity, and as soon as I was on my legs again :

"'Shake hands,' said she, ' I like you ; you like me, and I'll promise to be a good wife to you.'

" Grandmother Coussac, who's now asleep at Louyat, was still alive then ; Catherine's wedding was her last joy, poor old woman ! No, I'm mistaken, her last delight was the trial of the scoundrel who had killed her son the master-mason.

" He was a bricklayer named Massaloux, from La Souterraine, in the department of the Creuse, and having called at Monsieur Sabourdy's to try and get some work, he had heard mention made of the money which had been entrusted to Leonard Coussac. That excited him, and he said to himself, ' There's a good stroke of business to be done ; ' and he did it. All alone too. He hadn't any accomplice. He was an idle ne'er-do-well as a rule, but energetic whenever he thought fit. After the crime he had made off to Paris and led a gay life with some hussies there ; but the money being at last all spent he had come back, first to Guéret, then to Limoges, trying to get some work to do. What kind of work, you may ask ? Oh, any sort, no doubt, even in the knifing line. He scarcely defended himself when he was put iu the dock at the assizes. He seemed to say ; ' You've caught me. You know what you've got to do. So much the worse for me.'

" Of course, he was condemned to death. But before that, he had tried to batter his brains out by knocking his head against the wall of his cell ; and he kept on saying : ' All the same, the executioner sha'n't have me.'

" But the executioner did have him. I don't pity fellows of that kind. It serves them right to go to the guillotine. They don't let us escape, providing they can do for us. As for that chap, his hand, that wonderful hand you know, is preserved in a glass jar, in spirits of wine, at the Medical School in Paris. You can see it there if you like. It will well repay the trouble of a visit.

" During the trial—I don't say this out of vanity—the presiding judge complimented me on my behaviour. I merely mention it, because it's the truth ; but I had no need of his compliments, I had no need of anything, for Catissou had already become my wife. However, on my wedding day my captain made me a present—he gave me my sergeant's stripes, and I must say that I felt pleased to have them.

" And since then, if you want to see a happy man, just look at me ! Catissou has had ever so many engagements offered to her as a ' Silurus Woman' at circuses. Even a party in Australia wrote to ask whether she would go and join a company out there. The newspapers had related her story you see, and that made the managers anxious to get hold of her as a ' great attraction.' But whenever anyone talks to Catissou about that she begins to laugh. Silurus Woman, indeed ! No, no, she has other things to attend to—the brats to wash, my epaulets to clean, the fowl yard to see after, and the whole place to keep tidy. And everyone and everything obey her orders, and walk straight, the youngsters, the fowls, and the ducks, and even the sergeant as well ! No, no, Catissou isn't an artiste now-a-days ; and yet, dash it all—if ever a crime was committed in Limousin, and the culprit couldn't be found—ah ! then, *fé dé Di,* by my faith in God, I should put more trust in her than in all the bloodhounds of the police. Catissou has keen eyes, I can tell you, and you won't ever see a frightened look in them."

V.

THE sergeant tapped his pipe upon his left hand thumb-nail, on which the warm ashes soon fell, and he was preparing to fill his "comrade" anew, when Catherine Tharaud, beautiful and gay, her face lit up by a warm ray of the setting sun, returned and leant her bare elbows upon the window-sill, standing in the framework formed by the twining creeper. In a cheerful voice, and with a hearty laugh, she said :

"Come, Martial, I'm going to take the 'clafoutis' out of the oven. The 'brégeaude' is smoking! Call the little ones!"

Martial Tharaud rose up, formed a speaking trumpet of his two hands, and called out to the playful youngsters :

"Hallo! there, my little flies. Right about wheel! The soup's ready, you young rascals."

The three little fellows hurried up at once, already sniffing the savoury smell of the cabbage soup and the cooked cherries. Pushing the two younger ones on ahead, the worthy sergeant took the eldest between his legs, and the urchin well nigh disappeared amid the full folds of his father's blue regimental trousers, which had a black stripe on either side. Then, lifting his blue képi, adorned with white braid, Martial Tharaud bade us good-day, and gaily went off to partake, at the same time, of Catissou's warm soup and her fresh loving kiss.

At the end of the street, a wooden-shoe maker sat at work, singing the old song :

> "Limoges is our pride
> With its lads so fit to please !
>   Love shall e'er abide
> 'Neath its spreading chestnut trees."

And in the meanwhile, the setting sun cast its last ray upon the zinc flag of the good gendarme.

AUNT ES.

I KNEW her when I was staying with one of my friends at Amsterdam. Every one in the house called her Aunt Es. Her real name, I fancy, must have been Estelle or Esther. She was getting on for sixty, but her hair, which was quite white, alone indicated her age. She had a fine, unwrinkled skin, her glance was full of fire, her teeth were superb. She displayed them, moreover, with a certain amount of coquetry frequently allowing her lips to part in a smile. She must have been very pretty when she was young, and she was still good-looking; her latter-day beauty being accentuated by unusual quickness of motion, and perception.

Her bright eyes, her brisk expression, her hasty gestures, her curt words, her swiftness in everything, all indicated that charming Aunt Es, so alert, and so trim, had led a life full of activity, with many duties to attend to. In point of fact, she had been in business—no, I make a mistake, she was in business still; and her relatives foresaw that the old lady—unwearying toiler as she was—would never retire to take a little rest.

But, although Aunt Es was really established in business, on her own account, she was not a millionaire by any means; she had always lived in poverty, absolute, though independent, poverty. She had never asked anyone for anything; and repeated pressing was necessary to induce her to accept an invitation to dine with her relatives once a fortnight. She made her appearance, dressed in a grey woollen gown, invariably the same, summer and winter alike, with its sleeves fitting tight at her wrists, its long body forming a point in front, and with a few little flounces on its skirt.

Whenever the old lady came, she generally brought the children a few sweetmeats, and showed herself very sociable and gay; and if she was questioned about business, she invariably replied that it was "pretty fair." Her "business" was not, however, an important matter. The poor old woman lived in a cellar—one of those frightful Amsterdam cellars—damp and unhealthy, perfect fever nests, where the tourist is quite astonished to find clean little shops installed—shops occupied by fruiterers, milkmen, cobblers, coopers, fishmongers, and even publicans. It was necessary to go down some twenty steps to reach Aunt Es's stationery shop, which was about as large as the cage of an ascensor. A little, very little table did duty as a counter; there were three or four cardboard boxes, containing letter paper of various sizes, and an old glove box, in which some steel pens, quills, and wretched pencils indiscriminately found room. In addition, there were, perhaps, half-a-dozen bottles of ink, and three or four rulers—that was all. It would not have taken long to draw up a list of the stock-in-trade.

When business was prosperous, Aunt Es managed to earn from twelve to fifteen florins a month. Of an evening her shop was transformed into a dining-room, at night-time it served as a bed-chamber. She dined on her counter, and slept in a wardrobe at the further end of the cellar—a wardrobe with two doors, and one solitary shelf upon which a mattress was spread out.

When I became acquainted with her, she had been living for forty years in this dark basement. She had been living there, in an honest, thrifty style, without owing a halfpenny to anyone in the world, but actually managing to save up some money in view of providing herself with a dowry. For I must tell you that Aunt Es had a sweet-heart.

II.

BEFORE proceeding any further, it is necessary that I should state what a "betrothal" is in Holland. When a young Dutchman meets with a young Dutchwoman to his taste, when their respective families have been duly consulted and have consented, when the marriage is finally decided upon, it is first of all determined that the young couple shall be betrothed for a year or two.

That matter being settled, they live one for another. They can come and go, and walk out together as they please. They are to be met at the theatre, or on some little pleasure trip, leaning lovingly one on the other, the future wife already confiding in the protection of the future husband. This preliminary intimacy has never shocked anyone in Holland, and this matrimonial prologue has never lost its purely prelusive character.

One day, when Aunt Es was eighteen years of age, she introduced to her relatives the young man whom she had selected, and who had asked her for her hand. He was in business like herself, only in a still smaller way. Aunt Es at least had a shop, a counter, some cardboard boxes, full of note-paper, and an old glove-box, full of pens, whereas, the man of her choice had no shop at all. His stock-in-trade was so small, that he carried it about with him under his arm.

Karel was a dealer in cigars—not one of those wealthy merchants who import direct from Havannah the wherewithal to stock their extensive warehouses. His repository, a portable one, consisted of a little box, which before falling into his hands, had contained some high-class regalias, and in which he scattered, with somewhat cunning ostentation, a few selected cigars, worth just a farthing a-piece. He went about offering his goods to retail dealers, never having more than a hundred cigars at a time, and taking a fortnight or so to get rid of them.

He did not earn more money by these dealings than his betrothed did with her intermittent business in pens, pencils, and notepaper, so that they were exceptionally well matched, so far as equality of position went. It was a love match, since they were fond of one another. It was a fitting match, as they were both on the same footing as regards means, and it was also a reasonable match, since they were only to marry when they had saved up a little money, enough to start housekeeping without being charged with want of foresight.

III.

THIS last matter was uppermost in their minds. Aunt Es had formally declared, that they would not marry until they were able to make up a thousand florins between them. This was the least they would need to take a larger shop, to combine the tobacconist's with the stationery business, to sleep elsewhere than in a wardrobe, in which, by the way, there was not sufficient room for two, and to bring up properly a troop of youngsters, who would need a deal of air and space.

And so, as soon as she was betrothed to Karel, Aunt Es, whom the neighbours had been accustomed to hear singing in the depths of her cellar, with as much gusto and gaiety as a nightingale on the top branch of a poplar tree—Aunt Es, who, in the opinion of all the people round about her, had never shown herself sufficiently serious, Aunt Es became perfectly transformed. She showed marked eagerness in disposing of her various commodities, and marked eagerness in realising as handsome a profit upon them as was possible. Nothing equalled the zeal and ardour which she displayed in her business, unless, indeed, it were the zeal and ardour of Karel.

But business was not lively. All the custom went to the large firms. And the joint efforts of Karel and Aunt Es did not lead to any great result. He tried to open a trade in medium priced cigars, and she endeavoured to speculate with the famous "Bath superfine," then just introduced into Holland. However, both of these commercial ventures had disastrous results, and the marriage almost collapsed as well as the subterranean stationery shop, and the infinitesimal cigar business.

"Don't let us go too fast," they then said, frightened by their audacity. "Don't let us launch out into adventurous enterprises. A bird in the hand is worth two in the bush. We must be patient. In due course we shall end by attaining our object, sure enough."

And so they waited. They continued living on the same footing, in the tender, discreet intimacy which their betrothal permitted, rich in love and especially in hope. Their hearts, indeed, were full of hope, of illusions that nothing could destroy, of dreams of the future which they had long cherished, sempiternal plans which they discussed over and over again of an evening, she, seated behind her counter, and he in front of it, gazing at her in ecstacy. Sometimes it was a question of a deal chest of drawers which they had seen in a shop in the Kalverstraat, and which they would buy for their bedroom on the day when they could begin house-keeping; on other occasions it was a question as to how they should bring up their children. He wanted to have a little girl first of all, and she would prefer a little boy.

One evening she had a whim. "Do you know," she said to Karel, "do you know what we ought to do? You will perhaps think me unreasonable, but it's a fixed idea of mine. Well, it's this, we ought to buy a lottery ticket between us."

I should mention that the Dutch Government carries on a lottery from which it derives large profits. The drawings take place by series, and they last during several weeks. The grand prize of a hundred thousand florins is drawn on the last day; and as the ticket, which Aunt Es's betrothed had purchased, did not win any of the earlier prizes, it had a chance of securing the principal one.

It is easy to imagine how the young couple's plans progressed as the day of the grand prize drew near !

"If you see me drive up in a cab to-morrow," said Karel to Aunt Es, on the eve of the final drawing, "it will mean that our number has won !"

On the morrow, Aunt Es stationed herself at her door at a very early hour. How impatient she was ! Each time that she saw a cab approaching, her heart beat quick and loud. Fortunately, but few vehicles pass along the quays of Amsterdam. And yet, at one moment her head fairly swam, and she realised that she was turning quite pale. A "vigilant," as the Dutch cabs are called, had just drawn up, and she saw Karel looking out of the window.

In the space of a few seconds, all the plans which she had been forming for so many years flashed before her mind. At last the longed-for happiness was hers ! For there could be no mistake. They had won the prize since Karel arrived there in a cab. Aunt Es ended by running to the vehicle, the door of which had been slowly opened. Karel sat inside looking overwhelmed.

"What is the matter?" asked his betrothed. "Have we won the grand prize ?"

"No," answered Karel, "I have just broken my leg."

IV.

AUNT Es tended her lover in her subterranean abode, placing the wardrobe at his disposal, whilst she herself slept upon a chair. When his leg was healed, he turned his attention to business again, limping about the quays of Amsterdam, and offering his bad cigars to sundry retail tobacconists ; whilst Aunt Es sat in her darksome little shop, waiting until any of the petty tradespeople of the vicinity had occasion to purchase a quire of letter-paper or a few steel pens. And thus it was that during years and years, with illusion after illusion fading away, but without losing aught of their firm faith in a better future, they grew older and older, living on, in close intimacy, without noticing that their foreheads were becoming wrinkled, that their hair was growing white, that she was sixty-five and he seventy, and that even their health was failing them.

Aunt Es was ill, and did not speak of it. A decline was carrying her off, but all the same she somehow contrived to attend to her little business. In point of fact she did not suffer very much, and she never complained, nor did she even dream of consulting a doctor.

One day, however, feeling rather weaker than usual, she detained her betrothed, although by a fortunate chance he had five-and-twenty cigars to deliver to a purchaser. They talked together for a long while, and their sempiternal hopes seemed more justifiable than ever. Busybees that they were, they had ended by putting some money by, just one half of the sum that they had intended to get together. In a few years' time they would no doubt have the remainder.

Whilst they were chatting in this fashion, the twilight fell. It was a warm autumnal evening, and Aunt Es was beginning to feel comfortable again.

"I have an idea," said she. "After all, we have grown old, and we sha'n't have any children now, so suppose we content ourselves with the money we have saved, and marry ?"

Karel thought the proposal a very reasonable one. After all, what was the use of waiting any longer? Yes, yes, they would marry, said he, and whilst he spoke, Aunt Es took hold of his hand and pressed it warmly. Then with a sweet smile she closed her eyes.

"It's agreed, then," said Karel, rising from his seat at last. "I will attend to everything."

She did not give him any answer, however, and he went away on tip-toe, thinking that she had fallen asleep.

But she was dead.

· · · · · · · · ·

When I returned to Amsterdam, I met at my friend's house a tall, sturdy old man who was dressed in deep mourning. He was Aunt Es's betrothed. Her relatives had taken him to live with them; they treated him with affectionate care, and tried to comfort him with touching words. He had become one of the family.

AN IDOL.

THE window was open. The pale gleam of the stars stole over the amber-tinted silk of the hangings, which lost much of their effect amid the purple glow of the lamp. The fresh, salt air from the beach stirred a bouquet of tiger-lilies blooming in a horn-shaped vase of silver, inlaid with enamel. One could hear the orchestra of the Dieppe casino playing a lively waltz.

And yet, the Countess de la Merced, attired in evening dress, and quite ready to start for the villa, where her dear enemy, the Princess Catherine, was giving a concert, remained motionless with her eyebrows lowered, and an anxious expression upon her pale face. What petty worry had disturbed her delightful nonchalance? Since her departure from Paris, everything that had happened, had seemed to correspond with her desires.

In London, she had had the honours of the season. An exalted personage—H.R.H.—had been pleased to notice her, and paid her two compliments—the first on her wit, and the second on her dress. And not unnaturally, the latter had proved most to her liking. On her arrival at Dieppe, the first thing she had noticed on the table had been a huge bouquet of edelweiss, despatched from the Alps by the Grand Duke, who was " doing " Switzerland. Moreover, although she numbered twelve or fifteen summers more than the pretty Duchess d'Alérions, no attention had been paid to the latter since she, the countess, had arrived.

Young women of twenty do not know how to dress. They adopt whatever their dressmakers are pleased to advise. But, in reality, there is no art, no pleasure, in wearing the same things as other people ; and so she, Germaine de la Merced, had pondered deeply, and devised a special toilet, calculated to display her goddess-like figure to full advantage. The attire in which she last appeared at the casino was still talked about. Over a skirt of a tea-rose tint, covered with old Malines lace, she had worn a garment of " shot " taffeta of scarabæus hue, which with its lace muffler, tight sleeves, and graceful cut, had reminded one of the surtout worn by Marie Antoinette, in the celebrated portrait painted by Madame Le Brun. Moreover, daintily sat on the countess's dark hair, a high hat with a green aigrette, and a border of tea-roses, recalled the head-gear worn by the ill-fated Queen of France. Thus attired, Madame de la Merced had promenaded up and down the terrace, escorted by gallant and illustrious cavaliers. Ah ! what fury she had seen blazing in the eyes of all her envious feminine acquaintances.

A number of waltzes, novelettes, and sonnets had been dedicated to her, and her portrait had been *the* success at the last Fine Art show in Paris. Her most detested rival was now unable to show herself on account of a cold which had made her nose swell most outrageously. She, the countess, had just received the most delightful little toy terrier in the world, in the daintiest gilt basket that it is possible to imagine ; and, accompanying the present, there had come a glowing declaration from the most distinguished member of society at Dieppe, an imperial highness, if you please. So what could possibly trouble her ? Was she not flattered, petted, and admired, treated like a queen ? Was not her existence a succession of delights, without a care, without a worry?

At all events, a crease had appeared upon her white brow. She was looking at herself and saw this crease, and was unable to smooth it away. At the same time she beheld her straight Grecian nose, her mouth admirably formed though somewhat hard at the corners, her grey fascinating eyes which glowed like two lamps, her long graceful neck, and all her proud elegant figure arrayed in a moonlight tinted dress. She remembered some verses which had been addressed her, verses comparing her to Venus rising from the ocean, and enveloping her nudity in precious antique lace and creamy pearls. She wore some of that antique lace now, and the pearls of her necklet, and her silken train with its silver embroidery on a pale blue ground, gave her a resemblance with that terrible Diana of Poitiers who held two kings enthralled. She had oft time been compared to the Primaticcia's famous model, but of course she did not pass her time with astrologers and symbolical rhymsters ; her companions were gentlemen of high life, "philosophers for ladies," good-natured princes and beauties of either hemisphere.

As she sat there, in the purple glow of the lamp, it could be seen that there was a newspaper lying at her feet—a newspaper containing a paragraph round which a red line had been traced.

"Yesterday evening," said this paragraph, "at the Artistic Alliance Club, a stormy dispute took place between Baron von Alberg and Monsieur Ralph Reynold. A duel is spoken of as being inevitable ; and we hear that the quarrel was in reference to a lady of high birth whose name has not transpired."

It was this paragraph, ominously framed with red, that had brought a frown to Germaine de la Merced's forehead. Ralph Reynold was going to fight a duel on her account. The Baron von Alberg, an ill-bred Austrian nobleman, who drank deeply and who constantly forgot good manners, had grossly insulted the countess at a semi-political dinner, at which a foreign prince, several diplomatists, and two or three celebrated writers had been present.

No one had taken the countess's defence. Some of the guests did not know her, and the others did not like her. But it happened that the baron's remark had been repeated to Ralph Reynold, who for a fortnight past had been anxious to constitute himself the countess's champion. Who was Ralph Reynold you may ask ? He was a poet, but scarcely known as yet, a poet who had obtained but a semi-success with his drama in verse "The Duke of Alba." The son of an officer, who on dying had left no fortune behind him, he had been quietly brought up in the provinces by his sorrowing widowed mother.

Handsome as a poet should be, with his pale creamy complexion and large black eyes, he had remained for one whole evening in contemplation before Madame de la Merced, at a château near the town, where he had been born. He had been invited there, as some of the guests intended to perform a little comedy which he had written. But he paid no attention to the performance ; he gave no thought either to the young lady who was to play the part of the heroine, or to the annoying manner in which his verses were "murdered" by the amateur actors. He was indeed wholly absorbed in the most beautiful dream of his life.

He gazed in admiration at Germaine de la Merced, with her gold coronet above her haughty brow, and her lovely statuesque figure. He asked to be introduced to her; and his admiration, mute at first, finally became eloquent.

It was a warm September evening, and after the performance, most of the guests scattered through the grounds, while Madame de la Merced, draped in a lace shawl, remained upon a terrace gazing at the garden below her, at the flowerbeds illuminated by countless lights, at the dark romantic pathways, and the quivering water of the pond, which was streaked with white gleams between the dark herbage of its banks.

Seeing her there alone, the young poet drew near and spoke the language of his heart. For the first time in her life, perhaps, the *blasée* countess felt the breath of poetry upon her brow. Everything seemed changed by the imagery, the fire of Ralph's words. You would have said that he was studding the sky he spoke of with diamonds, and that flowers sprung up at the sound of his voice exhaling perfumed incense at the countess's feet. She took the young fellow's arm and strolled with him towards the dark pathways. Like children to whom a fairy tale is told, she felt inclined to exclaim: "More, more," as she listened in rapture to his musical language. And when she returned to the terrace again, Ralph, on his side, shuddered. Was this evening—the one ideal moment that life had granted him—already over? However, in answer to his request, the countess authorized him to call upon her.

On the following day he sent her a sonnet. She read it, and found it very pretty. The second one also seemed to her very nice, but the third was, to her mind, rather confused. As for the subsequent ones she did not read them at all. She was prevented from doing so by highly important matters. Her mornings were fully occupied in composing a series of six toilettes for a visit which she was to pay to some English friends in Devonshire, upon her departure from Dieppe.

But the spell was not broken as yet. Ralph did not bore her when he talked. His youthful emotion, his ardent love, titillated the countess's nerves in the most delightful fashion. Timid and ever fearful of displeasing her, he proved as submissive as a dog; and so she allowed him to see her whenever she had a spare moment, on which occasions his delight was so manifest and so exuberant that she felt positively ill at ease. It was years since she had experienced such sensations. The young fellow's intense bright love imparted renewed youth to her jaded heart.

Ralph Reynold certainly did not dress in an elegant style, he was not of high birth, nor was he gifted with that ready wit which shines most in society, but there was something unusual about him. He did not talk or make love like other people did. All the same, she, Germaine, ought to have reflected earlier, she ought to have foreseen the scandal which was now about to occur. It had been certain all along that Ralph would do something foolish one day or other; and that day had come. To fight a duel with that idiot Von Alberg for a remark which he (Ralph) had not even heard—and to let people guess that he was fighting on her account! All that was in extremely bad taste, it was ridiculous, it was, indeed, the very height of clumsiness.

Had she asked him to fight on her account? By what right had he undertaken her defence? A fine thing it would be, indeed, when all Paris learnt that her most devoted admirer was a petty poet, whose works had been refused at the Comédie Française. And to think that the archduke was to be introduced to her that very evening; and that she had even thought of inviting him to the lunch which she meant to give on the morrow !

If Ralph had even consulted her, she would then have had some responsibility in the matter. But no, this young commoner of the nineteenth century was as susceptible as a knight of olden time. He had been pleased with the thought of giving Baron von Alberg a lesson. When Germaine had written to him, reproaching him for having concealed his intentions from her, he, usually so submissive, had curtly replied: "In matters of this kind, my dear countess, a man does not consult a woman." And then he had taken the train which was to convey him to the Belgian frontier.

Nevertheless Germaine has dressed for the Princess Catherine's concert, being well aware that in most cases of the kind honour is easily "satisfied." She hopes that such will have been the case in the present instance, and yet she cannot make up her mind to start until she has received some news of the encounter. She looks at the clock—ten has just struck, and the duel must have taken place four hours ago. What can have happened? Oh ! no doubt the telegram has merely been delayed. That often occurs ! But a quarter past ten arrives, and then the half hour strikes ; and meanwhile the countess examines the flower on her dress-body, smoothes her hair, smells her salts, and toys with her fan, feeling terribly anxious despite herself.

"What can have happened?" she repeats once more ; and at that very moment her maid enters the room, exclaiming, "Here is a telegram for madame."

"Give it me quick," replies the countess, whose hand is trembling and whose heart is beating fast. Poor Ralph ! how happy he would feel could he witness these signs of the interest which she takes in him.

She has torn the blue paper open, and now she reads :

"He is very grievously wounded. Would like to see you. Am afraid you would arrive too late.

"DR. CONSTANT."

At this perusal she sinks back in her chair with her face extremely pale. "Very grievously wounded," she gasps. "He so young, so talented, so fond of me ! "

Something like a tear gathers in her eye. However, as for going to see him, that is quite impossible. That doctor must have lost his senses, and Ralph as well. And, besides, it would, no doubt, be useless. The telegram was sent off at seven o'clock.

But, supposing he died, how grievously afflicted his poor old mother would be. She is alone in the little country town where she has retired ; and her heart is full of her absent son—that handsome young fellow of four-and-twenty.

"Ah ! if he dies," thinks the countess, "I must send a wreath of violets to be laid upon his tomb."

He had seemed charming on that evening when they had first chatted together in the garden of the château. Yes, indeed ; on that evening she had perhaps really loved him. He was possessed of talent, undoubtedly. There was too much gush in his style, perhaps, and yet it was often very captivating. Unfortunately; however, he had no idea of life. He was clumsy, he dressed badly, he was but imperfectly acquainted with the manners and customs of society.

Then the countess continued thoughtfully : "At all events, I will send a telegram to the doctor—tell him to promise his patient a visit from me, that is if the poor fellow is still alive. I at least owe him that consolation. But am I to remain here like this all the evening, alone with my thoughts? What will the people think at the Princess Catherine's? I am expected there—some one will, no doubt, come to fetch me. Perhaps they are already whispering that I was interested in that duel, and that I don't dare to show myself—for Von Alberg may have sent a telegram to one of his friends here—a telegram giving the result. But, after all, did *I* ask Ralph to fight that duel? It places me in great embarrassment. I can't help it if Ralph is in love with me. It isn't my fault if he is wounded. Besides, love makes everybody suffer more or less. I remember that when I was eighteen years old, I was madly in love with my cousin Jacques. But he married another woman, an ugly one by the way ; and later on, I exerted my pride to hide what I felt. Why has Ralph asked to see me? It is folly, it is the height of impropriety ; of course, he will either die or survive. Well, if he dies, my visit would be uselesss—and if he survives I shall know how to console him. It is already bad enough that this affair should be talked about everywhere. And to think that I have all this worry on account of a man who is below me in rank, who doesn't belong to society, in whom I condescended to take a little interest, and who assumes the defence of my reputation without being in any way asked to do so ! After all, life is a very wearisome affair ! An early death is almost a form of happiness—and to be killed in a duel fought for a woman's sake 'tis a grand ending, such as a real nobleman might be proud of."

The countess has reached this point in her reflections when, once more, the door opens, and her maid appears bringing a second telegram.

"Another one !" murmurs Germaine de la Merced. "Haven't I had enough emotion for one evening?" And she hesitates to open this second telegram ; it seems to her as if there were a black veil before her eyes.

For the third time the drawing-room door is opened. "Prince Godenoff," says the maid "has called to inquire whether Madame la Comtesse is not indisposed."

"I indisposed !" exclaimed Germaine. "Why should I be indisposed I should like to know? Show the prince in."

"I have come to carry you off, countess," says the Russian nobleman as he crosses the threshold of the room. "Everything is terribly dull and gloomy at the Princess Catherine's without *you*."

"The fact is "—begins Germaine ; but the prince interrupts her by asking: "Can't you come?"

"Oh ! yes, I can—yes indeed," replies the countess ; and whilst her visitor leans forward to inhale the perfume of some flowers, she crumples up the telegram, which is burning her fingers, and throws it into the fire. Then, with her cloak about her shoulders, she exclaims: "Let us start !"

"To the princess's !" replies the Russian magnate gaily.

And she, once more in full possession of her grace and spirits, smilingly repeats : "Yes, to the princess's."

But as she and her cavalier turn to leave the room, the maid, inquisitive like all servants, leans over the fireplace and rescues from the flames a scrap of charred paper, upon which she reads this one word :

"Dead."

THE END.

www.ingramcontent.com/pod-product-compliance
Lightning Source LLC
Chambersburg PA
CBHW031111020726
47495CB00007B/2153